WHERE THE LIGHTNING GOES

ISBN: 978-1-958362-04-4 (hardback)

ISBN: 978-1-958362-02-0 (paperback)

ISBN: 978-1-958362-03-7 (ebook)

LCCN: 2022950126

Derealization Press: 1120 Bloomingdale Pike, Kingsport, TN 37660

www.jackarysalem.com

Cover by Kim Dingwall

Dedication:
To my dad, who always believed in me. I love you.

1

When Elle was little, she fell out of the sky. Her only memories were of an expanse of black and a horizontal flash of light. She'd been Inside ever since.

"I can't believe you're really going."

Elle looked at Quincy, who worried and whined by the door of her room. He fidgeted with the ratty strip of sheet tied over his empty eye sockets, straight black bangs parting around skinny fingers.

A smile touched Elle's lips. The dilapidated gray walls of her room, always so dark and claustrophobic, felt brighter. The empty floor, unfurnished save for the sheet Elle slept with, looked almost homey. Quincy's annoying lack of confidence and can't-do attitude only made her grin wider.

"The only reason I can even think about going is you." She held up the hammer, uncaring that he couldn't see it. "You and this hammer. I mean, saying you wanted to help was one thing, but stealing from Miss Cynthia?" She shook her head. "You're incredible."

"I wish you could have been there. It was really scary."

"If I could have gone with you, I would've. You know that." Elle glanced at the door. It was thick enough that the volunteer guard on the other side couldn't hear them. She lowered her voice anyway. "They don't even let me go to the bathroom alone."

"Maybe if you stopped trying to escape all the time, they'd let you out more."

Irritation darkened Elle's good mood. "They're the ones in the wrong, Quince. They have no right to keep me here."

"In your room?"

"In this house!" Quincy flinched. Elle grimaced at her own stupidity. She glanced around to see if her outburst had attracted anything dangerous. When no shadow demons leaked from the walls, she lowered her voice to its usual whisper. "Besides, you know that old crone hates me. Even if I was the picture of obedience, she'd find reasons to punish me."

"Maybe." He didn't sound convinced. "Or maybe she's just trying to keep everybody safe."

"And if she is? How does that make it okay?" Elle's voice rose in pitch but not volume as anger and incredulity flooded to the surface. "She's torturing me, Quincy. How can none of you see that? Leaving me locked in here. Only letting me chat with one person for one hour every few days. It's inhumane!" Tears stung the backs of her eyes. "Even if she didn't like seeing me suffer, which she does, this isn't okay. I don't care what her reasons are. No one deserves to be tossed in a room to rot."

Elle waited breathlessly for a reaction. For understanding. Rejection. Anything. Quincy fisted his fingers in his shirt and said, "Oh."

"Oh?"

"Sorry, Elle. I didn't know it was that bad." He hunched like he was waiting for a reprimand.

She sighed, and the frustration she felt for him flowed out with the air in her lungs. It wasn't his fault he didn't get it. Rather than continuing to unload her emotional trauma onto his innocent eleven-year-old shoulders, she said, "I just wish I could fight back. If I had even a little magic, she'd think twice about doing this to me."

Quincy shook his head hard. "No way. Don't even joke like that. Magic attracts . . . you know."

"Demons."

He ducked his head. Elle blew a lock of frizzy brown hair away from her face, wishing he'd chosen something else to be sensitive about. It made sense, what with demons having gouged his eyes out and all. It was just counterproductive. They lived in a world filled with demons. He was going to have to get over it eventually.

He murmured, "Yeah. That."

"Miss Cynthia does magic. It's how she gets the supplies and lights the house. If she can do it without getting eaten, so can I."

"Maybe you should ask her to teach you again. It'll be safer if you know how to do it first. Before you have to fight the . . ."

"Demons." Elle crossed her arms, doing her best to pretend they hadn't had this argument a million times already. "I've tried, Quince. I've begged. She just laughs in my face. Which is exactly why I need to go Outside. My teacher's out there somewhere. I just have to find them."

"But why? Why's magic so important?"

"Have you ever been around Miss Cynthia when she does magic?"

"No."

Elle scrunched her nose. She wasn't sure how that was possible, considering how packed the house was. But then, she didn't think she'd ever seen Quincy and Miss Cynthia in a room together, either.

"Well, it's amazing. Not the things she does, but the way it feels. Just being near her when she does magic is like, I don't know, being alive? Like I live every moment of every day in a constant state of drowning. Then she does magic, and I can breathe again." Elle looked to Quincy for some sign of comprehension. He twisted his hands together, obviously lost, and her willingness to open up to him died. She shrugged. "It's everything, and I want it for myself."

"Okay." He smiled, but she could tell he didn't understand. "You go and learn magic, enough to protect us both. Then when you come back for me, it'll be easier."

"Or you could get it over with and escape now. There's no telling how long it'll be before I can come back here again. Or if I'll survive long enough to come back at all."

Quincy's thin black brows rose above his blindfold. "And you think I'll be okay out there? I'm only eleven. You're . . ." He hesitated, tugging on his overlarge shirt. "Well, I don't know how old you are, but it's older than me. You're practically an adult. Besides"—he gestured embarrassedly to the cloth on his face—"I'll only get us killed faster."

"And? It's a monster-infested wasteland out there. It's not like my chances of survival are great to begin with." Elle rubbed the back of her neck. "I'm not going because I want to live. I'm going because I want to live *better*. Just think about it, Quince. Magic. Adventure. Furniture." She waved her hammer in a half circle to emphasize the bare walls and empty floor. "Plus, if you escape with me now, I don't have to come back later."

Quincy whined. "I can't. I'm not as brave as you, Elle." His lips wobbled. He sniffled. Elle wondered if people without eyes could cry.

Once it became clear he wasn't going to cheer up on his own, she huffed. "You're stupid for wanting to stay, but it's not like I can make you leave."

Quincy perked up. "You mean . . . ?"

"I go. You stay. When I'm strong enough, I'll come find you."

"And then we'll go on a huge adventure? Together?"

"That was the deal."

A ridiculously happy grin dimpled his left cheek. "You're gonna be so surprised when you see me again. I'll be older, and you'll be stronger, and we'll work together to take down bad guys. Like, pow pa pow!" He punched the air a few times.

She snorted. "I don't know about all that. I'll be happy just to survive."

"And get your memories back. Don't forget about that."

Elle stiffened. Resentment and yearning roiled to life inside her.

All her memories from before she fell out of the sky were blank. Not blank like paper but blank like a pit. Like a void had opened up within her and hollowed out the base she was supposed to be built on. She'd once thought her need to find out who she was would fade with time, but a decade of emptiness had taught her otherwise. Every day she went without knowledge of her past was another layer of herself scraped from the inside of her skull. Piece by piece, layer by layer, she was being devoured.

While she wasn't positive retrieving her memories would make it stop, she couldn't think of any alternatives, either.

"Elle?"

"Yeah. I heard you. Learn magic, return to the sky, get my memories back, then come find you." Fear prickled in Elle's stomach. Each task sounded more impossible than the last. "What could possibly go wrong?"

"You could die."

"Not helpful."

"I think you'll do good. Prob'ly. You're smart and super brave." Quincy bit his lip. His fidgeting fingers stilled. "Please be careful."

"I will." She closed the distance between them. The urge to hug him blossomed within her, but it felt too intimate. Too awkward. She laid her hand on his shoulder instead. "Thank you for helping me. Seriously. I don't think I could've survived in here much longer."

"It's not for free. You're gonna help me, too."

Elle flicked him on the side of the head.

He giggled. "Okay, okay. You're welcome. Just don't . . . don't forget about me, okay?"

"I won't." Elle squeezed his shoulder, and he tilted his head to nuzzle into her hand. She glanced restlessly at the flat gray ceiling. It was impossible to tell time, as there were no windows and the magical lighting in the house never changed, but it felt late. "You should get going."

Quincy nodded. "I'll miss you."

"I'll be back. And hey"—Elle cracked a humorless smile—"I might fail before I even open the door. Then they'll lock us both in here, and there won't be anything for you to miss."

He didn't laugh at her joke, which was fair because it wasn't funny. She pulled away and tucked the hammer into the back of her pants. Quincy turned and felt around until he found the door. He whispered, "I believe in you," then knocked for the volunteer guard to let him out.

A second later, Elle was alone.

Bitterness sank its claws into her heart. She curled her fingers into a fist, trying to will it away. Much as she was thankful for Quincy's help, she hated the way he treated her escape like a game they couldn't lose. Like if she failed to open the door, the only consequence would be trying again.

He didn't understand how suffocatingly small her room was or how staring at the same four walls day-in and day-out played tricks on her mind. He didn't have a ravenous void in his chest tormenting his every waking moment. He didn't need to leave. Elle though?

She'd die if she stayed. Maybe not in a day or a week or a year, but two years? Three? Elle could already feel her will to fight slipping away. Every day she went without human contact was a day she considered giving in. Giving up. They'd locked her in her room to break her, and if she didn't escape tonight—if they doubled the guards and took away her visitation rights—they'd succeed.

She'd told Quincy she wasn't sure how much longer she could survive Inside, and she'd meant it. Her sanity chipping away. Her hope shriveling. Her dreams dead. When she blinked, she could see herself sitting placidly on the living room floor, playing yet another rousing round of Guess Which Book Is Behind My Back, and that scared her more than the demons.

Anxiety squirmed in her stomach, nauseatingly thick. She squeezed her eyes shut and thought of the lightning instead. A single horizontal flash across a pitch-black sky. Beautiful in its intensity, with a dozen sharp edges and limitless warmth. The memory filled Elle with a sense of love and belonging, momentarily dulling the horrors in her heart.

She didn't know what the lightning was or why it made her feel at peace. She didn't know where it had come from or where it'd gone. She did know she'd find it again. So long as she could get Outside—so long as she had air in her lungs and strength in her legs—she'd find it.

She had a hammer. She had a plan.

She'd find it.

2

Elle sat in the middle of the floor with the hammer in her lap. She fiddled with the worn wooden handle and tapped bitten-down fingernails against the long, flat side of the metal head. Muffled voices sounded on the other side of the door, and Elle didn't have to listen to know Quincy was complaining of a nightmare. Something about demons gouging out his eyes or being forced to watch his parents die. Something about a warm glass of milk.

It didn't matter what he said so long as he said it while crying: snot pooling on his upper lip, voice wobbling—the whole nine yards. Empathy would cause the night guard to falter, willingly abandoning their post, and Elle would make her escape.

She squeezed the hammer's handle, adrenaline making every little movement seem both too loud and too fast. The moment of truth crept closer, terrifying and addictive. Elle forced herself to breathe. She closed her eyes and thought of the house.

Five dank, gray bedrooms. One cold, hearthless kitchen. One small, often-broken bathroom. One bleak, useless living room. Two glorious wooden doors: boarded shut.

Four of the bedrooms and the bathroom were upstairs. The doors would be closed while fourteen of the sixteen other occupants slept. Quincy and the night guard would go down the stairs and to the right, toward the kitchen. If Elle wanted even a chance at escape, she'd have to follow them out of her room, down the stupidly creaky staircase, and into the living room. She'd hide until Quincy and the night guard went back upstairs.

From there, it would be a quick jaunt down the hall to the back door. Miss Cynthia slept on the lower floor, bedroom situated between the kitchen and the front door, but so long as Elle was quiet, it wouldn't matter. They were still on opposite ends of the house. The likelihood of Elle waking her was microscopic.

(And, realistically, if Elle got loud enough to wake anyone, a few missing boards would be the least of their problems.)

The lock on Elle's door clicked, signaling Quincy had completed his end of the bargain. Elle's heart thundered in her chest. Her legs shook as she stood. She tried to draw on the lightning for courage, but the reality of what she was escaping *to* suddenly required more than a derisive scoff or a puffed-up chest.

Even if she managed to get out, she could be running to her death. Demons were sadistic beasts with bottomless stomachs. The world was a wasteland. And no matter how much Elle hated the house, Outside could be worse.

She shook out one hand, then the other. She rolled her shoulders and cracked her neck. She crossed the room. The hammer weighed heavy in her hand and heavy on her heart, cautioning. Going Outside meant more than changing her own life. It would change the lives of every other survivor, too. There was a chance they'd go on as they were, affected by her departure only in terms of a new bedroom opening up, but it was more likely they'd be slaughtered. She laid her free hand on the knob, fingertips full of consequences.

A deep breath in. A slow breath out.

She turned the knob and pushed.

The hallway, much like the rest of the house, was gray. Emptiness tangled with silence. Elle stepped out into the hall, and despite the enormity of the moment, nothing changed. The magical lighting didn't flicker. The temperature didn't rise. The other survivors didn't wake.

Elle tucked her hammer into the back of her pants and covered the head with her shirt. Cool metal pressed into her lower back. She eased her bedroom door closed.

The lifeless hall greeted her with indifference, and she returned the sentiment in full. She crept to the left, where two flat gray walls bracketed worn wooden stairs. If Quincy and the night guard returned before she made it to the bottom, there would be nowhere to hide.

Elle brushed her fingers over the wall to her right, smooth only in appearance. Tiny pockmarks and minuscule bumps caressed her skin. She used her free hand to press the hammer to her spine and slid one bare foot over the edge of the uppermost step.

Thirteen planks of wood mocked her efforts, promising to creak and give her away, but Elle had played this game before. She pressed her toes to the far-right side of the first step, foot flush with the wall. The wood held steady under her weight, silent as the grave.

She tiptoed down the stairwell, muscle memory steering the way. Only one stair could be trusted center-plank. Two stairs couldn't be trusted at all. Elle danced past those traps, trusting her body—her own knowledge and skills—above all else. She touched down on the bottom floor without a single whisper of protest from the wood. She released her hold on the hammer.

Quincy walked out of the kitchen.

Panic jammed Elle's heart into her throat. She skittered to the left. A loose floorboard groaned beneath her. She rounded the corner and threw herself against the living room wall.

The solid metal head of the hammer smacked the wall with a resounding thud. Her heart dropped into her stomach. She sandwiched her hand between her back and the wall, palm cushioning metal, but it was too late.

A loud whisper echoed through the house. "What was that?" The voice was high-pitched, the words accented and enunciated. *Terri*.

Elle clenched her eyes shut as Quincy asked, "What was what?"

The air near Elle's left shoulder drastically cooled. She shivered, icy terror sinking into her blood. She looked up.

Black mist dripped from the corner of the ceiling like translucent sludge. It puddled on the floor next to her feet, twisting and hardening to form disembodied claws. Hopelessness settled in her lungs as the claws connected with a palm.

Terri said, "I could've sworn I heard something."

Quincy whimpered. "Do you think my nightmare was real? Are the d-demons going to come kill us?"

A long, skinny arm sewed itself to the other end of the palm. The claws inched toward Elle's foot. Tears beaded in her eyes, and she held her breath, refusing to call for help.

Terri spoke in a low, soothing tone. "No, sweetie. There are no demons here. I, um—you know, I probably just imagined it. That's all. Even adults get a little spooked sometimes."

Elle looked from the malformed demon on the floor to the rest of the room. Twenty-eight well-read books, half a pack of cards, and a board game with no board decorated the center of the otherwise empty floor. A cylindrical sandwich-sized torso wriggled into existence. A claw nicked the side of Elle's foot, drawing blood. And it occurred to her, in a moment of almost bland morbidity, that there was an upside to being killed rather than captured.

At least if she was dead, she'd never have to play Guess Which Book Is Behind My Back again.

Terri offered another soft reassurance. Quincy sniffled. The stairs creaked, announcing their departure. Elle waited one breath. Two. The torso and the arm melded together, claws scraping wood. Elle darted around the corner, out of the living room. She snuck down the hall as quickly as she could, heartbeat denting her ribs.

The only person capable of banishing the demon was Miss Cynthia, but Elle would die before following protocol and waking her up. If demons invaded, they invaded. If the other survivors got caught in the crossfire . . .

Elle stopped by the back door. Guilt slithered under her skin. She glanced over her shoulder, down the drab gray hall, and toward the open archway of the living room. She told herself demons hunted by sound, not sight or smell. So long as she escaped in silence, the thing in the living room would sit harmless and still until morning.

(Probably.)

Elle curled her fingers into a fist, nails digging painfully into flesh. She retrieved the hammer from the back of her pants.

Both the front and back doors were boarded up in the same way: two slats of wood parallel to the floor, bracketing the doorknob, and one plank at a diagonal. Nails held the boards to the wall, one small gray circle per corner. That made twelve nails between Elle and freedom.

She laid her hand flat over the diagonal board and wedged the forked end of the hammer up under the lower-left nail. The edge of the hammer didn't scrape wood. The wood didn't creak. She pushed the handle of the hammer down, leveraging her strength against the solid wooden door, and the nail slid soundlessly free. Elle caught the little sliver of metal before it could hit the ground, and for a singular second, she knew something was wrong.

Taking the nail out had been too easy. Too quiet. Like thrusting a knife through bread, it hardly took any effort at all. She squeezed the nail in her fist. An invisible, microscopically thin layer of *something* flexed around the metal and abutted her palm. It shot the distinctive order to *be quiet* straight to her brain, as clear as if someone had pressed their lips to her ear and spoken aloud.

Warning bells went off in the back of Elle's head, labeling her escape a trap. She opened her palm, panic rising. A rolling fog invaded her thoughts.

Elle swayed on her feet. A thimble's worth of anxiety squirmed under a cloud of exhaustion, and though Elle knew whatever she'd been thinking about was important, she couldn't for the life of her remember the topic. It sat on the back of her tongue and in the farthest corner of her mind, a distant dream. She tried to retrace her steps from the demon to Quincy's uncertain fate to the door. She unfurled her fingers, revealing a thin cylinder of metal.

Elle's thoughts flitted back into place, settling around how strange it was that such a tiny thing could have kept her trapped for so long. She'd always imagined nails to be bigger. Stronger. More ominous.

She twisted the little piece of metal between her fingers, distinctly unimpressed, then set it on the floor to her left. Her focus recentered around a quick, quiet escape.

She started on the next nail.

The first board came down easily. It weighed less than she'd thought it would, but its length killed maneuverability. She gripped both sides of the wood, careful not to scrape the floor or bump the walls, then laid the plank down in the hall.

The second board joined the first, easy as breathing. Eight nails dotted the floor to her left, then ten. Twelve. She held the final board in the crooks of her elbows, forearms flat to wood and fingers hugging her hammer. She stared at the wholly uncovered door. The weight in her arms took weight off her shoulders. She stepped back. Something sharp pierced her heel. She flinched and hissed. She turned.

The edge of the final board smacked the wall, deafeningly loud.

Anxiety and fear made a dizzying brew. Elle stumbled to the left, blood-tipped nail falling from her wounded heel to the floor. Her other foot knocked into the two boards in the hall. They twisted and crashed. Panic flooded her veins and drowned logical thought. Black smoke oozed from the crevice between ceiling and wall.

Every ceiling.

Every wall.

Elle dropped the board, no longer concerned with a silent escape. She glanced at the floor *(eleven nails off to the left, one nail lying bloodied on its side in the middle of the tiny foyer, impossibly separate from the rest),* then to the exit. Scratching echoed down the hall, frantic and quick. The demon from the living room rounded the corner, six thin limbs ending in overlarge claws. Its small cylindrical torso hadn't changed. The simple circle of its skull housed more teeth than face.

Elle's blood pounded in her ears. She leapt for the door. The demon sprinted down the hall, claws trampling over its still-forming kin. Elle grabbed the knob with the hand not holding her hammer. She twisted her wrist.

Locked.

Terror coiled in her gut and brought tears to her eyes. She swiveled, hammer at the ready. The demon opened its maw, revealing rows and rows of sharp black teeth. A second mouth opened above the first, then a third. Its head twisted so the mouths were vertical.

Something invisible threw the demon into the wall, black skin swelling as it screeched and writhed. It burst into a cloud of smoke. Miss Cynthia appeared at the end of the hall, toes stopping just shy of the bubbling black floor.

Elle's arms trembled, adrenaline edging on exhaustion. Unformed demons coated the walls and soaked the floor. Cold, wispy tendrils lapped at her ankles, the beginnings of sharp talons piercing soft skin. Elle tried to pull away. The pecks of pain dug deeper. Miss Cynthia clapped her hands, fingertips toward Elle, then spread her arms wide. The demon smoke pooling around Elle's feet reared back, clearing a small circle around her.

Relief blossomed without Elle's consent. She stared at her savior, hatred kissing gratitude, and asked the only question she could.

"Where's the key?"

"Elle." Miss Cynthia stepped forward, the bottom of her thin blue nightgown dragging through black smoke-sludge. Hollow cheeks highlighted eerily bright blue eyes. Thin biceps shook from the effort of keeping the demons at bay. "Elle, stop. This is . . . this is bad, but it's not too late. Quick. I'm going to teach you a spell, and we can—"

"Where's the key?" Elle raised her voice. The demon smoke in the center of the hall thickened: not a writhing mass of body parts, but the torso of a singular, massive beast. A scream sounded from upstairs, igniting a chain reaction of shouts and bangs. *Quincy.* Elle glanced at the ceiling, heart cracking. She pointed the hammer at Miss Cynthia. Her voice sounded hoarse, even to her own ears, as she said, "Give it to me. Now. I'm leaving."

Miss Cynthia raised both brows, forcing already wrinkled skin to bunch near gray-white hair. "What part of 'you can't' do you not understand? Even if I open the door, there's nowhere for you to go." Miss Cynthia raised one hand, fingers shaking. "Please, Elle. Please. If you'll just . . ." Tears cascaded down her cheeks. The smoke-sludge nearest Miss Cynthia's legs molded itself into claws as big as hammers, signaling the approach of something gargantuan. Miss Cynthia's voice cracked, panic bleeding through. "I'm sorry we locked you up. I am. But it was a choice between you and everyone else. I couldn't—"

Sobs cut off speech, and for the barest moment, Elle believed her. Guilt doused determination. Elle's grip on the doorknob loosened. Then Miss Cynthia glanced up through thin gray lashes, and her eyes were *cold*. The fear, the concern, the apology: they were all fake. Miss Cynthia wasn't scared.

She was enjoying this.

Fury crashed into Elle like a physical force, and she reacted without thinking. She raised the hammer as high as she could and brought it down on the knob. The clank of metal on metal echoed through the hall. The demonic torso on the floor gained another limb, sharp claws scraping the thin magical barrier around Elle's feet. The door bled black.

This close, Elle could feel the demons' intent to harm. It seeped into her bones, promising cruelty and pain. She shivered, terrified. She struck the knob again. Once. Twice. Three times. The old bronze sphere dented, then bent. It fell to the ground with a heavy thump, instantly swallowed by demon smoke.

Elle opened the door.

A deep black emptiness stretched as far as she could see in every direction, leaving no distinction between sky and ground. It was with a sinking feeling that she thought there might not *be* any ground. Dread lanced through her, skewering any dreams of escape. She gripped the doorframe like a lifeline. The sweat on her palm wet the handle of her hammer. She reached past the doorway, into the nothing.

Bitter cold bit into her skin. The air felt both empty and thick, like negative space. It hurt to keep her hand Outside, but she couldn't pull it back in. Whatever was out there, it wanted her to move forward. To accept the nothingness. To die.

This was where things went to die.

Fear filled Elle to bursting, and she choked on the desire to flee. To cower in the safety the house provided. She tried to yank her hand Inside again. Outside tugged back. The hammer slipped from her fingers, a gray-and-brown fleck in a sea of black. It vanished. Elle slipped farther into the nothing.

She squeezed her eyes shut as her breathing stuttered, lungs pushing air out in quick uneven huffs. Horror and terror tangled, a thick blanket covering a slumbering beast.

Anger stirred.

She'd been tortured. Ridiculed. Humiliated. She might've just sacrificed her best friend. And for what? To give up right at the finish line? To give into her fear, just like the adults she despised?

Elle forced her eyes open, an animalistic noise crawling up her throat as she wrenched her hand back through the invisible barrier. It stung like nails scraping skin. Her head swam. Miss Cynthia spoke, but it sounded like gibberish. Looking down—down, down, down—made Elle dizzy, so she clutched the wall and turned.

"Are you satisfied yet?"

Elle focused on Miss Cynthia and the half-formed demon lumbering between them. The screaming upstairs grew louder, new voices joining old. Anger turned to nausea.

"Where are we?"

"Safe. Or at least we will be if you close the door. Close it now." Bright blue eyes glanced anxiously at the hallway-sized monster and its eight whip-like tails. Its head emerged from the muck, half as high as Elle was tall. Miss Cynthia's voice dipped low. "I'll help you board it up, and maybe, maybe if we do it together, we can fix this."

"No." Elle took a step back only to stop when her heel crossed the border. Outside grasped at her exposed flesh, gleeful and malevolent.

Miss Cynthia let one hand drop to her side, focus shifting from Elle to the beast. The black-smoke sludge swallowed Elle's toes, cold and unwelcoming. Miss Cynthia raised both hands, palms out. She shook her head, sad but sure. "Try to think clearly, Elle. Even if you somehow make it out there, you won't last. You have no magic."

"I'll find someone—"

"No one will teach you. The closest magic-anything is Adair, and he's more demon than human. Even if you don't die before you reach him, he'll kill you on sight. Now, please. I can't do this without you. I can't—" Miss Cynthia broke down crying. Sweat slid from her forehead down to her temple and into sleep-tousled hair. The demon's head attached itself to the body, all eyes and teeth. Elle couldn't tell if this was all part of the show or if Miss Cynthia was genuinely outmatched. She wasn't sure if it mattered. Even glancing at the bleak nothingness Outside was enough to convince her that whatever fantasies she had of survival were just that.

Still, she tested the air beneath her heel. Whatever she chose, she would never get the chance to choose again.

Staying meant claiming this house as her home. It was an acknowledgement that the other survivors were right all along and a promise never to try again. It was welcoming defeat. Going, on the other hand, meant death.

Stay or go. Life or death. Containment or freedom.

Elle spun to face the abyss, braced her hands on the doorframe exactly long enough to admit this was crazy, and leapt.

3

For the second time in Elle's life, she fell out of the sky. She remembered all of it.

First there was darkness surrounding and consuming her until she felt suffocated by the nothing. Then there was light. A pinprick grew and gave way to startling shades of blue she hadn't known existed. Puffs of white interrupted the endless expanse of blue, though none were close enough to touch.

The longer she fell, the more she got to see. Blue opened to make way for browns and greens, which Elle instinctively identified as land. Trees and grass and dirt, just like the books described. Her imagination didn't begin to measure up to the real thing, and now that it was practically at her fingertips, she wasn't sure how she had lived so long without it.

She was equally unsure how long she'd be able to live with it because she wasn't slowing down.

It was here that Elle could admit she hadn't thought things through. She wasn't entirely sure what she'd expected. Maybe for a hero to show up and pluck her from the air or for magic to slow her fall to a gentle drop.

What she got was the ground, hard and fast and all at once.

Agony lanced through her bones, punishing her for surviving. She lifted her head, migraine pounding behind her eyes. It hurt to breathe. It hurt to *think*. She propped herself up on shaking arms, and the world spun.

Blue. Green. Blue. Green. Blue. Green. She closed her eyes again, nauseated. Her thoughts jumbled. She heard Miss Cynthia telling her, in no uncertain terms, that Outside was unsurvivable. She heard screams echoing down the stairs as the other survivors—as *Quincy* paid for her selfishness. She heard birds.

Elle opened her eyes to see the world had settled. Pain still throbbed in her skull and scraped along her skin, but she could see. She could stand.

She pushed herself to her feet, wobbly but able. Her right heel twinged, reminding her of the nail she'd stepped on and the discomfort her adrenaline had ignored. She pressed her sole flush to the ground, acclimating herself to the pain rather than avoiding it. Dirt stung her open wound. She rested her hands on her hips, her breathing labored, and looked around.

Blue colored the sky above her, decorated only by white splotches and a blindingly bright yellow sphere. The sun. Elle craned her neck, seeking some sign of either the House or the pitch-black void from which she'd fallen. Blue and blue and more blue stared back.

To her left, a forest stretched out to infinity. A bird hopped on the ground near the forest's edge, red feathers darkening in the shade. A small, fuzzy creature with a long tail skittered up a nearby trunk. The bird chirped, uncaring of the noise it made. No demons dripped down from the bright green foliage.

The area to her right had no trees. Green grass and swaths of white, yellow, and purple flowers decorated the rim of a large body of water. Sunlight sparkled off the translucent surface, yet another new shade of blue. Wind cooled her cheek, causing flowers to sway and the water to ripple. Awe warmed her heart, gentle and yearning.

She'd dented the ground when she fell, creating a small crater in an otherwise well-kept, winding dirt path. The dusty-brown strip stretched as far as she could see in either direction, cutting a clear line between the forest and the field.

Paranoia bled into wonder as the years spent locked in a tiny room, the demons she'd seen slither from the walls, and the void outside the House clashed with fresh water and clear skies. She hunched her shoulders, the outside world suddenly feeling too open. Too bright. She squinted at the sky, then the forest. The urge to take cover burrowed beneath her skin. She dug her nails into her palm, embarrassed by her own cowardice, and turned the other way.

Elle hadn't risked everything to cower in the shade, clinging to some vague notion of safety. She'd done it for freedom. Thus, despite everything in her screaming to duck under the canopy of trees and hide, she shuffled toward the water.

It was bigger than the leaky bathtub by far. Bigger than the entire House. She'd guess it was a lake, maybe, or an ocean. A sea? The books in the House hadn't differentiated between bodies of water other than to say that oceans were salty.

Elle dropped to a crouch. Her legs shook. She pressed her knees to the ground, thin blades of grass parting around her shins and tickling the tops of her feet, then lowered her hands into the water. It felt blessedly cold, which informed Elle that she was warm. She glanced up at the sky, trying to spot the source of the heat. White smeared over blue and yellow gleamed. If a witch or wizard controlled the temperature, she didn't see them.

Staring at the sun made her headache worse. She turned back to the water, wondering if temperatures were as stable Outside as they were in the House. Sweat trickled from her hairline down to her chin. She hoped not.

The water above her fingers shimmered, begging her to go deeper. To dunk her arms in up to her elbows, then to soak the short sleeves of her patched-up shirt. She cupped her hands and brought the water to her lips instead. She drank from her palms, so thirsty that the water actually tasted sweet. Cool and smooth and not at all salty. *Not an ocean.* She drank two more palmfuls, then another after that. Her belly filled, her headache lessened, and for the first time since her fall, her mind cleared enough to feel the world.

Not the world as a physical thing, with its jutting trees and over-warm air, but the spirit of it. The *potential*. The water sang to her, a lullaby lost to a dream. The earth hummed with strength. Elle tilted her head, and the wind whispered past: a ghost dancing in the ether.

Potential thrummed all around her. It lived in everything, everywhere, filling an already gorgeous world with wonder. Elle laid her hand over her heart, wet skin soaking faded cloth, and felt that same potential in herself. Beautiful and bright. Sparkling. Elle had never felt anything like it. Not in the rough wooden flooring or the crumbling gray walls of the House. Not in the other survivors. Not in herself. And like being connected to her own soul—like asphyxiating for an eternity, then drawing her very first breath—she felt alive.

Tears burned behind her eyes as the painful void of her lost memories loosened its grip, and gratitude overtook her. She folded her torso over her thighs and cried into the grass. The potential of the earth stretched out beneath her, endless and forever. Quincy's whispers of encouragement twisted with the survivors' terrified screams and echoed in her heart.

She cried harder.

Her shoulders shook. Her throat ached. When her tears ran dry, her headache returned. She wiped her face on her sleeve and drank more water. She stood.

Fatigue fluffed up behind her ribs, filling her to the brim, and though her situation hadn't changed, she felt better about it. She looked from the clear blue water to the dirt path, then the forest. There was no telling which direction would lead her to a wizard capable of teaching her magic and which would lead to death. Miss Cynthia's cryptic warning about Adair bobbed in the back of Elle's mind, pointing out that the answer could be 'both.'

Elle studied the sky, still bereft of black holes and floating houses. Her distrust of the old witch battled with the fact that she had nothing else to go on. She still needed to learn magic and locate her memories. She still needed to figure out both where she was and where she'd been. Whether or not she needed to avoid someone named Adair on the way was irrelevant. Either she'd run into him or she wouldn't.

Elle stepped back onto the path to the left of her crater. The potential of the world flowed around her, present in everything but especially strong by the forest's edge. It molded to the trees and condensed in the air. It beckoned her closer.

She crossed the gap between the dirt and the trees. Low-hanging branches reached out. Soft, itchy grass bent under bare feet. And though sticking to the path presented her best chance of finding other people, adventure called from the woods. She stepped forward, for the first time free to make her own choices and bear her own regrets.

She allowed the forest to swallow her whole.

4

There was a girl in Adair's backyard.

Adair didn't generally like it when people trespassed on his property, and the penalty was generally death. This girl, however, was special.

She'd fallen out of the sky.

While her plunging through the air was odd in and of itself, the fact that she had enough magic to survive the impact was what had actually caught his attention. Adair had stood off to the side after she'd landed, unsure if she was an enemy, a refugee, or a reckless idiot. He'd waited almost patiently for her to notice him and declare her intentions. But she never did. The girl drank from the pond, cried, then wandered into the mirage in his yard.

Fifteen minutes of pointless meandering. Twenty. Thirty. He might've thought the innocent act a trick if not for the determined way she circled the trees.

Much as he would've liked to attribute her enchantment to his magical prowess, the mirage was relatively simple. It was only made to trap the magicless and the weak. Anyone with an ounce of mirage knowledge or even a good sense of direction would quickly realize the forest was fake. It wasn't that difficult to see the same four trees were being repeated indefinitely.

Yet the odd girl didn't see. She wove a determined path through the "forest," never once stopping to question her surroundings. Adair momentarily toyed with the idea of setting her free, if only to ask where she had fallen from, then let it go. If she couldn't get through his half-assed mirage with the impressive amount of magic at her disposal, she deserved to stay lost.

He returned to his cabin without sparing her another thought.

"You sure you want to leave her out there?"

Adair tensed. A man with straight black hair, a strong jawline, and flawless skin lay sprawled across the couch, looking irritatingly relaxed for someone invading Adair's home. His feet were perched on an armrest while his arms cushioned his head, and if not for the fact that he had spoken, Adair might have thought him asleep.

Then the man blinked, and Adair knew him. Or at least knew his eyes. They were a bright, vibrant blue boasting not of warm, sunny days but of blizzards that ravaged the land and ruined its people. He—it—was the embodiment of death and every fearful thing that came thereafter.

Demon.

Annoyance prickled on the edges of Adair's consciousness. "What do you want, Cypress?"

Cypress grinned, and the perfection of its smile gave away its status as a shapeshifter. "You know, I was hoping you'd be the one that remembered me. You were always my favorite."

Adair frowned. "Get out."

"So soon?" Cypress's grin turned sideways. "You don't even know why I'm here."

Adair summoned fire, intent to burn the demon alive. Cypress disappeared from the couch and breathed cold wind onto Adair's ear. Adair spun, but no one was there.

The room looked empty—felt empty—but Cypress wasn't one to flee so easily. Adair commanded the magic of the world to spark again, filling the entire house with electricity. A grunt sounded to his left. He reflexively targeted the source.

The electricity dissipated to reveal Cypress standing in the dining room, watching the flesh of its burned palm repair itself. It looked more interested than upset, which Adair expected but didn't enjoy.

Cypress said, "She's desperate to find someone who will teach her magic."

"So?"

"So desperate people do desperate things."

Cypress's gaze flicked from its wounded hand to the only painting in Adair's house, and the void in Adair's chest momentarily filled with fury. He summoned enough fire to burn down a forest, but by the time the air ignited, Cypress was gone.

Adair loosed a string of vulgarities, none of which properly relayed his anger. Rage fueled him, and he hated that he clung to the feeling. Shame curled around his fury, but it was still better than the boredom and the nothingness, so he leaned into that, too. He cursed harder, until the harsh words were empty echoes that once again meant nothing.

He strengthened the wards around his house. Anyone slipping into his home unnoticed was undesirable. For a demon of Cypress's caliber to do so was unacceptable. Even without precautions in place, Adair should have been able to sense that kind of power long before it approached.

So why hadn't he?

Adair looked out the window to watch the daft girl still lost in his mirage. Frizzy brown hair clung to sweaty skin and brushed thin shoulders. She wore a faded, patched-up brown T-shirt that looked like it'd never been washed and equally shabby brown cargo pants. She was relatively short and too skinny to be anything but malnourished. Dramatic entrance aside, there was nothing special about her.

He leaned against the wall, wondering what he'd missed. Demons weren't known for their honesty, and Adair was better versed with Cypress's sick sense of humor than most. The girl could be an assassin.

Adair watched her climb halfway up a tree, slip, and land face-first in the dirt. He dismissed the possibility of assassination. Still, she could be a shade or any number of other nefarious creatures charmed to look human. The only way to know for sure was to interact.

He breathed a heavy sigh and left the cabin, dragging his feet the entire way to the mirage. She jumped when she spotted him, and he felt miraculously less impressed.

She asked, "Where'd you come from?"

"I should be asking you that, trespasser."

"Trespass—" She narrowed her eyes and curled her lips, surprise giving way to confusion. "What's a trespasser?"

Adair opened his mouth, then closed it again. He shook his head. "Where *did* you come from?"

"The House."

Adair cocked a brow, and the girl pointed helplessly upward. He scanned the sky for any signs of a house or, more reasonably, a portal. His search came back empty, but the girl didn't strike him as a liar, either.

"This house . . . it's in the sky?"

"I think so. Or above the sky, maybe. It's a dark place."

His frown deepened. "What's your name, girl?"

"Elle. You?"

"Adair."

Elle paled, already wide brown eyes growing wider. She took a step back. It wasn't an uncommon reaction, all things considered, but he did find it curious that she'd heard of him and not trespassing.

"Are you going to kill me?"

"Maybe." He shrugged because he hadn't decided yet. She turned and ran, but so long as they were in the mirage, it was useless. She rounded the second tree, no doubt unaware of her own trajectory, and came straight back to him.

When she saw him again, her lips twisted. She made a frightened noise with the back of her throat and raced past. He allowed it, well aware that she would circle the other two trees and end up where she started.

Elle repeated the process an irksome number of times before coming to a stop in front of him, chest heaving. "How are you doing that?"

"I'm not doing anything."

"You are! You keep . . ." She panted. "Keep appearing in front of me."

"No, you're in a mirage. A rather simple one at that." Adair shot her a pointed look, just in case she wasn't aware of her own stupidity.

She scowled. "Well, let me out."

"No."

"Why not?"

"Because I don't have to. You entered my domain. Brought a demon to my home. I can do what I want with you."

She flinched, heel tapping the exposed root of a nearby tree. "I didn't do any of that."

"You did. You trespassed on my land. Entered without my permission. Cypress came with you."

Adair took a threatening step forward. Elle tried to flee. He bade the roots to entrap her ankles, slamming her into the earth.

She squirmed onto her back, eyes on the roots curling up her calves. "I didn't know. I'm sorry!"

"Why are you here, Elle?"

"I didn't mean to come here. This is just where I fell." She tried to wedge her fingers between bark and skin, desperate to free her feet. The roots didn't budge.

He asked, "Yes, but where from? Why?"

"I already told you. I came from the House. I came to learn magic and to find my memories and—and—" She bared her teeth. "And you aren't going to stop me."

She kicked out, and despite Adair's magic, the roots broke. Elle tossed a surprised glance between the broken roots and Adair, apparently unaware of her own capabilities. She scrambled to her feet and took off at a sprint. He walked out of the mirage before she could circle the trees and face him again.

An unfamiliar spark of hope lit the void where his heart should've been, a dying ember on a cold night. Much as he loathed to admit it, he owed Cypress for pointing her out.

Elle, at least for Adair's purposes, was the perfect mix between powerful and ignorant. She was both strong enough to instinctively protect herself and unrefined to the point of uselessness. That meant he could expose his weakness to her without fear of being killed. And, if they were both lucky, she could survive long enough to fix it.

He watched her loop the trees for another few minutes, unsure she understood what being in a mirage actually meant. The longer he looked, the less he cared. Trapped was trapped, and at the rate she was going, she'd still be there in the morning. He turned and walked away.

Hopefully a night in the cold would be enough to curb her attitude.

5

Elle was beginning to think the forest might never end.

Night had distracted her for a bit, with a show of darkness and cold that she had never experienced in the House. Exhaustion brought forth patches of sleep, though none were restful. She feared Adair's ability to appear out of thin air, and as much as she imagined standing brave against him, it was hard to think up a scenario where she left alive.

That did not, however, mean she was going down without a fight.

The sun rose, and the heat returned. Hunger coiled in her gut, but she was used to living off meager portions and scrounged supplies. She waited. When Adair reappeared, she attacked. A forceful lunge. Her shoulder in his stomach. A surprised grunt. She'd meant to shove him to the ground, but he was solid as stone. He stumbled back, barely a step, then grabbed her waist.

Pressure turned to agony as fire laced his fingers, the sickening smell of burned flesh wafting upward. Elle kicked and squirmed, but he only held her tighter. Reactionary tears blurred her vision. A scream scraped its way up her throat. She craned her neck to look at him, meaning to beg or bargain. Her breath caught in her throat.

Dark brown eyes watched her, empty and uncaring. There was no anger, wariness, or self-preservation. No empathy, either. Adair wasn't hurting her out of instinct or obligation, but just because he could.

Fear ratcheted up. Pleas died on her tongue. He threw her to the ground, the pain of her landing numbed by the pain in her sides, and she cried into the dirt.

"Did you really think you could kill me?"

"No." Elle raised her head, every brush of her shirt against her wounds a fresh wave of torment. She forced a grin. "Doesn't mean I can't try."

He stared at her, infinitely tall and built with brawn. Black hair lay short on the sides and fluffed out on top while a five o'clock shadow darkened his jaw. He sneered. "You're a fool. And were this any other time, any other place, you'd be a dead fool."

Elle blinked, not understanding. "You mean . . . ?"

"I'm not here to kill you. I'm here to offer you a deal."

She perked up. Her sides screamed. She hunkered back down. "What kind of deal?"

"I need you to run an errand. Do it successfully, and I'll teach you magic."

"What's an errand?"

He gave her the same odd look as when she'd asked about trespassing, then said, "It's a favor."

"What kind of favor?"

"Does it matter?"

Caution whispered that *yes, it very much did matter,* but longing was louder. If she wanted to learn magic, she had to be brave. To dive into the unknown as many times as it took, regardless of risk. She shook her head. "No. I guess not."

"Then follow me, and know that if you attack again, I will kill you."

There was no bluff in his tone, no lilt of playfulness in his voice. She nodded and stood. Pain seared her sides, finger-sized holes in her shirt revealing burned, bloody flesh, but she didn't complain. Adair took two steps, then vanished.

Frustration flared. She gritted her teeth, hating him for not helping her out and hating herself for needing the help in the first place. Adair materialized out of thin air, just to the left of where he'd vanished. He looked her over, equal parts disdainful and disinterested, then poked her between the eyes.

The majority of the trees ceased to exist. The path reappeared to her left, and the water beyond that. On the other side of the remaining trees sat a wooden building. Smoke billowed from a small stone tower on the roof.

Amazement overrode her ire, bathing the world in wonder. "What did you do to the forest?"

Adair grunted and again motioned for her to follow. This time, she could see him striding toward the wooden building.

Feeling braver now that he officially wanted her alive, she caught up and repeated, "What did you do to the forest?"

"There was no forest. You were in a mirage. Remember?" He said *remember* like it was a threat, but getting a response at all only served to encourage.

"A mirage is a fake forest?"

"No."

She waited for him to elaborate. He clenched his jaw and ignored her. She walked even closer.

He pushed out a breath through his teeth. "A mirage is a trick of the eye. Something that looks real but isn't. In this case, it was a forest. You were running around those trees"—he gestured to four unimpressive trees—"but thought you were in a forest."

Awe spiraled into excitement, imagination blooming. Elle asked, "Will I be able to do that some day?"

Adair shrugged. He led her into the wooden building, and curiosity made way for delight. Adair had *furniture*.

A blue couch sat across the room, cushions partially facing the door and partially facing the hearth. Bookcases bracketed the fireplace, though most of the books were on the floor. The rest of the walls were bare. In a connected room to her right stood a long, heavy wooden table and four comfy-looking chairs. Books littered the surface of the table by the far wall, directly in front of a door-sized painting. Words she didn't know and equations she couldn't understand were written on the wall surrounding the frame.

The painting depicted a field, a woman sitting at a little table, and a sunset. What drew Elle's attention, however, was the amount of potential surrounding it. Was the painting a mirage, like the forest?

She stepped forward, fingers itching to touch the couch or the chairs. "How did you get all this?"

"I bought it."

"Bought?"

"Again, where did you come from?" He shook his head and held up a hand, palm toward Elle. "Actually, you know what? No. I don't care. Go sit at the table, and I'll explain your task."

He walked into the next room. She rushed after him, fingers curling around the chair nearest the painting before he could change his mind. The potential in the chair felt sturdy and reliable, much like the trees and the ground. She pulled it from the table and plopped into the seat.

The curved back of the chair offered support in a way leaning against the wall of her room could never hope to emulate. She stretched out her legs, knees settling in a comfortable bend. And oh wow.

Furniture was amazing.

Adair grimaced, like her happiness somehow made his day worse. She slumped and let her hands fall to her sides, spine happily contouring to the wood of the chair. He ran his hand through his hair, messy black locks catching between his fingers, and muttered something in another language. He pointed to the painting in front of the table.

"See this painting?"

"Yeah."

"You're going to go inside and retrieve my heart."

She waited one beat, then another. Too much time passed for there to be a punchline. "I . . . what?"

"The painting."

Elle nodded, showing she understood.

"Go inside."

"Inside the painting?"

"Yes. Go inside, get my heart—"

"From the painting?"

"Yes. Get my heart and bring it back to me."

Elle deadpanned, "From the painting."

Adair's disdain broke through with a snarl. "Yes. From the painting. Or do you have a problem with that?"

His cold, empty eyes said he'd kill her if she did, so she shook her head. "No. No, no problems here. I just. . . . Don't I need to learn magic first?"

Adair pressed two fingers against his temple, and the only word Elle could think to describe him was *impatient*. He said, "This painting is enchanted. Anyone can enter it, magic or no."

"Seriously?"

"Seriously."

Elle glanced between Adair and the painting. She didn't know whether to be terrified or amazed, so she went with both. She sat up straighter, heart thumping, and gestured weakly to the canvas. "And your heart is in there?"

"Yes."

"Why?"

He pressed his lips into a thin line, genuine irritation flashing. "Question time is over. Are you going or not?"

"Now?"

The potential in the air around Adair flexed, and she knew, on some instinctive level, that he was the cause. He spoke, voice flat with warning. "Now."

Nervousness combined with fatigue, making her legs feel weak. She stood and walked to the painting. Even without taking its magic nature into account, the art was impressive. Textured green grass paired with the pinks and oranges of an eternal sunset, and the woman at the table looked serene. Even the painting's frame was eye-catching, with little flowers carved delicately into the wood. Elle ran her fingers over the designs before swerving to touch the scribbles on the wall. Were these the spells that let Adair put his heart in the painting, or were they his attempts to retrieve it?

She glanced covertly at Adair, who met her gaze head-on. He definitely looked heartless, but not necessarily like the type of person whose heart required protection. If not to keep it safe, why risk taking it out in the first place? For fun? And more importantly, how was Elle supposed to get it back?

She'd only just gotten Outside, and her ability to defend herself was nonexistent. She had no idea what had happened to Quincy or the other survivors. The circumstances surrounding her time in the House had grown more mysterious rather than less. Could she really move forward without first resolving what she'd already done?

Did she have a choice?

Adair's crossed arms and expectant stance said she didn't. She toyed with the idea of asking for more time to prepare—hot food or a short nap would do wonders—but he didn't strike her as the catering type. With her luck, he'd kill her for asking.

She stuck her finger through one of the holes in her shirt, careful not to touch her wounds, and nodded. "Okay. I'll go."

"Go then." He canted his head toward the painting.

The nervous fluttering in her stomach intensified, more fear than apprehension. She shuffled her feet. "One more question."

He joined her in front of the painting. "What?"

"Why not get it yourself?"

Adair's smile was a cruel wisp of a thing. "The heart wants what the heart wants." His hand warmed her back, and the next thing Elle knew, she was falling.

6

Elle's journey through the air was swift, and she met the ground with a crack.

If not for the fact that the wind had been knocked violently out of her, she would have cursed Adair. As it was, she had to suck in a few gasping breaths before condemning him. She inhaled deeply. She swore. The magic of the painting sank into her bones, and *oh*—

She couldn't breathe.

Magic swelled around her on all sides, clogging every pore until it not only surrounded her but filled her. A little whine slipped from her throat as her head began to fog, normally clear thoughts replaced by a barrage of images.

Four walls, a ceiling, a floor—the parameters of the painting. It was smaller than the House, but only barely.

There were three silhouettes: two in front of her, one at the far end of the box. Two were made up of the same nothingness as the painting, one was human. One was normal, one tied to the painting and leaking magic, and the last one cursed.

Elle thumped her fist on the grass, desperate for air in ways she had never imagined possible. The images were dense pieces of knowledge shoved where they had no business being, delivered with no signs of stopping. Pain filled her chest and flooded her brain.

A smaller box stood next to one of the nothingness silhouettes, the one with all the magic. A rectangle floated inside the box. The rectangle felt like the other human: real in a way nothing painted could imitate. The exit.

The rest of the painting was a void: an empty mimicry of death. Unnatural desolation carved a hollowness in her chest while magic jammed itself between her lips and swam down her throat. Her vision turned spotty, and she thought Miss Cynthia was probably right.

She was going to die out here.

Blunt pressure sharpened with purpose. The magic sifted carelessly through her soul, seeking her atrocities, and her mind convulsed with the knowledge that there would be no forgiveness. If the magic found what it sought, it would rip out her heart.

Anger scraped the inside of her skull as she realized Adair had known. That he'd faced this same test and *failed*. Injustice pointed her toward a hurtful betrayal, but panic was stronger. It informed her that she, too, was going to fail.

By opening the door to the House, she'd betrayed everyone inside. She'd acknowledged the risks and the danger, then done it anyway. She'd left them all to die. Even now, with her soul on the line and her chance to repent at hand, the only thing she regretted was being caught.

Elle felt her soul as clearly as her physical body, beaten and bruised and splayed to be judged. She imagined curling around the darkness within her—the selfishness and the lack of remorse—and prayed for the magic not to see.

It didn't work, of course.

The magic coiled around her internal projection and threw her away, small and useless. The painted world slid into focus for half a minute. A hand on her back, moving. A hand on her neck, grasping. The hand on her back rubbed soft, soothing circles. A smooth voice spoke, but its words were lost to the haze. She began to burn.

Everywhere the magic touched sizzled and crisped, skin melting into muscle and bubbling against bone. She slapped at the flames, terror escalating as her skin came off in her hands. Hyperventilating sobs caught in her breathless chest. She held only a vague, secondary awareness of her real, physical arms lying by her sides, useless but intact.

Sharp, deadly magic positioned itself over her sternum, ready to rip out her heart. She barely felt it. The little cuts in her soul were nothing compared to the pain in her body, and it was as she accepted defeat that the magic stilled. It saw something—it *knew* something—and flung her away, heart and all.

The black dots dancing across her vision merged and blurred until they were all she saw while the pressure in her head reached a crescendo. Elle's aches dulled as her consciousness slipped. Air entered her lungs, unimpeded.

Finally, blessedly, she passed out.

7

There is a castle in the sky. Its walls are great, and at its center sits a magnificently large sphere of lightning. Elle sees this sphere, knows it is important, but angry voices draw her attention away.

Two men and a woman are arguing. The woman is familiar, overly so, and it only takes Elle a moment to recognize herself. Older by a decade and dripping with magic, but still her. She does not question how she can see herself out of body and out of time. She moves closer.

The first man is covered in tattoos, all words Elle doesn't recognize, and he is powerful. His name comes to her, unbidden.

Perun.

Elle feels her elder counterpart, and she wishes Perun dead without knowing why. The second man stands off to the side, uninvolved. She cannot see his face, but he is displeased, and she feels his displeasure is somehow more dangerous than the battle brewing between her older self and Perun. Elle wants to tell herself not to get distracted by the wizard when a true beast lies in wait, but the world spins fast and hard enough to tear her apart, and suddenly she is flying.

No, falling.

Elle jerked awake. Nausea roiled in her empty stomach. She pushed herself up and started heaving. Her mind filled with a blurry version of the painting's knowledge. The three figures. The emptiness. The exit. The heart.

Fury surged through Elle, first for Adair, then for herself.

He hadn't put his heart in the painting for safe keeping. He'd lost it. Whatever atrocities he'd committed tore him from the painting and barred him from trying again, and Elle—

Elle was a sacrifice. There was no way he could have known she was purehearted (or, more accurately, that she wasn't pure-hearted but the painting would spare her). He hadn't asked, hadn't hinted, and likely hadn't cared. Either she would do his bidding, or he would kill whatever was sent back.

Worse still, she'd gone along with it. She'd known something was off, and as much as her departure was inevitable, she could have stalled. Blindly agreeing to a task wasn't brave. It was stupid and arrogant. *She* was stupid and arrogant. And now she was paying for it.

Another dry heave forced tears from her eyes. A warm hand rubbed circles on her back.

"It is okay. Let it out."

Elle jerked away from the voice, then wobbled and retched. The man patted her back and whispered baseless reassurances. Reactionary tears and spit dripped into the stiff, plush grass, but there was nothing she could do about it. When her stomach finished attempting to throw itself up, she groaned.

"There you go. Now, that feels better, does it not?"

She shifted away and used her shirt to wipe her face. The wounds Adair had given her hurt less, which made sense once she saw her midsection had been bandaged. She snuck a cautious glance at her new companion.

The man looked both curious and gentle, with kind brown eyes and a crooked smile. Golden-brown hair fell in a perfect wave over his ears, and despite their obvious difference in height and musculature, she felt no fear. If this were a children's story, he would be the prince.

He stood, showing he was at least as tall as Adair, and offered her a hand. Elle frowned and stood without the help. The world spun, brief but disorienting. She swayed on her feet.

He held out his hand, palm to the side. "I am Leslie. It is nice to meet you."

She hesitated for half of a second, then shook his hand. "Elle."

"Like the letter?"

Elle hummed in affirmation.

"How are you feeling, Elle?"

"Bad. What was that?"

"That?"

"There was magic and a map and . . . I don't know what else. It's gone now."

"Ah. You are referring to the painting's enchantment. Have no fear. While entering this world is a rather unpleasant experience, it requires no repetition."

Elle squeezed her eyes shut and attempted to recall what was apparently the magic of the enchantment. Her memory blanked.

She looked at her feet, thoughts a foggy mess. The grass was neither warm nor cold, and its texture was completely different from that of Adair's yard. It didn't make her skin itch, regardless of how she shifted. The blades clumped and curled rather than standing free.

She turned her attention to the horizon, where the sky remained unnaturally still and the field abounded in silence. The potential of the painted world stretched stiffly in every direction, the feeling of the sky indiscernible from that of the ground. Unlike the real world, this potential projected no strength or whimsy, and she knew without question that if she tore up the grass, there would be no dirt underneath.

Behind Leslie sat a small table, and at that table sat a beautiful woman. Dozens of long, dark brown braids cascaded over one shoulder while equally dark brown eyes stared unseeingly outward. She neither blinked nor breathed. Delicate fingers held a plain white teacup in a perpetual state of ready-to-drink, forearm hovering peacefully over the table. Her body was made of the same stiff potential as the rest of the world, and it didn't take a genius to see that this was the subject of the painting.

Elle leaned closer, entranced by the serene smile decorating still lips. She wondered if this woman existed in the real world, too, and if the real version had eyes anywhere near as stunning as the painted one. Even the void inside of Elle recognized the woman as something special, though Elle had no idea what the consequences of such an acknowledgment could be.

"That is Clarrissa." Leslie stepped between Elle and Clarrissa with a smile that didn't match his protective gait. "May I ask how you got here?"

Thoughts of Adair jostled Elle's anger. She grunted. "I was pushed. You?"

"Pushed?" Leslie's voice pitched high with concern. "By whom?"

"Adair. But I agreed to it, sort of. What about you?"

"I entered willingly, though for Clarrissa, not Adair." He glanced at Clarrissa's motionless form, both loving and wary. "Are you. . . . Did he send you to retrieve her?"

"What?" Elle scrunched her nose. "No. I'm here for his heart."

Leslie stiffened. "Adair's heart?"

"Yeah. Any chance you know where it is?"

It took him a few seconds too long to say, "No." A weak apology followed the obvious lie. Elle narrowed her eyes. He fiddled with the hem of his long-sleeved shirt and continued, "Even if I did know, it would not help. At this point, his heart and the painting are one and the same. You cannot separate them."

Elle crossed her arms. "Well, I have to try, don't I?"

"No. I could escort you to the exit and help you evade the Painted Lady. You could leave."

"If I go back without his heart, Adair will kill me."

Leslie pursed his lips, surprise melding seamlessly with concern. "He intends to kill you regardless of your success. Surely you know that."

Disquiet cooled the blood in her veins. A lead weight dropped into her stomach. She shook her head. "No. He's going to teach me magic. We made a deal."

"All due respect, Elle, but deals made by Adair's hand are meaningless. He is not one to leave his weaknesses exposed."

Dread joined the disquiet. She thought of Adair in all his strength and how much more powerful he would become once he had his heart. She said, "But that doesn't make any sense. Once I give him his heart, he won't have any weaknesses. Will he?"

Leslie flicked a glance at Clarrissa, and the puzzle pieces clicked. Adair's obsession with the painting—the crazy scribbles on the walls and the time he'd spent sitting in front of it—had as much to do with the subject as the enchantment.

"She's his weakness?"

"Why do you think he was willing to risk traversing the painting in the first place?"

Frustration bubbled under distress. Elle pressed her palm to her forehead and dragged it down her face. "It's not like I'll use it against him. I can't—"

"I am telling you it does not matter. When you return, he will kill you. Your best bet is to go quickly and attempt to flee."

Attempt to flee. *Right.* "Thanks, but I've tried that already." She motioned to her sides and the wounds they both knew were there.

He grimaced. "And you do not know any magic?"

"No. That's why I'm here." Resentment for her situation stumbled over the knowledge that it was too late to do anything about it. She was already in the painting. Assuming she ever wanted to leave again, she'd have to face Adair eventually. She buried both hands in her hair, ruffled the fluffy mess, and huffed. "You know what? It's fine. He said he'll teach me, and he will."

"He was hardly a man of his word even before losing his heart."

Elle raised her head to look Leslie in the eyes, and for a single, heart-wrenching moment, he reminded her of Quincy. Always kind and well-meaning. Always discouraged and so, so pessimistic. She said, "I haven't committed any atrocities *yet*, Leslie. If I have to hold his heart hostage, I will."

He blinked a few times, uncomprehending. His lips twitched with silent laughter. "You? How?"

"I'll have it when I get out of here, so I guess I'll just, I don't know, refuse to give it back?"

"Do you know how to fight? Physically?"

"No."

"So no physical advantage and no magic. Even if you manage to outwit Adair, his heart is strong. I highly doubt your ability to 'hold it hostage.'" His voice lilted with good-hearted condescension.

Elle wanted to hit him.

She said, "If you're so positive I'll lose on my own, why don't you come with me? Help me beat him."

Leslie's smile dropped. "I cannot."

"Why not? Can't you fight? Physically?"

"Well, yes, but that is hardly the point."

"Then what is the point? Because you seem to have a hell of a lot of opinions for someone who can't do anything." She balled her hands into fists, frustration overflowing. Leslie took a shameful step back, attention flitting once again to Clarrissa. Elle jeered. "You can't be serious."

"She needs me."

"She isn't real."

"You know nothing!" Leslie strode into Elle's personal space, suddenly on the offensive. "She is the only real thing left. It is the rest of the world that crumbled while she remained. She talks to me and comforts me. She—" He cut himself off, voice trembling. "You do not know what you are talking about."

Fear of what Leslie might do *(of his physical strength; of his anger)* encouraged Elle to run. The sorrow glistening in his eyes held her still. Apology seeped into her tone even as she asked, "There's a real Clarrissa, isn't there?"

Leslie paled, wide eyes and trembling lips negating any remaining threat. "No."

He took a step back. Elle took a step forward. "There is. Why else would you care so much about a painting? Why else would Adair have tried to come here, knowing what he might lose? What happened to her?"

"She . . ."

"Did she die?"

"Stop it!"

"Did you love her?" Elle took another step forward, bare toes abutting leather boots. "Did Adair?"

Leslie shoved Elle hard enough to send her sprawling. She hit the ground hard, forearms and back taking the brunt of the impact. Her sides burned. Anger ate her surprise. She opened her mouth, but Leslie was already shouting.

"Of course we loved her! She was kind and perfect and wonderful, and it is our fault that she . . ."

Elle watched Leslie break from her place on the ground, a dull picture of three childhood friends forming in her mind. His sobs were muted. His shoulders shook. She wanted to feel sorry for him, but there was nothing.

Whatever his reasons, he was choosing to stay in the painting. Choosing to be trapped in this pretty box, just like the survivors had chosen to stay in the House. They clung senselessly to their fantasies of happiness, and the only emotion Elle could muster for any of them was disgust.

She pushed herself off the ground. "You want to stay here? Fine. Stay here. Just don't act like you're doing it for her."

"Clarrissa needs me."

"No. You need her." Elle glanced past Leslie to see Clarrissa still staring at the other side of the table, still smiling. "Adair sent me in here because he wants his heart back. He's ready to move on. Maybe you should be, too."

Leslie's lips twisted in a vicious snarl. "You have no right!"

Elle didn't respond. She faced the empty field to her right, impossibly sure of which direction led where, and started walking.

Maybe the person near the exit—the Painted Lady?—would be more helpful.

8

Elle stared at the painted version of Adair's home, unamused. She knew he couldn't be there and yet . . .

"Adair?"

No response.

She crept forward. "Adair, I swear if I. . . . If you're here, I'm going to be pissed."

Silence settled in the artificial grass and the breezeless air. She pressed her face against a window, which had the same odd, plush texture as the ground, and peered inside.

Where Adair's home had been sparsely decorated and spacious, this place was cluttered. Used canvases covered the floors, furniture, and walls, some stacks touching the ceiling. If a path through the mess existed, she couldn't see it.

"Who's Adair?"

Elle's heart thundered. She skittered to the right, away from both the person who spoke and the window. A painfully thin, androgenous figure watched her go. The person—the Painted Lady, most likely—stood taller than the door and wore nothing but a formless, white-white dress. Her skin matched her clothing, and flowing, whiter-than-white hair draped over her shoulders. Even her eyes were colorless, with nothing but a thin black outline separating the irises from the whites. The only real splash of color Elle could find rested in her pupils, which were exactly as black as the void outside the House.

"When did—"

"Did I scare you?" The Painted Lady sounded curious but unrepentant. Her impossibly large eyes had yet to blink.

The hairs on Elle's arms stood on end. She slid her right foot behind her left, just that little bit farther away. "I . . . yeah. I didn't hear you coming."

"Were you supposed to?"

"Yes?"

The Painted Lady swayed on her feet, unnaturally fluid. "Should I try again?"

"No, that's okay." Elle offered a smile that felt more like a grimace. "There is something else you could do for me, though."

"Oh?" The Painted Lady leaned closer, too-tall frame bending like hot wax to hover over Elle.

Foreboding settled in Elle's bones. She rubbed her bicep and fought the urge to flee. "I'm looking for a heart. Adair's heart. Do you know where it is?"

"Everyone knows where the heart is."

Excitement colored over apprehension. Elle straightened. "Where?"

"With what it wants."

"What does that mean?"

The Painted Lady blinked for the first time, long and slow, before crowding farther into Elle's space. Elle craned her neck to maintain eye contact, doing her best not to cringe at the acrylic smell of the Painted Lady's breath.

"Your eyes are stunning. I've never seen such rich browns before. And those copper flecks . . ." The Painted Lady sighed wistfully, revealing white-white teeth to match her white-white skin. "May I have them?"

"My eyes?"

"Your colors."

Long, sinewy fingers reached for Elle's face. Elle took quick steps back to avoid the caress. "You said you know where the heart is."

The Painted Lady deflated at the redirection. "The heart, the heart, the heart. Why seek such a selfish thing?"

"Adair asked me to come get it."

"A friend?"

Elle glowered, then grunted. "Something like that."

The Painted Lady swooned. "I've never had a friend before. Is it nice?"

"Yeah. Real nice. Which is why I need to get the heart for him."

"Will you be my friend, too?" Elle opened her mouth to say she didn't have time for any more friends. The Painted Lady beat her to the punch. "I'll give you the heart."

Time seemed to slow as Elle's objective came into focus. In the span of a second, she thought of giving the heart to Adair and learning magic. She imagined retrieving her memories, returning to the House, and finding Quincy miraculously alive. Her voice came out hoarse. "You have the heart?"

"It is all I have. All, I feared, I ever would have. But your *colors*."

Elle shifted uncomfortably. "Where is it?"

The Painted Lady grinned, her gums the same color as her teeth, and unfurled her arm to mark a clear path toward the door.

A chill swept down Elle's spine, warning her not to go, but it was pointless. Both the heart and the exit were inside. The only way out was through.

The Painted Lady curled long, spidery fingers around Elle's shoulder. Her skin had the same plush, taut texture as the grass and the window, and it occurred to Elle that everything in the painted world was likely made of the same thing.

The Painted Lady opened the door and ushered Elle inside. "You won't regret this. I'll be a good friend. You'll see."

Elle nodded absently, already scanning the messy room for the heart. The Painted Lady closed the door behind them. Logic caught up to Elle's single-minded nature too little, too late, and—

Oh, hell.

She didn't know what a heart looked like.

It would be red, probably. Like blood. And small. Adair's heart was bound to be small, considering what an awful person he was. Except hearts were physical things, weren't they? And Adair was a big man: tall and broad. So maybe his heart was big, too.

Elle put a hand to her chest, half hoping she'd be able to feel the shape of her heart. She couldn't.

"So where is it?"

"This way."

The Painted Lady squeezed Elle's shoulder, powerful and eager. Elle tried to shrug out of the tight grip, but the Painted Lady was stronger by far. Elle licked her lips and asked, "Would you please let go of me?"

The Painted Lady stared at Elle with wide eyes, not seeming to understand.

Elle clarified. "You're hurting me. Friends don't hurt friends."

"Oh." The Painted Lady released her. "Is that better?"

"Much." Elle rolled her shoulder, preferring to focus on the pain over the Painted Lady's manic stare.

"What do friends do together?"

"I don't know. Hang out. Talk. Where's the heart?"

"Can we do those things?"

Elle frowned. "We're doing them right now." She waited for the Painted Lady to perk up, then asked, "Where's the heart?"

"This way."

The Painted Lady glided to the right. Elle followed at a more sedate pace. The rooms were cluttered to the point of only having a thin walkway between towering stacks of paintings, but the general layout mirrored Adair's actual home. A couch still sat near the fireplace. The room to the right still contained a heavy wooden table. Elle had hoped the exit would be in the same place the entrance had been, but too many paintings were hung too closely together to see the wall or door or *whatever* underneath.

Elle stepped carefully over what looked to be discarded painting supplies and turned sideways to avoid bumping into the paintings on the table. A voice in her ear said, "Here."

Elle jumped. The Painted Lady had once again invaded her personal space and was once again unrepentant. Bony fingers coiled around the edges of a book-sized painting, canvas a hair's breadth from Elle's skin.

Elle accepted the small square with care, not entirely sure what should and shouldn't be done with it.

"You're welcome."

"What?" Elle looked up from the painting, more than a little distracted, then said, "Oh, yeah. Thanks."

The Painted Lady smiled like Elle had praised her. Elle returned her attention to the painting. An ugly, odd-shaped red thing with a line not-quite down the center and tubes coming out of the top filled the majority of the square. It looked familiar, and Elle only had to glance up once to understand why. Every painting in the house depicted the same thing. They were different sizes, angles, and colors, but the subject was unmistakable.

"Is this a heart?"

"Oh, yes." The Painted Lady grinned, an excited child. She dipped her hands into the painting. The previously solid picture rippled like water around her fingers, and when she withdrew her hands from the painting, a heart beat in her palms.

The canvas that had once held the heart was blank. Elle tossed it to the side and leaned closer to the heart. She raised a hand, fingers trembling, but didn't touch it. The power she held over Adair thrummed in her veins, reminding her that every move she made had a consequence. Be it on accident or on purpose, a single, hard press could kill him. She clenched her fist twice to still her quivering fingers, then traced a feather-light line down the body of the beast. It felt like the grass, the window, and the Painted Lady.

It was fake.

"This isn't Adair's heart." Elle pulled back, eyes accusing. "Where's his heart?"

The Painted Lady's smile fled. She cradled the heart to her chest with the care of a parent hugging their child. "You asked for a heart, and I gave you one. The best one."

"I didn't ask for a heart. I asked for Adair's heart. Where is it?"

The Painted Lady frowned, small and tight. "You're not being a very good friend right now."

Elle gritted her teeth, then plastered on a less than friendly smile. "I'm sorry. I just thought you said you knew where the heart was." When the Painted Lady started to present the heart in her hands, Elle quickly corrected, "Adair's heart. The one from the real world."

The Painted Lady's frown gained a petulant twist. "It's with what it wants. I already told you that."

"But that doesn't make any sense."

"Hearts come here to be with what they want. There is nothing else." White-white fingers dug into the sides of the heart, nails piercing muscle and fingers sliding inside. It stopped beating. "The last heart was selfish. It only wanted what it wanted. It never spoke to me, not even once. You're a better heart. A heart and more. A friend."

Elle took a careful step back. White-white eyes zoned in on the movement.

The Painted Lady spoke, voice low and flat. "You are my friend, aren't you?"

The next few seconds extended indefinitely as Elle became aware of both her closeness to the Painted Lady and her distance from the door. There was no clear path to freedom, with paintings jutting out in every direction and the floor covered in discarded supplies. Her fingers tingled as her muscles tightened, a string pulled too tight. Elle's lungs filled to bursting while adrenaline pumped straight to her calves.

Time started moving again.

Elle made a run for it. One step. Two steps. Four. The Painted Lady grabbed her shoulder and yanked, throwing her to the floor. Paintbrushes dug into Elle's back. She kicked a stack of paintings, toppling it between them

The table stood sturdy between Elle and the exit. She rolled under it, arms and legs scrambling beneath her in a wild attempt to gain ground. She launched herself forward, the balls of her feet pushing off the floor so forcefully that she stumbled.

She bumped into another tower of paintings, overcorrected, and smacked into the table. Pain shot through her hip. Adrenaline smothered her discomfort. She could see the door. Elle sprinted across the room, blood pounding in her ears. Her fingertips grazed the knob.

A hand snaked into Elle's hair and yanked. Elle yowled, pain momentarily overriding all else. The Painted Lady dragged Elle from the door. Elle clawed at the hand in her hair. If the Painted Lady felt pain, she didn't show it. Panic bubbled.

"Stop it! Stop it! Let me go!"

The Painted Lady lifted Elle by her hair. Another animalistic noise vaulted from Elle's unwilling mouth. The Painted Lady frowned, markedly unsympathetic. "If you're not my friend, then I'm not your friend, either."

"This isn't about friendship, you crazy—"

Elle's head hit the table with a *crack*, panic vanishing under a nauseating wave of pain. She groaned, low and tearful. The urge to plead for her life blossomed, but anger got in the way. She kicked savagely backward. Her foot connected with something taut and plush. The hand in her hair tightened, forcing her up again.

Crack.

Elle's vision blurred. The pain intensified. She thought she might have been crying, except—

Crack.

9

Leslie stared dazedly in the direction Elle had gone, for once expecting to see movement.

Surely she would return once she realized the extent of the Painted Lady's power. Elle was magicless and physically defenseless, not to mention painfully thin. If she engaged in an altercation with the Painted Lady, she would die.

Surely she knew that.

He turned back to Clarrissa, who smiled at the sunset frozen on the horizon. His leg bounced nervously beneath the table. "Elle has been gone a long time. Do you think she is alright?"

Clarrissa smiled past Leslie, warm and approving. She always liked it when he worried about others.

"It is just, she is small. You saw her. Not short, per se, but tiny. Like she has not had a good meal in years. And young. Barely touching the age of majority, I think."

Clarrissa continued to smile, loving.

"I am not saying I wish to help her. Even if I wanted to, which I do not, it is not like I would be of any proper use. The Painted Lady is made of magic. Practically invincible."

Clarrissa's smile filled with silent laughter.

Leslie ducked his head. "It is not funny. She is going to die."

A small, skeptical smile.

"Alright, alright. So maybe I do wish to help her, but I cannot."

A smile tinted with disbelief.

Leslie rushed to defend himself. "You heard her. She is determined to take me back to Adair, and there is no way he will be willing to separate a second time. You and I will never see each other again." He traced random patterns on the table, determined not to know what kind of smile Clarrissa was presenting. "She reminds me of me, you know. Or Adair, I suppose. Forceful and charismatic. Definitely more logical than emotional, what with the way she spoke to me."

Leslie glanced up through his lashes to see an encouraging smile. He wished she would say something. Wished she would tell him what to do. Hearts weren't made for decision-making, and Leslie was no exception. He hesitated before reaching forward, aware that he should call on her sparingly but unable to hold himself back.

He drew a line in the air, from her eyes to her clavicle, then pulled away. There was no immediate reaction, but that was to be expected. The more he called on her, the longer she took to come to him and the less time she was able to stay. He tapped a rhythmless tune on the tabletop as he waited, the disconnect between a visibly wooden surface and the feel of canvas beneath his fingertips barely registering.

Then she breathed.

Clarrissa's arrival was always something of a marvel. Her previously still chest moved, achingly empty eyes filled with life, and Leslie fell in love all over again.

"Hello, Leslie. I didn't expect to see you again so soon."

"I apologize." Leslie leaned forward, content just to breathe the same air as his lost love. "It is an emergency."

Her smile was understanding. "How can I help?"

"There is a girl, here in the painting. I fear for her safety."

"A girl." Clarrissa stared dreamily at the sunset. Her teacup touched the table. Her smile softened. "Oh yes. I see her now."

"Where is she? Is she okay?"

"She's with the Painted Lady." Mahogany eyes refocused on Leslie. "Is she Adair?"

"What? No." He paused, knowing his time was running short but too curious to leave it be. "Why?"

"She feels like you. A little hurt, a little broken, but strong."

"Strong enough to survive?"

"I don't know." Her smile twitched wider. "Is that important?"

Leslie stiffened, horrified. "How could you even ask that?"

Clarrissa canted her head, looking soft, beautiful, and confused. "Did I say something wrong?"

Her smile tilted apologetically, and it occurred to him, possibly for the first time, that she was smiling not because of her gentle disposition but because it was painted to her face. His righteous anger plummeted, leaving him with nothing but sick truths and Elle's echoing accusations.

There's a real Clarrissa, isn't there?

What would the real Clarrissa have said? Something about the worth of a human life, probably. Or maybe she wouldn't have said anything, too busy rushing off to help. She had always been too kind for her own good. Selfless in ways that rarely benefited her.

Leslie tried to remember what Clarrissa sounded like when she was angry. When that didn't work, he widened his parameters to how she had sounded at any point while alive. A sudden desperation to know if her real voice matched up with the painted Clarrissa's flooded him, but those details were long gone.

Tears welled in his eyes. A profound sense of loss swallowed him whole. When he blinked next, it was like seeing for the first time. His placid worldview shattered while a spark along his skin burned away the thick, stifling desire to stay put. And there, in the farthest corner of his awareness: magic.

It was dust on the wind for its subtlety, but Leslie had lost his ability to manipulate magic in the split, not his sensitivity to its presence.

He was cursed.

The information both weighed him down and freed him. He stood, knees weak, and walked around the table. Clarrissa's eyes followed his every move. Her fingers twitched near the cup, but her control was clearly slipping. He pretended not to notice.

"Clarrissa." Leslie's confidence faltered as she offered him a beautiful, expectant smile. He fisted his hand in his shirt. "May I kiss you?"

Her newest smile was charming. Loving. Encouraging. Playful. She said, "Of course," as though he hadn't avoided touching her for the last decade. He leaned forward with confidence he didn't feel. His eyes closed, their lips met, and he cried harder.

Kissing Clarrissa was like kissing the table, taut and plush and *canvas.*

He pulled back, prepared to apologize, but she was already gone. Her lifeless husk smiled serenely at the sunset, waiting for him to take his usual seat across the table. She either didn't know that he knew, or she didn't care. *Couldn't* care. Leslie could no longer interpret her smiles, and even that small admission left him desolate.

"I have always loved you." He looked away from Clarrissa, toward Elle, the exit, the Painted Lady, and his other half. "And I always will."

If her smile changed as he left, he didn't see it.

10

Elle awoke to pain behind her eyes and a ticklish feeling on her cheek. She groaned and attempted to turn away. Long, strong fingers clutched her jaw.

"Hold still."

Awareness returned in a disorienting rush. Adair. The heart. The Painted Lady. The *table*. Elle tried to jerk away, but her arms and legs were pinned. Metal-looking shackles hugged her biceps, wrists, and ankles, the plush material clinging as tightly to her skin as muscle did to bone.

The hand on her jaw migrated down to her throat and squeezed. Elle stopped struggling.

"They won't break. I painted them on myself." Fear mixed with dread. The Painted Lady smiled and released Elle's neck. "That's better." She picked up a paintbrush. "Isn't that better?"

Elle glanced around the room for anything that could help her escape. There was nothing. "What are you doing to me?"

"Hmm?"

Elle tugged discreetly at her restraints, but they may as well have been a part of the table for all that they budged. The Painted Lady paused, gaze sliding down to Elle's cuffed wrist. Elle distracted her with a quick, "You're, uh . . . you're painting something on my cheek. What is it?"

"I'm not painting. I'm harvesting."

Elle froze. "Harvesting?"

"Your colors." The Painted Lady's large, black-and-white eyes moved back up to Elle's face. She pressed the brush to Elle's cheek. "You have beautiful colors."

Elle jerked away as best she could, both terrified and infuriated. "You can't do that. You have no right."

"I don't need rights. I have colors."

"They're *my* colors." Elle thrashed against her restraints. "You can't have them."

The Painted Lady returned her palm to Elle's throat and pressed down. Elle sucked in a wheezing breath, pain stained with humiliation. The ease with which the Painted Lady pinned Elle emphasized her weakness and mocked her effort to change. Pressure built in her lungs, horrible and unrelenting. The worse it got, the less she believed it was her need for air.

The thing compressing in her chest wasn't vulnerability, but power. It was anger, burning hot in her soul because she *would not* die like this. Fury and hatred fused in Elle's core, then surged outward. Her legs, her arms, her fingers, her toes. The hatred phased through her skin and shattered her shackles. The hand at Elle's throat tightened, a useless threat swatted away by the apex predator that was Elle's rage.

Elle sat up in tandem with the Painted Lady's body smashing into the wall.

Her burst of power flickered and died as the need for it abated, leaving her empty but fulfilled. She jumped off the table and ran. Her bare feet slapped the not-really-wood floor, headache pounding in time with her steps. She clutched the doorknob—solid contact that couldn't be taken from her—then flung the door open.

Leslie stood on the other side.

"What—"

"Duck!"

Elle dropped into a crouch as Leslie punched the air above her. Something hit the ground behind her. He grabbed her wrist and started running. She followed him in a near-stumble, daring to look over her shoulder only once and spinning back around just as quickly.

The Painted Lady raced after them, a flurry of white-white limbs and hungry hands. She reached for Elle, lanky arms and spindly fingers seeming longer than ever. The fury in her eyes promised ruin. A fingernail caught on the back of Elle's shirt as Leslie tugged her forward. Fear throbbed as she realized he was the only reason she hadn't been caught already.

Her lungs ached. Her legs wobbled. She couldn't keep the pace. Elle opened her mouth to say as much, but Leslie was a step ahead. He stopped running.

Panic overrode fatigue. She squeezed his hand and tried to pull him along. He didn't budge.

"It is alright, Elle. We have crossed the border."

"The what?"

Leslie pointed back the way they came, and Elle followed his finger to see the Painted Lady stalking an invisible line. Her too-large eyes were trained on Elle. Thin white lips parted in a snarl, baring her blunt teeth and white-white gums to the world.

Elle looked away. "Why isn't she coming after us?"

"Painted things cannot move too far from their points of origin without changing the actual painting, and the enchantment is not strong enough for that. This"—Leslie toed the grass in front of them—"is the edge of the painting. She is a part of the enchantment, not the painting."

"She can't enter the actual painting?"

"No. She can roam the edges, but nothing can change what was painted."

"But we—"

"Are not made of paint. We do not show up on the canvas."

"Oh, of course." Elle rolled her eyes, emotional exhaustion kicking in. "Why would . . ." She stopped, pain and anger jumbling her thoughts. Their sprint left her breaths heavy. "Why would Adair make her? What's the point?"

"It was not a choice. All magic is sentient, and when an enchantment as detailed as this is created, that sentience gains shape.

In this case, as is the case with most portal spells, the shape is a gatekeeper."

Elle frowned. She shot another glance at the Painted Lady, who stared obsessively back. Her headache hit its peak. "Could we talk somewhere else?"

Leslie nodded and led them in a new direction, away from both the Painted Lady and Clarrissa. Elle wasn't sure how he could tell where the edge of the painting was—there were no visible markers, and the world had no obvious end—but she trusted him to steer them away from it. Once the Painted Lady was out of sight, Leslie said, "I apologize for taking so long."

"Huh?"

"My intent was to rescue you from the Painted Lady, but I accomplished my task in only the barest sense of the word. You are alive, not unharmed. I admit that I . . ." He paused, a soft blush dusting his cheeks. "I dawdled when I should not have."

Elle grimaced. "It's fine. Honestly, I didn't think you'd come at all."

"It is not the expectation to do good that binds me. It is the good that needs done."

She snorted. "If you say so."

He walked a little closer. His forehead crinkled with worry. "How are you feeling?"

"Fine."

His brows shot up to his hairline. "You are not fine."

"Excuse you?"

"Pardon my rudeness, but your head. And your *face*."

Elle made an indignant noise, but the way her head throbbed said he probably had a point. She pressed two fingers to her scalp where her head hurt the worst. Pain shot through her skull. She winced. Leslie quit walking, his fingers encircling her wrist. She glared at his hand, ready to snap, but stopped short. Blood coated her fingers.

"Do not touch it. You will aggravate the wound."

Elle pulled her hand out of his grip, and he let her. She wiped her fingers on her shirt, then scanned the empty field. Aside from the silhouetted trees in the far distance, they were alone. "How bad is it?"

Leslie frowned, overly empathetic. "Very."

"Can you fix it?"

"If we were in the real world, certainly. Herbs and potions are my area of expertise. Here, though, I fear I am rather useless. Even if we could find the necessary ingredients, they would not have the same properties." He released her wrist. "I could feasibly bandage it, as I did the wounds on your sides, but it may do more harm than good."

Elle licked her lips. Her mouth felt dry. "I figured as much. What about my face?"

She rubbed her lower cheek and jaw, where the Painted Lady had been harvesting. Leslie looked off to the side, the guilty tug of his lips telling her everything she needed to know. He said, "I doubt it is reversible."

Elle prodded her jaw. "It doesn't hurt. Is it really that bad?"

"It is white."

"White?"

"White-white. As in completely devoid of color. Not your entire face, of course, but a patch of it." Leslie gestured to the lower-right side of Elle's face. "There."

"That's all? It's just a weird scar?" Tension bled from her shoulders, relief a palpable thing. "You made it sound like something bad."

"You do not care how you look?"

"No. Should I?"

He drummed his fingers against his thigh, contemplative. "I suppose not."

Elle waited for a better explanation, but he seemed content to leave it be. She changed the subject. "What about Clarrissa?" Like flicking a switch, Leslie's entire body slumped. His lips trembled. His eyes glistened. Confusion kick-started irritation, and Elle shook her head hard. "No. Stop it. You can't just start crying every time something upsets you."

Fat tears rolled down Leslie's cheeks. "Well, how should I know that? I was never upset before you came along."

"Never? You're like thirty."

"Thirty-seven." He sniffed and used the heel of his palm to wipe away tears, abruptly less upset. "Or perhaps twenty-seven. I suppose I could have stopped aging upon entering the painting."

Elle narrowed her eyes. "What is wrong with you?"

"I do not understand what you mean."

"Why are you so, so . . ." Elle motioned disgustedly to Leslie as a whole.

He crossed his arms, affronted. "So what?"

"Emotional."

Leslie pulled his lips together in what could only be described as a pout. "I am a heart. I am supposed to be emotional."

"Wait, what?"

"I refuse to apologize for my natural inclinations, and on that note, I find your crass assessment of my personhood genuinely offensive—"

"Shut up. You called yourself a heart. What did you mean?"

"I meant what I said. I am only a heart, and I cannot be expected to abide by the same social rules as those who have minds to guide their emotions."

"You—are you Adair's heart?"

"Leslie Adair, technically. We went by Adair before the split, but once I had my own body, I felt I deserved my own name as well. Also"—tears gathered in his eyes—"Clarrissa used to call us Leslie. She was the only one."

His voice sounded watery and pathetic, which Elle found more annoying than empathy-inducing. "How do you have a body? And how are you talking if you're only a heart?"

"The physical part of me is Adair's heart, yes, but I am also part of his soul. No matter our differences, we must be the same."

"That doesn't make any sense."

"It is impossible, yes." Leslie nodded like they had reached an agreement.

Elle breathed a deep, calming breath and moved on. "Why didn't you say you were his heart earlier?"

"Because I did not wish to return to Adair." Leslie sighed as he ruffled his hair, visibly conflicted. "That is to say, I do wish to rejoin him, but when I leave this place, I will never be able to return. And Clarrissa—"

Elle interrupted before he could start crying again. "Why tell me this now? You know I can't leave without you."

"Nor shall you have to." He stepped forward, all negative feelings apparently forgotten as he cupped Elle's hands with his own and offered an encouraging grin. "You have inspired me, Elle. Freed me, even. I will not allow you to go unrewarded."

She unclasped their hands and cocked her head, skeptical both of his new outlook and the odd interpretation of events that led him to it. "You'll go back to Adair then?"

"Better. I shall escort you wherever you wish to go."

She blinked once, slow and stupid. "What?"

"Without my intervention, Adair will kill you. Even if I were to merge with him, our mind has always overruled our emotions. It is doubtful I would be able to influence him enough to spare you."

"So you'll just, what, not merge?"

"For a time. Long enough to take you where you need to be."

"What I need is someone to teach me magic."

Leslie frowned. "Unfortunately, I am no longer capable of such things. When Adair and I split, he retained our magic. I retained our ability to fight physically, identify plants, and make potions. My current knowledge of magic and magic manipulation is vague, at best."

"Why?"

"It is . . . complicated. I assume the differentiating factor is my love for Clarrissa. Everything I know, I learned for or from her. Magic, on the other hand, was something we dedicated ourselves to purely for personal enjoyment."

"How does magically dividing up your knowledge even work?"

Leslie offered a helpless shrug. "You would have to ask Adair. In the meantime, think about my offer. If a teacher is what you seek, I promise to help you find one. If there is something else . . ."

Flashes of Elle's dream flitted through her mind. Her older, powerful self. Perun. The sphere of lightning. Having a guide would be helpful, but even Elle could recognize the unfairness of that request.

She had no idea how long her journey would take or how dangerous it would be. She couldn't say for sure that the dream had been real.

"Elle?"

"I'll think about it." Her voice came out more clipped than intended. Leslie tried to catch her eyes, but she looked past him, toward the distant silhouette of the Painted Lady's house. Her head throbbed, her throat ached, her sides burned, and as much progress as she'd made, she was practically back where she'd started.

She rolled her shoulders and ran a hand through her hair, purposefully relaxing. There was no point in getting bent out of shape thinking about the next adventure with the current one still flexing its claws inside her. Without looking away from the Painted Lady's house, she asked, "Any chance you've got a plan to get us out of here?"

"That depends."

"On?"

Leslie took his place next to Elle, smile blinding. "How much do you trust me?"

11

"This is a bad plan."

"Relax. You will be fine."

"Easy for you to say. You're not the one buddying up to the psycho." Elle glared at Leslie. He gnawed on his lower lip, attention never straying from the Painted Lady's house. Elle sighed. "Can you at least pretend you think this will work?"

"It will." He paused. "Probably. And if it does not, we shall simply escape again and come up with a new plan."

"If it's that easy, why do you look so nervous?"

"Oh, I do not know, Elle." Leslie rolled his eyes. "Perhaps because I am nervous?"

"Well can't you hide it?"

"How many times must I explain to you that I am a heart? I feel emotions, not filter them."

She mocked him under her breath but let it die. They'd known each other less than a day and the argument was already old. "You're sure she won't notice you?"

"Not so long as you distract her properly."

Elle frowned at the uneven distribution of responsibility, but Leslie had already gone back to worrying his lip in the Painted Lady's general direction. "I'll distract her, so stop brooding."

"I already told you—"

"We can do this." Elle waited for Leslie to look at her. When he did, she used confidence she didn't feel to say, "We're strong, we're smart, and she's just an enchantment. We can beat her."

The edges of Leslie's lips curved down in a preemptive crying frown. The worry watering his eyes traded places with gratitude. He leaned forward like he wanted to hug her, then squared his shoulders in a show of strength. He said, "Of course."

Elle breathed a soft sigh, unconvinced that her pep talk would be enough to carry him through. The more time she spent with Leslie, the more it seemed that his mood swings were the only reliable thing about him. She patted him on the back because he seemed like he needed it, then stood.

"Painted Lady!"

Leslie's poise melted into fidgety panic. Elle motioned for him to run before he ruined the plan for the both of them. When he failed to move, she cupped her hands around her mouth and shouted, "Painted Lady! We need to talk!"

Leslie stiffened, openly terrified, then took off. Elle pretended not to notice the way he chewed his lip as he went.

"Painted Lady!" She raised her voice again, ignoring the way it scratched her already sore throat. "I'm sorry for running away!" Something white moved on the horizon. Elle ignored the burning in her esophagus and yelled louder. "Please!"

The white splotch became a silhouette and eventually the Painted Lady. Elle glanced at the tree line denoting the edge of the painting and resisted the urge to retreat.

The Painted Lady stopped just shy of the border. "Why are you over there?"

"Because you scare me."

The Painted Lady leaned to the right, overly large eyes on Elle. "I'm not scary."

Elle opened her mouth, but she couldn't think of a polite way to inform someone that they were horrifying. She motioned to the bloody wound on her head instead. "You hurt me."

"You hurt me first!"

Cruel, angry words crowded behind Elle's teeth. She swallowed them down. "How did I hurt you?"

"I thought we were friends." The Painted Lady sagged, seeming more confused than upset. "Didn't you want to be my friend?"

"I did." Elle took the smallest step forward, toeing the line of safety. "I do. I was scared is all. You were such a good friend that I didn't think I'd be able to, uh . . . to live up to your standards."

The Painted Lady stared, a hair's breadth from inanimate. "That's not true."

"It is." Elle's smile was kind, encouraging, and almost genuine. "You were so good to me. Better than Adair ever was. I convinced myself that he'd be better if I got his heart for him, but I met his heart, and you were right. It was awful."

Enough time passed that Elle feared the worst. Then the Painted Lady straightened, long fingers primly adjusting her white dress. "The heart is a selfish thing. I told you that."

"Yeah. You did tell me. I'm sorry I didn't listen." Elle folded her hands in front of her and lowered her head, apologizing in the only manner Miss Cynthia had ever accepted. "You were a good friend."

The Painted Lady crooned. "I was a good friend, yes. I am a good friend. I can show you how to be a good friend." White-white palms splayed against a barrier Elle could neither see nor feel.

Elle smothered her disgust with a pleasant grin. She raised a hand to mirror the Painted Lady's. "You have to promise not to hurt me again."

"I promise."

The agreement was too eager to be honest, but this was where trusting Leslie came into play. Elle was the distraction, the bait, and going with the Painted Lady was part of the plan.

Elle held her breath and stepped over the border. She told herself everything would be fine. The Painted Lady latched onto Elle's bicep with enough force to rip that thought from her head, and *holy shit* this was a bad plan.

"I missed you, friend."

Elle smiled, but it was weak. "Yeah. Me too."

The Painted Lady tightened her grip, blunt nails piercing soft skin. She half led, half dragged Elle back to the house.

Anxiety crawled under Elle's skin, and she had to forcibly remind herself that this was the plan. She'd distracted the Painted Lady long enough for Leslie to break in, find the exit, and hide somewhere safe. Once Elle joined him inside, he'd signal in the direction of the exit, and they'd escape. The plan was so simple it would take a complete and total idiot to muck it up.

The Painted Lady opened the door with too much force and closed it the same way. She squeezed Elle's bicep painfully tight while reaching for the nearest brush, then painted a padlock onto the door. Elle's stomach sank. The Painted Lady grinned. Elle forced herself to smile back.

She prayed she wasn't working with an idiot.

Once the door was secured, the Painted Lady released her. Elle rubbed her sore arm and looked for some sign that Leslie hadn't chickened out and left her to die. The couch looked the same. The stacks of paintings looked the same. The room with the table—

Elle choked on her own spit.

The wall behind the table, once covered in canvases, had been cleared to reveal a door-sized painting. The positioning was the same as the portal in the real world. The picture was different. Instead of Clarrissa in a field, this painting depicted Adair reading a book at the table. There was no way the Painted Lady could miss it and no way she wouldn't think Elle was involved. Two steps in, and their *(really very bad)* plan had already failed.

The Painted Lady screeched. "You! You tricked me!"

Elle backed away. "Leslie!" The Painted Lady swiped out. Elle ducked and swerved. She tripped over an easel and steadied herself on a stack of paintings. They wobbled and fell. "Leslie, help!"

Silence settled. Terror tainted her blood. She took off toward the exit. Images of Leslie biting his lip, drumming his fingers on his thigh, and crying fluttered behind her eyes, and she knew calling out a third time would be pointless.

More likely than not, he was already gone.

The portal was too far. The Painted Lady was too close. Elle would've crawled under the table again, but the paintings once stacked atop the table had been moved to the floor, likely to make room to tie Elle down. She vaulted over the table instead.

Her feet hit the ground with a thud. She rushed toward the exit, but the Painted Lady was faster. White-white hands cut her off, fingers grasping. Elle twisted and ran the other way.

A mistake.

The Painted Lady stood in front of the portal, unmoving. Elle looked around for a weapon, but all she saw were paintings, paintbrushes, and empty tubes. She fingered a shard of broken shackle on the table, but it only looked sharp. It felt the same as the rest of the world. Fear tried to clog her thoughts, encouraging her to panic. She breathed through it.

"If you were really my friend, you'd let me go."

"If you were really my friend, you wouldn't keep trying to trick me."

Elle canted her head. *Fair enough.* She picked up one of the larger paintings leaning against the wall, canvas as tall as her torso and twice as wide. It wasn't sharper than anything else, but it was heavier. "So, we're not friends. Let me pass, and I promise never to bother you again."

The Painted Lady snarled. Elle raised the painting like a shield.

"I don't want you to go away! I want you to—"

Elle charged. She slammed both the painting and herself into the Painted Lady, then shoved hard to the side. The Painted Lady stumbled. The painting dropped. Elle turned to run only for two bony white arms to snake around her waist. She reached out, not even close to touching the exit.

Alarm bells went off in Elle's head. She thrashed in the Painted Lady's hold, near hysterical. The Painted Lady walked toward the table, and Elle's next move was born not from a well-thought-out plan, but the instinctive need to live. She scrunched her neck and lowered her head, lips aligning with the Painted Lady's bicep. She sank her teeth into white-white flesh.

The Painted Lady howled. Something thick and acrid poured into Elle's mouth, more chemical than blood. One of the arms around Elle's waist vanished. Knuckles smashed into her head wound.

Pain translated to nausea, which translated to more pain. Elle opened her mouth, removing teeth from flesh. The Painted Lady spun her around so they faced each other. The room kept spinning even after Elle stopped.

Three Painted Ladies snarled at Elle, all equally furious. Behind them stood three Leslies, each of which held the bottom of a folded easel. Elle didn't have to be lucid to understand what was about to happen. She leaned as far from the Painted Ladies as she could, and the Leslies swung.

Every easel cracked every Painted Lady in the side of the head. The Painted Ladies hit the ground, and the Leslies dove for Elle. They grabbed Elle's hand and pulled, apparently unbothered by the nauseating way the room tumbled, wall over wall and ceiling over floor. The Painted Ladies yelled something unintelligible.

A single Leslie hauled Elle the final few steps to the portal and exited with a graceful leap, their clasped hands leaving her no choice but to tumble in after him.

12

Elle had never been more thankful to be dumped on a hard, unforgiving floor.

"Wood. Leslie, it's real wood. We did it!"

"What did you call it?"

Elle jerked her head up so fast that the room seemed to tilt. Her glee fled in the face of Adair. "What?"

"My heart. What did you call it?"

"Leslie." Elle glanced at Leslie, who looked anywhere but at Adair. "And he's a him."

Adair's dark glare moved from Elle to Leslie. He sneered. "How quaint."

"Adair . . ." Tears filled Leslie's eyes and an apology twisted his lips.

Adair knelt in front of his heart, gentler than Elle had ever seen him. She knew she should move away, if only to give them privacy, but curiosity kept her still. Adair splayed his hand flat against Leslie's chest, and a sparkling light spread from his touch. It was bright edging on blinding, forcing Elle to squint. Leslie gasped, his eyes locking on Adair's, and a moment of understanding seemed to pass between them.

That moment was broken as Leslie jerked back, out of Adair's reach. The light died, leaving the room dimmer than ever. Elle scooted to the side as Adair snarled. For the first time since she'd met him, he looked genuinely angry. He grabbed Leslie's shoulder, but the light didn't return.

Adair asked, "What are you doing?"

Leslie attempted to wriggle away, but Adair held him in place. Leslie said, "I . . . I made a promise."

"Who gives a flying fuck about your promises? Merge with me."

"I will not."

"You're my heart. You don't have a choice."

"Yes, I do." Leslie gripped Adair's wrist, meek nature replaced by anger-fueled confidence. "I promised Elle I would escort her where she needs to go, and unlike you, my word actually means something."

Adair's murderous gaze swiveled to Elle. Her heart beat in her ears. His free hand shot up, palm toward her, and she felt the fire before she saw it. She dove to the side. The floor rumbled. She jumped to her feet.

The ground lurched, throwing her against the wall. Her head felt like a spike had been driven through it. Her entire body ached. She couldn't win this fight.

She stumbled to her feet, room swaying, and ran for the door. A crash sounded, but nowhere near Elle. The house didn't try to attack her. The potential in the air didn't twitch. She wrapped her hand around the doorknob, then looked back.

Leslie and Adair were wrestling on the floor. Adair was larger, but it looked like Leslie had been right about retaining their knowledge of physical fighting. Adair bucked and struggled, but it was Leslie who came out on top. He straddled Adair's waist, his chest to Adair's back, and pinned both Adair's hands to the floor. He wrapped his legs around Adair's, stopping the other man from kicking out.

Elle waited for Adair to use magic to throw Leslie off. Seconds ticked by, motionless, until it hit Elle that Adair couldn't risk it. Hurting Leslie meant hurting himself, and who was to say how that kind of damage would transfer once Leslie was a regular heart again?

Leslie spoke in a low warning tone. "Are you finished?"

Adair gave a single, sharp nod, cheek flush with the floor. Elle let go of the knob and slid to the ground, adrenaline giving way to dizziness, fatigue, and hunger. When was the last time she'd eaten?

Leslie untangled himself from Adair and rushed to Elle. He turned her head to check her wounds, skin cool and fingers gentle. "Are you alright?" He didn't wait for an answer, instead turning to Adair to ask, "Are our potions fully stocked?"

"Obviously."

Leslie nodded and, to Elle, said, "Wait here. I am going to retrieve some salves for your wounds and a potion for your concussion. Adair, will you please make something to eat?" Elle stared slack-jawed at Leslie, in awe of his audacity. Adair's responding glare said that Leslie may as well have asked him to chew off his own arm. Leslie huffed, more exasperated than angry, and clarified, "I require nourishment as well."

Adair cursed, pushed himself off the floor, and left. Elle barked out a laugh. Leslie shot her a soft look of disapproval, to which she tried and failed not to look as smug as she felt.

Leslie disappeared for a few minutes only to return with an arm full of rags, bottles, and jars. He used the rag to clean her head wound, every careful dab and gentle swipe birthing a new shock of pain. She bit her cheek to keep from whining.

Minutes passed like hours, then he smeared something cold on her wound, and the pain vanished. She relaxed against the door, barely blinking as Leslie lifted her shirt to move onto her sides.

He prodded her stomach. "Perhaps you should bathe first."

Elle glanced down, confused until she saw her bandages had reverted to paint. She scratched at one of the thick white lines, then nodded. "Good call."

"Would you like to do that now or after you eat?"

Soaking in a cold bath sounded like hell. Eating and not going to bed immediately afterward sounded worse. "Now is good."

Leslie led Elle down a hallway and to the right, into a small but sleek bathroom. He turned a knob and tested the water before putting the stopper in the drain. "Towels are in the closet. You may adjust the temperature as you see fit."

"I can . . ." Elle crouched by the tub and dipped her hand into the water. It was fantastically warm. "Oh wow. I've never had a hot bath before." She leaned over and fiddled with the knob, upping the heat.

"You only take cold baths?"

"I thought everyone did." The water in the tub steamed, near scalding. She shook her hand out over the tub and asked, "What's a closet?"

Leslie stared at her for a second too long, then pointed to a thin door partially hidden behind the door to the hall. Elle crossed the room, closed the door to the hall, and opened the smaller door. It led to a tiny room with shelves full of cloths and pretty bottles. Not even Quincy would've been able to squeeze inside. She tilted her head, unsure why such a little room existed.

Towels and washcloths were on the second shelf, colorful and aplenty. She picked green ones. Leslie watched the entire process with furrowed brows and parted lips.

"Elle, where are you from, exactly? If you do not mind my asking."

"The House."

"What house?"

"*The* House." Elle shrugged and pointed to the ceiling. She walked past Leslie to turn off the water. "You mind if I wash up now?"

He fiddled with the hem of his sleeve, obviously torn between asking more questions and leaving her to bathe. She preyed on his empathy by twining her hands together in front of her and pitching her voice low. "Please? I've never had a hot bath before."

Leslie's shoulders slumped, predictable and pity filled. "Of course." He opened the door to the hall and shouted, "Adair?"

Adair appeared in the doorway a minute later. "What?"

"Would you please imbue the water with healing properties?" Leslie shifted to the side so Adair could see the bath. Adair made a small counterclockwise circle with his finger, and the water tinted blue. He was halfway out the door when Leslie flatly repeated, "Healing properties."

Adair turned back around, expression unreadable. The two men stared at each other, neither one amused. Elle thought the standoff might stretch on forever, then Leslie reached for the water, and Adair's blank mask broke. He scowled, hand doing a quick clockwise flip. The water turned pink.

Leslie smiled. "Thank you."

Adair left without saying anything. Leslie rolled his eyes, tossed Elle a playful wink, and followed his counterpart. He shut the door behind him.

Elle laid her towel on the edge of the sink and stripped, careful not to touch whatever Leslie had smeared on her scalp. She dropped her clothes on the floor and stepped into the bath. She groaned in relief. The hot water stung the wounds on her sides, but not enough to ruin the experience. She leaned against the edge of the tub.

They were out there talking about her, she was sure. Adair wanted to kill her, as Leslie had predicted, and Leslie was likely defending her right to live. She thought Leslie would win, if only because Adair seemed to need him more than he needed Adair. Not that Leslie would hold out forever, but he at least seemed intent on keeping his promise to be Elle's guide.

She sunk deeper into the warm, comforting water, thoughts lulling. She'd never been this tired before, and she hoped never to be this tired again.

Was it okay to trust Leslie? His determination to help was suspicious, but it wasn't like she had other options. Adair had obviously never intended to teach her anything, which meant she wouldn't be able to protect herself for a while yet. Turning down an escort, practically a bodyguard, would be stupid. Not to mention running away with Adair's heart seemed like the quickest and most effective path to petty revenge.

The only real question was where she wanted to go. Finding a teacher would take the least amount of time but would also require the least amount of help. She could ask him to help her find her memories or the castle from her dreams, but there was no telling if either of those things actually existed. As much as she wanted to make Adair miserable, forcing him to live without his heart indefinitely seemed a bit extreme.

The pink water fogged from the paint on her abdomen. Her thoughts were running in circles, and her fingers were starting to prune. She grabbed a rag and started scrubbing. Elle washed her face, then cleaned the paint off her back and abdomen as best she could.

When the water got too cloudy to see her hands beneath the surface, she pulled the plug from the drain.

She climbed out of the bath and grabbed her towel, water pooling by her feet. Getting dressed took a stupid amount of time, her sides once again too tender to touch. She brushed her hair, careful not to touch the wound on her scalp.

Water marked her path back to the table.

Adair occupied the head of the table on the left, Leslie the one on the right. Elle's plate sat to the left of Leslie's, looking as delicious as it smelled. Adair flicked his wrist, drying both Elle and the trail of water behind her.

"Thanks."

The downward tilt of Adair's lips said he hadn't done it to be kind. Leslie motioned to the plate of food and a bottle of something brown. It was Leslie who said, "Please, have a seat." He waited for her to take the proffered chair, then continued, "The potion is for your concussion. It is best consumed with food, so I suggest eating first."

The meat, rice, and vegetable combo melted in her mouth. The potion tasted like refuse. Elle stuffed her face and pretended not to notice the awkward silence stretching between them. Adair glared at Leslie, who sent strained smiles to Elle. Whatever they'd talked about while Elle bathed clearly hadn't gone over well.

When Elle swallowed her last bite, Leslie cleared his throat. "Elle, I have a bit of a personal question for you. That is, if you do not mind."

"Go for it."

"Right. Yes." Leslie sipped his water. His leg bounced beneath the table. "You mentioned you came from a house and alluded to that house being in the sky. Could you tell us a bit more about it?"

"Sure." Elle leaned back. The burns on her sides twinged. "It had an upstairs, a downstairs, a kitchen, a living room, a bathroom, and five bedrooms. There were two doors, but they were both boarded shut to keep the demons out."

Adair cut in. "Who told you closed doors stop demons?"

"Don't they?"

"No."

Elle's worldview tilted as yet another facet of her reality turned out to be a lie. She swallowed hard. "The other survivors said opening the door was deadly. That's why they wouldn't let me leave."

"Survivors?" Leslie laid his forearms on the table, granting Elle his full attention. "What did they survive?"

"The fall of the world."

Adair raised a hand and motioned to the green grass and sunny skies just outside the window. "I don't know if you've had time to look around yet, but the world's just fine."

Humiliation bubbled in Elle's stomach. She snapped, "I know that now. But maybe I traveled back in time, or—"

Adair laughed, loud and derisive. Leslie coughed into his hand, likely to hide his own snickering. Elle flushed, more embarrassed than ever.

Leslie lowered his hand, a small smile still playing on his lips. He ignored her time-travel comment to say, "And this house. Where is it?"

Elle pointed up.

Adair said, "That's not an answer."

Leslie asked, "Could you clarify further?"

Elle hugged her stomach, hands resting on her hips to avoid touching her burns, and said, "I really don't know. There weren't any windows, and when I opened the door, there wasn't anything outside. No sky. No ground. It was just empty." She looked off to the side, unwilling to let them see how much the bleak nothingness scared her. "It's got to be up there somewhere, though, or else I wouldn't have fallen here."

Leslie wrapped both hands around his water glass. He smeared the condensation with his thumb. "And how did you arrive there initially?"

"I fell out of the sky. I don't remember anything before that."

Adair scoffed, disdainful. "So you fell out of the sky, into the sky? You do realize how ridiculous that sounds, right?"

She hugged herself tighter. "You asked me what happened, and I told you. What else do you want?"

"I want you to start making sense." Adair tapped the table. "Tell the truth."

His disbelief hit Elle like a smack in the face. She raised her voice. "I am. I came from the sky."

"The sky in the sky?" He raised his brows, both haughty and apathetic. "If you're going to lie, at least lie better."

"You know, Miss Cynthia said you were more demon than human, but I think she was giving you too much credit. All you are is annoying."

"Says the girl too stupid to tell which way is up."

Anger shoved logical thought to the side. Adair wanted to fight? Fine. She'd fight. Elle turned to Leslie and said, "Take me there."

Leslie drummed his fingers on the side of his glass. "Where?"

"The sky. I want to go back."

Adair scorned. "You can't be serious."

Elle ignored him in favor of watching Leslie. The heart-turned-human twisted his cup back and forth on the table, neither accepting nor declining. She pressed on. "You promised you'd take me wherever I want to go, didn't you?" She reached across the table and tucked her fingers between Leslie's hand and the glass.

Adair protested. "This is literal nonsense. The sky isn't a destination. It's not somewhere you can just *go*. It's infinite."

"No. There's a castle up there. It's magic, with a tattooed man and a sphere of lightning. That's where I need to be." She squeezed Leslie's hand. "Please."

Leslie glanced back and forth between them, posture hunched and nervous. Adair said, "Do not."

Elle countered, "Leslie, you promised."

Leslie pulled his hand away from Elle's, and she knew she'd pushed too far. He said, "I need to think about it. May I just. . . . May I have some time?"

Elle smiled through her frustration, determined for Leslie to see her as more compassionate than Adair. "Of course."

Adair waved a hand in Elle's direction, blatantly dismissive. "Isn't it your bedtime?"

She opened her mouth to argue, but what came out was a yawn. Elle blinked twice, confused as to where the sudden wave of exhaustion had come from. Suspicion spiked, then dissipated. Her head fogged. There was a bleary moment where she thought about raising a hand to rub the sleep out of her eyes, but her limbs were too heavy. She laid her head on the table, barely aware enough to avoid using her plate as a pillow.

She bid Leslie goodnight, but it was in a dream.

13

"How did you . . . ?"

"Sleeping draught in her food coupled with a compulsion charm." Adair tapped the table, forcing air under the dishes and ordering they levitate to the kitchen.

Longing and wonder fought inside Leslie, his fingers itching to perform the same feats. "I miss being able to do magic."

"Then merge with me."

Adair caught Leslie's eyes. Leslie looked away. Adair left him for the kitchen.

Elle slept peacefully at the table, thin chest rising and falling in time with her breaths. Under the influence of both a draught and a compulsion charm, she'd be impossible to wake before morning. Leslie rubbed the back of his neck, secretly thankful.

The girl was similar to Adair in a lot of ways—scarily so, in fact—and Leslie wasn't quite sure what to do about that. He wanted to keep being a person, at least for a little while longer, but trading one Adair for another seemed a dangerous deal.

Not to mention she wanted to go to *the sky*.

He hooked one arm under Elle's knees and the other behind her back, then lifted. She was exactly as light as she looked. He pondered over nutritional potions while carrying her to the guest bedroom, toed open the door, and froze. It looked exactly the same as he'd left it, with its dusty-blue bedspread and hand-sewn pillow. Sorrow crashed into him, heavy and unavoidable. His throat tightened around loneliness, and tears flowed over.

Once upon a time, Leslie had argued with Clarrissa over the necessity of a guest room. They never had anyone over, and he'd wanted to utilize the space to brew potions. Clarrissa hadn't cared. She'd wanted the drafty cabin to feel like a home, and to her, that meant having a guest room.

Leslie clutched Elle's thin frame to his chest and took deep, wobbling breaths. He missed Clarrissa—missed her kisses, her laugh, her smile—and the knowledge that he would never get to experience any of those things again was crushing. He wanted to apologize, but there was no one to apologize to and nothing to apologize for, so he just cried harder.

A warm hand on his back startled him. He jumped, grip on Elle slipping, but Adair was prepared for his clumsiness. A gust of wind lifted her from Leslie's arms and tossed her on the bed. She didn't even twitch.

Leslie rubbed his eyes with the heel of his palm. The tears kept coming. "It looks the same as when Clarrissa. . . . When she was . . ." He inhaled a sob, unable to finish his sentence.

"Yeah." Adair didn't sound like he cared, and without Leslie's emotions, he probably didn't. "I've been told it makes the place feel more like a home." A watery giggle slipped out of Leslie's mouth. Adair squeezed his shoulder, comforting rather than controlling, and said, "Hurry up. We need to talk."

Leslie wiped his tears on his sleeve, grateful even as Adair walked away. The sadness in his chest hadn't magically vanished, but it was more manageable. Entering the guest room didn't feel nearly as unbearable as it had minutes prior. He crossed the room and repositioned Elle's limp form so he could access her sides. He rubbed salve on her burns, which were fresh enough that they might not even scar.

It crossed his mind that he should sit by Elle's side and watch for an allergic reaction, but being surrounded by reminders of Clarrissa hurt too much. He placed the salve on the bedside table and left her to sleep.

Leslie followed Adair's magical signature out of the cabin and into a shabby mirage. Adair sat on the grass, knees to the sky. Leslie said, "This is new."

"I didn't want company."

Leslie touched one of the trees. He didn't have the magic necessary to dispel the illusion, but he knew enough to escape, regardless. "This mirage is . . ."

"Shitty?"

"Yes." Leslie sat cross-legged beside Adair. "Did you outsource?"

"No."

"Then why is it so terrible?"

"What can I say? My heart just wasn't in it." Adair tossed Leslie a sidelong glance.

Leslie looked away. "I wanted to come back."

"What stopped you?"

"There was a gatekeeper. The Painted Lady. She was powerful."

"Powerful enough that a clueless sixteen-year-old could bypass her in a day?"

Leslie swallowed his excuses. It was true that he could have gotten past the Painted Lady on his own, had he really wanted to. He'd considered it often enough. Rather than admitting any of that, he said, "We are cursed."

"We split our soul. Of course we're cursed."

"No, I mean to say that there is a secondary curse. It prevented me from seeing that the Clarrissa I was with and the Clarrissa we loved were different."

Leslie left out both the part where he knew Adair must have been hurting and the conscious decision he'd made to cater to himself rather than go back for his other half. He didn't mention the endless, all-consuming guilt that decision had spawned, either. Adair had too much ammunition already, and the only thing coming clean would do was provide him with more.

Adair made a few complicated hand signs in front of his eyes, and dark brown irises gained a golden glow. Leslie let him look, momentarily caught on the oddness of staring at a face he used to wear, listening to a voice he used to use, and saying a name he used to go by.

The downturn of Adair's lips said Leslie had been right. "That's not possible."

"Did you identify the curse?"

"No." Adair leaned closer, eyes searching. "It's soul magic. I would go so far as to call it a side effect of what we did, if not for the magical signature. But again, that isn't—" Adair broke off to list a string of obscenities, ending his tirade with a snarled, "Cypress."

"Who is Cypress?"

"You don't remember?" When Leslie shook his head, Adair said, "It's a higher demon. We met it in a bar, back when Clarrissa was diagnosed. It offered to save her in exchange for our soul." Adair paused, the tension in his posture bleeding into the magic in the air. Wind rustled the trees. "You really don't remember?"

Leslie blinked a few times, perplexed. "Not at all."

Adair swore again. "Our memories up to the point of separation shouldn't differ."

"What does that mean for us?" Leslie worried his bottom lip between his teeth. "How do we fix it?"

The angry set of Adair's jaw was familiar enough that Leslie's hope faded even before his counterpart said, "I don't know. Soul magic is high-risk, low-reward. We never touched the stuff before enchanting the painting." He paused. "Do you remember that much, at least?"

"Yes. I believe my lack of memories only extends to . . . Cypress, was it? Or demons in general, perhaps. I cannot recall any information on them."

"We don't know much. They're rare and steeped in soul magic. Immortal. There might be a way to kill them, but I haven't heard of it."

"And Cypress?"

"It showed up again when the girl fell out of the sky."

Surprise blossomed. Leslie sat up straighter. "Wait. She really did fall from the sky?"

"She did. Then she got lost in this mirage. I was going to leave her to die until Cypress showed up and hinted at using her to get you."

"But that means—"

"We're being played." Adair punched the dirt. "That bitch."

"Now hold on a minute. Even if Elle did play a role in this, I highly doubt it was purposeful. It is far more likely that she is a pawn, the same as us."

"All the more reason for us to merge and get rid of her. Whatever's going on, she's at the center of it. We're better off together—with all of our knowledge, all of our abilities—and far, far away from her."

"No."

Adair threw his hands in the air, expressing a frustration that didn't reach his eyes. "Why not?"

"I promised—"

"You can drop the nice-guy act, Heart. Elle is not the reason you're refusing to merge."

Leslie scooted farther away, affronted. "Why would you say that?"

"In a choice between helping myself and helping someone else, I always choose myself."

There was no accusation in Adair's tone. Leslie still felt attacked. Defensive anger covered shameful truths, and he shouted, "I am not you!"

Adair didn't respond to the outburst. He canted his head, emotionless brown eyes seeming to say, *Do you really think you can lie to me? I'm you.*

Self-loathing boiled in Leslie's veins. He pushed off the ground and stomped to the edge of the mirage.

Adair didn't understand—wasn't *capable* of understanding. When they merged, it was Leslie's personality that would be lost and Leslie who would have to give up his individuality for the sake of the whole. And for what? So Adair could go back to ignoring their emotions—ignoring Leslie—in favor of logic?

Even thinking about giving up his personhood made Leslie sick with anxiety. Refusing to merge with Adair made him sick with guilt.

Taking Elle on a journey was supposed to have been the compromise, but *the sky*.

That was a long, long way from where they were. Leslie had only wanted to take a short detour, to make his own decisions and experience his own adventure, before merging. Agreeing to escort her to some impossible castle could take months or even years.

He dug his nails under the bark of a nearby tree and tried to imagine what a castle in the sky would even look like. Crumbling stone and winding ivy. A tattooed stranger. *The lightning.*

Hope seeded in Leslie's chest, primary emotions trading out with the ease of breathing. To the cool night air and the endless forest, he said, "Maybe it is not a coincidence that Elle came to us."

Leslie saw Adair stand out of his peripherals. His counterpart joined him by the edge of the mirage. "What do you mean?"

"You remember it, right? The night Clarrissa died?"

"Don't even think about it, Heart."

Leslie ignored Adair's warning tone, guilt taking a back seat to love. "Her lightning struck across, not up. Clarrissa may still be—"

"No."

"She may still be where the lightning goes."

"Clarrissa is dead!" Adair grabbed the collar of Leslie's shirt and spun him around, genuine grief flashing in empty brown eyes. "We've already torn our soul apart in an attempt to reunite with her. What else do we have to do before you accept that she's gone?"

"So what? You expect us to move on? To forget?"

"I could never forget. That doesn't mean I want to spend every minute of every day remembering."

Guilt prodded Leslie again, but his love for Clarrissa was stronger. "This is a sign, Adair. What are the chances that Elle needs to go to the only place where Clarrissa might be?"

"Exactly. What are the chances?" Adair shoved Leslie away, out of the mirage. "It doesn't take a genius to see that this is a trap."

"I am going." Leslie said it on impulse, but pride mingled with anticipation, and he realized he meant it, too. Adair didn't appear anywhere near as at peace with Leslie's decision. His mouth opened and closed, soundless. It took him a full minute to say, "You can't."

"I am." Leslie smiled. "Do not worry, Adair. I shall return, and when that time comes, we will merge. I promise."

"I won't let you leave me again." Adair's voice was rough like sandpaper and dark with promise, but Leslie wasn't worried.

He was going to the sky.

14

Cypress was bored.

He'd been bored for 324 years, give or take an interesting soul or two. The reason for that boredom stood in front of him: a man-god with the gall to cheat death.

"Do you know why I called you here, demon?"

Cypress picked another nonexistent speck of dirt out from under his nails. Of course he knew why he'd been summoned. "No, Master."

Perun stared at his precious sphere of souls, one arm folded behind his back, the other kneading his abdomen. Short black hair had been slicked back, as it was always slicked-back. Tattooed toes poked out from beneath clean white slacks. He rolled his shoulders, drawing attention to the names of various lightning gods tattooed across his skin. They were written in different fonts, sizes, and languages.

Cypress glanced from his nails to the rest of the large circular room. It was drafty, as all old stone buildings tended to be drafty, with the only furniture being two overfull bookcases, a large wooden table, a throne-like chair, and the sphere.

Tattooed fingers curled into a fist. "My scar hurts today."

Cypress hummed, having guessed as much. "Is there anything I can do to help, Master?"

Perun looked over his shoulder, hazel eyes sharp. They both knew the only currency he had left was time, and while the wizard was arrogant and impatient, he wasn't stupid. He said, "I want to hear about the girl."

"Elle?" Cypress raised both brows, purposefully apathetic. "She escaped."

Perun's anger was a physical force. His magic lashed out with care only for the sphere of souls behind him. Cypress went back to examining his nails.

Despite his violent magic, Perun sounded calm as he asked, "What do you mean 'escaped'?"

"Broke out. Ran away. Departed. Left. Is no longer accounted for—" Cypress stopped as the wizard's wild magic shattered the solid wooden table.

"I know what escaped means!" Perun turned from his sphere, manic gaze finally focusing on Cypress. "What I want to know is *how*. I ordered you to keep her trapped forever."

Cypress's lips turned down in a minute show of displeasure. "You said, and I quote, 'Lock her up and throw away the key.' I did."

"Then how?"

"A hammer."

Perun sneered, disgusted and entitled. Cypress wanted to point out that imprisoning Elle at all had been an act of charity rather than a component of their agreement, but that would ruin their game. He kept his mouth shut.

"Find her, and this time, I want her dead."

"No."

"What did you say?"

"No, Master."

"Demon." Perun was never amused by Cypress's sense of humor. How dull. "You cannot deny me."

"Our deal compels me to protect you until the day you die. She's not threatening you."

"She could."

"A lot of things could. She isn't." Cypress caught Perun's gaze. "Unless you'd like to adjust the terms of our agreement?"

Perun's eyes dilated, a half second of fear squirming free before arrogance buried it. "You know I don't."

"Then are we done?"

"No." Perun returned his attention to the sphere of souls, tattooed hands clasping behind his tattooed back, inadvertently flexing the large *Apocatequil* written across his shoulders. "You may not have to physically protect me before I am threatened, but you do need to be aware of approaching threats. Find her. Make sure she hasn't had contact with the others."

Cypress nodded. "Yes, Master."

"And demon?"

"Yes, Master?"

"Do take care to complete your task correctly this time. I am not always such a gracious god."

Cypress bowed his head to hide bared teeth, his fingers itching to tear out a soul long overdue.

"Yes, Master."

15

There is a castle in the sky. It is grandiose to the point of egotism. Elle is watching her older self again, and she knows she does not belong. Her bones are tired. Her armor is worn. Her mind is sharp. The weight of her sword rests heavy on her back, encouraging her forward. She touches the hilt, aware that the master of the castle will not welcome her.

This is for the best, as her intentions are not kind.

Elle is a shadow of her older self, and their bloodlust is shared. She has been wronged. Her vengeance is deserved. They kneel, feeling the magic of the castle like a three-dimensional map, and their course is set.

"Wait for me, Clarrissa."

Elle opened her eyes slowly, savoring the taste of a distant dream. She didn't think she'd ever slept so well in her life, though that might've had more to do with the soft, cushy bed than any lingering sense of exhaustion. She snuggled into the cocoon of thick blankets, content to close her eyes and go back to sleep.

That contentedness faltered as she realized she had no idea how she'd gotten to bed. She remembered asking Leslie to take her to the sky, and then . . . Adair, maybe? Sleep left smudges on her memories, and all she knew for sure was that her exhaustion had hit too suddenly. One moment she was fine. The next?

Elle cursed and tossed the blankets away.

"Adair!" She stormed out of the room, not sure what he had done but more than positive he was the one who'd done it. "Adair!"

"Elle, what is wrong?"

She shoved past Leslie to see Adair sitting at the table. He didn't bother to look up from his book. She asked, "What did you do to me?"

Adair turned a page. Her temper flared. She marched forward, intent on snatching the book from his hands. She reached out. An invisible force tugged at her abdomen, and a single blink later, she was outside.

Elle spun around, but all she could see were four familiar trees on repeat.

"Adair!" Humiliation burned in her stomach. She turned in circles, but the house was nowhere to be seen. "You can't just leave me in here!"

The silence that settled around her said otherwise. Tears stung the backs of her eyes. For Adair to be able to incapacitate her without even looking up was embarrassing verging on demeaning. And worse: she respected him for it.

If she were even half as capable as Adair, she'd never have been trapped in the House in the first place.

The void inside Elle ached at the acknowledgment. Jealousy welled around the feeling that she should be able to do complicated magic, too. *Why was she so weak?*

"Elle? Are you alright?"

Leslie appeared out of nowhere, much like Adair had done days prior. Elle wiped her eyes with the back of her hand. "I'm fine. Can you get me out of here?"

"I can show you how to exit a mirage, yes." He looked anywhere but at her eyes, fingers tapping a nervous rhythm on his thigh. "Before that, however, I would like to speak with you. Is that alright?"

Elle made a broad motion to the infinite trees. "Not like I have anywhere else to go."

Leslie smiled, but it was halfhearted. "Fair enough. I wish to warn you against provoking Adair."

"Provoking. . . . He did something to me last night. Forced me to fall asleep."

"Yes." Leslie nodded. "He did."

"That's not fair." Indignation smoldered. She raised her voice. "He can't just make me go away whenever he feels like it."

"There are many societies in the world that feel the same. They ban and regulate magic as they see fit, and within their borders, your complaints have weight."

His tone was kind but unsympathetic, and her anger sunk under the weight of discontented understanding. "We're not in their borders, are we?"

Leslie smiled again, softer this time. "We are not. If you would rather I take you to one of those places, I can. If you wish to travel to the sky, however, you must let go of your pride."

"You mean you'll—"

"I am willing to escort you, yes."

Elle bounced on her toes and pumped her fist in the air. She grinned so wide it hurt. Then logic kicked her joy in the back of the knees, and her celebration stumbled. She let her arm drop. "Hold up. Adair isn't coming with us, is he?"

"No, but the laws governing magical beings are vague in the sense that they very rarely exist. People with power do as they please until people with more power decide to stop them. There is a general notion of courtesy, most often seen at Impossible Markets and in small magical settlements, but the final say goes to whomever has the greatest power. A castle in the sky is an impossible place, which means we will be bound to the rules, or lack thereof, of those with magic."

"Like Adair."

"Precisely."

"How are we supposed to survive out there if magical people are running around, doing whatever they want?"

"We will be smart. There is no other option." Leslie offered a comforting smile, and Elle couldn't help but think he was wrong. They had another option sitting ten meters away, reading a book. Leslie must have mistaken her disagreement for nerves because he offered a gentle reassurance. "I promise you that we will be fine. People survive without magic every day."

Elle smiled, hollow and fake.

She wasn't worried about surviving. If anything, it excited her to take part in a system where the powerful were rewarded and the weak got smart. Power was something Elle could understand. Something she could work toward, bend to, and die by. Her only real issue came from being at the bottom of the food chain, and that wouldn't last forever.

Leslie shifted closer and asked, "Do you think we can go back inside and, at the very least, refrain from purposefully inciting Adair?"

Elle made a lackluster noise of agreement. "I can try."

"That is all I ask." He raised a hand to point at the trees. "Do you see the repetition of trees? How the branches all point in the same directions and the leaves all move in tandem with one another?"

"I get that there are only four trees. I just don't know how to see it, too."

"The only way a mirage can be visibly dispelled is with magic. Once you recognize a mirage for what it is, however, you can always locate the border. This one is particularly easy to navigate, as Adair put very little effort into its creation. Instead of looking forward, at the trees, I want you to watch your feet. Can you do that?"

Elle looked down and wiggled her toes.

"Good. Now walk forward."

She shot him a suspicious glance, not entirely convinced he wasn't making it up as he went. He responded with an encouraging smile. She went back to staring at her feet. The first step was normal. The second step was normal. The third and fourth steps were normal, too. On the fifth step, her foot turned left. She stopped.

From somewhere behind her, Leslie said, "You found the border. Now walk through it."

She licked her lips and straightened her foot. Her fifth step met no resistance, and her sixth step was the same. On her seventh step, the trees vanished.

"I'm out. Leslie, I did it!" Elle turned to see the forest still existed behind her. Leslie appeared a moment later, though his eyes were notably on Elle and not his feet.

"Very good. The weakness of a mirage is that it can only fool your eyes. Adair coupled this mirage with a compulsion charm, which makes you want to follow a certain path. Magical compulsions mimic urges in that they can be overcome with mindfulness. While not all mirages are coupled with compulsions, it is not uncommon."

Elle beamed, high on her success. "Can you teach me more? I know you can't use magic, but can you tell me how?"

"I am afraid not. The knowledge I retained is general. While I could recite to you the basics of magical transactions, I could not explain the specifics of any spell, charm, or curse. Just as Adair, I am sure, could name any plant we knew but would be unable to list its uses."

Elle chewed at the fat of her cheek, only mildly disappointed. They walked to the house in silence, and Leslie shot her a pointed look before opening the door. Her attention narrowed on Adair, who had yet to look up from his book.

Her stomach squirmed. Her blood pulsed in her ears. She curled her hand into a fist to stop it from shaking and took a deep, steadying breath. She was tired of being weak, tired of waiting for strength to be handed to her, and tired of her own entitled whining. If she wanted things to change, she needed to work for it.

She had to prove she was willing to go the distance. "Adair?"

He didn't look up from his book, which hit the same as if he'd called her worthless and insignificant. She bit back a number of hateful comments and, before she could talk herself out of it, dropped to her knees. "Please come with us."

Leslie squeaked. "What?"

Adair raised his head.

Elle caught his eyes and said, "You want to protect your heart, right? Protect him and merge with him. If you come with us, you can keep him safe the whole time, and you won't have to wait for him to come back to you."

Adair closed his book, thumb marking his place. "If you think I'll protect you along with my heart, you're incorrect. I would consider your death an acceptable loss."

"That's fine." She kept her arms to her sides. Open. Vulnerable. "I don't want you to protect me. I want you to teach me how to protect myself." Adair didn't respond. She lowered her head to the floor and begged. "Please. I won't argue. I won't irritate you. Name your conditions, and I'll agree."

Footsteps sounded beside her. *Leslie, not Adair.* "Elle . . ."

He laid a hand on her shoulder. She shrugged him off. "Stay out of this, Leslie."

She heard him take a step back, his voice making a noise akin to a whimper. He was probably close to tears. She kept her forehead to the floor, refusing to be swayed. This wasn't about Leslie and his hurt feelings. It was about Elle.

Filling the void.

Finding the lightning.

Adair didn't answer immediately. For all she knew, he'd gone back to his book. She didn't dare check. This was as much about showing her commitment as it was acknowledging his superiority, and raising her head could ruin that.

Seconds ticked into minutes. The silence thickened. Her heart thumped like a drum, and she wondered if they could hear it. She decided Adair probably could. Her nervousness twisted into anxiety, and humiliation climbed on top. Was he laughing at her? Was he dragging this out just to enjoy the sight of weak, useless Elle prostrating herself? It was impossible to tell. She took deep, even breaths and awaited a verdict.

Eventually, Adair said, "I thought you had more pride than this."

"I don't need pride. I need a teacher." She clenched her fist tighter. Pressed it against the floor. Squeezed her eyes shut.

Adair spoke, unenthusiastic and unforgiving. "You'll do what I say, when I say it." Elle's head shot up, too surprised to be excited. He continued, "We do things my way. It won't be easy or fun. If I catch you complaining, even once, we're done. I refuse to waste my time teaching someone who doesn't want to learn. Understood?"

Elle nodded, breathless.

He said, "Words are important, so I'll answer any question you ask, but *only* what you ask. If you want to know more, rethink your question. Pay attention. Remember what I say. I will not repeat myself. Are we clear?"

"Yes." Elle nodded again. "Thank you."

"I planned on accompanying my heart either way. Teaching is a way to keep you quiet."

Leslie spluttered from his spot to her left. Joy painted a permanent grin on Elle's cheeks, and she pushed herself off the floor. "When do we start?"

"Go outside."

She glanced between Adair and the door. He opened his book again, then laid it face down on the table. They both crossed the room, though only Elle went outside. Adair raised his hand high above them, curled his fingers into a fist, and released.

Like an overfull bucket flipped upside down, freezing water poured from the sky, drenching nothing but Elle. She screeched. Her body hunched on its own, teeth starting to chatter. Surprise mingled with anger, but if this was the first step to learning magic, she could take it. She swallowed the urge to curse, choosing instead to ask, "W-what now?"

"Think warm thoughts."

He shut the door in her face.

16

"What do you mean neither of you have a plan? How did you intend to get to the sky?"

Elle felt her cheeks warm. She looked at Leslie, who refused to meet her eyes. He was still angry over her betrayal. Adair's house towered behind Leslie, and the mirage behind Elle. Adair himself stood next to the path, facing away from the lake. Elle went back to watching the water drip from her fingers.

"I expect an answer."

Elle didn't know if Adair was capable of feeling real irritation, but he was certainly good at faking it. She cleared her throat. "I was kind of hoping it would just . . . work out?" She risked a glance at Adair, whose disbelieving stare made her wish she'd kept her eyes on the ground.

"And you, Heart?"

Leslie shuffled his feet, indenting the grass beneath his boots. He whispered, "Follow the lightning."

Adair said something in another language, tone exasperated. He thought they were idiots.

Elle shoved her hands in her pockets, shame burning bright, and asked, "Now that you're with us, can't we just teleport there?" Leslie barked out a condescending laugh. She elbowed him in the side, secretly thankful to have a break from Adair's berating, and used a distinctly unapologetic tone to say, "Sorry if that was a stupid question." She caught Leslie's eyes, daring him to comment on her childhood.

He cringed. "There are no such things as stupid questions."

Adair cut in. "No, she's right. That was a stupid question." He didn't explain why, and it took Elle a shameful amount of time to realize she was supposed to rethink her question and ask again.

"Why can't we teleport?"

"Magic is about give and take. Teleportation is one of the most difficult subtypes because it requires knowing exactly what you're teleporting in both directions. I didn't only put you outside. I also moved the air from the space you were about to occupy inside. You swapped places. Do you understand?"

"Yeah."

"I had to know I was moving air. If I had accidentally teleported you to a spot occupied by a deer, what do you think would've happened?"

"What's a deer?"

Adair rubbed the bridge of his nose. "A tree. Let's say I placed you in the same space as a tree. What would happen?"

"You would have a tree in your house?"

"No. I would have part of a tree in my house, and you would have part of a tree in your body."

Elle grimaced at the imagery. "Right. So no teleportation. Got it." She looked first to Leslie, who'd apparently remembered he was angry with her, then to Adair. "How do we get there then?"

"We'll need a guide."

"And where do we get one of those?"

"The same place you get all impossible things."

Adair started down the path to the left without clarifying what that meant. It was Leslie who said, "The Impossible Market."

They trailed after Adair together. Elle said, "You mentioned that before. What is it?"

Leslie made a visible attempt to stay angry as he looked anywhere but at Elle. She didn't mind. She'd seen firsthand how quickly his emotions flipped on themselves. So long as she was nice, kind, and interesting, he'd come around.

Minutes passed in silence before he said, "Impossible Markets are magical settlements where impossible things are bartered. They can be reliably found near non-magical settlements, as those without magic are always seeking the impossible."

"How does that work? Is there a value system or something?"

"No. The two most common factors in determining price are need and time, but it varies from trade to trade." Leslie must have seen Elle's confusion because he continued, "For example, someone with an infected wound needs a healing salve more urgently than someone who simply wants to be prepared. The greater the need, the greater the price. Does that make sense?"

"I think so. What about time?"

"The amount of time an impossible commodity stays in effect is the easiest place to begin a barter. Say you would like a pie that tastes like freedom."

"Freedom isn't a flavor."

"Exactly. That is what makes the pie impossible. So, again, you would like a pie that tastes like freedom. The pie itself might sustain you for a day. You could feasibly trade a headache potion for that pie, as it would heal their headache for around the same amount of time. They might awaken with a headache tomorrow, just as you might awaken hungry tomorrow."

"What about trading a possible thing for an impossible thing?"

Leslie hit Elle with a hard, angry glare. "That, Elle, would be a very stupid thing to do. Possible things have little to no value when compared with impossible things, effectively giving the owner of the impossible thing the right to name his price. All of your material possessions. Your memories. Your *heart*." He fisted the strap of his brown leather satchel hard enough to turn his knuckles white.

She stepped away, confused by his sudden fury. "Leslie, why are you—"

"You are lucky Adair does not care for swindling children because 'name your conditions and I will agree to them' is one of the most foolish things I have ever heard. Bargains like that will get you killed. Or worse."

Leslie bit out a curse and stormed ahead of her.

Shame pooled in Elle's stomach, cold and sickening. What she had thought was bravery had been dumb verging on deadly, and both of her companions knew it.

Anger blossomed within the void to feast on Elle's self-deprecating thoughts, and she hated herself. Hated that she was too much of a coward to go after Leslie and apologize for pushing him away. Hated that she was too mortified to approach Adair and thank him for not taking advantage of her. She focused on her hands, still trembling from the cold water, and thought warm thoughts.

The blankets in the House. The fire Adair had nearly killed her with. The sun. She tried to imagine them (any of them, all of them) in her palms, but the imagery was ridiculous. She funneled her frustration with her situation into her lack of progress and switched tactics.

The dirt path was uneven but relatively straight. She closed her eyes, trusting she'd feel the grass beneath her toes if she veered off course, and imagined heat. The overbearing heat of the sun. The scorching heat of a fire. The heat of her own body.

A new potential sparked in her hands, painful and bright. Unlike the strength of the earth or the whimsy of the air, this potential was wild. It singed her palms and vanished. She opened her eyes to red skin and empty air.

Leslie and Adair were locked in a heated conversation up ahead, voices too low for Elle to hear. She opened her mouth to call out and share her success, then remembered they didn't actually like her. The pride she'd felt for her accomplishment dampened, though she didn't understand why. She looked again at the red marks on her hands.

It was fine that they didn't like her. Aside from Quincy, no one in the House had liked her. She had never been the best with words (with human interaction in general), but she didn't need to be. There were other ways to prove her worth.

She focused on pulling heat into her hands, fed the feeling with every pulse of her heart, and this time when a flame flickered to life, she held it closer.

This, she could do.

17

The Impossible Market was busy.

Vendors shouted from beneath colorful tents and outside mismatched buildings. The people crowding the wide dirt aisle between tents shouted back. Elle tried to get a closer look at the nearest booth, but a hand encircled her arm and yanked her backward.

"Don't." Adair kept his eyes on the path ahead, grip painfully tight. "They'll try and trick you into a deal, and you've got nothing to trade."

She glanced over her shoulder, and the creature manning the green booth—a short fat blob-looking thing with long ears and a large nose—smiled at her. Adair tugged her none too gently in the other direction.

"What's wrong with looking? I want to know what they're selling."

"They're selling everything. Knowledge. Wealth. Health. Imagination. Food. None of it is interesting."

"Sounds interesting to me." She tried to tug her arm free from his steel grip. A sharp shock pierced her bicep. "Ow! Stop that!"

"Then stop resisting. You do what I say, when I say it, remember?" He pushed through the crowd with a roughness that had people complaining. Leslie trailed behind them, still angry at Elle for bringing Adair along and freshly angry at Adair for who knew what.

Elle frowned. "Where are we going?"

"A bookstore."

"Books? Books aren't impossible." Adair didn't respond. She rolled her eyes and rephrased. "How can books be impossible?"

"Impossible books are usually regular books charmed to resist damage. They can be burned or dunked in the sea and come out fine on the other end."

"Why do we need that?"

"We don't."

Elle groaned. "Why are we going to a bookstore if we don't need a book?"

"We don't need an impossible book. We need impossible information, which may have been written down in a book."

A woman, taller than Elle but shorter than Adair, stepped in front of them. She held out cupped hands, palms empty. "Air for the lovely lady? Twenty minutes of breathing, anytime, anywhere. Under water? She can breathe. In a smoke-filled chamber? No problem. Taste refreshing mountain air for just—" The air crackled around them, bright even in the daylight, and the saleswoman's smile dropped. "No need to be rude." She returned to her booth without a fuss. Adair kept moving.

"What was that?"

"Air."

"No, I mean, what did you just do?"

Adair glanced at Elle, expression as unreadable as ever. "I summoned electricity."

"It looked like lightning."

Adair didn't respond.

Elle asked, "Was it lightning?"

"It's akin to lightning, when lightning comes from storms. It also powers my home, and it hurts to touch."

"Will you teach me?"

Adair squeezed Elle's arm, and when he released her, frigid water poured from the sky. It soaked her clothes and hair, leaving her shivering. She whispered curses under her breath but didn't complain.

Elle craned her neck as they passed stalls selling bottomless bags and sympathetic diaries. She caught Leslie's gaze only once, by accident. He looked away. The farther into the market they traveled, the more buildings replaced tents. No two buildings looked the same, and few were as well-built as Adair's home. Some were round, others square. Roofs were lopsided, and materials varied from one floor to the next.

A lumpy human-esque creature emerged from a stone building to their right, all four hands offering something shiny. A single look from Adair had it swerving to show off its merchandise to someone else.

Elle tried not to feel resentful when they entered a calmer part of the market without actually interacting with anyone, but it was hard. Places like the Impossible Market *(rough and wild with everyone out for themselves)* were what she had craved in the House, and Adair was ruining it. They stopped outside a building that had four blue-gray books floating over the entrance, and Adair walked inside. Elle tried to follow him, but a plump man rushed over and shooed her out. "No! No, no, no. I'll not have some shoeless orphan ruining my books with her greasy, grubby fingers. Back to the poorhouse with you."

Elle shivered and looked at Adair, who stared unapologetically back. When it became clear he didn't intend to help, she turned her eyes to the ground and took another step away from the store.

Leslie's brown boots stopped beside Elle's bare feet. "Do not feel bad. Adair does not expect you to be able to dry yourself anytime soon."

She brought her pointer finger to her lips and gnawed on the nail. Her problem wasn't lack of ability. It was lack of control. If she ruined a bunch of impossible things with her magic fire, she'd never be able to pay the debt.

Leslie must have mistaken her brooding for the silent treatment because he shifted so the toes of his shoes faced her bare feet. He said, "I apologize for my earlier outburst. I was out of line." Elle looked up, meaning to disagree. He held out a hand for her to shake. "Let us begin anew. I am Leslie Adair, at your service."

From somewhere in the building, Adair shouted, "Not at her service."

Elle huffed out a laugh. She bypassed Leslie's outstretched hand to rub the back of her neck. "It's fine. You were right."

He let his hand fall to his side. "Yes, but I should have been more considerate of your situation. Clarrissa grew up in a magicless society, and as such had a similar lack of understanding." He tossed a hesitant glance at the bookstore, then lowered his voice. "And so did we."

"Seriously? I figured you grew up in one of these markets."

"Quite the opposite. We were born from magicless parents in a magic-restricted society."

"What happened?"

"Nothing spectacular." Leslie's shoulders rose and fell. "We always had a knack for the impossible, and while our parents attempted to support us, their lack of understanding and blind enthusiasm were more burdens than gifts. We spent an ever-increasing amount of time at the nearest Impossible Market until one day we just decided not to go home. We were capable of enough impossible things to make a living, and life was better that way." Leslie's smile stretched wide, joyful tears decorating his lashes. "We met Clarrissa there. She was magicless, and her father was sick. She came running into the market with wild deals on the tip of her tongue, much like you. The difference is that she wanted a cure, and I could not provide."

"Is that why you learned how to make potions and salves and stuff?"

"Yes." His smile softened. "But before that, I helped her by performing impossible feats for another vendor in exchange for her cure. That transferred the debt of her father's cure to me, of course, but I was already half-in-love. She could have handed me a pebble off the roadside, and I would have considered it fair trade."

"What did she give you?"

"Lessons. Her father owned a dojo, and she taught me how to fight. By the time I surpassed Clarrissa, her father had healed, and he took over as my instructor." He leaned closer to Elle, mischief sparkling in his eyes, and said, "I never really cared for hand-to-hand combat—and why would I, when I could set someone alight from twenty meters—but it was a fantastic excuse to spend time with Clarrissa."

Elle grinned, momentarily swept up in their childhood romance. "Did you teach her magic, too?"

"We attempted, but she was incapable of performing even the slightest magical feat."

"Why?"

Leslie hummed, fingers tapping a soundless tune on the strap of his bag. "That is a difficult question. I suppose I should first inform you that everyone, on a technical level, is capable of performing magic. It is a person's capacity for magic that varies. Some have capacities so low that they may as well be magicless, like Clarrissa. Some seem to be limited only by their imaginations."

"Like you and Adair."

"Yes. We are on the higher end of the spectrum. Capacity, unfortunately, is nothing without understanding. Most people, regardless of their capacity, focus on a single type of magic and spend their entire lives perfecting it."

"But I've seen Adair do all sorts of magic. Water, earth, fire, air, electricity. Those aren't the same, are they?"

"No." Leslie shook his head, tone indulgent. "We have always been more sensitive to magic than most, and that lent itself to our greater understanding of magic theory. Where other people need to visualize every little detail, Adair and I operate largely by feel. We want the ground to move, so we call on the soil. We want wind, so we pull the air. There is magic in everything, and if you can feel that—feel the differences in every element and every lifeform—the possibilities become endless."

Elle must have looked as starstruck as she felt because Leslie raised both hands in a stop motion. He said, "Not that we expect you to be able to do what we do. To have our natural affinity for the ebb and flow of magic is rare to the point of incredulity, and you should not hold yourself to our standards. Right now, Adair is testing your talent for fire, and if you do not respond, he will move on to another element."

"What if I want to be held to your standards?"

Leslie's encouraging expression faltered. He twisted the strap of his satchel and looked away. "Elle, we were making the wind blow before we could walk. If you were like us, you would know it." He spoke in a low, soothing tone that offered more pity than comfort. "Not that you should be worrying over such matters regardless. It has been less than a day. Your lack of progress is nothing with which to be concerned."

She looked at her hands, imagined the fire she knew she could create, and said nothing. What did a single flame matter to someone like Leslie Adair? They had grown up bending the elements to their will while Elle . . .

Elle had no idea how she'd grown up.

She clenched her fists, discontent and ashamed. Adair reappeared. He said there were no books mentioning a castle in the sky, but there was a rumor that when lightning traveled, it traveled west.

Adair and Leslie set their course for another Impossible Market two days to the west. Leslie bought their dinners with half a jar of invisibility cream, and Elle's meal tasted like success. She assumed Leslie chose the flavor on purpose, as some strange form of encouragement, but all it did was remind her that the food in her mouth was impossible.

Did she owe them now? Would her debt build with every meal until Elle was more servant than girl? Or did the rule of trading impossible things for impossible things only count inside the Impossible Market?

She voiced her fears only for Leslie to smile and laugh, assuring her that she owed them nothing. "It is a gift," he said.

She hated that even more.

Adair seemed to understand her discomfort (or at least he wasn't as generous as Leslie) because he cut her no slack. When he created a small earthen house to take shelter for the night, he told Elle to go make her own. Leslie argued against it, pointing out the impossibility of the task, but Elle was already walking away.

In truth, she preferred Adair's harsh treatment to Leslie's kindness. It meant, at least in her mind, that he hadn't yet written off her potential. That the high standards to which she held herself could still be attained.

She chose a spot within viewing distance of Adair's makeshift house and pressed her hands against the dirt. The ground here was harder than where Elle had initially fallen, but she appreciated the firmness. It was easier to imagine moving the earth—real and solid beneath her—than it was to create a wisp of fire from nowhere.

She dug her fingers into the dirt, felt small clods of it stuff themselves under her bitten-down nails, and closed her eyes. The earth was dense and heavy, stretching endlessly downward. The air was cool and refreshing, raising gooseflesh on her skin. She knew the potential of the air and the earth were fundamentally different, but not what that differentiation could mean. Still as the earth, Elle sat, listened, and waited.

Leslie had said they felt the magic in the world around them, so that was what Elle would do, too.

18

There is a castle in the sky. It taunts Elle with high walls and thick defenses.

Elle hates this castle. She hates it for the deeds of its master, and she hates it for failures all her own. Her older self drops an empty bottle on the ground, and Elle realizes she is unprepared.

Perun is inside, and he is strong. If she is not careful, she will die.

She tells her older self to turn back, to wait, but depression and anger form a self-destructive spiral she cannot escape. If it means saving Clarrissa, no price is too high. Her body moves helplessly in time with her older self, and they stride toward the castle, unafraid.

Fire lights her fingers, heats the air, and blows a hole in the oppressive wall of the castle she hates.

"Elle? Elle, did you do this?"

Elle groaned, still half-asleep, and swatted at the general direction of Leslie's voice. "Go away."

"Elle, can you wake up, please? I need to know if you built this hut."

She tucked her knees closer to her chest, stone pillow doing little to increase her comfort, and said, "Yeah. And it took a long time. So can I sleep some more? Please?"

The potential in the earth shifted a split second before the ground under Elle jutted up, ejecting her from the little building. She hit the ground outside her hut and rolled, shoulder taking the brunt of the impact. Elle, now wide awake, cursed Adair for all he was worth and then some.

Adair was too busy inspecting the inside of her hut to care what she said. Leslie offered her a hand, which she reluctantly accepted. He said, "This is very good work, Elle. How did you do it?"

"I felt the magic, like you said." She rubbed her aching shoulder and admired her work in the daylight. Thick twisting pillars of earth held up a grassy ceiling while the intricately decorated door (which couldn't be closed but looked spectacular) stuck out to the side, offering a view of the admittedly shabby interior.

"You felt it? What does that mean?"

She shrugged. "I don't know. It's like seeing with your eyes closed, maybe? Everything out here has a sort of potential, and I could be wrong, but I think that potential is magic. Like, you know how you said all magic is sentient? It took me a while, but I think I know what you mean. When I was making this hut, the earth had a presence all its own. And when I focused hard enough, I could talk to it. Or maybe it talked to me? I don't know. It doesn't really make sense when I say it out loud."

Leslie's pupils dilated. The smile he offered was weak. She wanted to ask what was wrong, but Adair stole her attention by emerging from the hut. She crossed her arms, silently daring him to insult her work.

After a staring contest where Adair appeared neither disappointed nor impressed, he said, "It's not the worst thing I've ever seen."

Elle grinned, pride flourishing.

Leslie argued. "Not the worst you have ever seen? Adair, this is amazing. She only started yesterday—"

"Put it back."

Leslie and Elle exchanged a glance. She asked, "What?"

Leslie said, "There is no way."

Adair pointed to his own dirt house and drew an invisible line toward the ground. The house fell in a cloud of dust, leaving the earth just as it had been before they'd set up camp.

"Adair, you cannot genuinely expect her to—"

"I'll do it." Elle caught Leslie's eyes and shook her head, telling him to let it go. To Adair, she said, "How much time do I have?"

"None. Do it now."

Leslie made a disgruntled noise. Elle hurried to her hut. She didn't understand how Adair used magic from a distance, but she would learn. She would prove herself capable of learning.

The ground felt rough under her feet and rough under her fingers. She slid her hands from the twisting pillars up to the low grassy roof and closed her eyes. The "taking" part of give and take had been easy, but she had no idea how to give it back. The earth thrummed below and in front of her, alive in its own way. It offered her strength, for it had plenty to spare. She splayed her fingers against the roof of her hut in what she hoped was a respectful declination.

Where does this go?

The hum of the earth swelled and breathed out, exposing more and more of itself to Elle. A map of the ground beneath her feet formed in her mind, as real as any physical picture. She saw dense minerals and expansive caves. She saw burrows where animals once lived. The map stretched out until she could feel emptiness deep beneath them. She smiled *(grateful, connected, alive)*, and returned what she had borrowed.

Her hut disappeared in a flash. Dust billowed. She opened her eyes to find Adair staring at her. His eyes didn't look any less cold or empty, but his expression was decidedly more interested. The pride she'd felt before dismantling her hut doubled.

She turned to smile at Leslie. He returned her elation with a broad grin and a simple thumbs-up. Their celebration ended as freezing water fell from nowhere, soaking her to the bone. She screamed.

Adair said, "Don't forget to—"

"Think warm thoughts." She hugged her arms to her chest and glared, teeth already chattering. "I know."

Adair didn't respond, but Elle caught a glimpse of a smirk as he turned away. She cursed, mostly at Adair, and hoped that her success with the earth would translate over to her sad attempts at controlling fire.

It didn't.

Over the next day and a half, Elle managed to singe both her hands, burn a hole in her shirt, and dry nothing. By the time they reached the next Impossible Market, Leslie had officially, embarrassingly, gifted her the healing salve.

The second Impossible Market looked much the same as the first, with its cobbled-together buildings and colorful tents. The only ostensible difference was the vendors.

Elle tilted her head, gathered her hair in both hands, and wrung out some of the water. She said, "I think we should split up."

"What? Elle, no." Leslie touched her bicep, eyes wide. "Have we not been adequate guides?"

She squinted, confused, then clarified. "I meant for this market. I want to explore without Adair scaring off all the vendors."

Adair tilted his head, both aloof and judgmental. "There's no need for you to talk to the vendors. Unless you've forgotten you have nothing to trade?"

"I'm not looking to trade. I just want to see."

"See what?" Adair gestured to the Impossible Market in the same way Elle might've gestured to her bedroom in the House. "There's nothing here."

She crossed her arms, defensive. "I won't know what I want to see until I see it. And what matters isn't what I'm looking for. It's what I'll find. I don't want to miss out on learning something new just because you two think I can't handle myself." She focused on Leslie, if only because his potent emotionality made him more likely to cave. "I know better than to try and trade something possible for something impossible now. I can do this."

Leslie adjusted the strap on his shoulder and tapped his fingers on the leather flap. He said, "It is not that we believe you incapable, Elle. You are doing spectacularly well in your training." Adair scoffed. Leslie ignored him. "Larger than the issue of your knowledge is the issue of our location. We are days from any non-magical community, which encourages those with prejudices against the non-magical to gather."

"But I do have magic."

"Barely." Leslie leaned closer, maintaining eye contact. "If you were to be tricked into an impossible exchange, it is unlikely we would be able to save you. Even if you were to avoid all trades, the care for courtesy here is weak. You could be attacked for bumping into someone, being barefoot, or even your gender. It is not safe."

Adair countered by pointing farther into the market. "There's an inn on the other side of the market called The Rabbit Hole. Meet us there by dinner's end, or we'll assume you're dead and move on."

"Adair, no."

"We're not her parents, Heart. If she wants to get herself killed, that's her prerogative."

Adair spared her an apathetic glance before disappearing into the market. She locked her thanks behind grinning teeth. Leslie looked between them, brows furrowed with worry, then hurried after his counterpart. As soon as the sound of Leslie berating Adair faded into the distance, she darted inside.

If the last market had been busy, this one was *full*. She could barely move without bumping into a stranger or tripping over a stray tail. She pushed her way through the crowd, the majority of the other patrons towering over her but some only as tall as her knees. When her hip knocked the edge of a striped white-and-yellow booth, she stopped.

Colorful glowing rocks were scattered across the table. The space behind the booth was empty. Elle leaned over the table without touching the rocks and asked, "Is anyone here?"

A thin sallow man in a black suit flickered into existence. He stood on the other side of the table, but his nose brushed Elle's cheek. "My apologies. I sometimes forget to disillusion myself." He smiled, teeth as sharp as any knife.

Elle straightened, putting more space between them. "What are you selling?"

"Empathy stones."

"What do they do?"

"Make people feel." His already raspy voice lowered. Elle stepped closer so she could hear. "You want someone to fear you? Love you? Worship you? Press the stone to their skin, and they will." He leaned farther over the table, into Elle's space. His breath warmed her temple. "The price is low, and the reward is high. What do you offer?"

"Nothing. I was just curious."

"Convenient." He twisted, neck and torso elongating so that he was behind Elle, too. He spoke into her other ear. "Curiosity is the best way to bait a trap, and is thus always in demand. What's your price?"

"I'm not selling."

"Everyone is selling." His head moved toward the rest of his body, torso pushing Elle forward until her hips knocked against the booth. "And I pay well."

Elle ducked away. "Thanks, but no thanks."

She slipped back into the crowd. Not a minute later, a human-looking man grabbed her wrist and tugged her toward another booth. He was taller than her. Stronger, too. Curly blond hair fluffed out around his ears, and his smile sparkled. They stopped under a black tent.

He waved his free arm over an array of glowing bottles, each more colorful than the last, and said, "Tell me, have you ever seen anything more beautiful in your entire life?"

"Erm, yes?"

"Then you must have been looking in a mirror. But I can promise that the second most beautiful thing you've ever seen is right in front of you. Behold, one hundred percent pure sunlight in a bottle. Think about all the nights you've spent trying to find objects in the dark. All the stubbed toes and broken knickknacks. This little bottle"—he lifted a square bottle, forcing her to squint—"is guaranteed to light up your life for months to come! And for a beautiful little lady like you, I'm willing to offer a great discount. So what do you say? Let me light up your life?"

Elle shuffled her feet, still held uncomfortably close by the man's tight grip. "Couldn't I just light a fire?"

He blinked once, confused. His smile dropped. "You're a firemonger? Why didn't you start with that?" He shoved her away with a muttered, "Ugly bitch," then slapped his smile back on and rushed after someone else.

She stood by the sunshine booth a minute longer, strangely contented. The Impossible Market was loud and cluttered. The people inside were untrustworthy. And still, she felt at home. She inspected other booths, which sold everything from seeds that grew gold to lie-detecting pendants. None of the vendors cared about her beyond what she was willing to buy. The second they accepted she couldn't be enticed into purchasing their wares, they moved on.

Rather than being offended, she appreciated the candor. They wanted what they wanted, and they weren't going to waste time on people who couldn't help them get it.

Admiration and ardor soothed the void within her, and she decided the next time she saw Quincy *(if she survived this journey, if her opening the door hadn't killed him)* she'd tell him about Impossible Markets.

"Hey, wait! Stop!"

A large black beast barreled into Elle, knocking her feet out from under her. She hit the ground spine-first, breath leaving her in a huff. The rest of the Impossible Market moved on, patrons stepping over and around her while Elle stared dazedly up at the sky. A big sloppy tongue dragged her out of her stupor.

The beast licked her face from chin to forehead and back again. Its tongue dipped into her mouth and wet her nose. She sputtered and pushed it away. It licked her ear.

"Cyrilla, stop! Get off her!" A frantic woman pulled the beast—Cyrilla—away by the collar around its neck. She was short and thin with pretty green eyes. Straight brown hair piled atop her head in a complicated-looking updo. "I am so sorry." She offered a hand, which Elle immediately regretted accepting. The woman tugged her up and started dragging her through the streets.

Elle asked, "What are you doing?"

"I'm sorry. Just bear with me for a minute."

Elle, who'd never been blessed with physical strength, had no choice but to comply. They jogged until the booths turned to buildings and the crowd thinned to an occasional passerby. The woman pulled Elle into one of the smaller shops and stopped. Elle doubled over, palms pressed to her knees, and panted, lungs burning.

The woman released Cyrilla, clapped her hands together, and bowed. "I'm sorry. I'm so sorry. I'm really sorry."

"Why would you do that?" Elle pushed locks of sweaty hair out of her face and looked around the room. It was large and empty, with the only furniture being a wooden counter to the right of the door. On the counter sat a single piece of plain black paper. Brick walls were bare. "Who are you?"

"I'm Dani, and this is my dog, Cyrilla. Look, we're really, really sorry, but I need you to keep this quiet. I'm not exactly supposed to have her here, and it would really help me out if you'd, you know, not tell my landlord."

Elle's first thought was that Dani was stupid because how could Elle have known any of that to be able to take revenge? Her second thought was that this market was impossible for a reason, and it was probably smart of Dani to cover all her bases.

"Why aren't you allowed to have a dog? I thought they were supposed to be nice."

"Well, she's not exactly a dog, per se, but she's really close."

"What is she?"

"A lesser demon?" Dani fell to her knees and hugged Cyrilla's big, fluffy body. "But she's different! She's nice and sweet, and all she wants is to live in the daylight. She's never hurt anyone, I swear. I don't know why she went after you like that."

Elle recalled something similar from her first conversation with Adair, where he'd claimed a demon had followed her to his home. She wondered if she attracted them somehow.

Deciding it wasn't her place to punish Dani for breaking the rules—especially if it was Elle's fault that Cyrilla had taken off in the first place—she said, "It's fine. I won't tell."

"Really? Oh, thank you. Thank you so much. You won't regret this."

Dani released Cyrilla to stand, which ended up being a mistake as the overly large dog once again tackled Elle. She stumbled but didn't fall. The dog went up on its hind legs, big paws using Elle's chest for balance, and licked Elle's face.

Elle scrunched her nose and looked Cyrilla in the eyes. Her heart stuttered. For a split second, she was once again in the abyss outside the

House. Then she blinked, and the world returned to normal. Cyrilla's eyes were a regular, albeit frigidly cold, blue. Elle forced a laugh to cover her discomfort.

Dani hooked her fingers under Cyrilla's collar and tugged. She apologized again. Elle held up a hand and said, "It's fine. Seriously. Just keep a better eye on her, yeah?"

Elle walked to the door. Dani said, "No, please. Let me repay you."

"That's really not—"

"Please. Just take one word. It'd make me feel a lot better about this whole mess."

"Words? That's what you sell?" Elle looked around the seemingly empty building, curiosity piqued. "What do they do?"

"It varies from person to person." Dani smiled, all business. "Words determine the ways our lives move forward, and everyone needs them. A single word can sometimes sell for upward of twenty smaller impossibilities."

"Wouldn't it be easier to buy a book?"

Dani's smile stiffened, letting Elle know she found the comparison insulting. Her voice stayed sugar sweet. "Words on their own are much more powerful than words in a sentence, or worse, in a book. A singular word can mean anything. Can be anything. A book's path is already decided. Its end already met."

"Then, no offense, but why give one to me? It doesn't seem like fair trade."

"Believe me, it's more than fair."

Dani released Cyrilla again, and this time, the dog stayed put. She walked past Elle to pluck the paper off the counter, then turned and held it out. It radiated magic.

"What do I do?"

"Touch the paper. Pick a word. It'll be what you need, I promise."

Elle joined Dani by the counter. She lifted her hand, fingers hovering over the pitch-black paper, but didn't touch. "And all I have to do is not tell your landlord about Cyrilla?"

"You got it."

Elle worried her bottom lip between her teeth, unsure. All the books she had seen thus far contained the same magic as the earth. This paper felt more like a person. She pushed a breath out through her nose, caution winning over curiosity, and decided to decline. Cyrilla knocked into her from behind.

Elle stumbled, and her fingers touched the paper. She jerked her hand away. Foreboding weighed heavy on her shoulders as she remembered both Leslie's and Adair's warnings about agreeing to strange deals. She flipped her hand over in time to see little black letters crawling down her fingers. They lined up to write the word *cursed* on her palm. Her stomach sank.

"Cursed? What does that mean?"

"I don't know." Dani took a step away from Elle, personality abruptly devoid of both kindness and interest. "It varies from person to person, remember?"

"Yeah, but. . . . Do the words apply to the people? Am I cursed?"

"Didn't you say you needed to get going?"

Elle hadn't said that, but between the word on her palm and Dani's cold smile, she figured it was probably true. "Um, yeah. You're right." She rubbed the thin calligraphic letters with her thumb, positive she'd missed something but not sure what. "Thanks for the word."

"It was my pleasure." Dani's tense smile and dismissive tone said that it'd been anything but. Elle nodded and left. As her toes touched the ground outside, she heard Dani say, "Are you happy now?"

Cyrilla barked.

19

Losing his heart had decimated Adair's ability to feel emotion, but it made him think clearer. Logical thought came more easily, and for those rare social moments where he was required to fit in, he could evaluate the situation and fake whatever they expected him to feel. Emotions, while pleasant, were not a requirement of survival. Disregarding the horrific void in his chest, Adair was fine.

Mostly.

"What do you think it means?"

"It means you're cursed." Adair peeled the word off Elle's hand and placed it in the book he'd bought. It dried on the title page as though it had been printed. He closed the book so he wouldn't have to look at it again.

"Yeah, but how? I think I would remember getting cursed." She hesitated, worry clear in the way she scanned The Rabbit Hole. They'd situated themselves at a small round table in the far-right corner of the pub to avoid eavesdroppers. A large stone fireplace crackled near the entrance. A bar stood on the other side of the room, and behind it, the stairs to the inn. Mismatched tables, rickety wooden chairs, and inebriated patrons filled the space between their little group and the bar. "Wouldn't I?"

Adair's heart used a voice softened with empathy to say, "It depends on the curse. Perhaps your lack of childhood memories can be attributed to this. Or perhaps it occurred during your childhood."

"Is there any way to know?"

Both Elle and Adair's heart looked to Adair.

"No."

She turned back to his heart, which frowned, upset. Without looking away from Adair, it said, "You can examine her curse. It may not tell us when she was cursed or exactly what the curse does, but we will gain knowledge of its nature." His heart sounded insistent. Adair weighed the effort it would take to look at Elle's curse against how boring listening to his heart's lecture would be. His heart nagged him. "Adair."

Adair raised a hand to perform the proper focusing motions. A line for insight, two petals for seeing magic, an open palm to access the soul, and a three-fingered, circular motion to tie them together. The spell slipped into his eyes with a light, ticklish feeling and stained the world gold. The table gained a swirling, glittery sheen. The air brightened. Magic became visible.

Unfortunately, everything had magic, and being able to see it—all of it, all at once—gave him a headache. Adair sighed, wishing he could feel frustrated.

Brilliant white light radiated from Elle's skin, filling the entire room. A rainbow of colors shimmered in and out of view, dancing through the light. Adair's headache pounded. Her power, regardless of her ability to use it, was immense. It was also curse-free, so he moved past the cacophony of colors to peer at her soul.

"What the fuck?" Adair leaned closer, genuinely interested, only to have her aura flare bright enough to blind. He ended the spell before she could do any real damage.

The panic in her aura bled through to her face. "What did you find? What's wrong with me?"

Nearby tables quieted to listen in on their drama. Adair pressed his lips into a thin line. He knew he should approach the situation delicately, with care for both Elle's feelings and whatever time she might require to process the news, but god did that sound boring. He sighed through his nose.

Clarrissa had always harped on his inability to commiserate with others, and that had been back when he actually had empathy.

He pointed at the fireplace. "See the fire?"

She glanced over, eyes wide from either adrenaline or fear, and nodded.

"Good. Go stick your hand in it."

"What?"

"Adair!"

Adair ignored his heart to watch Elle. She narrowed her eyes and bared her teeth, angry and disbelieving. He said, "Your control of fire is abysmal. It'll help if the fire is already there rather than you having to create and sustain it."

"No." She shook her head, frizzy brown locks slapping her cheeks. "You can't tell me I'm cursed and then send me away like some—"

"Are you complaining?"

Elle's eyes dilated. Her lips parted and curled down in a furious, soundless snarl. Her hands clenched into fists. He maintained eye contact, daring her to defy him.

She didn't.

Impulsive nature aside, Elle was smart. Instead of giving in to her obvious desire to punch him in the face, she stood and stomped to the fire. Both Adair and his heart watched as she plopped down on the floor, cross-legged, and stuck her hand into the flames. As soon as she was properly distracted, his heart scolded him. "That was cruel, Adair. She deserves to know—"

"Her soul is shredded."

His heart yelped. "It what?"

Elle twisted around to glare at them. Adair matched her glare until she returned her attention to the fire.

Quieter this time, his heart asked, "It is what? What do you mean shredded?"

"I mean what I said. It's in tatters."

"Like . . ." His heart swallowed, lowering its voice to a barely there whisper. "Like us?"

"Worse than us. We've got damage on one side, where we separated. She's ruined from every angle." Adair paused, tempted to take another look at her mess of a soul. His migraine decided against it. "The thing to focus on here is that she didn't do it to herself. She tangled with someone dabbling in soul magic, and she paid the price."

"We have to help her."

"No. We have to get away from her."

His heart reeled back, appalled. "She needs us."

"She's not the only one in danger here. I let it slide when a demon pointed her out and her destination happened to be the last place Clarrissa could exist. For her to also suffer from the same curse as us with no idea how she got it? This trap couldn't be any more obvious if we'd laid it ourselves."

"Or perhaps this is fate. Her memory loss is likely the result of having her soul torn, and it is up to us to help her restore it."

"Restore it?" Adair sneered. "The likelihood that the rest of her soul wasn't destroyed on the spot is infinitesimal, and even if it weren't, we have no way to identify the soul pieces. In all likelihood, not even they would recognize themselves as parts of her soul."

"How could they not—"

"If her enemies are capable of ripping someone's soul apart, they're more than capable of implanting false memories. The only thing I don't doubt about her is her name."

His heart shifted in its seat, eyes on Elle. "Is that not something which can be changed?"

"It's possible, but adjusting smaller details is tedious and generally leads to noticeable inconsistencies. While Elle may not be her given name, it's almost guaranteed to be a part of her original identity."

His heart whimpered. "Do you think the house she came from is fake?"

"Worse. I think it's real." Adair paused as a group of raucous, drunken boys stumbled past their table. "I think she could have been neutralized with false memories of loyalty or a happy family, but was instead trapped in a house with nothing."

"So her lack of memories is purposeful."

"I wouldn't be surprised. You've met her. She jumps at the chance to learn something new and hates being restrained. Taking away her knowledge and trapping her in a static environment are Elle-specific tortures."

"You're saying the House wasn't made to keep demons out."

"It was made to keep her in."

His heart's breath hitched, worry replaced with empathetic sorrow. Fat tears perched on long lashes before sliding down trembling cheeks. "Oh, Elle."

Adair swatted the air in front of his heart's face. "Don't feel bad for her. Not remembering what she did to deserve this doesn't clear her of responsibility."

"She is a good kid."

"She's not a kid. She's an adult. And if we stay with her, she could get us killed."

"Clarrissa would help her."

Anger sparked in Adair, brief but powerful, and he hated his heart for using Clarrissa against him. Like it was his fault he didn't love her anymore. Like he wouldn't kill for the chance to mourn his loss.

"Clarrissa is dead." He leaned forward, into his heart's personal space. "And I'm not looking to join her."

"You are . . ." His heart blinked out more tears. Its voice cracked. "You are only saying that because you cannot feel anything anymore."

"And you're only saying that because you can't think things through."

Adair wrapped his fingers around his heart's wrist. He felt the brief bliss of their soul beginning to mend itself. Then his heart realized what he was doing and jerked away, carelessly thrusting him back into the void. It said, "I am staying with Elle, and that is final."

Adair had lived with his heart long enough to know how stubborn it could be. He nodded. "Alright."

"No! You—what?"

"I said alright. We'll stay with Elle. For now."

His heart narrowed its eyes, suspicious, but it had always been too eager to trust. When all Adair did was go back to watching Elle, it relaxed. It even said, "Thank you."

What it should have done was look under the table to see Adair's fingers twitch. Maybe then it would have noticed the fire leaping from the hearth to singe the two intoxicated boys by the door and, by proxy, been able to warn Elle of their oncoming grievances. As it was, his heart could only watch as the boys turned, angry for reasons it didn't understand, and rounded on Elle.

"Oi! The fuck d'you think you're doing?"

Adair watched Elle crane her neck, not yet aware she should pull her hand out of the fire and run. "What?"

"Think you're funny, do you? Think just because we're not firemongers, we'll sit here and take it?"

One of the boys—stocky with barely two decades under his belt—strode toward Elle until she was nearly sitting in the fire. Adair's heart shot up, indignant. "Leave her alone!"

The stocky one's friend—a little older but no wiser—raised a hand, palm toward Adair's heart. Ice crept along tan skin, thin but there. Other patrons cleared the way, unwilling to get involved. It seemed to take that show of mass caution for Adair's heart to remember it could no longer perform magic.

"Adair, help her."

Adair didn't move. If Elle insisted on risking their lives, she needed to prove she could pull her weight.

The stocky one grabbed hold of Elle's hair, grip visibly painful, and yanked her to her feet. He grinned at Adair. "That's right. Sit there nice and still, and your girlfriend might come back to you in one piece." Elle gritted her teeth and looked past her assailants, toward Adair and his heart. Adair responded to her silent plea by crossing his arms and leaning back in his chair.

Your move.

Elle grabbed the stocky boy's wrist and stepped into the fire. He said something about her liking having her hair pulled. She kicked out, shaping the flames into a blazing semicircle. Her stocky attacker released her with a pathetic yip.

The older one pressed his wrists together, palms toward Elle. He pooled his energy into a ball of icy air that would cause frostbite on contact. The sphere took long, slow seconds to form, and the execution was weak. He threw it at Elle. Instead of dodging, as Adair expected, Elle reached out to catch the thing. She redirected it to the stocky boy with a graceful twist. As the icy air left her hand, her bare foot clapped against the floor.

The earth responded with vigor, a jagged chunk of ground bursting through the wooden flooring. It punched the older boy in the chest and flung him across the room. He hit the wall by the staircase, slid to the floor, and stopped moving. Elle's attention shot back to the stocky boy, who had curled into a whimpering, shivering mess after being hit by his friend's attack, and it was in her victory that she allowed her control to slip.

The half-ring of fire latched onto the floorboards, igniting everything in reach. She cursed, panicked, and reached out to calm the flames. Unfortunately for everyone involved, her understanding of fire only extended so far. The flames climbed the walls and engulfed a nearby table. Those closest to the brawl shuffled backward, readying to run.

Adair's heart grabbed him by the bicep and shook. "Help her!"

Adair cracked his neck, annoyingly aware that this moment of not-boredom wasn't worth the lecture he would receive for letting the place burn. He stood and opened his hands in an unmistakable call to the fire, demanding it stop.

The will of the fire hissed and spit, refusing to be tamed. Adair let his magic flare. His aura, when not held in check, was an oppressive force. The nearest patrons staggered, overwhelmed. Adair paid them no mind. He ordered the fire to stand down a second time, along with the underlying message that he *would not ask again*. It molded to his will, sweet as a cat in heat.

He waved his fingers, and the flames took their rightful place in the hearth.

The way Elle struggled just to stay on her knees reminded him to reconceal his magic. He swaddled his aura around his soul and sat back down. Her shoulders slumped as the pressure receded, and Adair acknowledged that he should've been impressed. Most people could waste their lives studying magical theory and still only touch on one element. For Elle to command three in less than a week was insane. It also reinforced Adair's decision not to like her. She was too powerful. Too talented. Too lucky.

He said, "Get up and fix the floors."

Elle stared at him, eyes blown wide with awe and respect, lips tugged down with the knowledge that he had set her up. She didn't complain.

20

"You don't feel anything, do you?"

Elle watched Adair for a reaction—for surprise, irritation, anything—but his expression remained blank and bored. Leslie drummed his fingers on the table, clearly uncomfortable with her line of questioning, and said, "Elle, that is a very impolite thing to ask."

She ignored him. "At first, I thought you were just a little dead inside, and that balanced out with him being overly emotional, but it's more than that. You don't feel anything. And he"—she jabbed her thumb at Leslie—"feels everything. Right?"

Adair gave a half nod, half shrug. "Basically."

"Basically? What does that mean?"

"We share a soul. Regardless of our bodily forms, we must be the same."

Elle recalled Leslie saying something similar in the painting, and it made as much sense now as it had then. She waited half a minute for Adair to clarify. When he didn't, she rephrased her question. "What does that have to do with your emotions?"

"Everything. Memories, inclinations, and personhood are all embedded in the soul. While it takes an intense stimulus to force my emotions to the surface, they can exist. Just, as I'm sure, my heart is capable of thinking things through, so long as the situation is dire enough."

Adair's tone was bland, but his eyes were alert. She pushed on. "Me fighting with those guys wasn't enough to make you feel though, right?"

Leslie chided her again. "Elle."

Adair said, "Correct."

She nodded, having figured as much. "Then I forgive you."

Adair's raised brow said he had nothing to be forgiven for, but they both knew what she meant. She had sensed his fire, felt it burn the two men who'd attacked her. Even without an actual sense of guilt, he was smart enough to know what he'd done was cruel.

Leslie asked, "What are you forgiving him for?"

"Nothing." Elle tossed Leslie a smile. "Adair and I had a disagreement, but I'm over it."

Leslie pursed his lips, unconvinced. "What was the disagreement about?"

"Training tactics." Elle glanced at Adair, wondering if he'd disagree. Most people would hide what they'd done out of shame or for fear of the consequences, but an emotionless man? She said, "But again, I'm over it. Whatever he throws at me, I can take it."

For a moment, she thought Adair would argue. Then his lips tipped in a smile that was all the more unsettling for its lack of cheer. He said, "We'll see."

Leslie splayed his hands flat against the tabletop, physically interrupting their banter. "I may make decisions based primarily on emotions, but I am not stupid."

Elle kept her eyes on Adair for a quick, silent exchange.

A tilt of his head. *He doesn't know.*

A press of her lips. *He'll disapprove.*

Slightly raised brows. *Will you tell?*

Adair didn't—couldn't—care about what Elle would do. She covered for him anyhow. "Adair could've beaten those guys in two seconds flat, but he let them fight me. I think it was to test what I could do."

Leslie turned his glare solely on Adair and asked, "Is that true?" Adair shrugged noncommittally, which Leslie seemed to take as a confirmation because he swiveled back to Elle, apologetic rather than angry. "I am so sorry. Those men could have seriously hurt you, and I am a failure as an escort for believing Adair would help you instead of interfering myself. It is generally unwise for the magicless to fight sorcerers, but at least I knew what I was doing. If there is a next time, though hopefully there shall not be, but if there is, I swear on my life that I will—"

"It's fine, Leslie." Elle placed a reassuring hand on his shoulder. "I can handle myself, and Adair knows it."

That wasn't strictly true, but it was enough to end his monologue. Leslie went back to berating Adair, who looked like he couldn't have cared less if he tried. She pulled her hand away, unsure if she felt comforted by Leslie's protective nature or embittered by his hypocrisy.

How could he so eagerly reprimand Adair for wronging her while also keeping the secret of how she was cursed? Would her knowing make it worse? Somehow, she didn't think so.

For all that Leslie was sincerely kind, he was also selfish. He preferred warmth and safety, and if not for the fact that he was incapable of getting on Adair's bad side, Elle doubted he would defend her at all. She wondered, briefly, vindictively, what Leslie would do if she asked about the curse again, but her curiosity was moot.

As much as she felt like she deserved to know, she also accepted that if her knowing would be helpful, Adair would tell her. And part of her—the part still struggling to breathe under the inescapable pressure of Adair's magic—wanted him to *want* to tell her. To acknowledge her strength in the same factual manner that she had acknowledged the strength of the earth, and to trust that she wouldn't ruin things just by being involved.

Either way, Elle wasn't a child. She wouldn't complain. "I'm going to get a drink. Do you guys want anything?"

They both said, "Whiskey," without looking at Elle. She snorted because *of course* they liked the same things. She stood from their table in the corner and made her way to the bar.

After she had finished repairing The Rabbit Hole, the owner approached them, declaring they could take whatever they wanted for free. Elle had thought it odd to be thanked so heartily considering she was the one who'd messed everything up in the first place, but Leslie explained the generosity stemmed more from fear than gratitude. If Adair wanted, he could take everything by force, and they all knew it.

"Excuse me." Elle raised her voice to get the bartender's attention. "Could I get two—or no, three whiskeys?"

The bartender turned, and his eyes were *blue*. Bright enough to have stolen the light from the sun and cold enough to make Elle yearn for the fire. She instinctively stepped away.

He smiled, a single dimple crinkling his cheek. Pin-straight, dark brown hair cascaded over one shoulder, all the way down to his waist. A black vest with a white apron emphasized his slim build. "Is that all?"

She blinked, taken aback by the disconnect between his terrible eyes and his geniality, before realizing his eyes were familiar. Suddenly more interested than afraid, she pressed her stomach to the bar and leaned in. If the man—his name tag read Cycero—cared about her invading his space, he didn't show it. He stayed perfectly still, their noses near to touching, and allowed Elle to examine him.

His eyes were worse up close, with a devastating cold that sank into her bones and raised gooseflesh on her arms. A gravity in them warned her not to linger too long, lest the choice to leave cease to be hers. She leaned even closer.

"Are you a lesser demon?"

He blinked once, twice, then laughed. The sound was loud and jovial, another contrast to the death in his eyes. He said, "I apologize. I've never been asked that before."

Elle scrunched her nose. "Really? Because I met a lesser demon earlier today, and your eyes are the exact same." He blinked again, and Elle stood close enough to see long dark lashes brush high, angular cheekbones. "Don't worry. I won't tell." She pushed off the bar, curiosity sated. "You guys aren't supposed to be here, right?"

His kind smile flickered, momentarily revealing something intense bordering on obsessive. When his smile returned, it was twice as friendly. "How kind of you. Surely there's something I can do in return?"

"Three whiskeys?"

Cycero motioned to the counter, and three full tumblers appeared between them. Elle glanced over her shoulder to make sure Adair and Leslie weren't looking, then picked up a single tumbler. She lifted it to her lips, and a pungent chemical smell wafted upward. She paused.

Was she really supposed to drink this?

Cycero watched her, openly amused. She downed the shot. The taste was so-so. The acrid burn in her throat made her sputter. She spat half the shot back out, throat convulsing, and spent the next ten seconds coughing onto the bar. Cycero's pleasant laughter said he'd expected as much.

"Ugh. Why do people drink this?"

"It's an acquired taste."

"Not a taste I could ever acquire." She grimaced at the smell still stuck in her nose and nudged the empty tumbler back toward Cycero. "Sorry for the mess."

"It's no problem." He flexed his fingers. The spilled whiskey and spit disappeared. She nodded in thanks and picked up the remaining shots. Before she turned to go, he said, "Ask for something else. I would have given you the whiskey regardless."

Elle shook her head. "I don't know a lot about demons, but making a deal with you sounds like an all-around bad idea."

"Not a deal, then. A gift. I'd expect nothing in return."

She stared into eyes the color of despair, then smiled, humorless. "Somehow I doubt that." She raised the drinks in a makeshift salute and took a step away.

Cycero said, "You're looking for a castle in the sky, right?"

All thoughts of leaving fled. She swiveled and asked, "How did you know that?"

"You could say it comes with the territory." This time, it was Cycero who pressed his abdomen to the bar. He rested his forearms on the wooden tabletop and leaned over. "If you want to get there, you'll need a guide."

"I know."

"Her name is Honeycutt. She's the only dwarf aboard *Las Estrellas*." He smiled again, gentle enough to comfort and sharp enough to cut. Without ever taking his eyes off Elle, he said, "Your friends are waiting for you."

"I. . . . Thanks." Elle nodded, uncomfortable. She left before he could gift her with anything else.

Leslie and Adair were still arguing at the table. She jogged over, whiskey sloshing out of the tumblers and dripping down her fingers. By the time she set the little cups down, they were half-empty.

"You are literally the worst waitress I've ever had the displeasure of meeting."

"Shut up, Adair. I know who can take us to the castle in the sky."

She waited for them to ask who. Adair said, "How?"

"The bartender. He told me—"

"Which bartender?"

Elle huffed and rolled her eyes but obediently spun around to point at three unfamiliar men.

Cycero was gone.

21

Leslie missed Clarrissa.

He missed seeing her face, of course, and he missed her kisses. More than that, though, he missed their talks. They'd known each other since they were children, and Leslie couldn't remember the last time he'd made a crucial decision without her input.

If she were still alive, he would thank her for always keeping him grounded. He'd hold her close and run his fingers through her hair. He wouldn't have to gather the courage to request her help because she'd already know. She'd ask, "What's going on?" or maybe she'd already know that, too. If so, she would tell him to "Buck up, Les. You can do anything, including this."

He remembered her hand on his cheek, soft and frail, as she assured him that he'd be fine without her. He remembered getting angry at her for giving in so easily. Young, stupid Leslie had rejected her offer of comfort with the bitter declaration that she was going to live. He might've even gone so far as to promise that they'd travel when she recovered—that she would finally see the world outside of her hometown and the nearest Impossible Market. The memory was a blur of pain and regret, and he could no longer say for sure.

He knew she would've loved an adventure like this. She'd have bounced on her heels and packed way too many things into a bottomless bag. And if the question ever came up over whether or not they should abandon Elle, she'd have smacked him over the head.

Don't you even think about it, Leslie Adair. She's a good kid.

But the circumstances surrounding Elle, even to Leslie's overly emotional brain, were too convenient. Demons didn't give away crucial, impossible information for nothing, which meant Adair had been right. This was a trap.

So? If anyone can walk into a trap and come out on top, it's you. And just look at her. She's so earnest it hurts. If you leave her to fend for herself, she'll die.

Leslie blinked through his tears and sucked his bottom lip between his teeth. The campfire warmed his shins, forearms, and face. Elle and Adair sat across from him, facing each other, training. Leslie dried his eyes on his knees.

He knew Adair was right, and he knew Clarrissa was right, too. Elle was eager and honest, putting her all into everything she did. Even without the storm currently brewing around her, she'd likely get into more trouble than she could handle and require help. She needed them.

Then what's the problem?

Leslie turned to Clarrissa, meaning to tell her that *impending death* was the problem. Empty air stared back. He knew, technically, that she'd never been there (that she was dead, and she'd never be there again), but for a single second, he'd felt her hand on his bicep. It hurt all the more for that second to have passed.

He choked on a sob, feeling stupid for even thinking of using death as an excuse. Clarrissa had known she was going to die years in advance, and she'd never been so pathetic about it. If anything, she'd say the added risk of Elle's enemies made the journey that much more exciting.

If it's worth killing for, it's worth dying for, too.

She'd always been stupid like that. Stupid and positive and loving. Like the whole point of being alive was to either run into the sun or clear the way for someone else to do the same.

How many sunrises had they watched together? How many sunrises had he slept through, too tired to enjoy those extra minutes with Clarrissa while he still had the chance? He wished he could remember, to know with certainty that he'd utilized more time than he'd wasted, but life wasn't that easy.

Clarrissa was dead. Elle was being targeted. They were all cursed. And to what end?

The urge to run away stuck in Leslie like a barb, but honoring Clarrissa's memory—living in a way that would make her proud—meant seeing this through.

He contemplated asking Clarrissa for a second opinion, but he knew deep inside that a decision had already been reached. Abandoning Elle was no longer an option. She was too adventurous, too stubborn, and he cared about her too much. She was like a younger sister or, if he and Clarrissa had ever decided to go that route, a daughter. He needed to see her safe.

He just didn't necessarily want to be the one protecting her.

Leslie wiped his tears on his sleeve and looked across the campfire. Elle and Adair sat cross-legged in the dirt, facing one another. She held her hands out between them, palms up, and though Leslie couldn't see exactly what they were doing, he knew it was some type of magic. They'd been training nonstop ever since the incident at The Rabbit Hole. Mornings, evenings, nights. Training, training, training. Half a week of hellish exercises, offered and accepted like being pushed to the limit was the norm. Adair ran her ragged, uncaring of her health or stamina. And Elle, never satisfied with her progress, let him.

Adair said, "Again."

Leslie leaned to the left until he could see Elle's empty palms. Adair swiped his thumb across his pointer and middle fingers, creating a small sphere of electricity in her palms. Her hands trembled, and sweat beaded below her hairline. She held it for four seconds before it dissipated. She jerked back with a hiss.

Adair called her back to position. "Again."

She held out her hands, and Leslie realized her palms weren't red from the firelight. They were burned.

A spark lit the air above her hands. It lasted for three seconds rather than four. She flinched and mouthed a curse but kept her hands steady. Adair created another sphere, and she tried her best to hold it. Her best wasn't enough. She whined through gritted teeth as another shock of electricity sank into her palms.

Leslie jumped to his feet. "Adair!"

They both turned to him, Elle seeming confused but relieved and Adair as emotionless as ever. Adair asked, "What?"

"You are hurting her."

Adair stared at him, unmoved. Elle turned away and said, "Again."

Leslie shook his head. "Elle, no. You need to understand how electricity feels, but not like this."

"Shut up, Leslie. I can handle it."

"Perhaps I have not mentioned this enough, but you are doing incredibly well. Most sorcerers—"

"Don't you get it?" She caught Leslie's eyes, fierce and determined. "I don't want to *be* most sorcerers. I'm different. I can feel it. And maybe it hasn't occurred to you yet, but this journey won't last forever. We'll get to the castle, you two will merge, and we'll probably never see each other again. Until then, I'm going to learn as much as I physically can. I like being taught by Adair, and I like being held to his standards." She refocused on Adair and held her hands out, palms up. "Again."

Adair returned his full attention to Elle, shoulders squared with approval. Leslie sunk to the ground, uneasy but outnumbered, and watched them return to their task. What did it say about Adair—about *Leslie*—that he was proud of her for choosing to learn magic over all else? And what did it say about Elle, to have gained the approval of a man who was literally without a heart? Leslie supposed, from the determined set of Elle's jaw, the uncaring glint in Adair's eyes, and the turmoil of his own emotions, that he had little choice but to find out.

22

Perun hadn't always been a god.

Once upon a time, in a land far, far below, he'd been a child like any other. His mother and father had doted on him. His younger sister had idolized him. They ate together, played together, and prayed together. Then lightning struck, and they'd burned together, too.

Flames licking up the walls. Smoke on the ceiling. Screams in the air. His family had perished that day while Perun walked out unscathed.

He hadn't understood it at the time, mind addled by tragedy and thoughts steeped in mortal woes, but the lightning had chosen him. It'd said that if he worked hard enough—if he proved himself worthy—then he could be its god. Others had come before him, and their successes were tattooed across his skin. The names were reminders that he was not the only one capable of rising to godhood and, more importantly, an acknowledgment that if he died, a replacement would be chosen soon thereafter.

Perun caressed the thin magical barrier containing his collected souls. There were eight of them all together, though only two still glittered with any real level of power. One had withered to a thin twinkle, as all souls who spent too long in his sphere eventually withered, and he knew it would soon be time to collect another.

He laid his hand flat on the barrier. The souls inside flashed to the opposite end of the sphere, cowering. Perun had designed the sphere to feed him a continuous stream of magic and youth, but it could be operated manually, too. If he focused on a particular soul, fed his intentions into the spell, and tugged, he could siphon out an extra six months, easy.

The additional feeding wouldn't make him younger or stronger, but it felt fantastic. And what was the point of being a god if not to do as he pleased with those below?

He focused on the weakest soul and gathered his magic. He demanded the sphere bring him energy and pleasure. Then the demon appeared, its inherent darkness devitalizing the otherwise vibrant room, and the moment was ruined.

He lifted his hand from the barrier. "What did you find?"

"Do you want the good news or the bad news first?"

Perun turned to see the demon standing by the remains of his table, strong arms folded behind its back. Blue eyes sparkled with mischief, and Perun's patience ran thin. It always wanted to play games. It always thought it was funny. He frowned in warning. "Demon."

"She's headed this way."

"Is she by herself?"

"She is."

Perun nodded, and a sliver of the anxiety coiling in his stomach unfurled. "And the good news?"

"That was the good news."

Irritation seeded. He worked his jaw. "The bad news then."

"That was also the bad news."

Fury laid its hand over his eyes and whispered in his ear. His magic lashed out, narrowly missing his throne. The wall cracked. The demon remained upright in front of him, unaware of how lucky it was to serve such a forgiving god. He clenched his fist and imagined wringing the demon's neck. When his temper receded, he asked, "Do you think yourself clever, demon?"

The demon didn't answer.

"I personally believe all dogs think themselves clever. This is because they have yet to understand the true power of their masters. One day, I will teach you that lesson, and you will realize that the only reason I have allowed your sharp tongue for so long is because it amuses me to watch you gnaw on your chain." He strode forward, stone floor cool against bare feet, and pressed the backs of his fingers to the demon's perfectly attractive face. He traced its cheekbone. "Do you understand?"

"I do."

Perun smiled and gave the demon two solid, condescending pats on the cheek. "I thought you might."

The demon didn't outwardly react to Perun's show of dominance, but the room grew colder. Perun stepped away, a dismissal on his lips. The demon said, "I've met souls like hers before."

"Oh?"

"They come once a generation, if you're lucky, and they always make an impact. A will like hers can topple nations."

He raised both brows, unamused. "You don't believe I can defeat her?"

"I wouldn't bet my soul on it."

The taunt was petty but sharp, and it struck true. Perun lashed out physically, magic lacing his backhand for a more powerful impact. He swatted empty air. The room brightened, affirming that the demon had left, and Perun roared.

The crack in the wall deepened to a fissure. The door flew off its hinges and crashed in the hall. He took long, purposeful strides out of the room, uncontrolled magic flinging bits of broken door out of the way.

The demon thought it was smart. It thought Perun couldn't see its discontent—its burning desire to rip out his soul—but he could. He knew for a fact that it was rabid, constantly looking for an opportunity to bite the hand that fed. Its betrayal wasn't a question of if but when.

Unfortunately for the demon, Perun was a god. He could not be fooled by a silver tongue or well-placed gibes.

He walked into his storeroom and retrieved a bottomless pouch filled with soil from the graves of his kin. It took him a moment to find his ever-fill bottle, enchanted to take water from the air with the same efficiency as dipping a container into a stream. He returned to his throne room.

The demon's faith in the girl was genuine, and Perun could understand why. Where she used versatile, elemental magics, he only dabbled in magic pertaining to the soul. In a physical, one-on-one fight between them, he would lose. Unfortunately for both the demon and the girl, brawn was not everything. Perun had always known that there would be magicians who could outpace him, which was why he'd enslaved the demon.

Brawn could be found, hired, made. Brains, on the other hand, were hard to come by. If Perun could not win against the girl in a one-on-one fight, then he would not fight her one-on-one. He would not fight her at all.

He dumped the contents of the pouch onto the floor in front of his sphere, dirt piling into a waist-high mound. When the pouch emptied, he tossed it to the side and tipped the ever-fill bottle over the mound. It poured and poured, softening dirt into mud. As soon as the soil was moldable, he capped the ever-fill bottle and knelt.

Should the girl make it to the castle, his deal with the demon ensured it would protect him. But Perun had no desire to place his neck so close to the sword. He could not trust the demon, and he would not gamble with the girl.

He buried his hands in the muck, coating the names of his predecessors in mud, and shaped the mound into something usable. Two thick arms and four grubby fingers. A rectangular torso and two stubbed legs. A head with no neck, rounded like a dome. He dug his thumbs into the face, creating pits for its eyes, then used his pinky to carve a smile. His magic danced beneath his skin, anticipation riding high.

Perun was always a god, yes, but it was rare that he had an excuse to perform tasks as stereotypically godly as creating life.

"Dirt stolen from the dead. Rain fresh from the sky." He reached inside the sphere for the dimmest light. "A soul free of a body."

The soul struggled in Perun's grasp, weak flickers burning mud-covered skin, but Perun held tight. He folded his magic around the soul to keep it from escaping, then thrust his hand straight from the sphere to the heart of his sculpture. Mud crawled across his skin and encased his wrist.

It was only in moments like this, deep in the bowels of spell manifestation, that Perun could feel the spirit of the elements. The will of the earth held strong against him, refusing to merge with the will of his proffered soul. The will of the water raged, momentarily indignant, then receded. It understood, on some basic level, that its only requirement had been to make the earth more pliable, and that once it evaporated, it would be free.

Perun used the weight of his own soul to pressure this small piece of earth into opening and making room for the spare. The weakened soul melted into the crevice, and both the soul and the earth screamed. Sentient beings were not meant to merge, and the unnatural lilt of it created a chasm between this being and the rest of the world.

The earthen portion of the creature panicked and tried to rip out the unfamiliar soul, but it was too late. The soul in his hand merged with the mud, and that mud shaped itself into an anatomically correct heart.

"You are my creation. You obey my will and my will alone."

The creature's mouth stretched open in a pained groan. Its heart started to beat. Perun squeezed the heart, and its cries echoed.

"Quiet, golem. You are my creation. You obey my will and my will alone." He used his own magic to grab hold of the golem's freshly formed soul and twisted. Fat limbs twitched and flopped, powerless. He dug his thumbnail into its heart. "Agree to my terms."

Slowly, with a voice like the wind through the trees, it said, "Yes."

Warmth flourished in Perun's soul, and an invisible tether formed between them. Their bond solidified with him as the master, and the horrible, misshapen thing on the ground as his servant. The golem attempted to curl in on itself, pained by every breath and every twitch.

Perun pulled his hand from the golem's chest and smoothed mud over the hole. He stood. "To be of use to me is an honor. Treat it as such."

The golem must have thought otherwise because it convulsed, their bond automatically punishing any perceived disobedience. After a few seconds of seizing, the bastardized soldier settled and stood. It had drawn its gruesome mouth into a wide, tortured smile, which Perun supposed was the most he could expect from the last dregs of a dying soul.

"I will release you only when you complete your task. Is that understood?"

The golem's breath sounded like the crunch of dead leaves on frozen soil. It opened its still-smiling mouth and said, "Yes."

"Good. Now go find the girl with only a third of a soul, and bring me back her head."

23

Las Estrellas was docked at Grenadine Port. Grenadine Port was a part of Grenadine Harbor, which connected the ocean to the town of Grenadine. This was important because Grenadine was a magic-restricted community, and if they ever wanted to reach *Las Estrellas*, they'd have to pass through it. Considering Elle's control of magic was unpredictable, at best, she should have been the one most wary of walking through the town.

She wasn't.

Elle didn't care about Grenadine, its rules, or its risks because the ocean was barely six kilometers away. It called to her with sweet promises of knowledge and adventure, and her ability to resist that call was weak. She bounced on her heels as the line to enter Grenadine shortened.

Leslie laid a strong hand on her shoulder, forcing her still. He said, "Tell me again what crossing the Grenadine border means for us."

Elle kept her eyes on the ocean as she said, "No magic without a permit."

"Correct. And do we have a permit?"

"No."

"And what happens if you perform magic?"

"The town puts a bounty on my head."

Adair didn't turn from where he was being checked in. "And?"

"And you'll kill me and collect the bounty yourself."

Adair hummed in affirmation. Leslie smiled and whispered, "He is joking."

Elle didn't think Adair was joking, but it was easier to let Leslie believe what he wanted than to argue. Adair made it through the check, and the guards waved Elle forward.

Getting through the border check was simple. People in blue uniforms patted her down, noted her magical artifacts, and took her picture. At least, Leslie said they were taking her picture. All Elle actually saw was a box and a flash, then they ushered her inside.

When Leslie got through the border check, he said, "First things first, we need coin."

"Coin?"

Leslie watched her for a confusing minute before the answer seemed to dawn. They stepped to the side so the other people entering the border check could get through, and he said, "Oh. That is right. You have never bought anything before, have you?"

Elle scrunched her nose at the semi-familiar word. "Bought is what you do to get furniture, right?"

The way Leslie tilted his head, endeared, let Elle know she was wrong. "Not quite. You do recall what bartering is, yes?"

"Yeah. You trade stuff for other stuff."

"Yes. Most communities have moved away from bartering to use a system of currency—in this case gold, silver, and bronze coins—to purchase what you desire."

Elle stared at Leslie, uncomprehending. Adair said, "Impossible Markets deal in impossible goods. Everyone else wants coin. If we want to board *Las Estrellas*, we need coin."

"Oh." She nodded. "Alright. How do we get that?"

"I'll get it." Adair raised a hand, pointer and middle fingers outstretched. "You two are going to find *Las Estrellas* and reserve our places on board."

"Why?"

"Because it's a cargo ship that's willing to take passengers, not the other way around."

Elle scratched behind her ear, unsure what that meant. Leslie explained. "If we take too long, they may be unwilling to accommodate us. We would have no choice but to wait here until they return to port."

Adair cut in. "Exactly. So stop wasting time and go."

Elle didn't need to be told twice. She grabbed Leslie's hand, shouted, "Later Adair," and bolted toward the sea. Leslie laughed, surprised, and matched her pace.

Grenadine was different from the Impossible Markets in that it was mostly buildings filled with mostly humans. Where the markets brimmed with a colorful, cobbled-together atmosphere, Grenadine was filled with long lines of similarly designed, light brown rectangles. The buildings looked like they'd all been made around the same time and with the same material. The streets held fewer citizens than the markets did vendors. Leslie and Elle swerved around people on occasion, but for the most part, their path was clear.

The longer they ran, the more Elle was reminded of their time escaping the Painted Lady. Her legs hurt and her lungs burned. Leslie took a sharp turn, and Elle stumbled. He pulled her along.

"Leslie. Leslie, wait. I can't keep up. I can't . . ." She trailed off to focus on breathing.

He said, "Just a little farther." They raced around two more corners before coming to a dead stop. He released her wrist, and she doubled over, panting hard. He asked, "What do you think?"

She sucked in a deep breath, insults piling on her tongue, then looked up. Her ability to be cruel vanished in the face of wonder.

The ocean was beautiful.

She'd technically been able to see it for days, but the line of blue on the horizon was nothing compared to the waves crashing against the shore. Even the air had changed, becoming so salty that she could practically taste it. She walked forward. The ground turned soft and gritty. She jumped back.

Leslie laughed. "That is sand. It is safe."

She looked at the sand, not quite believing, and took a careful step out. Tiny golden grains warmed her naked feet. She wiggled her toes to burrow deeper.

"Do you know how to swim? If not, we could wade in the shallows. I have always loved the ocean and could teach you much about the plant and animal life within."

Elle glanced between Leslie and the ocean, yearning to touch it. "Don't we need to reserve our places on the boat?"

"*Las Estrellas* will still be there when we are finished. It is not due to set sail until dawn."

She shifted on her feet, and the sand shifted with her. "I thought you said it couldn't wait."

"I said it could not wait long. It can wait a little."

Hesitation huddled behind her ribs. She bit her lip. "I don't know. Adair seemed pretty serious."

"You have worked hard, Elle. You deserve a break." He gestured toward the ocean. "I will handle Adair."

Sunshine beat down on her neck and face. Crashing waves promised relief. Ocean-flavored wind blew, tempting her closer. She fisted her fingers in the hem of her shirt, resolve crumbling. "You're sure it's okay?"

"I promise." Leslie sat down to remove his boots, decision made.

Elle sprinted to the ocean.

24

As it turned out, reserving their spots could not wait.

Elle buried her face between her knees and listened to Adair argue with the captain for a spot on the ship. Humiliation churned in her stomach as the stranger once again turned down what seemed like a large amount of gold. She doubted Adair would ever forgive this screwup, and the possibility of losing whatever modicum of respect he had for her hurt more than she'd thought possible.

A gentle hand on her shoulder pulled Elle from her spiral. She jerked away.

"Elle . . ." Leslie's voice dripped with regret.

She pushed herself off the ground, refusing to look at him, and made her way over to the ship. Both the captain and Adair paused as she approached. Adair's expression remained hard and unforgiving, but the captain's gaze softened.

Elle knew she looked pathetic, with her too-thin frame outlined by still-wet clothes and her hair a tousled mess. She played to that pitiful picture by twisting her hands into her shirt. For once, she didn't have to fake the remorse. She said, "It was my fault we missed the cutoff time. I was supposed to come reserve our spots, but I'd never seen the ocean before, and I . . ." She blinked away tears that were neither entirely real nor entirely faked. She maintained eye contact with the captain as they rolled down her face. "I got distracted. I'm real sorry, Mister." A sob hopped in her chest, and she used the heel of her palm to wipe away stray tears. "Is there any way you can let us on just this once?" She sniffled. More tears fell. "Please?"

The captain cursed. He took off his hat and ran his hand through his hair, eyes swiveling to Adair. "I'm doing this for her. Not you." He jabbed a thick finger at Adair before gruffly demanding thirty gold. Adair handed it over without a fuss, and the captain stomped away.

Elle used the hem of her shirt to better dry her tears. The urge to cry remained even though the show had ended. She looked up. Adair caught her eyes, the slight curl in his lip bringing forth a new wave of shame, and she knew her act with the captain had earned her no points.

She lowered her voice and said, "I really am sorry." He raised a hand, and she squared her shoulders, resolving to take whatever lashes he deemed fit. He buried his fingers in her damp locks and pressed his palm to her scalp. She flinched.

He ruffled her hair.

"It's not you who should be apologizing." He strode past Elle, toward Leslie, and used the hand on her head to push her in the opposite direction. "Get on the boat."

"What?"

Adair didn't turn back, didn't clarify. Elle took the out for what it was and scurried up the ramp to the ship's deck. She ducked behind the railing nearest Adair and Leslie to listen in.

Adair said, "What the fuck are you trying to pull?"

Leslie grunted, likely because Adair was manhandling him. "I wanted to share with her the joy of the ocean."

"Bullshit."

"It is the truth."

"We'll be sailing for six days. She's got plenty of time."

"That is different, and you know it."

"You could've taken her to the beach after reserving our places. You could've waited until we dock in Norwich." A beat of silence stretched into an awkward pause. Elle resisted the urge to peek over the wooden railing. When it became clear Leslie didn't intend to respond, Adair said, "You're my heart. Like it or not, I know you, and I know you aren't this stupid."

"You know nothing." Leslie's enunciation slurred, as it always did when he cried.

"Heart—"

"My name is Leslie!"

"No. My name is Leslie. You don't have a name because you aren't a person. You are a single piece of my soul enchanted to appear human."

Elle heard Leslie sob, and her own heart winced. He asked, "How can you be so cruel?"

"You took my emotions—"

"Oh, please." Leslie choked out a humorless laugh. "If I cannot play the fool, then you cannot play the victim. We calculated the likelihood of our separation before entering the painting. We knew the risks. We—the *both* of us—decided that even living heartless would be better than the pain and the loss."

"We were mistaken."

"You are still mistaken."

Silence settled over them, but it wasn't until Elle heard the heavy clap of boots moving up the wooden ramp that she realized the conversation was over. She scrambled to her feet, as though that would make her look less like she'd been eavesdropping. Leslie rounded the corner. His lips thinned to a tight line while tear-reddened eyes closed, and guilt dug a pit in Elle's stomach.

She slid back down the wall. "Do you want to talk about it?" He opened his eyes, suspicious of her kindness. She patted the floorboards to her right. "I won't judge. I promise."

That seemed to be all he needed to hear. Leslie crossed the empty wooden deck and plopped down beside her. He changed positions a few times before hugging his knees to his chest, left bicep pressed firmly against Elle's right. His fingers tapped a tuneless rhythm on his knee, and his eyes never strayed from the center mast. He said, "Adair is not incorrect. I am a small piece of the larger whole, and it would be in our best interest for me to merge with him."

"And?"

He ducked his head. "And I do not wish to merge."

"Because he's a jerk?"

"No."

"Are you sure? Because I have a crazy amount of respect for Adair, and I still wouldn't want to merge with him."

Leslie cracked a smile and shook his head. "He is me, and I like the way he is."

"Then what's the problem?"

"I am me, too, and I like the way I am."

"Is that why you agreed to take me to the sky? You're stalling?" His head shot up, apparently surprised that she wasn't a complete idiot. She smiled. "It's alright, Leslie. I'm not mad. I always knew you were getting something out of being my escort. I just wasn't sure what."

Big brown eyes flooded with tears. He curled his lips into an ugly crying frown and blubbered. "You are so kind." He leaned more heavily against Elle, head twisting so he could cry into her shoulder.

She reached up with the hand not pinned between them and patted his head. "There, there. You're okay."

Leslie cried harder, chest hopping. "I do not know what to do."

Elle turned her eyes to the stars. Leslie was always emotional, tending to cry at least once or twice a day. This crying fit, however, felt different. It made her chest ache and her fingers twitch. It made her want to help. She said, "Well, you don't have to decide right now. You said you'd merge with Adair after getting me to the sky, and who knows how long that'll take? And, okay, you holding his emotions hostage is kind of cruel. But him forcing you to stop being a person is also cruel. So you guys are . . . I don't know. Even?"

He sniffled and rubbed his nose on the sleeve of her shirt. "You believe I should wait?"

"Yeah. Take your time. Think it over. Why do today what you can put off until tomorrow, right?"

She'd hoped her joke would cheer him up, but he only cried harder. He twisted so his legs stacked one atop the other, and his upper body bent. He pressed his forehead to her neck and his face to her chest. As he wrapped her in a tight hug, trapping her right arm between them, she promised herself she'd never comfort anyone ever again.

They were still in that position when Adair found them. Elle used her free hand to point at the still-crying Leslie and mouthed "Apologize."

Adair raised a brow, doubtlessly claiming he had nothing to apologize for.

She jabbed her finger first at Adair, then at Leslie and mouthed, "Fix this." Adair turned away. She straightened her bent leg to kick his ankle. He spun, emotionless eyes narrowed, but she had bigger, sadder problems. She mouthed the word "Now."

The corner of Adair's upper lip lifted in a sneer, but he did turn his attention to Leslie. He watched his other half cry, contemplative, then stepped forward. He pressed the bottom of his boot against Leslie's calf and shoved. Leslie lurched toward Elle, who collapsed beneath him.

Leslie whined and raised his head. Before he could complain, Adair said, "I won't call you Leslie because you're not Leslie. You're my heart."

Elle pushed Leslie off her so she could sit up. Under her breath, she said, "Real mature."

Adair kicked her in the shin. Pain lanced up her leg, and she hissed, positive it would bruise. He continued, "That being said, I accept that you believe you're a person, so I'll make an effort to treat you like one."

Leslie straightened, bottom lip still trembling. "Really?"

"Really."

Elle scooted away, more than ready to have her personal space back. Leslie jumped to his feet. He said, "I accept your offer."

"It wasn't an offer. I'm going to do it regardless of what you want."

"Thank you, Adair." Leslie threw his arms around Adair in an overly friendly hug, which Adair neither rejected nor returned.

Elle snickered at Adair's expense. A sharp pain zinged the back of her neck. She cursed and slapped at the flame. Her amusement went out with the fire, and she reached for her healing salve. More to the salve than any actual person, she said, "This is nice and all, but shouldn't we be trying to find Honeycutt?"

Adair said, "She's the only dwarf on the ship. We already know where she is."

Elle rubbed the salve onto the back of her neck. "Where?"

Leslie turned so he and Adair stood side by side. One arm stayed slung over Adair's shoulders, the other held his pointer finger perpendicular to smiling lips. They waited and, after a moment, the faint sound of shouting floated over. He dropped the shushing motion and pointed toward the source.

"There."

25

They found Honeycutt in the ship's mess hall, arguing with a cook. She was short, the top of her head barely brushing Elle's shoulder, and had long, wavy brown hair. Her beard was curlier than her hair and stretched all the way to her abdomen. Both her hair and her beard were streaked with thin braids. Leather armor clung to her muscular figure. Spittle caught in her mustache as she shouted, "What do ye mean you're cutting me off? I'm your best customer."

Elle cringed because Honeycutt was *loud*. The cook said, "My best customers can pay."

"I've got coin."

"You *had* coin. You can come back when you've got more."

Adair stepped forward, coin pouch in hand. "I'll pay."

The cook, Honeycutt, and Elle all turned to Adair. Honeycutt gave him a hard slap on the back. "Attaboy! That's another pint over here. No, a gallon."

The cook looked between Adair and Honeycutt, openly skeptical. Adair opened his pouch and took out two gold coins. "Whatever she wants."

Honeycutt pumped a fist in the air, mood drastically improved. The cook tucked his hands into the pockets of his white apron and said, "I'm not one to turn away business, but are you sure you want to waste that much coin on this drunkard?"

"Positive." Adair's tone left no room for argument. The cook shook his head and accepted the payment.

"Good man." Honeycutt reached up to grab Adair's bicep. She dragged him to a nearby table. "Ye really saved me back there, ye did. He was going to cut me off."

"So I heard." Adair sat next to Honeycutt, and Elle took the seat on his other side. Leslie followed the cook into the kitchen. When he returned, it was with a pint and three shot glasses. He took the seat between Elle and Honeycutt.

Both Leslie and Adair downed their shots. Honeycutt chugged her pint so fast it dribbled out of the sides of her mouth and streaked down her beard. Elle twisted her tumbler between her fingers, still grossed out from the last shot she'd tried, and waited for one of the others to speak.

Honeycutt slammed her empty mug on the table, bright brown eyes trained on Adair. "So, to what do I owe the pleasure?"

"We want to hire you."

"No." Honeycutt stopped as the cook approached. He placed a pitcher of frothy yellow liquid on the table, wordless, then left. She refilled her mug. "Ye found me, which means ye must know I'm the head guard on this here ship. I'm no' looking for a job."

"Name your price."

Honeycutt laughed long and loud, right in Adair's face. "Ye've never met a dwarf before, have ye?" She didn't wait for him to respond. "We dinnae do things for coin. We do it for glory."

Adair's empty eyes slid from Honeycutt's face down to her drink. "If you're going to refuse us based on your culture, you should do it without a pint in your hand."

Honeycutt stiffened, mustache curling down in displeasure. Elle nudged Leslie and asked, "What's he mean?"

Leslie shifted uncomfortably. Adair said, "Dwarven culture forbids drinking alcohol. They believe readiness to do battle directly correlates with being rewarded in the afterlife, and alcohol dulls the senses. To have even a sip of mead is supposedly on par with blaspheming."

Elle blinked, only understanding half of that. Honeycutt raised her glass in a mock salute. "Well aren't ye knowledgeable?" She downed another few mouthfuls, then pressed the cool glass to her ruddy cheek.

Her heavy, lilting accent slurred as she said, "I've already earned my glory, and I can nae return to my clan. The way I figure it, all I've left to do is die and wait for the great waters to carry me to the Motherland." She stared unseeingly at the table, sounding exactly as defeated as she claimed not to be. Her voice lowered to a bitter murmur. "There's no need to be sober for that."

Adair opened his mouth, but it was Elle who said, "Seriously?"

Leslie laid a warning hand on her shoulder. Honeycutt waved his interference away with an unconcerned swish of her mug. "Say your piece, lassie."

Elle batted Leslie's hand away and leaned over the table. "So you got your glory already. So what? I don't know if you've noticed or not, but this world is fricking huge. You should be exploring it, not sitting here waiting to die."

Leslie used a firm, disapproving tone to say, "Elle."

Honeycutt laughed. "Well said!" She lifted her mug in a toast that no one returned. She drank regardless. "I like your spirit, lassie, so I'll make ye a deal." She drew out the word *deal*, lips curved in a derisive smile. "If ye can tell me how I'm supposed to face my clansmen without the counter-curse I swore to find, I'll consider taking your job."

Elle hesitated, unsure how to respond. Adair saved her by saying, "You're in self-exile."

Honeycutt raised her glass again, smile gone.

"Oh, Honeycutt." Leslie sniffled, tears shining in his eyes.

Elle shook her head. "Wait. I don't get it."

Adair barely spared Elle a glance. He said, "Pride is everything to a dwarf. Honeycutt made a promise, and she can't return to her clan until she fulfills it."

Elle shrugged, not seeing the problem. "Okay. What if we help you? Would you be our guide then?"

Honeycutt smiled at Elle again, more sympathetic this time. "That's a right kind offer, but I could nae ask ye to do that. The cure I need is a long ways off, and the road there's near as dangerous as the destination."

"Where is it?"

Honeycutt's smile tilted mischievously. She released her pint and pointed up. "The sky."

Excitement molded itself to Elle's spine. She grinned. "That's where we need to go, too."

Honeycutt banged her fist on the tabletop, all good feelings gone. Elle stilled, wary. Honeycutt said, "Ye can nae go there. That place is hell. A wee lass like ye could get struck down just thinking about it."

"You're wrong." Elle pushed on, determined. "I'm from the sky—"

"The only things up there are a god and a demon, and neither of them like company. Wherever you're from, it's no' there."

Elle's anger burned. "That's not true. I've seen it. There's a castle and a tattooed man and a huge ball of lightning—"

"Sweet gods." Honeycutt lifted her mug only to find it empty. She shook her head. "I'm telling ye this because if I don't, your blood's on my hands. Ye will nae survive."

"You did."

"I had a sword built for killing demons." Honeycutt waved a hand through the empty air behind her head. "Now I dinnae."

"We'll get you another one."

Honeycutt snorted. "There is no 'other one.' I crafted that sword myself to earn glory, and the materials alone took years to gather."

"Okay, so we'll go get that one. Where is it?"

Honeycutt tossed a look at both Adair and Leslie, very clearly asking if Elle was touched in the head. To Elle, she said, "Ye think I have nae tried retrieving my sword? When the god defeated me, the demon took my sword and hid it in a dragon's hoard. That dragon's got my scent, and now I can nae go within ten meters of the place without getting sniffed out. It's no' possible."

Elle splayed both hands on the table, resolute. "The dragon has your scent not ours. We'll get it for you." She looked to Leslie for confirmation. He stared at his hands, saying nothing. Adair shook his head no. She turned back to Honeycutt, undeterred. "Alright. I'll get it for you."

Honeycutt sighed and tugged on her beard. "Lassie. Do ye even know what a dragon is?"

"Yes." Elle hesitated. "It's like a lizard, right?"

Honeycutt barked out a laugh. "I think we're done here."

"No. Please."

"I'm sorry. Ye seem sweet, but it's just no' going to happen." Honeycutt stood, snagged the pitcher, and wished them luck. She walked away.

Elle stood, ready to give chase. Leslie grabbed her forearm and said, "She is correct, Elle. We cannot defeat a dragon."

Elle furrowed her brows, unable to believe there was anything they couldn't do. She looked at Adair. He shrugged and said, "Dragonhide is impervious to magic. Our hands are tied."

She glanced between them, frustration burrowing deep. It didn't make sense that she would be hurt by their refusal, but she was. She jerked her arm out of Leslie's grasp. To him, she said, "So much for having a knack for the impossible."

She chased after Honeycutt again, and no one stopped her.

26

Leslie curled up on one of the two beds provided to them by the *Las Estrellas* crew. Their bedroom was laughably small, with three sides of each bed jammed against the walls and exactly enough room for the door to open in the middle. Adair sat on the other bed, back propped against the headboard, legs crossed. He read one of the books he'd bought at the last Impossible Market. If Elle ever came back to them, she would sleep on the bed Leslie currently occupied, and Leslie would share with Adair.

He told himself she would return soon. The clock ticked on. He imagined being brave enough to get up and go find her, but that bravery never reached his legs.

He hated himself.

"Did you know that we had to fight the guardian of the painting in order to leave?" Leslie spoke into the pillow, dry lips catching on rough cotton. Adair didn't look up from his book. "I say 'we,' but it was really only her. Elle was the one who bit, kicked, and scratched. She screamed for me, you know, and I . . ." Leslie's breath hitched. He snuggled deeper into the pillow, tears blurring his vision. "I remained hidden. I knew she needed me—knew she could not defeat the enchantment on her own—but the fear overwhelmed me. When the opportunity to save Elle arose, it was a matter of luck. The Painted Lady was distracted. They were both facing away. We were all right next to the exit."

Adair turned a page in his book. Leslie turned his face into the pillow. Cotton and goose feathers muffled his voice as he said, "I had been waiting not for the chance to rescue her, but the right moment to run. Had the stars not aligned, I likely would have fled alone."

Shame flushed through Leslie, acrid and inescapable. His tears wet the pillow. He wanted to take the admission back so he could go on pretending righteousness, and he wanted to bask in the honesty. The only sound in the room came from Adair's book. From the soft rub of fingers grasping paper and the quiet swish of a page being turned. Encouraged by the silence (by the lack of judgment), he pressed on.

"I told myself the cowardice was circumstantial. That next time—*next time* I would be brave. Then the sorcerers in The Rabbit Hole attacked, and I did nothing. They were larger and physically stronger. They outnumbered her. I even knew you would protect me should I step in to help. And yet . . ." His tears flooded over. His throat ached. He cried into Elle's pillow, and the knowledge that *nothing had changed* sank its knife in deep.

Adair had said Elle would change her mind once she realized the dangers a dragon presented, but Leslie knew that wasn't true. She would charge forward, determined to get what she wanted no matter the obstacles. And if Leslie refused to accompany her, so be it.

The shame clawed its way through his stomach, into his spine, and he admitted, if only to himself, that part of him would prefer that. If Elle left them, Leslie would be relieved of his responsibility to keep her safe. He would finish his adventure some other way, and she—

She would die.

Sorrow tangled with his shame. He was so tired of letting Elle down—tired of letting himself down—but saw no other options. If he left Elle, she would die. If he stayed with Elle, they would both die. And to what end?

His lifted his head from the pillow. "Adair?"

"What?"

"What are we going to do?"

Leslie heard the book close and Adair's rickety bed creak beneath him. "About what?"

"Elle. She wants to go to the dragon's den."

"So let her go."

Anger overrode shame. Leslie sat up. "Why are you always so horrible?"

"Why are you always crying?"

"I am not always—" Leslie's voice cracked, and he whined, momentarily incapable of comprehending why life had to be so *hard*. "Why does no one understand that I am a heart? I feel strongly, I feel often, and I am incapable of hiding it."

Adair watched Leslie cry, visibly unsympathetic. He clarified. "Why are you crying this time?"

"Because I do not want Elle to die."

"Then go with her."

"I do not wish to die, either."

"Then don't go with her."

Leslie ground the heels of his palms into his eyes, frustration mounting. "I cannot do both."

"Why not?" Adair reopened his book, all interest in Leslie's issues apparently lost. "This is hardly our first impossible problem."

Leslie blinked. Hope took root in his misery. He swung his feet over the edge of the bed. "This is our problem."

"I just said that." ·

"Yes, but this is *our* problem. The both of us." Leslie hopped up, excitement flowering. He started to pace. "If the dragon has Honeycutt's scent, she must have attempted to retrieve the sword already. That, by proxy, means she is willing to go into the dragon's den."

Adair didn't look up, but his eyes weren't scanning the page, either. He was listening.

Leslie grinned. "I have knowledge of potions and plants. You have magic. Separate, we are useless, but if we work together, I am positive we could hide Honeycutt's scent long enough to get her into the den. She could protect Elle while we stand safely outside, and we will still have helped."

Adair raised both brows, eyes on his book. "You can't honestly expect them to be able to kill a full-grown dragon on their own."

"What if you help them? Dragons' skin and scales are impervious to magic, yes, but they can be affected indirectly. You could help fend it off."

"No."

Leslie stopped pacing. "Why not? Do not tell me you believe yourself incapable."

"Do you have any idea how much work that would be? Fire doesn't hurt them, they're too far off the ground to effectively fight with earth or water, and even if I could feasibly overpower a dragon with air alone, it would be exhausting. I'm not doing it."

Leslie cringed, bothered first by Adair's priority list and second by his apt description of their task. He asked, "What if we do not confront it? We need the sword, not the dragon. So long as they are quiet, they will be fine."

"And what are you going to tell them?"

Leslie tugged at the hem of his sleeve. "Excuse me?"

"You don't want to die for Elle. I get it. I don't want to die for her, either. Question is: How are you going to explain that to her?"

"I will tell the truth."

"Oh?" Adair placed his finger between the pages of the book and flipped it closed. "You're going to look guileless Elle in her big brown eyes and tell her you're too much of a coward to shoulder the danger? Tell me, how do you think that's going to go over?"

Leslie opened his mouth to argue, but Adair was right. Even if his plan worked, he was taking the easy way out. Any positive opinion she had of him was sure to be shattered. His sorrow returned. "She will hate me."

"She doesn't have to." Adair set his book to the side, voice low and soothing. "You can tell them it's my decision, that I won't risk my heart on one of her ridiculous whims."

Gratitude fluttered, then crumbled. Rage reigned. "You are a terrible person."

"What?"

"You do not wish to help me. This is another ploy to indebt me to you so we will merge sooner."

Adair tilted his head, guilty but unapologetic. He reopened his book. "Worth a shot."

"No. That is not okay."

"So you won't blame me, then? You're going to march up to Elle and tell her about how you could feasibly help, but you'd really rather she risk her life alone while you wait safely outside?" Guilt and anger bubbled. Self-hatred fumed. Leslie turned away, thoroughly humiliated, and Adair said, "That's what I thought."

Leslie clenched his fists but didn't respond. As much as he hated Adair's tactics, he couldn't argue with the results. And if he was going to use Adair as a scapegoat, what right did he have to complain? From (beside him, inside him, nowhere at all), he could hear Clarrissa insist he *just tell the truth*. But then, she'd always had too much faith in him.

Another test of valor come and gone. Another failure tallied under his name. Fresh tears wet his lashes. Self-loathing soaked his soul. He held his voice steady and said, "Will you go find Elle?"

27

A full day had passed since Elle stormed off after Honeycutt, but it only took Adair three minutes to find her again. This was partly due to the fact that they were on a boat in the middle of the ocean and mostly due to his impatience. When he reached the upper deck and Elle's location didn't immediately present itself, he activated his second-sight.

Her obnoxiously large aura pointed him upward. He canceled the spell, headache already forming behind his eyes. The air whispered around him, rife with energy from the approaching storm. He bent his fingers, bidding it to lift him until he, too, stood in the crow's nest.

The platform was a small, circular thing with thin knee-high posts holding up an equally thin wooden railing. Elle sat with her legs hanging over the edge, arms folded on the rail. Without looking away from the horizon, she asked, "Did Leslie send you?"

"Yes." He took the few steps necessary to stand beside her. She patted the floorboards to her right. He remained standing. "He wants you to come to the room."

She looked up, impassive. "You're calling him 'he.'"

"As I said I would."

"Yeah, but I didn't think you'd actually do it." She turned back to the ocean and let her arms pillow her head. "You're making an effort. It's nice."

"Come to the room."

"Tell me why you never talk to Leslie about merging."

Adair didn't respond because her moronic prying didn't deserve a response.

She seemed to take his silence as an answer. "I guess you do talk about it, if bullying him and trying to trick him into merging counts. But I think you'd get a lot further if you just told him that not having a heart is painful, and you miss him. He's got a weak spot for the mushy stuff."

"In case you've forgotten, I only experience emotions in small bursts and in response to strong, anomalous stimuli. Not having a heart is a norm, not an irregularity to which I could react, and I have never missed people."

She hummed. "You know, I don't think that's true. I mean, I don't think you feel things like we do, but that doesn't mean you don't feel anything at all because . . . well, because it's got to hurt, doesn't it? To know that you aren't yourself and that the solution is right in front of you, but you aren't allowed to have it." She hugged the railing, eyes on the sky. "It's got to hurt."

She was wrong, of course.

The only pain Adair could feel was physical, and no amount of sentiment would change that. At the same time, the deep emptiness inside him did spawn a sort of discontent and, with that, a yearning to be whole. They weren't emotions, per se, but the parallel existed.

He tapped her thigh with the side of his boot. "It doesn't hurt. Now get up. My heart has something to say to you."

"Tell him I don't care if he comes. I don't care what a dragon is or how hard it'll be to get to the sky, either. I'm going."

He considered ending the conversation by saying they would accompany her, but he found her propensity for suicide missions admittedly interesting. He asked, "Why?"

"When I was a kid, I fell out of the sky. I don't remember anything before that."

"And?"

"And that's six years of me, gone. Leslie says you grew up in a magic-restricted society and chose to run away to an Impossible Market. That shaped who you are. Me though? I just woke up in the

House with a bunch of strangers and learned that I'd never be able to leave."

"You did leave, though."

"Did I? I know you think I'm stupid, but I'm not. I don't understand what went on in the House, but I know I wasn't picked up by accident. And this journey? Landing in front of you, finding Leslie, the painting sparing me—"

"What do you mean the painting spared you?"

Elle glanced up. "I opened the door to the House knowing it might kill us all. I don't know what happened to the others after I left. That's betrayal, at minimum, and probably a whole slew of other atrocities. But the painting left me alone. Then I got that free word, and the bartender told us about Honeycutt, and it's just all going too smoothly, isn't it?"

"What are you saying?"

"I'm saying I'm not the only person who wants me back in the sky, and I want to know why. Whatever I did, whoever I am, I want to know." She gripped the railing hard enough to turn her knuckles white. "Run away if you want. I'm going."

Adair watched her stare at the ocean. Her back was straight, her shoulders were squared, and he was reminded of the time she bowed to beg for his help. She was strong and willful, even at her lowest.

It was almost disappointing to know she was going to die.

Elle obviously didn't understand the enchantment around the painting, but Adair had created the thing. It worked like an alarm, and without a pure heart, she should have been ripped apart and ejected. Not even Adair had been able to outmaneuver it. So either her betrayal and possible murder were false, or she had some seriously powerful soul magic protecting her.

Considering the extent of her entrapment, Adair doubted the former, and considering the state of her soul, he doubted the latter. Either way, whatever she was racing toward was more powerful than she could handle. Maybe even more powerful than he could handle.

There were too many unknowns, and the playing field was skewed in favor of the opposition. If Elle were smart, she would stop and take stock. Refuse to fight until she had all the variables. If Adair were kind, he would tell her as much.

Unfortunately for Elle, delivering her to the sky was Adair's only way to merge with his heart, and he cared more about himself than he did her. Instead of warning her, he said, "We're still taking you to the sky."

She swung around, eyes wide. "Really? You're not just saying that?"

"My heart insists."

She breathed the words, "Oh thank goodness," and slumped against the railing, visibly relieved. In that motion, he realized that Elle was, in fact, afraid to die. She just wasn't willing to let that fear dictate her future. And now, with Adair and his heart by her side, she apparently thought herself safe. She believed in them.

Adair was blandly aware that this was where he should feel guilt, but his chest was empty.

He offered her a hand, and she accepted.

28

Honeycutt hadn't felt hope in nearly a decade.

Ever since realizing she couldn't defeat a dragon without her clansmen, she'd been an empty shell of her former self. The dwarven way said she should've kept going until she died in battle, but her gut said that dying without first finding the counter-curse would be the ultimate shame.

Her clansmen hadn't understood, of course. They believed running was reprehensible verging on sinful, and that no matter how strong the urge to flee may have been, she should've pressed on. Except this time, staying and dying had meant condemning her best friend along with herself, and Honeycutt couldn't do it.

She lived.

It was hard, and it hurt, but what other option did she have? No one else would step forward to find the counter-curse, and so long as Honeycutt was already damned, there was nothing to lose. She'd emptied the canteen at her hip, exiled herself in disgrace, and—on the off-chance she died before getting a chance at redemption—gotten a job at sea.

While waiting for that chance wasn't ideal, she'd grown used to it. Alcohol numbed the pain and blurred the days. Every sip was blasphemy, but it was *good* blasphemy. So long as she was drunk, the ache for home felt dull. It didn't do much for her humiliation or guilt, but they were as constant as the sound of water against the hull. She was desensitized to their presence.

Or at least, she'd thought she was desensitized. Then the waif girl mentioned the castle in the sky, and all of Honeycutt's hurt, disappointment, and indignity flared like fresh wounds. Like skin peeled from muscle and muscle exposed to sharp, cold air. It'd made Honeycutt sad and scared, which had made her angry, and she'd walked away.

Ran away.

The waif girl had chased after her, passionate and determined, but Honeycutt shut her out. She'd recognized the look in those eyes, had seen it plenty of times both in her clansmen and in the mirror, and knew without asking that there was nothing she could say to change the waif girl's mind. It didn't matter that the waif girl didn't know what a dragon was or if there were ten gods waiting for her at the castle instead of one. She would go.

Honeycutt both admired and envied that kind of spirit. She longed to throw herself into the fray, uncaring of the consequences, but that longing was buried under responsibility, and her responsibilities were heavy. When she did attempt to retrieve her sword again, she had to be prepared *(had to be sober)*, and a resolution like that couldn't be made on a whim. That meant not jumping at the chance to travel with the first group of adventurers to happen across her path.

"Please?"

Even if they outright refused to get off her path.

The waif girl clasped her hands together in a praying gesture, salty sea air ruffling frizzy brown locks. Honeycutt had come up on deck to finish her rounds, and the waif girl had followed. She *always* followed. And worse: now the waif girl's companions—a friendly man and an unfriendly man—followed with her. The waif girl said, "I promise you won't be disappointed. We can get your sword from the dragon, and if we all go to the sky together, I'm sure we can find your counter-curse, too."

"Ye don't even know what a dragon is."

"I do, though. It's a really big lizard with wings."

Honeycutt glanced behind the waif girl to catch the eyes of the friendly man, who offered a weak smile and a shrug. To the waif girl,

Honeycutt said, "Listen lassie, I'm right honored that a spitfire like ye sought me out, but ye dinnae know what you're asking for. If ye go on this journey, ye will die."

"We won't."

"I dinnae think ye understand. Fighting a dragon is deadly, and it only gets worse from there."

The friendly man raised a hand and said, "We intend to avoid fighting the dragon, if at all possible."

Honeycutt barked out a laugh. "So it's still just her?"

"No. We believe we can retrieve your sword without a fight is all. Why waste energy and resources where they are not required?"

Honeycutt straightened, hope ghosting through her drunken haze for an unbearably bright second. "Ye what?"

"I have a vast knowledge of potions, and Adair"—he motioned to the unfriendly one— "is a brilliant sorcerer. Together, we believe we could hide your scent from the dragon, allowing you to enter its den and create a distraction. Meanwhile Elle"—he placed a hand on the waif girl's shoulder—"will find your sword. So long as you can evade the dragon afterward, as it seems you have done on previous occasions, we should be able to get in and get out without issue."

Honeycutt looked between them, disbelieving. "Do ye have any idea how sensitive a dragon's sniffer is?"

"Yes, but I believe as long as we collect the ingredients from outside its den—using scents that it is accustomed to as your cover—we can do it."

Honeycutt shook her head. "Even then, the amount of magic it would take to completely smother my scent is massive. I seriously doubt ye can—" The ship lurched and shuddered. She stumbled and grabbed the nearest mast. The ship rose out of the sea, and adrenaline snuffed out her buzz. She raced to the bow, conversation forgotten.

Half the crew and counting were gathered on deck. Some headed to the bow, like Honeycutt. Some steadied themselves on the gunwale and peered over the sides. She ran to the starboard side and looked down.

"Oh gods . . ."

Ice jutted up under the ship, impossibly huge and also just regular impossible, considering they were in a tropical sea. *Las Estrellas* had been caught and lifted from the water, immobilized in a single unseen motion that sent cold fear trickling down her spine.

She tore her eyes from the iceberg and shouted, "Below deck! Everyone, now! We're under attack!" A few crewmates looked up. Scant few moved. She spun, determined to force the gawking crew into action. Empty brown eyes caught her gaze.

The unfriendly one, Adair, leaned against the mizzenmast with his arms crossed over his chest. He was too calm for someone under attack. He made no attempt to look over the edge. She swallowed thickly, mouth dry, then nodded.

Adair raised a hand and swiped his thumb down the pads of his other four fingers. The ship shuddered again, gentler this time, and Honeycutt didn't need to look to know they were sinking back into the sea.

Exhilaration lit fireworks in her chest, coloring the world with hope. Adair was powerful. Powerful enough to be relied upon in dangerous situations. Powerful enough to make their crazy idea work.

Powerful enough to travel with.

She took a step toward him. Crew members started shouting about the melting ice. Calmer now that she knew they weren't under attack, Honeycutt told the travelers to wait for her in her room and went about settling the crew. She spun a nonsense story about having set off a trap, stating that the ice had likely been meant for someone else. When their attackers had realized they'd caught the wrong prey, they'd released the spell. She called it a "run-of-the-mill catch and release."

The crewmembers who hailed from non-magic and magic-restricted societies accepted her explanation without question. Those who knew better eyed her, wary, but said nothing. She was the head guard for a reason, and when it came to the safety of the ship, she knew best.

They furled the sails and spent an hour checking the ship over. Once they confirmed the ice hadn't damaged anything, they took another hour to check again. Honeycutt worked with the crew through the whole process, thoughts constantly circling back to the three mysterious travelers awaiting her in her room.

When the sails unfurled, Honeycutt excused herself. She practically ran to her quarters, grin so wide it hurt. She threw open her door, and three sets of brown eyes looked up.

Her room was modest, with a creaky bed and an old wooden nightstand. The three travelers huddled in the tiny room: Adair next to the bed, the friendly man next to Adair, and Elle next to the friendly man. Honeycutt stepped inside and closed the door. She skipped the pleasantries to ask, "You're an icemonger?"

Adair radiated bored indifference. "I'm not an anything monger."

Elle glanced between them. "What are mongers?"

The friendly man said, "Monger is a slang term for sorcerers, usually used in concert with the element they control. Adair dislikes being called a monger because it implies he has only one elemental affinity, but if we are speaking in terms of favoritism, we are partial to electricity."

"Electricity?" Honeycutt leaned forward. "I was no' aware it could be controlled by a human."

"We are the first."

"We? You're both magicians?"

"Not technically." The friendly man motioned to Elle and Adair. "They are capable of magic, and I am Adair's heart."

Honeycutt glanced between the dark, broody Adair and his happy-go-lucky companion, genuinely surprised. "Oh. Er, meal do naidheachd?"

The friendly man flushed and said, "You misunderstand," while Elle turned to Adair and asked what meal do naidheachd meant.

He said, "It's a form of congratulations."

"Why?"

"She thinks my heart and I are sexually involved."

Elle laughed, a clear indication that Honeycutt had missed something. "You and Leslie?"

Leslie huffed, indignant, and dragged Adair closer to Honeycutt. He grabbed Honeycutt's hand and placed it firmly against Adair's chest, which was confusing until she realized he had no heartbeat. Honeycutt hissed in a breath through her teeth. "That's no' possible."

Elle shrugged, somehow unimpressed by the glory-worthy magical feat. "You get used to it." Leslie released Honeycutt's hand, and Adair removed himself from their huddle. To Leslie, Elle said, "They've got a knack for the impossible."

"As do you." Leslie smiled proudly at Elle, who grinned back.

Honeycutt interrupted their moment to say, "Ye can really do it then, can't ye? Ye can get me past the dragon."

"Yeah."

"Yes."

"Probably."

Both Elle and Leslie glared at Adair, who stared back, unrepentant.

Honeycutt jumped up, heels knocking together beneath her as she thrust her arms into the air. "Oh sweet, merciful gods. Ye have answered my prayers even through the barrier of exile." She pushed past Leslie to get to her nightstand and started stuffing her few worldly possessions into a knapsack. "We'll head off as soon as we dock. There's a teleportation station in Norwich that'll take us to Monty, and that's only a half-week's walk from the Halivaara Impossible Market. The dragon's den is six hours to the east of there. So long as ye can tromp the magicians at the market, we should be able to make our final preparations there before taking off."

Leslie said, "To be clear, you are willing to take us to the sky?"

"Are ye kidding? Ye help me get my sword back, and I'll take ye to the moon."

Honeycutt zipped her knapsack and turned in time to see Leslie and Elle exchange a high-five. Leslie caught Honeycutt's gaze, then held out a hand for her to shake. "That is wonderful to hear. Anything you need, simply let us know. We are at your service."

Adair smacked Leslie's hand down before Honeycutt could shake it. "Stop saying that."

Elle, apparently used to their antics, asked, "Why does it matter if we're stronger than the people at the market? Isn't there a courtesy thing in place?"

"No' that far from a non-magic society, and no' that close to a dragon's den. Anybody wayfaring in that area is looking for trouble, and everybody knows it. Prices are higher. People are rougher." Honeycutt tightened her grip on her knapsack, entire body thrumming. Her grin bared teeth. "Winner takes all."

Elle's eyes dilated, enamored rather than afraid. "How much longer until we dock?"

"Four days, give or take a few hours. But once I tell the captain I will nae be joining them on the return trip, I'm yours." Honeycutt nodded to them, then to Elle in particular, and made a silent promise to stop running away. Fear tried to bury itself under her conviction *(She would have to stop drinking. Could she handle life without alcohol? What if they failed?)*, but once Honeycutt had made up her mind, there was no turning back. She'd given her word, and this time, she'd be damned if she didn't keep it.

Like a key turning in a rusted lock, her determination opened a new door. Weight slid from her shoulders, and invisible hands pushed her forth. Her inability to help Clarrissa, her failure to keep a promise, and the disconnect between her actions and her ideals were no longer shackles holding her down but reasons to move forward. The entire world unfolded in front of her, rife with opportunity. Her relief was immense.

Almost, she thought wryly, *like being freed from a curse.*

29

The town of Norwich looked a lot like the town of Grenadine, with its bland brown buildings and mostly human occupants. Where it differed was the feel. Elle stood at the end of the harbor where *Las Estrellas* had docked and stared at the empty air separating them from the town. She said, "There's something there."

Leslie blinked. "What?"

Elle crept forward, arm out. She stopped when she felt the flat, solid press of magic against her palm. It reminded her of when Adair had taken control of her fire, only this was compressed into a thin, wall-like structure. "It's right here."

"There is nothing there, Elle."

"No, it's invisible is all." She splayed her other hand against the barrier, which felt both flimsy enough that she could push through it and firm enough to hurt. She focused on the barrier the same way she'd focused on the earth, feeling for where it might end. "I think it's a wall, maybe? But huge. It might cover the whole town."

Leslie laid his hand next to Elle's, brows drawing together. "It is faint, but she is correct. Adair?"

"It's a barrier." Adair didn't even pretend to examine the invisible wall. "Hardly a reason to be concerned."

"What are ye all blabbering on about?" Honeycutt marched forward, right through the invisible wall, and waved her hands around in what was apparently empty air. She'd been irritable ever since she finished detoxing, which Leslie had blamed on alcohol withdrawal.

He'd also said Honeycutt was liable to have mood swings, but that, too, was supposed to be a good thing, as it meant she hadn't relapsed. Elle personally thought there should be a potion for mood swings, like the one that helped Honeycutt through her detox, but apparently stifling a person's emotions tended to do more harm than good.

Leslie said, "There is a barrier here." He ran his fingers along the invisible wall. "A magical checkpoint, if you will."

Honeycutt rested her fists on her hips. "I dinnae feel anything."

"Most people do not. I may not have noticed it myself if Elle had not pointed it out." Leslie lowered his hand and walked through the barrier. "The more magic a person has, the more sensitive they become to the magic of others. For Elle and Adair, crossing the barrier will be somewhat uncomfortable, and it will inform the creator that two powerful sorcerers have arrived. It is the simplest way to be aware of magical threats entering and exiting the city without a physical checkpoint."

Elle dropped her hands. "I thought this place didn't use magic."

"No, they are magic-restricted. While they still disapprove of performing magic without a permit, they recognize how useful it can be. I do not doubt the person responsible for creating this barrier is paid by the city for its upkeep. The same goes for the operator of the teleportation station as well as the providers of numerous other magical amenities."

"Huh." Elle shuffled forward. Just thinking about crossing the barrier made her stomach squirm. She glanced at Adair. "I thought you said teleporting was a dumb idea."

"Teleporting at random is stupid." Adair moved behind Elle and placed a comforting hand on her upper back. "Teleportation stations are set up specifically for teleporting and are manned by practiced teleporters. They're fine."

"How's that?"

She turned her head to look at Adair, and he shoved her through the barrier.

For a moment, the world ceased to exist. A cold, oppressive force bore down on her from every angle, suffocating her. *Crushing* her. She lashed out on instinct, her own magic rushing to combat the threat. The familiar weight of Adair's power smothered her retaliation.

Then she blinked, and the world went back to normal. She lay on the ground, cheek pressed to the dirt, though she couldn't say when she'd fallen. "What was that?"

"Magic."

Adair stepped around her, seemingly unbothered by the hellish experience of crossing the border.

Elle pushed herself onto her forearms and knees. She felt woozy. "It attacked me."

"It assessed your capabilities. You, on the other hand, nearly tore it open in an attempt to get through faster." Adair gave her a pointed look that may as well have been a verbal insult.

She refused to believe it was that simple. "It didn't feel like an assessment. It felt. . . . I feel violated. What was the magic controlling?"

"Nothing. Magic is its own element, and you can only control your own. Using plain magic as opposed to using magic in concert with a more traditional element generally takes more concentration than it's worth. All of this"—Adair gestured to the barrier—"is part of a person, and the only thing it's good for is measuring the magic passing through. Any feeling of violation comes from your lack of preparedness, not its intent."

Elle scowled and stood. "Why didn't you prepare me then?"

"Don't blame me for your incompetence. Your magic is an extension of your soul, and the only person who can do anything with it is you."

Elle snarled, angry and hurt and *angry*, only to have Leslie step between them, peacekeeping smile firmly in place. He turned to Elle and said, "Your reaction to the barrier is normal. What you felt were your natural defenses—the magic in your soul—reacting to what it perceived as a threat. I suspect those natural defenses are also why you survived your initial fall from the sky. It is nothing to be ashamed of." He shifted his attention to encompass both Elle and Adair. "Now, let us remember where we are. Norwich, like Grenadine, is a magic-restricted society. If you two start fighting here, we will be banned from the city, at best, and hunted down, at worst. Do you understand?" He gave them both a hard, warning look.

Elle crossed her arms and looked off to the side. "Yeah."

"And you, Adair?"

"I won't use magic. I'm not an idiot."

Elle sneered at his not-so-subtle jab. Adair stared impassively back.

"Good." Leslie gave them both a hard pat on the back and turned to an amused-looking Honeycutt. "Which way is the teleportation station?"

A sharp smack to the back of Elle's head caused her to miss Honeycutt's response. Elle looked at Adair, who stared innocently at Honeycutt. She tried to punch him in the arm without Leslie seeing, but stealth had never been her strong suit. Adair dodged. Leslie saw. Elle tried to come up with an excuse that wasn't "he started it."

"Seriously, Elle? It has been less than a minute." Leslie rubbed little circles into his temple with his pointer and middle fingers. "I cannot believe I am doing this, but you two need to be separated." He gestured toward Honeycutt. "Walk with her. She knows the way."

"But I—"

"We cannot risk being banned before teleporting, and your control of magic is dubious, at best. Now go."

He pointed toward Honeycutt again. Elle rolled her eyes but complied. Honeycutt and Elle walked a few purposeful paces ahead, and Honeycutt said, "Dinnae worry. Ye can fight all ye like soon as we leave Monty." She patted one of the daggers on her belt with a daring grin. "I'll even help ye, if ye'd like."

Elle grunted. "Thanks, but I don't think that'll do much against Adair."

"'Course it will. Ye have to fight magic with magic."

"You can use magic?"

"No, but I'm known for my ingenuity. What I can nae do, I can build."

Elle eyed Honeycutt's daggers with renewed interest. "Your weapons are magic? How's that work?"

"For as long as there've been magicians, there've been people looking to cover their arses against magicians. Magical artifacts do just that."

"How?"

Honeycutt removed her dagger from its sheath and handed it to Elle. "Ye see those symbols on the blade? They correspond with spells, and so long as I've got both the dagger and the ability to speak, I can activate it. Granted, it's no' as strong as it would be if I had magic, but ye work with what ye've got."

"What if I used it?"

"Ye wouldn't need a spell to activate it, for one. The effect would be amplified, too. Stronger than what ye could do on your own, even."

Elle handed the dagger back. "Is your sword the same way?"

"Aye, though it's a wee bit trickier to use."

"Why's that?"

"Well. . . ." She scratched her beard. "What do ye know about demons?"

"Doors don't stop them."

Honeycutt laughed, sharp and short. "They certainly dinnae!"

Honeycutt seemed to be waiting for something else. Elle wasn't sure how much of her knowledge from the House was true, so she said, "That's all I know."

"Really? Lived under a rock until now, did ye?" Honeycutt grinned at her own joke, which made the dark bags under her eyes seem a little less severe. "No worries. I'll set ye straight. First, there are higher demons, intermediate demons, and lesser demons. Lesser demons are a copper a dozen: shadow-looking creatures that infest houses. They feed on fear and can make a right mess out of your head. Hallucinations. Crazy ideas. Nasty little buggers get mistaken for poltergeists all the time." Honeycutt made a noise that said she thought the mix-up was ridiculous. Elle didn't ask what a poltergeist was. Honeycutt continued, "So long as ye are nae afraid of them, they get bored and head out. Nothing to waste your worry on."

"They don't always look like shadows though, do they? I mean, they could look like other things, too. Like people or dogs. Right?"

Honeycutt's lips tugged down. "Who told ye that nonsense?"

"I met, I mean, I sort of met a lesser demon. Or two of them, I guess. One was a dog, and another was a bartender. They seemed nice enough."

Honeycutt groaned, both pitying and condescending. "Oh, lassie. Lesser demons are thick shadows and nothing else."

"But the dog's owner said it was a lesser demon. And the bartender had the same eyes, so I assumed—"

"What color?"

"What?"

Honeycutt grasped Elle's bicep and lowered her voice. "What color were the eyes?"

"Blue. Why?"

Honeycutt whistled lowly. She looked over her shoulder at Leslie and Adair, presumably to make sure they weren't paying attention, then shifted closer. She said, "Higher demons are shifters, the lot of them. They look like whatever they want, whenever they want it. The only thing they can't change is eye color." She glanced at their companions again, more discreetly this time. "There are nae many of them, and from what I can tell, they've all got different eyes. Now, I've only met Blue Eyes twice myself, but it's bad news. Badder than the rest."

Elle stiffened and turned, lips parting to call the others over. Honeycutt squeezed her arm, hard and tight.

"No. Those two are smart. If ye've told them what ye told me, they already know. And if they know ye've got a higher demon on your tail and they're still no' preparing ye for it . . ." Honeycutt shook her head. "I know ye like them, but maybe a demon is no' the worst of your problems."

Doubt and distrust seeded in Elle's chest. If she left them there, they'd grow into vines that twisted her guts and stuffed her throat. She pulled her arm out of Honeycutt's grasp and spun to face Leslie and Adair.

Honeycutt sighed, voice tender with sympathy. "Oh, lassie."

Elle ignored her. "Did you know I'm being targeted by a higher demon?"

"What?"

"Yes."

Leslie turned to Adair, lips twisted and brows furrowed. Horrified. His voice pitched high as he once again asked, "What?"

Elle waved Leslie off. "Why didn't you tell me?"

"This is neither the time"—Adair gestured to the curious passersby who had begun to gather—"nor the place." Dissatisfaction coiled in Elle's chest. She crossed her arms, refusing to move until he answered her question. He frowned. "Would anything have changed if you knew?"

The response was bland and unsatisfying. It was also the truth. Adair didn't hide things out of nefarious intent—he was just a lazy jerk.

Her shoulders sagged in relief, the doubt in her gut morphing into resentment for her own ignorance. She uncrossed her arms. "I have more questions."

"Later. After we leave Monty."

Elle nodded, not quite satisfied but close enough. Leslie held up a hand and said, "No. That is not okay. How could you not say anything?"

Adair started walking without responding, which told Elle that this exact reaction was his reason for not telling Leslie. She turned back to Honeycutt, who seemed more confused by their exchange rather than less, and motioned for her to lead the way.

They walked far enough ahead of their companions to tune out the sound of Leslie berating Adair. Elle asked, "What does having a higher demon after me mean?"

"Your guess is as good as mine." Honeycutt pursed her lips and gestured to the men arguing behind them. "How are ye okay with this?"

"The Adair thing?" Elle scrunched her nose. "It's just who he is. If it doesn't benefit him, he doesn't do it. And while that can be super fricking irritating, it also means he's probably not involved in some elaborate plot against me."

"What if the demon had killed ye?"

"Then I'd be dead. Look, Adair's never going to come running to my rescue, but that doesn't make him a bad guy. For whatever reason, a higher demon wants me to go to the sky. I also want to go to the sky, so in the long run, Adair is right. Me knowing wouldn't have changed much."

Honeycutt tsked. "If I were ye, I'd be right pissed."

"Oh, I am pissed." Elle grinned, wide and unkind. Self-hatred and disappointment simmered behind her teeth. "Just at myself, not him. I knew something weird was going on, and I never bothered to ask if he thought the same. I mean, I brought it up on the boat, but Adair has this thing about only giving the right answer if I ask the right question, and I knew that—"

"Lassie, this is nae your fault."

"It's not about fault. It's about ability. Right now, the only thing I can change is myself. If I want to get better, to become as strong as Adair, then I have to play by his rules." Elle stared at her fingers, imagined the fire she knew she could summon, then clenched her fist. "One day I'll be powerful enough to force people to give me all the answers, but not today."

Honeycutt cleared her throat and adjusted the canteen on her hip. "Wise words from a wise woman."

Elle hummed noncommittally. It wasn't wise to admit weakness any more than it was wise to admire power. If it were possible to reach the top of the hierarchy without ever acknowledging her current placement, she would.

"How much farther to the teleportation station?"

Honeycutt carded her fingers through her beard. "No' far. Have ye ever teleported before?"

Elle thought back to Adair teleporting her into the mirage outside his house. She said, "No."

"Right. Well, teleportation stations have two platforms. One's for arrivals, and nobody steps on that unless they want to get spliced with whoever's arriving. Same goes for wherever you're teleporting to. In this case, Monty. Ye pay the magician teleporting ye, then step onto the departure platform. Teleporting feels like a tug, quick and easy, but dinnae forget that ye will end up standing in an arrival zone. Linger too long, and ye won't live to regret it."

"Good to know."

They rounded another corner, and the dirt street opened to reveal what looked like a non-impossible market. The majority of the storefronts were indoors, selling things like food and clothing. Toward the middle of the market, under a large red banner reading Teleportation Station, stood the platforms Honeycutt had mentioned.

Adair strode ahead of them, no doubt to get away from Leslie, and spoke to the witch Elle assumed would be teleporting them.

Elle strode closer to get a look at the platforms, which were stone, circular, and came up to her shins. The base of the left platform said Arrivals, and the base of the right, Departures. Leslie stepped onto the platform on the right. Elle moved to join Adair over by the witch.

Honeycutt stopped her with a light touch on her forearm and said, "Ye know I was only looking out for ye, right? I did nae mean to come between ye and your friends."

"Yeah. I know that."

Honeycutt's shoulders slumped, visibly relieved. She opened her mouth.

Adair said, "Elle. Your turn," and motioned to the platform.

Elle walked backward to show Honeycutt she was still listening. She said, "Don't worry about it, okay?"

"Aye. And thank ye." Honeycutt fingered her canteen as Elle stepped up onto the departure platform. It was with a wistful, loving smile that she continued, "Counter-curse or no, Clarrissa would throttle me if she ever found out I'd hurt a sweet lass like ye."

The question, *Clarrissa?* caught in Elle's throat as trepidation solidified in her stomach. She glanced at Adair, who looked as tense as she felt, and it was with a whole new sense of dread that she was teleported away.

30

Elle waited impatiently for Adair to teleport in. As soon as he did, she dragged him off to the side. "How common is the name Clarrissa?"

"Shut up."

"What? No. What if it's the same—"

"Not the time. Not the place."

"You can't say that every time you want to avoid something."

Adair laid a hand on Elle's shoulder. A sharp shock of electricity burned through her shirt and forced her muscles to convulse. She flinched.

"Not the time." He met her eyes, then looked pointedly at Leslie. "Not the place."

"Are you two fighting again?"

Adair squeezed her shoulder as Leslie approached, warning her to keep quiet. She smiled. "Adair was actually just apologizing for pushing me through the barrier without explaining anything first. It's a bad habit of his."

Leslie raised skeptic brows. "Really?"

"No." Adair released Elle and strode toward Leslie. "I was reminding her that Monty is also a no-magic zone. It will likely have a similar checkpoint barrier around its border, and I refuse to continue fixing her screwups. If she breaks the barrier, she'll get a bounty, and I'll kill her for whatever meager amount of gold they deem her worth."

Adair's dark glare assured Elle that he'd kill her for a lot less than a bounty. Her sorry excuse for a smile fell, and she gritted her teeth to avoid starting another fight. Honeycutt appeared on the teleportation platform a few seconds later, pleasantly unaware.

A single look from Adair told Elle she wasn't meant to bring the Clarrissa issue up with Honeycutt, either. Elle kicked at the dirt and complied. After all, he'd made it pretty clear that the no-magic rule actually only meant not to get caught, and in a battle of subtlety, Adair would always win.

She attempted to busy herself by inspecting her surroundings, but non-magic societies weren't nearly as interesting as Impossible Markets. All the houses looked the same, the majority of the people were human, and even the plants were arranged in pleasant clusters of color. In a weird, claustrophobic way, it reminded Elle of the House.

She turned her attention back to Honeycutt and, after a knowing look from Adair, asked careful questions about not-Clarrissa. Luckily, Honeycutt was as knowledgeable as she was well traveled. The majority of their conversation revolved around Honeycutt's exploration of ancient ruins, the interesting bounties she'd hunted to fund her expeditions, and the concept of magical artifacts. Infusing items with magic was a large part of dwarven culture, and bringing new information to the clan was the second-most-celebrated honor achievable.

While it wasn't what Elle wanted to know, she couldn't complain about the extra information. Especially since recounting adventures seemed to significantly improve Honeycutt's mood.

Elle kept Honeycutt chatting until they approached the barrier. It felt slightly different from the one in Norwich, maybe because it was powered by a different person, and her stomach roiled at the thought of touching it again. That discomfort was joined by embarrassment as Leslie, Honeycutt, and Adair all passed through the barrier without issue. Elle avoided Adair's judgmental stare, and Leslie caught her attention with an encouraging smile.

"You can do this. Just breathe through it."

She grimaced because the advice was worthless, then nodded because she couldn't come up with anything better. She breathed in, long and deep, then crossed the border.

The barrier shifted to wrap around her. It felt thick and oppressive, though the weight seemed to be on her magic rather than her physical body. Anxiety spiked, and with it, the need to lash out. She suppressed the urge by drawing her magic closer to her core, which felt oddly similar to flexing a muscle.

It was only then that she remembered Leslie's advice. The foreign magic surrounding her felt like sludge, making it difficult to breathe. She had to work to push air out through her nose, which was surprisingly calming. She took another step forward. The magic around her faded. With a third step, she was free.

"Fantastic! That was wonderful, Elle." Leslie sounded as proud as he looked.

Elle's self-esteem plumed. She stuffed her hands in her pockets and grinned. Adair cut her moment short by asking, "Which direction is Halivaara?"

"West." Honeycutt pointed in the direction of the sun. "Then southwest in another day or two."

"You're sure?"

"As sure as my blade is sharp."

Adair nodded and started west. Elle hurried after him. "Is now the time?"

"No."

"When then?"

"Tonight."

He clenched and unclenched his fist, and freezing water gushed from the sky. Elle shrieked, entirely unprepared. Her clothes stuck to her skin. She started to shiver. She felt the magic in the water, strong but pliable. When she called to it, the water responded with a pulse. It peeled itself off her skin and leeched itself from her clothes. There was a second where it floated around her, as indulgent as an adult dancing with a small child, and she knew that it obeyed her not out of obligation, but affection. Water had existed since the dawn of time, and it made up the majority of the world. What did it care if a few droplets splashed over here or swallowed a city over there?

It offered her this knowledge in a blink, factual rather than patronizing. She thanked it for its leniency and requested it gather in her hands. The droplets in the air drifted down to her palms and formed a perfect sphere.

Elle considered throwing it at Adair. The magic of the earth thrummed, then shifted, raising a small circular platform directly in front of her feet. She tripped over it. The sphere in her hands lost its shape, water dripping over her palms. She called it back to form.

Adair said, "Don't drop the water."

Elle muttered every curse word she knew, including a few she'd picked up from Adair, but very distinctly didn't complain.

Honeycutt motioned to the sphere in Elle's palms. "What's all this about?"

"Adair's teaching me magic. This is one of the exercises." Elle hopped up onto the stone Adair had summoned, which was barely large enough to house half of one foot. She asked the earth to raise another stone in front of the first, and it complied. "I can only walk on these, I can't make more than three at a time, and I have to put them back in the ground behind me."

Elle stepped onto the second stone. She imagined another platform rising out of the dirt, and the earth matched her imagination. She thanked it for its cooperation and pictured the empty area where the first stone belonged. The water wobbled in her palms, requiring an entirely different sort of attention than the ground. She returned the first stone.

"Will that no' slow us down?"

"Nah. I'm usually faster than this. I've just never held water while doing it before."

"Is there anything I can do to help?"

Elle glanced from her feet to her hands and back again before creating another stone, farther way this time. She hopped carefully over to it, more than aware of the sizable distance Leslie and Adair had already put between them.

"No. I've got this."

Honeycutt grinned, teeth shining through the gap in her mustache and beard. She clapped her hands and said, "Ye have a dwarf's spirit, ye do. I'll leave ye to it then."

Elle nodded, only half listening. Her world narrowed to the sphere in her hands, the stones beneath her feet, and the guiding figures of her companions. Water demanded constant supervision while earth required short snippets of alternating requests and demands. It didn't take long for her arms to tremble or her feet to throb, but she paid them little mind. Cramped muscles were a small price to pay for the magic at her fingertips, and the aches of her overworked feet were negligible in comparison to the privilege of walking a path all her own.

Sweat dripped down her forehead and soaked the back of her neck. The sun crawled across the sky, casting shadows through the trees. The sky dimmed. Her abs quivered from the strain of staying too tense for too long. She breathed in slow, measured breaths as her concentration zeroed in on the increasingly restless water in her palms. Her natural inclination was not to provide continuous, tender guidance, and the water knew it.

Which made it all the worse that Elle didn't fail due to fatigue but a lack of attentiveness.

She raised a stone and took a step, the same as she'd done thousands of times before, only to find Leslie standing in her way. She jerked back, attention broken, and the water slipped through her fingers.

"Shit."

She tried to pull it back before it hit the ground, but her exhausted body lagged behind her overstimulated mind, and the water soaked into the dirt. Elle tried to crouch. Her legs trembled. She knelt instead.

Her hands shook as she held them over the dark patch of dirt, and Leslie said, "Leave it." Large, sturdy hands covered Elle's own. She tried to shake him off, rejecting his unsolicited compassion. He held her hands tighter. "We have stopped for the night. You are finished. You did well."

Elle raised her head. They were in a large clearing between thick patches of trees. The sky was dark but not black. A fire crackled in the center of the clearing, to the left of the path. Honeycutt sat next to the fire, sharpening her dagger. Adair stood on the opposite end of the clearing, manipulating the water in a nearby stream to bring fish to dry land. He only ever did that while setting up camp, which meant Elle really was finished. She let her arms drop to the ground, exhausted, and pressed her forehead to the cool, wet dirt. "Do you need me to—"

"Rest. You may help with breakfast tomorrow."

Leslie smiled, kind and understanding in ways Elle couldn't even pretend to emulate. She nodded, too tired to argue. He left to help Adair. She gave herself another long, motionless minute before pushing off the ground and making her way to the fire. Honeycutt had already started gutting the fish.

The dwarf patted the ground beside her. "Ye were right impressive back there, lassie. I never thought we would stop before ye did."

Elle dropped down next to Honeycutt, decided sitting up took too much energy, and flopped the rest of the way to the ground. "What can I say? I'm not a quitter."

"Ye certainly are nae. But ye dinnae make it easy on yourself, either." Honeycutt separated the fish from its spine with an easy flick of her dagger, then jabbed the tip of the blade toward Elle's feet. "Why do ye no' wear shoes?"

Elle lifted her head exactly enough to see her own feet. She wiggled her toes and let her head fall back into the dirt. "There weren't shoes in the House, and I guess I never really thought about it past that."

"The house?"

Elle turned on her side so she could see Honeycutt's face without lifting her head. "Oh yeah. I guess you don't know. So I fell from the sky, right?"

"That's what ye said, yes."

"Well, there's a house up there that isn't the castle. They trapped me inside and convinced me that everything outside was a wasteland. I only escaped a few weeks ago."

"They?"

"The other survivors. Or I guess they aren't really survivors, since the world never fell and there was nothing for them to have survived." Elle adjusted so she could use her bicep as a pillow. "Or maybe they survived getting to the House in the first place? I don't know. There was this weird bubble-thing around the House, and it was . . ." Icy tendrils of fear wrapped around her heart, as though the memory alone could send her back. She scooted closer to the fire. "It was cold and dark, and I thought, 'This is where people go to die.' And I know it sounds dumb when I say it out loud, but if you'd been there, if you'd felt what I felt, you'd think the same."

"Was the bubble empty? And I mean real empty. No ground, no sky, no nothing?"

Elle blinked, unsure whether to be surprised or confused. "How'd you know?"

Honeycutt shook her head. Her thick mustache turned down at the edges as she said, "I was hoping to be wrong."

"Wrong about what? What do you know?" Elle sat up, eager and anxious.

Honeycutt busied herself cleaning another fish. "It's no' for sure. It's no' even likely."

"What isn't likely?"

"I heard of a place like that before is all. But it's no' a place people go, and it's definitely no' a place they come back from."

Frustration and exhaustion twined, imbuing Elle with an overarching sense of helplessness. She raised her voice. "Where?"

Honeycutt's lips curled down, disapproving. She shook her head. "I call it the demon realm. It may have an actual name, but I dinnae know what. Even the wee bit of information I've gathered is nothing but rumor. Little things written in the deepest parts of the darkest caves and buried in the farthest corners of forbidden libraries. But ye have to understand that only demons and their souls go there. If that's where ye were, then ye either sold your soul or . . ."

Elle barely dared to breathe. "Or what?"

"Or nothing." Honeycutt raised her shoulders in a grim shrug. "It's like I said, lassie. People dinnae go there, and people dinnae come back."

Elle's first instinct was to rebel against the implication that she had sold her soul, but her inability to recall anything before the House was damning. Still, she said, "I wouldn't do that."

"No. I did nae think ye would."

"But you said—"

"That only demons and their souls go there. Ye are nae a demon, and ye are nae dead. Regardless of whether ye sold your soul, demons dinnae take the living." Honeycutt skewered a clean fish. Her mustache lifted in an apologetic smile. "I dinnae know where ye were. I only know where it sounds like."

"But I, um. . . . If that is where I was, what about the other survivors?"

"Souls, probably." Honeycutt shrugged and started on a third fish. "Maybe a demon or two, but they dinnae generally like each other, and I doubt ye would miss it if ye met one." Honeycutt tapped her temple with the tip of her fish-gut covered blade. "They can nae change their eyes, remember?"

Elle's heart stuttered and her vision blurred. She did remember. Bright, icy blue irises painting thin rims around dark, empty black pupils. A cruel, apathetic smile and punishments that never fit the crime. She steadied herself with a hand in the dirt.

Miss Cynthia wasn't a witch. She was a demon.

Elle's stomach churned, but there was nothing for her to throw up. Had the other survivors been dead all along? Did they know about Miss Cynthia? If so, why hadn't they said anything? Quincy's *(unwavering loyalty, encouraging words, bright smile)* request for her to come back for him flashed through her mind. Had he been a prisoner, too, or . . . ?

Tears burned behind her eyes as devastation loomed. She couldn't—wouldn't—believe that her only friend had been using her. If Elle had been trapped, alive and unaware, then others could've been, too.

"Lassie?"

Elle looked up, thoughts in a fog. The fire highlighted Honeycutt with a warm, orange-yellow glow. Leslie stood behind her, present but out of focus, and Adair behind him: a straight-backed silhouette. Elle heard her blood pulse in her ears, entire world tipping sideways. She sounded desperate as she asked, "How do you kill a demon?"

Honeycutt grimaced. "I did nae mean to scare ye, lassie. I dinnae really think—"

"Miss Cynthia has blue eyes. And it makes sense, doesn't it? She trapped me in the House. She saw me trying to escape but didn't stop me. And now she's leading me to the sky. Please, Honeycutt. I need to be able to defend myself."

Honeycutt's eyes dilated. Her lips parted, but no sound came out.

Elle shouted, "Honeycutt!"

Honeycutt held up both hands, defensive. "I'm sorry, but it's no' that simple. Even if ye were in the demon realm, the fact that ye were taken alive creates a whole slew of other issues. Demons dinnae act without reason, and they dinnae work alone."

Elle's worldview tripped over the notion that Miss Cynthia was working for someone else. She couldn't imagine fighting someone powerful enough to control a demon. Hell, she couldn't even imagine fighting the demon. She shook her head. "I don't care. Teach me how to use the sword."

Honeycutt heaved a heavy, frustrated sigh. "Do ye know what makes demons immortal?"

"No."

"It's the deals they make with humans. They trade an impossible thing for a soul, usually on a time limit. Once their time is up, the demons collect. Do ye know what demons do with those souls?" Honeycutt didn't wait for an answer. "They tie the souls to their own magical cores, right here." Honeycutt jabbed a thick finger against Elle's sternum. "They drain the souls slowly, over years and years, until there's nothing left. That's what keeps demons young, and that's what ye have to sever if ye want any chance of killing them. Because if they have even one soul left, they can run off and heal. Like nothing ever happened."

"So I have to hit her core?"

"No. Ye have to cut it out. And it's no' enough just to hold the sword, either. Ye have to activate the magic in the sword, and it's no' like anything ye've ever messed with before. It's soul magic."

Elle tensed. "You mean like what the demons use?"

"Fight fire with fire, lassie. I dinnae have magic of my own, so I activate the sword with a continuous chant. If I stop even for a moment, the magic dies. For ye, it will be even harder."

"But why? I won't have to say the chant."

Honeycutt ran her hand through her hair, clearly frustrated. Adair stepped into the firelight and said, "Soul magic is high-risk, low-reward. Instead of using the magic in the world around you, you're drawing off your own soul. If you use too much or don't put it back correctly, that's it. No more you." He held eye contact with Elle, tone unsympathetic verging on callous. "If you want to use that sword, it sounds like you'll need to command it with your soul."

Elle twisted her hands in the loose material of her pants, more confused than ever. "What does that mean?"

"It means if you aren't in complete control, if you don't have an unwavering resolution, then you're just as likely to cut your own soul as you are to cut the demon's. Understand?"

Elle looked down at her hands, realization dawning. Fear of a demon maiming her met with fear of accidentally maiming herself. "But I . . . I can just say the chant then, can't I?"

"The difference between you and Honeycutt is that she can't feel her magic. That, by proxy, means she can't feel her soul. Even if her soul rejects what she's doing, she can't feel it to be distracted by it. You can. And if you get distracted, even for a moment . . ."

"No more me."

Adair nodded.

Elle watched her fingers twist in the thin brown fabric of her pants until they disappeared. Terror touched resentment, and she didn't know what to do. Miss Cynthia could obviously find her wherever she went, and even if running away were an option, Elle wouldn't do it. Not with the void in her chest and the curse on her soul. Tears dripped onto the backs of her hands, and she accepted, regardless of consequence, that the only way to move was forward.

"Lassie." Honeycutt pulled Elle from her spiral with a gentle hand on her shoulder. "I know this is scary, but ye need no' fear. Ye are nae alone."

"You don't get it. Miss Cynthia is after—"

"Ye. Aye. But that does nae mean it will get to ye." Honeycutt grinned, confident and encouraging. "The only things that matter to me are glory and the clan. Until I get that counter-curse and we all leave the sky together, ye are my clan." She threw a glance over her shoulder, including Leslie and Adair in the generalized "you," then lifted the hand not on Elle's shoulder to point at the sky. "There's a god and a demon waiting for us up there. If ye think ye can handle a god, then ye can leave the demon to me."

Tears made warm tracks down Elle's cheeks. The fear festering inside her cracked, and gratitude stepped out. "You're serious?"

"I dinnae lie, lassie."

"And we are here for you, as well." Leslie crouched by Elle and placed his hand over Honeycutt's. "It may not always seem like it, but Adair and I care for you. Whatever awaits us in the sky, we face it together."

Elle returned Leslie's smile, weak and watery. "Thank you. Both of you." She glanced past Leslie and Honeycutt to see Adair, who had yet to move from his place by the fire. "All of you."

The fire crackled, warm and bright. The hands on her shoulder lifted burdens off her back. And Elle wondered, for the briefest second, if that was what it meant to have a family.

She hoped so.

31

There is a castle in the sky. Elle's older self has decimated its defenses, cornered its beast, and proved herself superior to its master. She is sure of her victory, and that arrogance is her undoing. The master of the castle rises from a fatal blow, scarred but otherwise unharmed.

Perun.

He knocks her away with wild, angry magic, and her sword is lost. The beast steps forward, no longer threatened. Elle's older self is pinned by malice potent enough to choke on, but she does not panic. Some part of her craves this ending: a masochistic yearning to be punished for her sins. She has the power to fight back, but she does not use it. She asks, "What are you going to do? Kill me? Put me in your precious sphere?"

"Oh no." Perun picks up her sword, admires its strength, and turns it on its master. "Sustaining my life is an honor, and you are not worthy. For your transgressions are great, and it is not a sorcerer you have offended, but a god. I am gracious, I am merciful, and I am fair." He presses the tip of the blade to Elle's sternum, and she spits at him. His magic rages. She writhes. He uses her sword to draw blood and sneers his first truth. "I also wish to see you suffer."

The world spins fast and hard enough to tear her apart, and suddenly she is flying.

No, falling.

Elle woke with a gasping breath, arms covered in gooseflesh and vision blurred with unshed tears. It'd been weeks since she'd last dreamed of the castle, with its high walls and terrible end. Guilt and regret sloshed in her belly, sickeningly thick. She hugged her knees to her chest and imagined the lightning.

A single, horizontal flash of light across a pitch-black sky. A blanket of love and benevolence. Warmth and care washed over her, natural as the tide rolling up the beach. The lightning eased the ache of her dream and dulled the void in her chest. It offered salvation.

But a flash was only a flash, and quick as it came, it vanished.

"Are ye alright?"

Elle swallowed around the lump in her throat and blinked away her tears. It took her a moment to remember that they were in her shoddily made earthen shelter, and that she and Honeycutt were alone. It was too dark to see Honeycutt, but she turned toward the dwarf's voice. "Sorry. Did I wake you?"

"No. It's been ten years since I've slept without the ocean beneath me. Takes some getting used to is all."

Honeycutt's voice didn't waver, but the assurance was weak. Adair had refused to let her sleep in his larger, better-constructed shelter specifically because recovering alcoholics were often plagued with insomnia, and he hadn't wanted her to keep him up, too. This moment showed he'd been right.

Elle cushioned her face with her hair so the dirt wouldn't chafe her cheek. She changed the subject. "What's it like being a dwarf?"

Honeycutt's clothes rustled as she shifted, presumably so they could face each other. "What do ye mean?"

"I guess, what separates you from humans? What's it like having a clan? Or being without them?" The memory of Perun's magic *(thick and blunt and digging into her skin like it belonged there)* made her feel used and dirtied. She curled in on herself like that might take his touch away. "Anything, really."

Honeycutt hummed. "I dinnae think dwarves and humans are too different. We're shorter, of course, and we dinnae have magic of our own. We live longer, two or three hundred years compared to your eighty. Our skin is tougher, too. It takes a right sharp blade to make me bleed even a wee bit." Honeycutt sounded proud, and Elle assumed she was grinning. "I dinnae think there's much else."

"What about the whole glory thing? What do you have to do?"

"Something legendary."

"Like?"

Honeycutt grunted. "It's hard to explain. Assume that if no bards are singing of your feat, it is nae glory worthy."

"And everyone in your clan seeks glory?"

"Aye. It's a rite of passage."

"Why'd you choose to make a demon-killing sword?"

"A demon guards Clarrissa's counter-curse."

"Oh." Elle licked her lips. "Clarrissa's your friend?"

"Aye. My best friend."

"How did you two meet?"

"Meet?" Honeycutt barked out a laugh. "It's so long ago now that I could nae say. We've been together since we were wee bairns."

Elle bent her arm so she could rest her head on her hand. "What's she like?"

"Perfect. Strong, crafty, smart, and a right bonnie lass on top of that. Kindest dwarf you'd ever meet. She insists on always doing the 'right thing,' and makes me do it right along with her. Even when she speaks of earning her glory, she chooses feats centered around helping others." Honeycutt scoffed, soft and fond. "Wants to make new medicines or some other centaur jobby."

"What did Clarrissa end up doing? For her glory, I mean."

"Nothing. We always dreamed about seeking glory together, but that was before the curse set in."

Elle paused, aware that she was stepping on fragile ground but too curious to turn back. She asked, "What did the curse do?"

"Nasty business, it was. Made her weak and frail like ye would nae believe."

"Is that why she didn't come with you to find the counter-curse?"

"Aye, though she did nae want me to go, either. And let me tell ye, I did nae see that coming. I thought she would tell me to buck up, then spout nonsense about how there's no' anything I can nae do, but Clarrissa . . ." Honeycutt stopped. Elle heard her take a long, deep breath. Her voice still cracked as she said, "She, uh, she begged me to stay. Said I could wait to seek glory until she passed and that she did nae want to die without me there. I did nae listen, clearly. Did nae even consider it. And how could I, when she was asking me to sit by and watch her die?" Honeycutt made a resentful noise just short of a whine. "We fought, I swore to find the counter-curse, and I left."

Silence settled between them. Elle didn't know what to say.

Honeycutt broke the silence with a chuckle that sounded more like a sob. "First time I try to do the right thing without Clarrissa guiding me, and look how it turned out."

"I . . ." Elle shifted uncomfortably. "I'm sorry. I shouldn't have asked."

"No! No, lassie. Ye are the only reason I'm no' still on that blasted boat, drinking myself into an early grave. If there's anything ye want to know, ye go ahead and ask. I owe ye that much."

Elle ruffled her own hair. She knew she shouldn't ask, but it came out anyway. "Clarrissa, is she . . . ? I mean, is she still . . . ?"

"I dinnae know. She used to write me letters, but they got shakier and shorter, and I have nae received one in years."

"Oh." Regret pooled in Elle's stomach, solid and sad. "I'm sorry."

"There's nothing for ye to be sorry for. I have nae letters from Clarrissa, but I have nae letters from my clan stating her fate, either. Until it's proved otherwise, I've got to believe she's still waiting for me."

Elle nodded. She wanted to say something encouraging, but the only thoughts in her head were about how *that was ridiculous* and *Clarrissa was probably dead.*

Honeycutt must have sensed the dip in Elle's mood because she tapped something metal and used a much lighter tone to say, "Ye know, before a dwarf leaves the clan, be it to seek their glory or to help with a hunt, we're given a canteen full of ancestral tea. While the tea's delicious, what really matters is the canteen. It's made from the finest ore in our homeland."

"What does it do?"

"For ye? It holds liquid. For a dwarf, though, it's the purest form of magic. Ye see, any time we miss home, we can drink from our canteens and know someone in the clan's drinking with us. I've no' filled my canteen since being bested by the dragon. But if we get my sword back, if ye help me go to the sky, I'll fill it again. I'll drink with my clan, with Clarrissa, every day for the rest of my life. And that . . ." Honeycutt patted the ground until she found Elle's hand. She threaded their fingers together. "That's a blessing."

Elle's chest tightened, empathy painful. She adjusted her grip to squeeze back. For as much as Honeycutt was strong and valiant, she was also desperate and alone. She didn't only need the counter-curse for Clarrissa, but for herself. To apologize for their argument and make the years of exile worth something.

Elle rubbed her thumb along the back of Honeycutt's hand and said, "You'll drink with them in person, too. Clarrissa, your clan, all of them. Just you wait."

Honeycutt sniffled. She pressed their palms together and said, "Aye."

Elle snuggled closer. She didn't ask anything else and, afraid Honeycutt would sense her doubt, didn't offer any more assurances. Honeycutt's hair tickled her nose. Elle's knee bumped Honeycutt's thigh. They fell back to sleep, hand in hand.

Elle didn't dream of the castle.

32

Adair entered the Halivaara Impossible Market alone.

The others had wanted to come with him, but he'd told them in no uncertain terms that their menial chatter was the bane of his existence. He'd been listening to them bond for four straight days, and if he had to hear one more story about either of their Clarrissas, he would light them all on fire. The group then came to the rather quick decision that *yes, maybe Adair should take some time to himself,* and in he went.

His honesty wasn't rewarded with silence, but at least none of the noisy strangers had the audacity to talk to him.

"Hey! Slow down there, buddy. You forgot to pay the entrance fee."

Correction: almost none.

Adair frowned as unfamiliar magic brushed against him, forcing his short stint of privacy to a close. He turned to see five lowlifes: three sorcerers and two sorceresses. Magic bristled around them, strong but untamed. *Presumptuous.* He said, "Fuck off."

The sorceress on the far right thrust both hands out in front of her in an overexaggerated motion meant to summon a blade of ice near his throat. Adair twisted his middle finger around his index finger, effectively hijacking her spell. He sent the blade to the sorcerer in the middle, instead. Said sorcerer swiveled to his friend, angry and afraid. Adair untwisted his fingers, and electricity lit the square. All five of them crumpled.

If Adair could feel, he thought he'd be disappointed. He'd always had a propensity for battle, and while there was a certain satisfaction in victory, it was the thrill of the fight that he'd loved. Then again, enjoying a fight came with the inherent stipulation of finding opponents powerful enough to present a challenge, and that had been an issue even before losing his heart.

Adair utilized the air, still thick with his magic, to pluck the coin pouch from one of the sorceress's belts. It flew into his hand, heavy with coin. Vendors and other patrons watched him from a distance. None met his eyes. This was for the best, as he was likely to strike down do-gooders as rapidly as assailants. He didn't linger to see if the thugs had survived his attack. If anyone came to their aid, it was after he left.

Adair's objective in the market was to gather supplies and secure them a place to stay for the night. The first thing he did was stop for a drink.

He ordered two shots of peace and quiet, then paid by fixing two broken floorboards. It wasn't a fair trade, necessarily, but Adair was too tired to haggle. He accepted his drinks and headed to a secluded booth at the back of the bar.

"Rough day, huh?"

Clarrissa sat down beside him, beautiful and perfect. Healthy. *Alive.* If he'd had a heart, it would've skipped a beat. As it was, he recognized her as an impostor, acknowledged a mild flash of discontent, and frowned to communicate his lack of amusement.

"Cypress." Adair drained his first shot. "Or is it Miss Cynthia now?"

Dangerously hungry, glacial-blue eyes clashed with Clarrissa's warm smile. "I was wondering when you'd figure it out."

"Does Elle have a deal with you?"

Cypress leaned back, pursed Clarrissa's lips, and said, "Of sorts. It's not for her soul, if that's what you're asking. Though her soul is collateral, should she fail to come through."

Adair narrowed his eyes. "Can you make a deal for something other than a soul?"

"It's uncommon." Cypress shrugged Clarrissa's shoulders. "So long as the energy I exert to fulfill the bargain is less than the energy I receive, anything's game."

"Is that why you trapped her in the House? She failed to fulfill her end of the bargain?"

"Goodness, no. That was"—it twisted Clarrissa's lips into a familiar, playful smile—"a favor for another client. Nothing personal."

"And I suppose dampening her magic was also out of the kindness of your heart?"

It propped Clarrissa's elbow on the table and rested her chin in her palm. "Dampening? What makes you think I'd do something like that?"

Adair leaned back in the booth, unamused. "That kind of talent doesn't go dormant on its own."

"No. No, I suppose it doesn't." It smiled with Clarrissa's mouth, and Adair knew that was as much as he would get.

"Why are you leading her to the sky?"

"Now that would be telling."

"So tell."

"I could." It leaned toward him, slid Clarrissa's hand up his thigh, and nestled Clarrissa's body against his side. "For you, I'd even give a discount. Just a sliver of your soul. A sixth."

"No."

Cypress pulled away and used Clarrissa's lips to pout. "Pretty please?"

"Clarrissa would never say that."

"Yes, she would." It traced Adair's jaw with one of Clarrissa's fingers. He focused on eager, deathly blue eyes. "She used to say it to you when she didn't want to make dinner or do chores. Back before she got sick. She did it because it worked. Because you gave in." It sidled closer, long braids falling over Adair's chest and plush lips brushing his ear. "Every. Single. Time."

Adair downed his second shot. "Why are you here?"

It tapped Clarrissa's middle finger on Adair's knee, seeming to think something over. Blue eyes flitted to Adair's face, then to the empty shots on the table. It moved out of his personal space. "You're too slow, love."

"Too slow for what?"

"You're a horse in a race, and while you're not necessarily falling behind, you aren't inspiring a lot of confidence, either. You know what I mean?"

"What race?"

"And normally I'd stay out of it, but I'm betting a lot on you. I'll be very disappointed if you lose." It looked at Adair through lowered lashes. The twist of Clarrissa's lips turned pleading. "You've already disappointed me once, Les. Isn't that enough?"

"You aren't Clarrissa."

It blinked, tears glittering on Clarrissa's lashes, then straightened. It said, "Nor do you want me to be. Clarrissa can't help you here. I can."

"You don't want to help me."

"Alright, I want to help myself." It lifted Clarrissa's hand, palm to the ceiling, as though the difference was semantic. "But you'll benefit."

"How?"

Cypress used Clarrissa's pointer finger to tap the side of her nose, and Adair hated it. He hated seeing that familiar gesture performed by her familiar face. He hated knowing she was dead even as she sat beside him. He hated that he couldn't actually feel hatred. Adair twined his fingers with Clarrissa's, and the demon's obsessive gaze zeroed in on their joined hands.

Adair said, "How about this, then? I'm going to bet the way demons teleport is similar to the way humans teleport, in that you can't do it while touching another person."

Cypress attempted to pull away, but it was in Clarrissa's body with Clarrissa's strength. Adair tightened his grip and sent a warning shock into Clarrissa's palm.

"I may not be able to kill you, but I can certainly make you waste a few souls repairing yourself. Now, you've got thirty seconds to tell me why you're here, or we find out how much electricity your body can handle before it burns. Deal?"

Arctic-blue eyes glanced from their intertwined hands to Adair's face, and the edges of Clarrissa's lips lifted in a mad grin. Cypress made Clarrissa's fingers clench around Adair's. "I knew you were my favorite for a reason."

"Twenty-three seconds."

"Demons are bound to the parameters of their deals. I'm no exception. The closer you get to Perun, the more pressure I'll feel to stop you. Understand?" It canted Clarrissa's head, and the beads at the bottom of her braids clinked. "If you come within a certain proximity, I'm going to have to kill you. All of you. Not that I want to, but, well, a deal's a deal, right?"

"You came all this way just to tell me you're going to kill us?"

"No. I came to tell you that you're slow. You're missing a key piece of information, and if you reach the castle without it, you'll die. I'll make sure of that."

"But you won't tell me what it is I'm missing."

"Where's the fun in watching a rigged race?"

Adair released Clarrissa's hand only for slim fingers to latch around his wrist. He blinked, and that was all the time it took for Cypress to morph. The man from Adair's couch replaced Clarrissa's slim, pretty figure. Cypress's grip felt like steel.

"Take your time, Adair. When I kill you, I want it to be because I'm harvesting your soul, not on the whim of a man-god."

Adair sent a bolt of electricity straight to Cypress's heart. The demon didn't even twitch.

"Let go."

Cypress squeezed harder. Sharp pain radiated out from Adair's wrist. His bones quivered under the pressure. He kept his face blank and his shoulders squared, refusing to react.

Cypress said, "There are things you don't understand yet, but you will. I'm betting on that." It maintained eye contact as it released his wrist. "Don't disappoint."

The demon vanished.

Adair clenched his fist. He wanted to be angry at Cypress or dissatisfied with himself, but there was nothing. He reached for a tumbler. They were both empty. He sighed in a way that projected the frustration he wished he could feel, then stood.

So much for having time to himself.

33

Leslie was prepared for Elle to ask why he wouldn't be joining her in the dragon's den.

He had five points of defense which, assuming she believed them, would leave Leslie inculpable. The first three points were a connected series circling his desire to help and Adair's refusal to let him. They were believable because Leslie really did care for her, Adair was capable of overpowering Leslie if he deemed it necessary, and Adair would confirm anything Leslie said.

His remaining points had to do with Elle's safety. With a mission this dangerous, it was important they all be on the same side. Not to mention they would need Adair to get to the sky after this, and pissing him off here could ruin it for all of them. Kind, honorable Leslie was staying behind for the good of the group. No one could fault him for that.

Or at least they wouldn't be able to fault him once they heard his excuses.

"Are you sure you are ready for this, Elle?"

Elle nodded. The warmth and trust in her eyes curdled the guilt in his stomach. Almost a week had passed since she'd been told she was going in alone, and she had yet to question it. He wished she would question it. He couldn't explain himself if she didn't question it.

Leslie looked around the wide grassy field outside the dragon's den and asked, "How about we go over the plan one more time?"

Honeycutt loosed an irritated groan. He ignored her. "First, you enter the cavern. This is important because . . ."

"Magic isn't foolproof, and your potion might fail. If Honeycutt gets sniffed out, I need to be able to grab the sword and run."

"Good. As soon as you go inside, we shall begin crafting the potion. It should take a few minutes, at most, and you should attempt to locate the sword within that time span. You will know the sword when you see it because . . ."

"It's got a white leather hilt and engravings all down the blade."

"Correct. Now, only Honeycutt will be joining you in the den." Leslie paused for a moment too long, in case Elle wanted to ask why. When she remained silent, he begrudgingly continued, "You are to wait for one of two things before taking the sword. What are they?"

"If I see Honeycutt or if the dragon wakes up. Either way, Honeycutt will be ready to draw the dragon's attention while I take the sword and run."

"Right again." Leslie picked at the strap of his satchel. "Do you have any questions?"

"Nope." Elle grinned and rolled her shoulders. "You worry too much, Leslie. Sneaking around's not really my thing, but even if I mess up, Honeycutt's got my back."

Leslie cringed. *Was that a jab?* "If you are sure."

"I'm sure. You guys have everything you need?"

"We do."

"Then I'm off."

Elle turned toward the large, rocky outcrop that housed the dragon's den, and Leslie was struck with the awful realization that she could really, genuinely die in there. He took a pitiful step forward, guilt feeding off terror feeding off guilt, then stopped. Panic and anxiety formed a tornado in his chest. The confession in his throat tore itself free and he just—

"Why did you not ask?"

Elle looked over her shoulder. She didn't stop walking. "Ask what?"

"Why I will not be joining Honeycutt. I have reasons. Good ones."

Elle tilted her head, confused. She paused when she reached the entrance to the cavern, thin fingers tracing dark stone, and said, "It's okay to be scared, Leslie."

Leslie's breath stuttered, overwhelmed by relief. Tears blurred his vision while a sob shook his chest. By the time he wiped his eyes, she was gone.

Honeycutt stood beside him, grinning in the direction of the dragon's den. "She's a good lass."

"Yes. She is."

Adair positioned their small cauldron over an equally small fire. He said, "Any chance you two can save the parental bonding until after we've retrieved the sword? Unless you're alright with the fact that every minute we waste is a minute that she's alone with a dragon. Then by all means, continue."

Leslie sniffed and rubbed his eyes with the heel of his palm. He nodded. "You are right. We have a job to do. Honeycutt, could you fetch us some of that feather reed grass?" Leslie joined Adair by the cauldron. Honeycutt hurried away. "Adair, keep the fire steady. We must stay between ninety-eight and one hundred two degrees. Any deviation will render the potion useless." Leslie knelt and pulled the ingredients from his satchel. He mixed two grams of powdered air with a half-talon of stillwater and three drops of molten gold. "Three counterclockwise stirs."

Adair forced the concoction to stir itself. Honeycutt returned with the feather reed grass. Leslie tore the tips off the grass and threw the sprigs away, then scooped up a handful of dirt.

"Honeycutt, I need one hair with the root intact. Adair, as soon as Honeycutt adds her hair, we will need a clockwise swish. Then I shall add this." He held out the grass and dirt. "When I do, we will need a counterclockwise swish."

"How large?"

"Three-quarters each way. Both swishes should be accompanied with a dash of magic to convince Honeycutt's scent that it is what it is not."

"A full dash?"

"A full dash."

Adair nodded, Honeycutt plucked one of her hairs, and Leslie motioned for them to start. Honeycutt added her hair, Adair swished, and the potion turned red. Leslie threw in the dirt and feather reed grass, Adair swished, and the red tinted orange.

"Kill the fire."

The fire went out. Leslie uncorked a vial of wind and tipped it over the potion. Thin copper-colored liquid splashed up the sides of the cauldron. When the potion settled again, it was the same soft, oaken brown as Honeycutt's hair.

She made a disgusted noise. "Is it supposed to look like that?"

Leslie shrugged. "I assume so."

"Ye dinnae know?"

"I have never needed to hide someone's scent from a dragon before." Leslie lifted the cauldron and tilted it to the side. He noted the potion's sludge-like consistency for future reference, then handed it off to Honeycutt. "Drink up."

Honeycutt scrunched her nose but accepted the cauldron. "Can nae be worse than orc ale, right?" She cracked an unsure grin at her own joke. No one laughed. She grumbled something along the lines of, "No funny bone on these two," then raised the cauldron to her mouth. "Alright. Down the hatch." She tipped the cauldron back, lips to the cast iron.

Both Leslie and Adair leaned forward, curious to see how, exactly, the potion would affect her. Leslie was sure that it would have side effects, as all new potions did, but those could range from turning her tongue blue to making her better at jumping. It was so unpredictable that he was ready for just about anything.

Anything, that is, except a golem barreling into Honeycutt's back.

Honeycutt hit the ground hard. The cauldron went flying. Leslie ran over, fear for himself tamped by fear for a friend. The golem atop her was a lumpy brown, human-like creature with thick limbs and a dome-shaped head. It was dwarf-sized.

"Honeycutt!" Leslie grabbed the golem's arm and pulled, but it was heavy as a mountain.

Adair said, "Out of the way."

Leslie jumped away on reflex. Two pillars jutted from the ground around Honeycutt, catapulting the golem into the air. It flew, fell, and crashed. The impact resounded, loud as thunder. The golem used clunky movements to get to its feet, visibly unharmed.

The pillars around Honeycutt receded. She pushed herself to her feet and unsheathed her daggers. "What in the devil was that?"

The golem lumbered toward them. It had shallow indents for eyes and a gouge for a mouth. It smiled.

Leslie grabbed Honeycutt by the arm and backpedaled. He said, "It is a golem. They are slow but strong and practically indestructible."

"My blades—"

"Will not even scratch it. Golems are soul magic of the worst sort, with a soul being forcibly tied to"—Leslie flinched as a spike sprung from the earth to skewer the golem through the chest—"a body that does not suit its needs. This one looks poorly made, which shows the creator did not even attempt to make the soul comfortable. Our only choice is to run."

The golem used a fist to smash through the thick spike connecting it to the ground. Adair stepped between them. It turned toward Honeycutt. If it cared at all that there was a spike sticking out of its chest, it didn't show it.

Stones levitated around the golem, then flew toward Leslie and Honeycutt. They dodged in opposite directions. The stones followed the dwarf.

"Why is it no' attacking ye?"

"It's part of the enchantment." Adair created a strong gust to push the golem back. It dug its stubby feet into the ground and stomped forward. "Golems are created with specific purposes in mind. It looks like this one's duty is to kill you."

"Well that's just—" Honeycutt yelped as the earth opened up beneath her. Leslie watched, horrified, as it swallowed her up to her shoulders and closed in.

The golem knelt on one side of Honeycutt, hands and legs flush with the earth. Adair crouched opposite the golem, palms pressed to the ground. Honeycutt's face reddened from the pressure, and a jagged rock nicked her throat, causing it to bleed.

Fear and worry curdled in Leslie's stomach, and he shouted for Adair to help. Neither Adair nor the golem moved. Honeycutt sucked in a wheezing breath. The sound of chanting filled the air, and Leslie's fear morphed into terror.

Adair was struggling.

It made sense to an extent—the golem was made of earth and thereby held more sway over the element—but the soul within the golem must've been a sorcerer in its last life to be able to access its power so readily. Leslie looked between them, knowing he needed to hurry and help but unsure how. Panic addled his thoughts. He told himself to *Go. Be brave. Do literally anything.* His legs trembled.

A tall man with straight black hair and cold blue eyes strode into the field.

Leslie stared at him, comprehension stuttering. The man paused in the middle of their fight, brows raised in surprise and lips dipped in amusement. He said, "Well, I'll be. Looks like he isn't completely useless after all."

The man looked from the golem to Leslie, and his eyes were horrible. They were a cold, hollow blue colored with whispered promises of never-ending torment. Leslie took an unconscious step back, mind numb with the knowledge that *this* was the demon after Elle.

The demon smiled at him and his open show of fear. Then he moved on, toward the open mouth of the cavern.

Adair paused his chanting to yell, "Don't touch her!" only for the strain of fighting the golem's magic to bring him to his knee. He resumed his mantra.

The demon shouted over his shoulder. "Sorry. I'd love to stay and chat, but you look like you've got your hands full. Maybe another time." He gave a two-fingered salute and disappeared after Elle.

Leslie's head swam. His stomach revolted. He imagined chasing the demon down and forcing it to stop because *(he wanted to protect Elle; they couldn't afford to disturb the dragon; he was tired of being useless)* everyone was depending on him, but his body refused. He twisted trembling hands together, the mix of fear and adrenaline freezing him just as it had every time before.

Adair's glare demanded he *do something* while Honeycutt's gasping breaths begged him to *help*. Fear shoved regret, which stumbled into self-hatred. His emotions whirled and multiplied: too many, too fast. Leslie fisted his hands in his hair, overwhelmed.

He couldn't fight a demon. He couldn't fight a dragon. He couldn't fight a golem. Without Adair to protect him, Leslie was as good as dead. He didn't want to die. *He didn't want to die.* Humiliation and anxiety beat hard in his chest until he cracked under the pressure, and Leslie did the only thing that made sense.

He cried.

34

The flame in Elle's palm flickered impishly, already bored despite having been lit less than a minute prior. She imagined strangling the stupid thing, and her magic—her will—used that sentiment to coil around the will of the flame.

Fire, unlike water, earth, and air, was always young. It didn't like to obey, it never wanted to listen, and it only responded to force. She compressed her will around that of the flame's, nearly smothering the thing. When she let up, it was with a demand for the fire to *brighten*. It complied without complaint, revealing a tunnel of rock.

She waved the flame behind her to see a similar tunnel and no sign of the entrance. The ground was slick and uneven. It sloped steeply downward. She clung to the wall with her free hand and lowered the flame in hopes of finding good stepping spots.

"This is ridiculous."

Her voice reverberated off the walls, and Elle extinguished the flame. Adair had warned her not to overwork herself before reaching the sword, just in case she needed her magic to run from the dragon. That meant only using one element at a time.

She pressed her palm to the ground, felt the earth's strength, and requested guidance. The magic of the earth swelled, ancient and knowledgeable. Elle felt more than heard the question of where she wanted to go. She tried to imagine a dragon's hoard or the sword they needed, but the pictures came out blurry. She changed tactics and thought of the dragon, her imagery stolen from one of the picture books in the House.

It seemed to be enough. The earth's magic ebbed away, a ripple expanding from a thrown stone, then flowed back. It pooled beneath her feet and urged her forward. She raised a flat stone and took a blind step toward it. Instinctual fear of falling slowed her progress, but the earth didn't mind. It had waited far longer for far less. Small swells of magic relayed the placement and dimensions of the stepping stones she should create, and she thanked the earth by returning the stones behind her.

Minutes passed slowly but steadily, and Elle breathed a sigh of relief as darkness made way for natural light. The cave opened up into a colossal chamber, with sunlight streaming in through a large hole in the ceiling. Walls of dark gray rock stretched up and up, to what Elle assumed was the top of the mountain-like outcrop they'd seen in the field. Piles of gold and tall slabs of stone decorated the floor between her and the giant, lizard-esque beast sleeping on the other side of the room.

The dragon was larger than Elle had ever imagined, with its body stretching from one end of the chamber to the other and both its tail and neck crooking for extra room. The majority of its scales were dark blue, but seemingly random patches mimicked the bright, happy blue of the sky.

She stared for a full minute before it clicked that scale color was determined by sunlight, and *oh holy hell*. The beast could camouflage. Elle swallowed around the lump in her throat, suddenly understanding why dragons being nocturnal was such a plus. She crept farther into the cavern.

Most of the treasure heaps were twice Adair's height, if not more. The narrow strips of earth between the piles were littered with overflow coins and gems. She checked and double-checked every spot before taking a step, often balancing on her tiptoes to avoid stray coins. Her heart pounded in her ears, and her calves ached, but she'd heard Leslie rattling around in his coin pouch one too many times to think the dragon would sleep through her stumbling into one of the piles.

She did her best to search the room as she went, but the sheer amount of treasure was overwhelming. Coins. Jewelry. Statues. Toys. Weapons. She passed a number of swords, none of which matched even one of Honeycutt's descriptors. Worry whispered in her ear, suggesting that she'd missed the sword, or worse, that it wasn't in the cavern at all. She stopped a stone's throw from the dragon's belly.

"Over here."

Elle jumped, terrified. She spun to the right, but no one was there. Her blood thrummed in her ears. She licked chapped lips, overly aware of the dragon sleeping a single gold pile away, and said, "Hello?"

No one answered. Elle took cautious steps toward the dragon. The voice had come from her right, she was sure, but it wasn't until she stood close enough to feel the dragon's body heat that she knew where it must have gone, too.

There, between a pile of gold and the dragon's stomach, was a small path.

Elle swallowed thickly and, knowing it was impossible, whispered, "Honeycutt?"

The dragon shuddered beside her. Elle stopped breathing. Seconds passed like minutes as she waited to see what the dragon would do.

She counted to thirty, then exhaled low and slow. The dragon kept sleeping. Elle crept closer to the beast.

It looked like the hardest part of traversing the path would be timing. Every time the dragon inhaled, its belly expanded, scales stopping just shy of gold. Elle crouched to get a better look at the trinkets littering the ground. There were seven treasure-free spaces between her and the other side of the pile. The dragon took five to six seconds for each inhale, which meant Elle needed to get across in four.

She wished she had spent more time learning to control air, as being able to lift herself without blowing away the gold at her feet would make everything infinitely easier, but that was a regret for later. If she wanted to pay more attention to the less fun elements, it would have to be after she got out of her current mess. Elle rolled her shoulders and cracked her neck, resolving to act as reliable as she claimed to be. She breathed with the dragon.

One.

A step to the right, next to a blue gem.

Two.

A hop to the left, inside a bejeweled circle of gold.

Three.

Half a leap forward, both feet on the ground.

Four.

Legs bent with pressure on the balls of her feet for a final spring.

Five.

She landed with too much force. Elle teetered forward, then threw her arms out to the sides. She caught herself on a smooth, warm wall of stone. Relief settled in her belly. Fear chased it out. The wall moved. Elle slowly *(slowly slowly slowly)* turned her head to look at the dragon's face.

A mouth large enough for her entire group to set up camp inside, nostrils taller than Elle on her tiptoes, and thick, scaly eyelids—still closed. Gratitude weakened her knees. Anxiety kept her standing. The dragon breathed softly under her palm. She stared at its face and oh-so-carefully peeled her fingers from its scales.

It didn't stir, and Elle didn't press her luck. She slipped into the next aisle of gold.

"Nice one. I didn't think you were going to make it there for a minute."

Elle's heart jumped into her throat. She craned her neck to see a man standing on top of the nearest pile of gold, then swung around to look at the dragon.

"Don't worry. We'll have to be a lot louder than that to wake her up."

Elle laid her hand over her heart and steadied her breathing. "Her?"

The man tilted his head toward the dragon, and it was in that motion that Elle caught sight of his cold blue eyes. Her breath hitched. He smiled.

"What's the matter, Elle?"

"I know who you are."

"Oh?"

Elle clenched her fist, anger overriding fear. "Miss Cynthia."

He laughed, low and pleasantly deep. His smile struck her as familiar. "I suppose you could call me that, but I tend to prefer Cypress." He held out a hand for her to shake, which emphasized the fact that she'd never actually be able to reach him. She shook her head. He dropped his hand. "Suit yourself."

"Why are you here? What do you want with me?"

"You never were one for small talk. Though I suppose that's partially my fault. It's not as though I ever taught you manners."

"You didn't teach me at all."

"Debatable." Cypress used the side of his shoe to tap a sword half-buried in the gold. "This is what you're looking for, right?"

Elle looked at the sword, with its white leather hilt and engraved blade. Frustration coiled around exhaustion and squeezed. Cypress was a demon. He'd never let her take the sword without a fight.

And she'd never be able to win.

She gritted her teeth, undeterred, and asked again. "Why are you here?"

"To help. I'm on your side, Elle."

"You kept me trapped in a house for ten years."

"Yes, and I also helped you escape. You're welcome for that, by the way."

"You didn't—"

"Do you want the sword or not?"

Elle dug her bitten-down nails into her palms. *Yes*, she wanted the sword. *No*, she didn't trust Cypress to get it for her. "Why are you doing this?"

"Do you want the sword"—he wrapped his fingers around the hilt—"or not?"

A thousand refusals wrote themselves on her tongue. She told herself she'd rather die than give Miss Cynthia the pleasure of seeing her submit, but the truth was crueler. Elle was neither strong nor fast enough to fight off a demon. They needed the sword. She swallowed her pride and said, "Yes."

Cypress released the hilt with a sunny smile. He raised both hands, fingers spread. "Luckily for you, I really am on your side, so I really will give it to you." He laid the bottom of his shoe flat against the exposed blade of the sword. "Unluckily for you, I'm also on your opponent's side." He kicked the sword, simultaneously freeing it from the pile and starting an avalanche of gold large and loud enough to wake the dead. "Good luck."

35

A horrible roar filled the cavern. Elle dove for the ground.

There was a single moment where she considered lying really still until the dragon fell asleep again. Then she remembered the whole reason she'd invaded the den alone was the dragon's terrific sense of smell. Her next thought was to run, but the sword was buried somewhere in the gold. She didn't have time to search carefully, and she couldn't afford to leave empty-handed.

She spared half of a second to glare at the spot where Cypress had stood, then used both arms to start shoveling gold and gems to the side. The avalanche had been loud, but the dragon was louder. Booming footsteps caused the ground to shake. Gold pelted Elle's back. She didn't dare look up.

When she found the sword, it was palm to blade. She hissed and adjusted her grip to pull the blade from the gold. It was both heavier and taller than she'd thought it would be. Hilt included, it probably came up to her shoulders. She turned it over, trying to find a good way to carry it, and her memory flashed. Elle recognized the sword.

She'd seen it in her dream.

It'd been strapped diagonally across her older self's back as she'd stormed the castle. It'd been used to corner the beast and, later, to kill its owner. Elle's hands trembled around the hilt. The void in her chest pulsed. Then a hot, rancid puff of air blew her into the gold, and reality played on.

Large green-gold eyes stared unforgivingly into her soul. Slit pupils dilated. Pure terror pulsed through her veins, potent and numbing. She told herself to run, but her legs wouldn't move. The sword wouldn't stop shaking, or—no. She couldn't stop shaking. She glanced at the sword, and water on the blade told her she was crying.

The dragon opened its mouth to reveal teeth half as long as Elle was tall. Panic drove her thoughts in circles. Even Adair had balked at the idea of fighting a dragon. What could she possibly do?

The heat in the dragon's mouth brightened into full-fledged flame, and Elle felt the will of the dragon within it. Strong, angry, territorial emotions demanded the fire go forth and burn what dared to disturb its den. The flames molded easily to the dragon's whims, and Elle understood why.

She could feel the dragon's will even without reaching out. As the flames raced up its throat, she knew without a shadow of a doubt that this fight wasn't about speed or strength. It was about magic. Whoever had the greater control—the greater will—would win, and Elle was outmatched by such a wide margin that there was hardly a point in trying.

But then, maybe that was just what death was. Giving up. Accepting defeat.

Are you satisfied yet?

Miss Cynthia's voice echoed mockingly in Elle's mind: a cool reminder that she really had been better off in the House. Everything she'd learned, everything she'd done, and for what? To die crying on her knees in front of a giant lizard?

Was she satisfied yet?

Elle scowled.

Never.

Terror and rage held each other so tightly that they became desperation, and Elle funneled that into her magic. She raised her hand and pushed back against the dragon's will, demanding the flames part around her. Hesitation joined the flames' usual vigor, but they didn't falter. Elle pressed harder still.

Go around me. Go around Me. Go Around Me. Go Around Me!

Flames burned her palm, hotter than any Elle had ever felt before, then split. Thick walls of fire burned around her, heat stifling. She released the sword and plunged her hand into the scorching-hot coins. Heated metal scalded her skin. Tears balanced on her lashes, then dried in the heat. Her fingers hit the ground first, then her palm. She felt for the earth's will.

It greeted her with a gentle swell, quieter and sturdier than the fire. Her magic folded around her will, and her attention with it. The earth awaited her request, but even holding off the flames stretched Elle to her limits. Parting her will from the fire to command the earth would mean burning alive. She offered instead her panic, and the earth understood. For unlike the fire, which lived and died with the whims of its master, the earth was old. It remembered Elle's respectful treatment and, in turn, offered her its strength.

Elle accepted.

Her control over the fire slipped as she focused more heavily on the earth, and with the cage of fire closing in on her, Elle thought of a pillar. She imagined it with parameters as large as the dragon was wide and as strong as the walls of the cave, formed with enough velocity to push out of the earth entirely.

The ground rumbled as fire singed Elle's hair. Coins clinked and chattered. Her skin started to burn. The rumbling evolved to full-on shaking, and she kept her eyes on the open maw of the beast, determined to face her death head-on.

The stone pillar from her imagination jutted from the ground beneath the dragon, hurtling it to the other side of the chamber. The dragon slammed into the wall with a deafening crash. Rocks tumbled from the ceiling. Elle dropped her hand, took a single, shuddering breath, and grabbed the sword.

She shot to her feet. The room blurred and spun. Exhaustion felt like pain, and it ran deeper than any muscle. She bit out a curse and pushed on.

Wading through treasure was like trying to run in the ocean. Her feet kept slipping. Her legs got caught in pockets of gold. She kept her eyes on the exit and sprinted as best she could. The dragon was enormous. If she could make it to the tunnel, it wouldn't be able to follow.

The dragon must have had the same thought. Its tail whipped across the chamber, striking the wall above the exit. The tunnel caved in, her only escape route filling with earth.

Horror crowded in her chest, making it hard to breathe. The tail whipped toward her. She flung herself to the side, the edge of the blade cutting into her thigh. Her back hit the wall hard enough to bruise. Adrenaline dulled the pain. She ducked behind a mound of gold and searched her scattered thoughts for a plan.

The only exit was blocked. Dragons were impervious to magic. Elle was tired. She needed to get to the others. There was no exit. Elle was tired. The dragon could smell her. It knew where she was. She needed to move. Elle was *tired*.

She leaned her head against the gold, overwhelmed, and squinted at the sunlight.

The sunlight.

An idea sprouted. Hope bloomed. Elle could leave the same way the dragon did. Getting to the top of the chamber would be difficult, but if she could do that, then . . . then the dragon could catch her anyhow because it had wings. If she wanted to take the sky route *(and she didn't really have a choice),* she'd need a head start.

The pile of gold she'd been leaning against exploded, the tip of a blue-scaled tail bursting through. She smacked into the wall. The tail speared the earth next to her face. Her hair caught on some of the scales, and terror abounded. She clutched the sword close and ducked under the tail.

The edges of the chamber felt safer, as she could hide or take shelter behind the scattered rocks and piles of treasure, but her best bet at surviving was under the opening in the ceiling. She made a break for the center of the room.

The dragon roared, furious. Elle leapt over a mound of artifacts. She felt the dragon's will flex in a tyrannical demand for fire to gather in its throat. She felt the fire respond. Her heart beat in her throat as she found a clear spot of earth, and it was with a great, terrified breath that she stopped. Earth's magic swept under Elle, reminding her of the fact that she hadn't fixed the pillar. She apologized because she probably never would.

The earth accepted her answer as it accepted all things. It shared the knowledge that humans often took more than they gave. It asked if she needed more.

She did.

The opening in the ceiling was large enough for the dragon to fit through if it flew vertically. Elle needed the hole to be larger. She dug her toes into the earth and felt the framework of the chamber stretching out and up. Chunks of ground connected, branched off, and merged again until they formed a single, complex cone. The ceiling as she saw it was more than she had known, with layers of rock, soil, and life piling one on top of the other until they made earth.

Elle located the support points with a twinge of regret. She twisted her foot, commanding they crumble. Fire surged behind her, as eager for bloodshed as the dragon who'd birthed it. She ignored the rush of heat to focus on the air.

The magic of the air flowed lazily around her, an impartial observer to her struggle. She grabbed its attention with a firm tug. Her overused magical core protested, pain similar to a cramp, but she didn't listen. She begged.

Up. Up, up, up. Into the sky until there's nothing but blue in every direction.

The air casually considered her plea and, with no objective of its own to convince it otherwise, folded to her will. Elle clutched the sword to her chest, took a deep breath, and jumped.

Air thrust itself beneath her and blasted upward. Fire warmed her feet for a fraction of a second, then vanished, leaving her to the mercy of her own badly worded request. Wind surged against her from every angle, too hard and too fast. The ceiling above her began to crumble.

Huge, jagged rocks fell toward her. The wind blew so hard she could barely breathe. She feared for a moment that her plan would be what killed her, but just as the wind was too strong for Elle, it was too strong for the falling stones. Cyclonic wind flung the rubble to the side. The dragon wailed.

She tried to look down—to see if her plan had worked and she'd managed to bury the beast alive—but the wind was too much. She sped past the still-collapsing ceiling, wind only growing more powerful. It took her up and up and up, far past what she needed or wanted, until the air was frigidly cold and the ground a distant memory.

Her teeth chattered as she slowed to a stop. For a single second, she and the air were one and the same. She leaned into its embrace, and it cradled her close: a thank you and a goodbye.

Then, with no objective of its own to convince it otherwise, the air let go.

And Elle fell.

36

Adair was fairly certain they weren't going to be able to save Honeycutt.

That was a problem because Honeycutt was the only one who knew how to reach the castle in the sky, and getting Elle to the castle was the only way Adair's heart would agree to merge. If Adair lost Honeycutt, he'd likely lose his heart, too. Which was stupid. Adair shouldn't have to suffer just because every other member of his group was weak.

Fighting the golem's magic was like fighting the earth itself, and even neutralizing the golem's will stretched Adair's limits. He couldn't break concentration, he couldn't quit chanting, and worst of all, he couldn't yell at his heart to *stop crying*.

Adair understood his heart was likely overwhelmed with emotions *(fear, humiliation, anxiety)*, but there was a limit to how useless a person could be. Not that Adair was sure what he would do in his heart's situation—it wasn't like the golem could be harmed—but he was positive he would do *something*.

It didn't help that Elle's mission had failed, if the dragon's roars and subsequent string of explosions were anything to go by. Whatever help she could've debatably offered reduced to nothing, and Adair was officially on his own.

The golem's will flexed, challenging Adair's control, and he mimicked the motion. Unlike the will of the actual earth, the golem's will felt rigid. It had only one thought, only one goal. *Kill the girl, bring back her head.* Adair ground his knee into the dirt and slid his palms along the ground, magic in constant flex. He had to keep his command both strong enough that the golem couldn't push through and soft enough that Honeycutt wouldn't be crushed by his defense.

Honeycutt continued to wheeze, no more or less crushed than when Adair had first intercepted the golem's attack. Her skin was stained a deep red. Her eyes bulged. His own arms trembled.

Adair didn't think he could win this battle of wills, especially when considering this was literally the golem's only purpose in life, but he'd never been one to give up without a fight. He scraped his fingers through the dirt, uprooting a palmful of grass, and slid his will along that of the golem's. The earthen portion of the thing felt strong and powerful. The soul shoved inside felt static and virulent. Like ink spilled on cotton paper, it spread through the body, infecting all else.

The golem's will spiked, taking advantage of Adair's distraction, and the earth surrounding Honeycutt tightened. Adair quickened his chant.

The air shifted as another will approached from above, strong and frantic. Adair glanced up only once, very vaguely hoping to identify what the air was cushioning. He was surprised (or maybe not, all things considered) to see Elle plummeting toward them. The golem recaptured his attention with a strong push to crush Honeycutt, which forced Adair to strengthen his own demands for the opposite. Elle hit the ground.

Hard.

She pushed herself up on shaking arms, blood seeping from her hairline and the corner of her lips. Her voice came out in a croak. "Dragon." She sat up, face unnaturally red and right hand covered in third-degree burns. The sword lay beneath her. Adair internally retracted three of his previous comments on her uselessness, then added four more as the roar of the dragon echoed above them.

Trust Elle to take a bad situation and set it on fucking fire.

"Adair, the dragon is—"

Adair chanted louder. Elle caught his eyes, pupils blown wide. He jerked his head toward Honeycutt and the golem. She turned to look, movements too slow to be anything but concussed, and he felt her will reach out. It slid between Adair's will and that of the golem, inquisitive.

He did his best not to react to how weak she felt.

Elle stood, then swayed. She took stumbling steps toward Adair's heart. "Leslie. Leslie, listen to me."

His heart looked up. The golem attempted to stand, and Adair commanded the earth to collapse beneath its stubby foot. The ground shifted. The golem countered. The earth stayed put, and the golem with it. Adair saw his heart hug Elle out of his peripherals. Still sobbing, his heart said, "You are alive."

Elle shook her head. "We don't have time for this." She pushed Adair's heart away. "There's a dragon coming. I'll hold it off. You kill that." She jabbed a finger toward the golem.

Adair's heart backed away. "I—I cannot. It is a golem. It cannot be—"

"It has a soul, doesn't it?"

Adair's heart nodded.

"Then use the sword and cut it out."

Adair's heart glanced to the sword with wide, panicking eyes. "I cannot—"

"You don't have a choice!" Elle turned to stare at something behind Adair. She twisted her feet with a command for the earth to hold them in place. Rock and soil covered her feet and crawled up her legs. The ground softened beneath Adair, pulling his foot, leg, and hands under. He was too stretched to fight it.

The command made sense a second later as wind from the dragon's wings rushed by, strong as a hurricane. The golem slid back a few steps before digging its stocky legs into the soil. It looked up at the dragon, gouge of a smile wobbling, then redoubled its efforts to crush Honeycutt. Its will flexed with an unsustainable rush of power, and Adair struggled to match the spike.

The moment Adair's heart saw the dragon was clear. He shielded his face with his arms, dropped into a crouch, and started hyperventilating. His sobs were interrupted only by broken apologies, excuses about not wanting to die, and the word "impossible."

If Elle heard Adair's heart panicking, she ignored it. Her attention zeroed in on the dragon, and despite the exhaustion Adair could feel at the very center of her soul, she squared her shoulders. Adair was reminded, however briefly, of the bravery she'd displayed in the crow's nest. He wondered if this show of determination was built on a similar base of fear.

The dragon's will tensed above them, angry and overwhelming. Fire responded with alarming swiftness, gathering in its throat without complaint. Genuine fear twinged in Adair's chest as he accepted that the only thing between him and death was Elle. He forced himself not to close his eyes as the dragon's will contracted in a clear command for the fire to *go*.

The fire rushed at them, fast and deadly.

Elle's will reverberated through the magic in the air, commanding the flames to part, but like a rule without consequence, the fire paid her no mind. Adair prepared to forfeit the tug-of-war with the golem to instead protect himself and his heart, but Elle wasn't finished. She unfurled her magic (her will, her soul) in a blatant show of force that leveled *everything*. The earth trembled. The golem stilled. The wind softened. Adair struggled to breathe.

Time seemed to slow as the flames recognized Elle was a threat. Adair felt another spark of genuine terror deep inside, though this fear wasn't of death. It was of Elle. Of how impossibly similar her magic was to his own. Of how she fought like him even when he hadn't taught her to do so.

He felt her ironclad order for the flames to *leave us be*, and against all odds, they did.

Fire flowed around them like water around a rock. Elle held her magic and will steady even as the strain caused her arms to shake. Adair chanted louder and faster, as though that would somehow rid him of the golem and allow him to help.

He wasn't sure how long Elle held her ground, but he knew the moment the attack stopped. The dragon's furious, deafening roar bent the grass and shook the trees. The fire dissipated, though the air remained thick with both heat and Elle's magic.

Elle went straight from defending against the flames to joining Adair. She stepped out of the ground like it hadn't been holding her down, and the almost thoughtless control of her surroundings set off warning bells in his head.

Her knees hit the ground next to him. She buried both hands in the grass. He felt her will against his own, seeking guidance, and he responded with a short pulse around Honeycutt's body. Elle molded her will to Adair's, an extra barrier between the golem's magic and Honeycutt's life.

The dragon's will flared behind them, angrier than ever. Adair wasn't naive enough to think Elle would be able to hold it off twice. He moved his will in a convex motion, relaying his intent to push both the golem's will and the earth away from Honeycutt. A thin, silken layer of Elle's will matched Adair's, motion for motion, as natural as breathing. She nodded.

Adair closed his eyes, tuned out both the aggrandized flames of the dragon and the broken sobs of his heart, and breathed. He pushed the circle of his will outward with a calm but firm request for the earth to *move*, and with Elle's will paralleling his own, the earth listened. He felt a reverberation of the golem's protest, but through the wall of Elle's will, it was negligible.

The next maneuver was complicated and required trust Adair hadn't known he was capable of producing. The moment Honeycutt climbed out of the earth, Adair broke ranks. He communicated with Elle's will the same way he would any other element, commanding her to *keep Honeycutt off the ground*. Then, without sparing a thought for either her exhaustion or the possibility that she didn't understand his order, he moved on.

He freed himself of his earthen bindings and stood, using a single, offhanded flick of his wrist to ward the wind away. The dragon treaded air above them, open maw bright with flames. An unnatural pause between the charge and the release rang out like a proposition.

Leave the girl and the treasure. Live.

Adair stepped over Elle, placing himself solidly between her and the dragon. He curved his will with the mocking counteroffer: *Go home. Leave the girl and the treasure. Live.*

The dragon, of course, responded with fire, and as Adair waited for the perfect moment to react—not only to divert the attack but to return it—he thought he might actually be excited.

It had been a while since he'd done anything *impossible*.

37

When air swept beneath Honeycutt's feet, her first reaction was to panic. She was sure the golem had changed tactics, and just as she couldn't fight against earth, she couldn't fight against air.

Confusion bled into her fear as she realized the air wasn't doing anything nefarious. It sat under her feet like a translucent platform, holding her above the ground. The grass swaying beneath her feet let her know the platform wasn't made of solid air but wind. She turned her attention to Adair.

"Sweet gods."

The crazy bastard was actually doing it. He was fighting the dragon.

Fire rained from the sky like pillars of judgment, and Adair met them head-on. Hands outstretched and feet planted, he grabbed the fire like cloth and spun to send it back. A solid wall of flames crashed over the dragon like waves upon the rocks. It howled.

Elle lay on the ground behind Adair, upper body propped on her left forearm. Her face was tinted a deep, sunburned red. Burns marred her right arm, fingertips to elbow. She held her right hand out toward Honeycutt.

Concern hopped in Honeycutt's chest. She'd left Elle alone with the dragon. Honeycutt moved to check on her, but a twitch of Elle's burned fingers coupled with a shift in the windy platform, and she stopped. It wasn't Adair keeping her off the ground, but Elle. Injured, exhausted Elle. Honeycutt nodded her thanks and turned, determined to finish this quickly.

If Adair had the dragon and Elle had her, that left Honeycutt with the golem. She scanned the field, praying Elle had been successful. The grass swayed in the wind. The dragon breathed its fire. The sun glinted off something metallic.

Joy sped Honeycutt's heart and lifted her weary soul. *Her sword.* She ran toward the shining blade, which rested in the grass just south of Adair. The air under her feet dipped with every step, like walking on a mattress, but it was no less reliable than the earth.

Her foot neared the tip of the blade. A boulder hurled past her head. She skittered backward only for another jagged piece of stone to fly toward her calf. She twisted out of the way, in the opposite direction of her sword.

The golem lumbered toward her, its status as an earthmonger confirmed. It spread its stubby fingers and summoned chunks of rock from the ground. The spike of earth from Adair's previous attack still jutted through its chest, emphasizing the golem's immortality. It threw the floating chunks of rock at Honeycutt. She jumped and dodged, the golem holding position between her and the sword. Two boulders soared toward her. She dove to the right, onto soft, wobbling air. Elle's elbow touched the ground, energy visibly draining.

Honeycutt ran to the left, eyes on the golem. She crashed into Leslie. With him crouched in the grass and her elevated on her platform, her knee rammed into his shoulder. She tripped. Her platform parted around Leslie to catch her. Leslie yelped, more surprised than pained, and cried harder.

Irritation sparked *(couldn't he see they were all scared?)*, but the need for cooperation trumped the need to berate. "Leslie! Leslie, go get my sword."

Leslie raised his head to reveal red-rimmed eyes. Quivering lips stretched in a bright, thankful smile. "Honeycutt. You are safe."

A rock grazed Honeycutt's arm. She turned back to the golem. "My sword. Now!"

He scrambled to his feet and ran for the sword. The golem pulled the spike from its chest and chucked it at Leslie, who backtracked so fast he ended up farther from the sword than where he'd started. Honeycutt utilized the distraction to run for her blade. Six steps away. Four steps. Two. She reached for the hilt. The golem stomped.

The air swept Honeycutt to the side just as the earth cracked and jutted, a rock sharp as any blade narrowly missing her spine. Her sword skidded away. The golem's attention moved to Elle and, with a groan that sounded like confusion, it changed targets.

The golem clunked toward Elle, who was in no position to fight. Care for a friend trampled over logic, and Honeycutt charged. She unsheathed her dagger. The golem turned its head but not its body, tortured smile unwavering. She drove her blade into its eye.

It didn't even flinch.

Two thick, rocky arms wound around her waist and pulled her flush to its chest. She twisted the dagger in its eye socket. It squeezed the breath from her lungs, painfully tight. Her ribs creaked. Leslie appeared behind the golem, sword in hand.

Hope soared as he swung. The blade caught the golem in the side of the head, carving a deep gash in its face. Leslie yanked on the hilt, but the sword stayed put, and a horrid mix of fear and anger tore her hopes from the sky.

He hadn't even attempted to activate the sword's magic, and without its soul-severing properties, it was as useless as a leaf.

The golem squeezed harder. Honeycutt couldn't breathe. She scrabbled at its shoulders and ground the dagger deeper into its eye, but it didn't care. It turned its head 180 degrees to look at Leslie. The idiot gave up on the sword and stumbled away, eyes glistening. The primal desire to live thudded against Honeycutt's ribs, begging for another chance, but for the second time that day, all she could do was gasp.

Her normally analytical mind shot out thoughts like confetti. Her vision blurred. She barely heard Leslie's sad, scared voice ask, "Do you not want us to kill you?"

The black spots dancing across her vision merged. The bones in her spine ground together. She felt numb. Then the pressure lessened. Honeycutt took gasping breaths, which devolved into ragged coughs. She dug her fingers into the golem's biceps, still caught in its grasp but no longer suffocating. She wanted to puke.

Leslie stood in front of the golem, large hands twisting in the strap of his satchel. He dug his upper teeth into his bottom lip, and tears spilled over his lashes. His voice wobbled as he said, "It must be painful. To exist in that body, that is. And we . . . we can free you. We can sever the connection between you and the earth."

The golem took a step toward Leslie, who flinched but didn't run. His arms shook, fists gripping his satchel strap so tightly that his knuckles turned white. Honeycutt tried to meet his eyes—to signal for him to grab the sword and try again—but he looked only at the golem.

He said, "Whoever put you in that body is cruel. You need not do them any favors." His right hand slid down the strap and back up again in a familiar motion that Honeycutt knew meant he was gathering his courage. He took a tentative step forward. "Please. Let us go. Let us free you." Leslie raised a hand, fingers shaking, but he didn't go for the sword. He laid his palm over the creature's heart. "Please."

A beat passed where the only movement came from Adair and the dragon, then the golem groaned. It opened its arms, dropping Honeycutt onto her platform of air. Relief splashed up her sides. Amazement stained her skin. She pushed herself up as best she could, back and abdomen aching. The golem loosed a long, sorrowful moan, then molded its hand around the hilt of her sword. It pulled the blade out of its skull and offered the weapon to Leslie.

He shook his head. "N-no. I cannot."

Leslie raised a shaking hand to point at Honeycutt. The golem turned and offered her the sword. Something inside it revolted. Its entire body convulsed, seizure-like, and it fell to its knees. A pained wail filled the air, and Honeycutt rushed forward. Helping her must go against its primary objective, which meant she needed to get the sword before it could change its mind.

She reached out, ready to fight for her blade, but there was no need. If anything, the pain seemed to have strengthened its resolve. The golem shoved the sword into her arms, then used a stubby hand to pound on its chest. She nodded and raised the blade. Honeycutt had dreamed of this moment for the past ten years, and now that she was finally here—

It felt wrong.

The sword she'd crafted by herself, for herself, felt off. The point of balance was too far away. She shifted her grip, but there was nothing wrong with her stance. The sword was just too long.

Like it hadn't been made for a dwarf, but for a human.

"Honeycutt?" Leslie's voice sounded small, his tone hesitant.

Honeycutt started to chant. The runes on the sword shone with the light of her soul, and she closed her eyes as she felt the magic flow through her. It heightened her senses to the point that she felt her soul as clearly as her physical body. Magic pooled in her eyes, granting her second-sight.

When she opened her eyes, it was to bright, disorienting lights.

She treated the other souls like background noise and focused on the golem. Its physical body made a dull outline around the metronomic beat of its soul. A jagged line of light cut down the center of a mud-crafted heart, and a curse flowed through it.

Honeycutt wrapped her soul so tightly around the sword that it became an extension of her arm. She steeled herself against any resistance the golem might present, determined that she would not break, and drove the blade directly into its heart.

The golem's soul clashed with Honeycutt's: one drained to the point of being sickly and the other lined with an iron will. Her sword cut effortlessly through the golem's defenses and, more importantly, the thick vein of soul tethering it to the soil. She withdrew her sword in a single, swift motion, not wanting her soul to interact with another's any longer than necessary.

The golem's soul flickered. She squinted and slowed her chant. Years of experience kept her blade at the ready, just in case. The golem's body slumped. The flickering dimmed and stopped. Her feet touched the ground. She held the spell for a full extra minute.

The second she stopped chanting, her soul retreated from the sword. Her second-sight took longer to fade. She turned toward Adair to see how he was holding up, then sucked a hissing breath through her teeth.

Adair's soul was mangled, torn on two sides and pulsing with a constant need to reconnect. His magic presented itself in the form of an aura so large and bright that it hurt to look at, and Honeycutt's heart skipped a beat as she realized Elle's was the same.

Not similar. Not reminiscent. *The same.*

The spell faded before Honeycutt could make sense of what she was seeing. Elle's outstretched hand dropped into the grass, unfocused eyes sliding closed. The dragon roared above them, angrier than ever. Honeycutt shoved the conundrum of their souls to the back of her mind and turned to Leslie. "Check on the lass. I'll help with the beast." She didn't wait for him to respond. She ran to Adair. "What do ye need?"

"Do you have the sword?"

"Aye. Did ye find its weak point?"

"I did."

Honeycutt squinted up at the dragon. Its scales blended near perfectly with the sky. Discolored scales could mean it was shedding, which would present the opening they needed. She cursed and shook her head. "I dinnae see it."

"It's not on the outside."

Honeycutt craned her neck to look at Adair, who had yet to take his eyes off the dragon. "What are ye suggesting?"

"Try not to get swallowed."

"Wha—"

Wind swirled around her legs and launched her into the air, straight toward the head of the beast. Honeycutt screamed.

The dragon opened its mouth, a fence of ridiculously large, needlessly sharp teeth protecting its vulnerable insides. Fear coursed through Honeycutt as she caught onto the plan, and she didn't know whether to hate Adair or to praise him. If she lived through this, she'd probably do both. Fire glowed in the monster's gullet while an unnatural heat saturated the air around its mouth. Honeycutt flew inside.

The wind surrounding her disappeared, but she didn't slow. She turned her sword perpendicular to her body and thrust it downward, into the dragon's tongue. Her momentum instantly lessened. Golden blood spurted from the wound as the dragon howled. Her feet hit the tongue, and she slid, cutting a line down the muscle as she went.

Fascination overwhelmed fear as the tongue started to writhe, and the insanity of what she was doing sank in. She gripped her sword tighter. The dragon tried to crush her against the roof of its mouth. Adrenaline replaced oxygen, and her blood sang for more.

She'd forgotten how thrilling battle could be.

The fight with the golem had been unsatisfying: the first half spent without her weapon, and the second half a mercy killing. This though—*this* was perfect. Even inside the beast's mouth, she was nearly outmatched. A single misstep would spell her death. A moment of hesitation. A miscalculation. An ill-timed swipe. Death, death, death. Blood coated her hands and slicked her grip, further lowering her chances of survival. She grinned.

There was only one thing to do in a place like this. Only one vulnerable spot that wouldn't end with Honeycutt in the dragon's belly. The dragon's tongue twisted and squirmed, trying to throw her off. She dug her boots into the firm, wet muscle and faced the back of the tongue.

Legends would be born from this encounter and, regardless of whether or not she succeeded, Clarrissa would hear of what she'd done. Honeycutt yanked her sword from the dragon's tongue, held it high above her, and yelled, "For glory!" She took off running.

Tastebuds dipped beneath the weight of her boots. Blood splashed up her calves. As soon as she reached the throat, she spun, took one last look at the sky, and threw herself off the edge. Gravity carried her down.

Her hair floated above her, and her stomach flipped. The world darkened. Death hugged her from behind as she raised the sword over her head, all ten fingers curled in a desperate clutch around the slippery wet hilt. A thrill twirled up her spine, the line between *clever* and *crazy* imperceptibly thin. She plunged the blade into the dragon's gullet.

Pain ratcheted through her body. Her arms felt like they'd been pulled out of their sockets. She screamed through clenched teeth and planted her feet against the squishy lining of the dragon's throat, leveraging her body to shove the blade deeper. The dragon's throat convulsed, nearly crushing her between walls of muscle and mucus.

It was the dragon's own throat, not Honeycutt, that pushed the blade through.

A loud, pained wail reverberated through muscle and bone. Its throat opened up. Honeycutt's arms shook, near numb with exhaustion. Her body dangled over the abyss. She planted her feet and adjusted her grip, then shoved downward. The sword barely wiggled, her weight nothing compared to thick layers of muscle and scale. She grunted and tried again. Her boot slipped. The sword started moving on its own.

It slit the dragon's throat in a smooth glide. Down and down and down, so fast that the hilt slipped from her grasp. Golden blood gushed from the wound, threatening to drown her.

The wound pried itself open, chunks of skin and scale pulled easily apart by two invisible hands, and sunshine streamed in. Honeycutt let out a victorious whoop. The dragon's neck twisted, revealing the quickly approaching ground. The corpse crashed, and Honeycutt crashed with it.

She hit the back of the dragon's throat with a wet smack, the solid ground with a hard crack, and passed out.

38

Clarrissa used to run her fingers through Leslie's hair. She'd occasionally do it when he was healthy, but always when he was sick. The gentle, repetitive motion made him feel soothed and cared for. It encouraged him to get better.

"Please wake up."

When he ran his fingers through Elle's hair, it was in hopes of her feeling the same way. Because Elle was strong and brave, and they'd used up the last of the healing salve on her hands.

"Please wake up."

Adair had called it magical exhaustion. He'd said Elle would either wake up or she wouldn't, and there was nothing else they could do about it. But Leslie couldn't just do nothing, so he ran his fingers through her hair.

"Please wake up."

"Would ye stop that?"

Leslie's teeth clicked together. He nodded. He ran his fingers through Elle's hair.

Please wake up.

Honeycutt huffed and shifted. A waterfall of coins tumbled down the pile of treasure on which she'd perched. "I know ye are worried, but telling her to wake up is nae helping."

Leslie nodded again because he didn't have the right to argue. The only reason Elle had used so much magic in the first place was because he was a coward. Because she had begged for his help, and he'd curled up and cried.

Please wake up.

Honeycutt went back to sharpening her blade. Adair had disappeared more than an hour prior to look for medical supplies with containers shiny enough for a dragon to steal, and he'd yet to return. Leslie kept his eyes on Elle's face and chest, determined that if she stopped breathing, he would be there to see it. He'd bear witness to the consequences of his weakness.

He lowered his voice and whispered, "Please wake up."

If Elle woke up, the first thing Leslie would do was apologize. Then he'd beg for her forgiveness. He'd beg because his righteous, reliable persona had been shattered the moment he'd abandoned her to save his own skin, and he'd beg *Elle* because she was the only one who could absolve him of his sin.

Adair didn't (couldn't) care, and Honeycutt insisted it was fine. Insisted, as though Leslie wasn't a heart and, by proxy, predisposed to identify emotions. Insisted, like he couldn't see the scorn in her eyes or hear the resentment in her voice.

She liked Elle better than Leslie. Adair liked Elle better than Leslie. Even Leslie liked Elle better than Leslie. If one of them had to die, it should be him.

"Please wake up."

Elle didn't move. Leslie leaned closer to feel the rise and fall of her chest, past echoing in the present. He'd done the same thing with Clarrissa, who had looked equally still and weak before dying. Tears weighed down his lashes and dripped onto Elle's cheeks.

"Please wake up."

"You're doing it again." Leslie raised his head to look at Honeycutt. He must have been a miserable sight because her irritation melted into distaste. She said, "If ye really want to help, try giving her some room to breathe."

"I . . ." Leslie sniffed. "I am sorry."

"I know. We all know how sorry ye are. So if ye could just quit crying—"

A sob hopped in Leslie's chest, too powerful to swallow down. He couldn't hear her advice over the sound of his own useless weeping. He couldn't see through his tears. He yelled. "I am sorry!"

"Move." Adair appeared by Leslie's side, all calm and strength. He laid a hand on Leslie's shoulder and pulled, putting space between Leslie and Elle. Leslie and Adair traded places: Adair going down on one knee next to Elle, Leslie standing to hover a single step away.

The despair deadening Leslie's chest lightened. Hope sparked. He asked, "Did you find something?" Adair waved his fingers, and the tears on Elle's cheeks vanished. Coins jangled as Honeycutt sheathed her sword and made her way down the mountain of gold. Anxiety twisted Leslie's hands together and, as though there was any chance Adair hadn't heard him, asked again. "Adair, did you—"

"No." Adair made complicated hand signs in front of his eyes. Dark brown gained a golden glow, allowing him to examine her magic.

Leslie glanced between Elle's sleeping face and Adair's impassive, golden eyes. "How does she look?"

Adair frowned. He cancelled the spell. "No."

Honeycutt swore and stomped away. Guilt and regret swelled to bursting, and Leslie's tears overflowed. Honeycutt swiveled back around. "Gods! Can ye no' go ten minutes without weeping?"

"I am a heart."

"Ye keep saying that."

"Because it is true."

"Aye, but as far as defenses go, it's getting a wee bit weak."

Leslie stuttered out a few unintelligible noises. His head felt too full. His lips tasted like salt. He said, "I cannot help what I am."

"Why no'?"

"Because I am not like you. I am not brave. I feel fear."

"Do ye no' think Elle was scared out of her wits when she squared off against the dragon alone? Do ye no' think I felt fear when this numpty"—she jabbed a thick finger at Adair—"tossed me into the maw of the beast? Bravery does nae mean ye are nae afraid. It means ye act in spite of the fear. And maybe being a heart means ye feel fear more, but it means ye can feel the need to fight back more, too."

Tears burned behind Leslie's eyes. His throat ached with the effort of holding them back. "I . . ."

"Ye what? Are sorry? Then stop handing out jobby excuses and do something about it."

Leslie's breath hitched in what was almost a sob. His lips trembled as he whimpered, "Like what?"

Honeycutt groaned and tugged at her beard. "I dinnae know. But if the lassie dies, her blood is on your hands. Heart or no."

A fresh wave of tears cascaded down Leslie's cheeks. Honeycutt turned away. Leslie looked to his other half, praying for support. Adair raised his brows, silently asking what Leslie expected him to do about it.

Leslie swallowed around the lump in his throat and gestured to Elle. "Can I?"

Adair stood, apparently done, and Leslie leaned over her again. He stared at her face and chest, determined to know either the moment she woke up or the moment she stopped breathing. He ran his fingers through her hair.

Please wake up.

39

It had been a long time since Honeycutt last watched a lightning storm. The sight of it *(here, now)* carved a dreadful hollowness in her chest. She hoped no lightning would strike horizontally tonight.

She hoped Elle would live.

Gold coins dug into Honeycutt's back as she shifted, eyes on Leslie. He hovered over Elle's motionless body and ran his hand through her hair. He'd been muttering useless pleas for her to wake up for three days straight, and Honeycutt had to wonder if that constant stream of hope wasn't what kept her breathing.

Thoughts like that made Honeycutt feel guilty for yelling at him, though not enough to apologize. Lightning flashed bright enough to make the gold-laden room shine, drawing her attention to the dark outline of Adair. He sat in the middle of a wide circle of stone half a pile away and sorted through artifacts.

She squinted. "What are ye doing?"

"Cataloging." Adair placed a bracelet to his left, then picked up a silver stick.

"And ye dinnae think that's . . . insensitive?"

"No." The silver stick joined the bracelet. He picked up a jewel-encrusted scimitar.

"I know ye can nae feel anything, but the lass could die. Does that no' bother ye?"

"No."

"No' even a wee bit?"

The scimitar went to the right. He picked up a gaudy necklace with a sapphire the size of Honeycutt's fist. "No."

"Then why do ye keep checking on her?"

"To gauge the length of our stay. My heart likes Elle, which means we'll be here either until she wakes or she dies." He dropped the necklace on the right and plucked another bracelet from the pile. "If I have to be here, I may as well be entertained."

Honeycutt blinked as she was reminded that Leslie and Adair were one and the same. In that way, she supposed he cared just as much as he didn't. "Do ye think she'll wake?"

"I don't know."

"Does it have anything to do with the sorry state of her soul?"

Adair raised his head, seeming as surprised as someone with his emotional impotence could be. He tossed the bracelet behind him. "Probably." He grabbed a diamond circlet, then cast it to the right. "Souls produce and restore magic. Her reserves are so massive that I doubt she's ever noticed the slow rate of replenishment."

"And yours? Ye fought the dragon, too, and your soul is in no better shape than hers."

Adair narrowed his eyes. "I'm not an amateur. Elle is capable of performing large magical feats, but she throws her entire self into it instead of the base amount of magic required. If she dies, it's because she's a wasteful fool."

Honeycutt snorted. She both doubted that was true and doubted Adair thought it was true, but there was no point in arguing. "How did it happen?"

"What?"

"Her soul. How'd it get that way?"

Adair shrugged. He picked up a dagger only to drop it in the same place. He stopped sorting. "I don't know."

"Did ye no' ask?"

"She doesn't know, either."

Honeycutt sat up, coins jingling. "How can she no' know?"

"You're aware that she doesn't remember anything before being trapped in the House?"

"Aye."

"That's likely, at least partially, due to a curse."

"How's that?"

"Memories are a part of the soul. Whenever you tear off a piece of someone's soul, you take memories with it. The remaining portion of her soul is so small and shredded I doubt many memories were left. Those that were likely got manually blocked off."

Honeycutt edged closer. "What about the rest of her soul?"

"Destroyed, most likely."

"Most likely?"

Adair stared at Honeycutt, seeming to contemplate how much he should share. "It's possible that the other pieces of her soul are out there somewhere. But even if they are, we'd have no way of knowing it. And even if we knew it, we'd have no way of tracking them down."

"If the other pieces have her memories, they'd know. They'd seek her out."

"First off, we don't know what form they would take, assuming they still exist. They could be lightning trapped in a bottle, sold at an Impossible Market. They could also be a book of sunshine, an absorbable sphere of youth, or any number of other innocuous objects. Second, just as memories can be blocked, they can be rewritten. *If* the rest of her soul is wandering around somewhere, it likely believes itself to be its own person. It wouldn't recognize that the memories it has are hers, and any inconsistencies in its beliefs would be glazed over by the curse."

Honeycutt grunted, uncomfortable with the turn their conversation had taken. She didn't want Elle to die, but living with that mangled excuse for a soul couldn't be pleasant, either. She rolled onto her side and wondered if the dragon had ever stolen a shiny flask. If so, did the flask have anything in it? Like gin or mead. Her stress-addled brain and worried heart both insisted that a drink would help her process things easier. A drink would help her sleep.

She distracted herself with another question. "Surely it'd notice, though. It's got to think about its life at some point, right?"

"Have you ever resisted a compulsion charm?"

"Aye."

"Curses like this almost always come with soul-deep compulsions. When you get too close to the truth, you get distracted. It doesn't matter why, and it doesn't seem odd. And unless you realize there's a compulsion on you . . ."

"Ye dinnae know to resist it." Honeycutt cursed.

"Exactly. And that"—Adair shot Honeycutt a pointed, warning look—"is why we don't tell Elle. If she realizes she's missing the majority of her soul, she'll likely spend the rest of her life searching for something that no longer exists."

Honeycutt's gaze softened. Fondness filled her chest, and she grinned. "Ye do care."

"No."

"All this time I thought ye were a heartless bastard, but here ye are sneaking around to protect the lass."

"No."

"Ye can nae hide it now. I see ye for the big softy that ye are." The air tightened threateningly around Honeycutt. She held up both hands in a show of peace. "There, there. Your secret's safe with me. I will nae tell Elle of what ye said." She waited for the air to relax, then changed the subject. "Do ye at least know what happened to your soul?"

Adair motioned to Leslie. "It was our decision to split. Once we get Elle to the sky, we'll merge again."

"Aye? And how'd the memories get divvied between ye?"

"Since we tore our own soul, we had more say in the separation. We remember it happening, for one, and all our large-scale memories are still in place. We split the details. I no longer remember how to identify plants, make potions, or fight physically. He no longer remembers how to use magic or how most magic works."

"Ah." Honeycutt nodded. "And what about the other side?"

"Other side?"

"Your soul is torn on two sides. He's one of them." She pointed at Leslie. "Where's the other?"

Adair's shoulders tensed. He pressed his lips into a thin line, normally empty eyes filling with something intense enough to be frightening. Honeycutt grimaced and scratched the back of her neck.

She said, "Sorry. I suppose even ye have things ye dinnae like to talk about." Adair didn't respond. Honeycutt considered letting the conversation die, but the only other thing to do was join Leslie in staring at Elle. She looked for yet another topic. How easily would Adair, with all his fancy magic tricks, be able to find a flask in this mess? Honeycutt tilted her face toward the sky and asked, "Do ye think Elle's lightning will flash across?"

After a long pause where Honeycutt very specifically didn't look at Adair, he said, "I don't know."

"I worry Clarrissa's will." She licked her lips as the need to reciprocate vulnerability warred with the stoic pride she'd been conditioned to uphold. She ended up mixing personal worry with general fact to say, "I know it's supposed to be something special. Only strong, powerful souls can be seen leaving the body, and only the most powerful of those strike across instead of up. But something about it feels . . . I dinnae know. Wrong."

Adair hummed in agreement. "How was she cursed?"

Honeycutt clenched her eyes shut, throat trying to close around the memory. She took a steadying breath, wished once again for even the smallest sip of ale, and said, "It made her frail, like she'd break by breathing, and so weak she could barely get out of bed. Thin as a spear with sunken cheeks and—"

"No. How did it happen?"

Honeycutt paused. "What do ye mean?"

"Dwarves don't leave their clans until they seek their glory, right? You said she hadn't sought hers yet, which means she was cursed while within the confines of your clan. Outsiders aren't allowed, and I've never heard of a dwarf killing one of their own outside of death matches and mercy killings. So what was it? A stray artifact? An accident?"

Honeycutt stilled as she thought back to the day of Clarrissa's curse. She remembered Clarrissa coughing, Clarrissa crying, Clarrissa begging her not to leave, but those were all toward the end. As for the day it began . . . ? Honeycutt curled her fists around handfuls of coins, memory blank. It seemed important—essential, even, considering she was seeking the counter-curse—but no matter how hard she thought, the answer remained elusive.

It was through ears full of cotton that she heard Adair ask, "Was that insensitive?"

"I . . ." Honeycutt trailed off because *yes, it was,* and also *how could it be* if she didn't remember?

Why didn't she remember?

Adair must have taken her stuttering as an affirmative because he said, "That's fine, then," and went back to sorting.

Honeycutt's lips trembled around questions she didn't know how to ask, but the time to voice them cut short as Leslie said, "Elle! You are awake."

Elle groaned. Honeycutt's heart leapt. She turned her head to see Leslie hugging Elle and Elle attempting to shove him away. "Leslie. Leslie, let go. I can't breathe."

Leslie pulled back, though his hands remained on Elle's shoulders. Honeycutt grinned, her own troubles momentarily forgotten. She sprang to her feet and raced over. "Lassie. Good to see you're alright."

"Yeah." Elle raised two fingers to rub her temple, thumb resting just above the odd white scar on her jaw. "Why wouldn't I be?"

"You—you . . ." Leslie sobbed and pulled her into another hug. "You almost died."

Elle stiffened. "I what?"

Adair approached from behind Honeycutt, eyes already backlit by a golden glow. "You used too much magic and delayed our journey a full three days." He canted his head, all signs of his previous concern lost. The glow faded away. "If Honeycutt's Clarrissa dies within three days of the counter-curse being delivered, it'll be your fault."

Honeycutt felt a sharp pang in her chest at the thought of Clarrissa dying. Elle turned her face so only her cheek and ear were pressed to Leslie's chest. She said, "I saved you from the dragon."

"Barely."

"And I got the sword. Without that, we'd be waiting way longer than three days."

Adair frowned, unimpressed.

Honeycutt said, "Aye, ye did. And I thank ye for it."

Elle lifted the hand less pinned by Leslie's hug and gestured to Honeycutt. "Exactly. And even if I was dying before, I feel fine now." She squirmed and pushed Leslie away, then swayed. He caught her before she could fall. Honeycutt stepped forward, a sliver of her anxiety returning. Elle held up a hand and said, "Mostly fine. I just need to eat, then we can go."

Honeycutt and Leslie shared a worried glance. Honeycutt lowered her voice and said, "Dinnae rush yourself, lassie. There's no point in storming the castle with only half a centaur."

Elle crinkled her nose and blinked. "What?"

"I believe she means to say that it is better to be prepared than it is to be early." Leslie glanced to Honeycutt for confirmation. When she nodded, he continued, "I am inclined to agree. You should eat and rest. When you are truly better, we will leave."

"But I am better. And the castle—"

"Is less than a week's walk from here. Waiting another day or two will nae hurt."

The set of Elle's jaw said she disagreed. She tried to sit up on her own again. She failed again. "You're sure?"

Honeycutt smiled. "Aye. We're sure."

Leslie rubbed Elle's back. "Not only are we sure, we insist."

Both Honeycutt and Leslie turned to Adair, who crossed his arms and said nothing. Honeycutt rolled her eyes. "We're finishing out the night regardless of how ye feel, so ye may as well relax. We can reevaluate in the morn."

Elle breathed a heavy sigh, then slumped against Leslie. She spoke with her face pressed to his shirt. "Less than a week, right? Even if we wait?"

Lightning flashed above them, only electricity. The storm started to pass.

"Less than a week."

40

It took them six days to reach Ferron, including the day and a half of rest forced upon Elle by her oh-so-caring companions.

The journey itself wasn't bad, just strange. Adair was oddly talkative. He continually asked Elle, Honeycutt, and even Leslie questions, though Elle couldn't make heads or tails of what he hoped to learn. When she brought up his sudden personality shift, he gave her extra work.

As if to balance out his chatter, Honeycutt became uncharacteristically spacey. Elle asked her about it more than once, but the dwarf always brushed off her concerns by rambling about memories. The only one acting semi-normally was Leslie, though his mood swings had grown impossibly less predictable. He monologued about kindness and bravery, then devolved into a sobbing puddle in the middle of the path. He begged for forgiveness Elle had already given, then refused her help because he was quote-unquote "fine."

It was exhausting.

Elle's initial plan was to corner them in Ferron—maybe at dinner or, if traveling took too long, a hostel—but that was before they actually entered the town. Ferron was smaller than the other cities they'd traversed, with only a few rows of small wooden buildings and no non-human entities. The townspeople they passed all stopped and stared.

"Why are they looking at us like that?"

"No' us, lassie. Ye."

Elle scrunched her nose. Three villagers—a middle-aged couple and an old woman—stood outside a small wooden house. They stared at her. She waved at them. They flinched.

Leslie looked at Elle. "What did you do to them?"

"I didn't do anything." She canted her head and watched them watch her back. "At least, I don't think I did."

"How reassuring." Adair broke from the group to greet the villagers. Elle tried to follow, but her feet were suctioned to the ground. She listed off curse words in her head, all aimed at Adair. He motioned back toward Elle and asked, "Do you know her?"

The middle-aged couple glanced nervously between Adair and Elle. The older woman shooed him away. "We don't know nothin' about the witch." She ushered the couple into the house, then hurried in after them. She slammed the door in Adair's face.

Nervousness fluttered its wings in Elle's stomach as she accepted this wasn't just another stop on the way. The castle she'd come from—the truth of her past—was here.

The void within her groaned, more ravenous now that the truth was so close. Elle tried to move toward the house, eager to find out what they knew, but her feet stuck tight. The strength of the earth hummed beneath her, uninvolved. The air laughed at her ignorance.

Elle commanded the air to *let go*, but it vastly preferred Adair and made no attempt to pretend otherwise. She turned to him instead. "Let me go."

Adair returned to the group and curled a domineering hand around her shoulder, then canceled the spell on her feet. He used brute strength to steer her down the street, opposite the direction of the house.

She jerked in his hold. He sent a shock of electricity down her arm. She flinched and hissed. "What are you doing? We have to go back. They know me."

"Look around. Everyone in this town knows you." He dipped his chin toward some of the other houses. Curtains parted, and curious eyes watched them pass. "The question is how, and if we want an answer, we need to find someone who's familiar enough in dealing with undesirables not to flee."

Elle stopped struggling to escape. She crossed her arms, mostly to let Adair know she still hated him, and asked, "Where are we supposed to find that?"

"We'll know it when we see it."

Elle sneered at the obscure answer, but in the end, Adair was right. A small run-down building with a hole in the roof and the door hanging off its hinges stuck out like a sore thumb. A drunk slumbered on the porch, dead to the world. The sign above the door read Perëndi's Pub.

Elle strode forward, and Adair let her. The large wooden door felt rough and unpolished beneath her fingers. The pungent smell of alcohol gave her pause. "Honeycutt? Do you want to wait outside? I mean . . ." Elle trailed off, not wanting to undermine Honeycutt's will but also worried for what being surrounded by alcohol could do to her sobriety.

Honeycutt's mustache lifted in a thankful smile. She shook her head. "Ye need no' worry about me, lassie. If it gets to be too much, I'll let ye know."

Something deep in Elle's gut doubted that was true. Honeycutt was too strong, too prideful, to ever admit to her struggle. She'd claimed to be fine while drinking herself into a stupor. She'd cracked jokes through her potion-induced detox period. And now, despite the fact that Elle had seen her shaking a few empty flasks in the dragon's hoard, she wanted to enter a pub.

Discomfort seeded in Elle's belly, and she had to remind herself that Honeycutt was an adult. Even if Honeycutt did end up drinking again, it was her life. Her choice. Elle nodded, took a deep steadying breath, and entered the pub.

The bar only had two patrons, both of whom did their best not to make eye contact. She turned from them, uninterested, and focused on the man behind the bar. He stood taller than Adair, with a thin chest and a wiry frame. Shaggy black hair fell over bored brown eyes, the tips of it brushing his stained black shirt. Wrinkles added texture to already leathery skin, and a thick mustache hid his upper lip. Gray peppered his hair, denoting he'd been around for a while.

The bartender spoke first. "You lot plan on standing in the doorway all day, or would you like to have a seat?"

Elle hurried to the bar, butt barely touching the seat before she asked, "Do you know me?"

"Not exactly. Any of you want a drink?"

Elle shook her head. Her companions mimicked the motion. She said, "We're not here to drink. We're looking for information."

"Information costs more than a drink."

"I figured it might." Elle pulled a handful of coins from her pocket and dropped them on the table. The bartender's eyes widened, letting her know he'd have answered for less. She asked, "Why is everyone afraid of me?"

He glanced between her and the gold. "Not of you. Of your mum."

Elle blinked. Her thoughts moved like sludge. "My mom?"

"I assume she was your mum." He shrugged and edged closer to the bar. Closer to the gold. "Hell, I'd say she was you, if not for your being so young and that weird patch on your jaw."

"But I don't . . ." Her tongue felt heavy. "I don't have a mom."

"Everybody's got a mum. Though I'm not surprised yours didn't stick around. Wench was more fire and brimstone than bedtime stories and home-cooked meals."

"What did she do?"

The bartender scoffed. "What didn't she do?" He held up a hand and counted offenses on his fingers. "Used magic without a permit, threatened half the town, defaced the shrine, stormed the castle, even killed a few people. We put a bounty on her head, of course, but no one's heard hide or hair of her since. I kind of assumed she died up there." He paused, then frowned, empathy an afterthought. "Sorry you had to hear it from me."

The condolence was cheap. Elle brushed past it to ask, "Why would she do that? I mean, she had to have a reason, right?"

"Not one that made any sense. She wanted to challenge Perun, the local god residing in the castle, and rescue someone named Clarrissa."

Adair, Leslie, and Honeycutt all looked at one another. Elle leaned forward, blood thrumming. "Clarrissa? You're sure?"

"Ferron's a sleepy, out-of-the-way town. And even if it weren't, a rampage like hers isn't one you'd forget."

Elle dug bitten-down nails into her bicep. She thought of her dreams and the way her older self—her *mother*—had been murdered within them. "Is there anything else you remember?"

"Nothing worthwhile."

"Every little detail helps."

"I might still have the wanted poster in the back somewhere, but like I said, she looks like you. Older. Scarier. Had a sword." He cupped his hand around the gold and slid it off the bar, into his open palm. "Poster might give a few more details about the kind of magic she used, but not much. We don't get many magicians around here, and we sure as hell don't know how to describe what they do."

Elle pursed her lips. She already knew what her mother looked like, and it didn't matter what type of magic she'd used because she was dead. "Don't worry about it." She hopped off the stool and left the bar, uncaring what anyone else had to say.

The sun beat down on her shoulders. The drunk slept on the porch. Nothing had changed, but everything was different. She could feel the void widening within her, taking more of who she thought she was. Questions invaded her brain and ate away at her thoughts. The castle. Perun. Her mother. Clarrissa.

Who was Clarrissa?

Leslie caught Elle by the wrist, two houses down from the pub. "We should talk about this."

Elle swung around to face him, and she hoped she looked angry. She hoped his deductive heart powers had failed him, and he couldn't tell she was sad. She said, "Let's go to the sky. Now."

"Elle, take a moment."

"For what? The castle is right there." She pointed straight up. "And our answers are there, too. So why wait?"

Leslie squeezed her wrist, pitying rather than upset. Adair stepped up and asked, "If she really is your mother, why weren't you with her?"

The word 'abandonment' flitted through her mind, but that only made her sadder. She leaned into her frustration and built a protective wall out of her anger. She sneered. "What part of me having no memories don't you understand?"

"I'm not asking you to remember. I'm asking you to think. How did you get to the sky?"

Elle pulled her hand from Leslie's grasp and hugged her arms to her chest. "I don't know."

"You remember the castle, so you must've been there, but he just said your 'mother' was searching for a Clarissa, not an Elle. So where were you?"

"I don't know."

"Well, think. Because we're missing something, and until we figure out what it is, none of us are stepping foot in that castle."

Elle's head snapped up. The void inside her cracked, staining the rest of her with that deep, black emptiness. She said, "What? You can't do that."

"I'm the strongest sorcerer here. I can do whatever I want."

Anxiety tightened Elle's throat and burned behind her eyes, but she refused to cry. Being emotional would make Adair less likely to listen to her, not more. "The answers are in the sky. If we go there—"

"It'll be too late."

"Too late for what? And how? The fastest way to get our answers is to go directly to the source."

"That won't work."

"Why not?"

"I don't know."

Elle waited for him to clarify. He didn't. She threw her hands in the air. "Seriously? That's it?"

"That's it."

"No. You can't put everything on hold for no reason."

"I have a reason."

"Then tell us what it is."

Adair stared impassively at Elle, seeming to gauge whether or not explaining himself would be worth the effort. Eventually, he said, "I met with Cypress. It warned against traveling to the castle without all the necessary information."

Elle narrowed her eyes, dumbfounded. "Cypress is a demon. Why would you even consider listening to him? Especially after what he did to me."

"It's because Cypress is a demon that I'm heeding the warning. Demons are only out for themselves, which means they don't go around sabotaging people for no reason."

"He's working for the enemy."

"And who exactly is the enemy? Cypress? Perun? Someone else? Because I thought you were here to discover your past, not avenge someone who may or may not be your mother."

Elle's temper flared. She tried to think of a logical reason why Adair had to be wrong, but her thoughts blurred until all she had was a headache. Anger from the void hijacked the argument with promises of how good it would feel to prove Adair wrong, and she eagerly conceded.

"I'm going."

"Excuse me?"

"Honeycutt's taking me to the sky. Right now. You can come with us or stay here and gather information. Or you know what? You can go home. You've taught me magic, found me a guide, and brought me to the castle. Consider your obligation fulfilled."

Silence coated the street. Two beats passed before Adair reacted, and even then, it was to turn away. "Heart, we're leaving."

Leslie's breath hitched. "What?"

"We're not entering the castle until we figure out what's going on." He motioned to the empty space at his side, tone brooking no arguments. "Come."

Leslie shifted on his feet. His fingers tapped an inconstant rhythm against his palm, and he looked anywhere but at Adair as he said, "I want to help Elle."

"You can't help her if you're dead."

Leslie's front teeth dug into his lower lip. He hunched in on himself and took shallow, shuddering breaths. Elle reached out to comfort him. Honeycutt held her back. Leslie whispered, "No."

Adair's eyes narrowed. "What?"

Leslie cringed, then said it again. Louder. "No, I will not look for information with you. I promised to take Elle to the sky, and that is what I intend to do."

"Are you deaf? She just released us of our obligation—"

"That is the same as running away, though, is it not? And I am so tired of running. Of being useless and afraid while everyone else fights." Leslie looked up, and the word *tired* didn't begin to cover it. Tears glistened in his eyes, but they didn't fall. "I am going with Elle."

Pride swelled in Elle's chest. This time when she reached for his hand, Honeycutt allowed it. Leslie offered Elle a wobbly, watery smile.

Adair muttered obscenities under his breath and glanced at Honeycutt. "And you?"

"I'm afraid so." Honeycutt patted the canteen on her hip. "I've kept Clarrissa waiting long enough, wouldn't ye say?"

Adair shook his head, then locked eyes with Leslie. "Something's wrong here, and Elle isn't the only anomaly."

"I do not—"

"There's a second tear in my soul. I don't know where it came from." Adair stepped forward, into Leslie's personal space. "What's the last thing Clarrissa said to us?"

At the mention of their Clarrissa, Leslie's tears spilled over. He said, "I—I do not remember. Why—"

"Because I don't remember, either. The love of our life, the reason we split our soul, and I can't remember her last words. Or what she was wearing. Or what season it was. Don't you think that's odd?"

Leslie shook his head so hard his hair whipped his face. "I do not wish to remember."

"Because it hurts? Or because you can't?"

"That's enough!" Elle pushed her way between them, furious that Adair would hurt Leslie just to prove a point. "You're done here,

Adair. We're going to the castle, and there's nothing you can say to change that."

Adair snarled at her, but just like it hadn't been anger in Elle's voice, it wasn't anger in his eyes. "You idiot. Can't you see you're being compelled to stop looking for answers? What sense does it make to risk your life fighting a god and a demon if you could get the same results with none of the risks?"

"Sometimes you have to think with your heart, not your head." She laid her hand on his chest, and nothing beat underneath. "But I guess that's not an option for you, is it?"

Adair looked at Elle like he was seeing her for the first time. He didn't reject her touch. He didn't bully or berate. He said, "You go now, you'll die. All of you."

And while Elle knew that was as close to a plea as Adair would ever get, patience had never been one of her virtues. "I'm sorry, Adair."

He cursed, and if not for the fact that his heart was crying beside her, she might've thought the fear in his voice was real. He turned and strode back toward town. Leslie cried harder, and disbelief shoved Elle into the realization that this was it. Adair really was going. Compromises piled on her tongue—too little, too late. Her pride refused to fold. She locked her apologies behind her teeth and allowed a declaration made in the heat of the moment to ripple out into reality.

Adair left.

41

Elle crouched by the small moss-covered stone embedded in the ground. "This is it?"

"Aye." Honeycutt scraped off some of the moss with the toe of her boot. "Just a wee bit of magic, and it'll toss us up to the castle."

"I thought dwarves couldn't use magic."

"No, but a little coin goes a long way. Convincing a magician to spare some magic is hardly a glory-worthy feat."

Elle hummed, interested but not engrossed. She stood and placed her toes on the edge of the rock. Cool moss molded to her skin. She looked at Leslie. "You ready?"

Leslie stepped forward and rested the toe of his boot on the outer slope of the stone. His fingers tapped a nervous rhythm against his thigh, but his voice held steady. "I am ready."

Elle turned to Honeycutt. The dwarf shifted but didn't place her boot on the stone. She said, "I'm with ye whatever ye decide, but I have to ask. Are ye sure ye want to do this without Adair?"

Elle frowned. No, she wasn't sure. But as the void inside her widened, desperate to be filled by memories, she found herself incapable of considering other options. "I'm positive."

Honeycutt scratched at her beard, ruffled her hair, then placed her boot solidly on the stone. "Lead the way, lassie."

Elle closed her eyes and sought the spell wrapped around the stone. It was strong but immobile, like a sleeping devil. She used her magic to probe it awake. The will of the spell responded with a reflexive offer of safe passage in exchange for a steady flow of magic.

An Adair-like voice in the back of Elle's mind said only idiots trusted spells they didn't know, but if Adair had wanted a say in how they proceeded, he shouldn't have left.

She opened herself to the spell in a silent acceptance of its proposition. It asked, *How many?*

She responded, *All.*

The spell surged forward, no longer content to exist but intent to do. Instead of ripping out a chunk of her magic, like she expected, it attached itself to her like a leech.

Like a funnel.

It wove her magic into a thin, flexible wire that circled her, Leslie, and Honeycutt before stretching up into the sky. The magic wire extended farther than Elle could see. The spell started sucking, and like water down a river, her magic flowed. She lurched forward, nauseated by its speed. Honeycutt caught her by the elbow while Leslie rubbed her back. She closed her eyes and breathed through it. As the suction slowed and finally stopped, the leech part of the spell detached itself, leaving only the wire of her own magic behind.

Elle blinked, unsure what she was supposed to do next. A strange tug in her belly pulled her off the ground. She levitated over the earth, bare toes kissing the tall grass, and a glance to her left showed the others were floating, too. Another, stronger tug in her belly flipped the world upside down.

Like gravity in reverse, they fell into the sky.

She yelped at the unexpected movement, but the bright wire of her magic promised safe travels. They were not falling ad infinitum, but in a particular direction, to a particular place. The wind rushed around her, and she stretched out her arms. The sky welcomed her home.

Honeycutt and Leslie, either unaware or uncaring of the magic guiding them, screamed and flailed. Elle craned her neck to follow the trajectory of the wire. She spotted a speck in the distance.

The farther they fell, the larger the speck grew, until it was a solid chunk of earth. Honeycutt shouted something, but the wind drowned her out. Her panicked pointing translated the notion that she thought they were going to crash. Elle shook her head, unsure how to relay that her magic would protect them. She tried to reach out, but the wind pressure was too much. Leslie covered his eyes.

It wasn't until they zoomed past the underside of the earthen chunk that the spell slowed their fall, and Elle saw the castle. The building took up the majority of the floating platform, and a thick wall of stone surrounded its base. Five towers jutted upward, each one a different shape, and intricate carvings lined the walls. A singular window in the center of the largest tower produced light.

They levitated over the ground to the right of the castle, no higher than if they had climbed a tree. Honeycutt stopped cursing. Leslie continued to mutter prayers under his breath. The magic wire encircling them retreated, and a final, hard tug in her belly ended the spell.

Gravity resumed.

Elle called to the air around her legs, ordering it to slow her descent, and it obeyed. Wind caressed her calves and thighs. She landed gently on her feet. Honeycutt tucked and rolled, her landing harsher but no less graceful. Leslie hit the ground with a smack.

Elle cringed, realizing she probably should've helped him, too. She jogged over and asked, "Are you okay?"

Leslie whined as he sat up. His palms were scraped and dirt had stained his white button-up, but he looked no worse for wear. He said, "I do not want to know how we get back down."

Elle laughed, joyful and relieved. She turned to Honeycutt. "What about you?"

Honeycutt pressed the heel of her palm to the side of her head, then checked on her sword. She said, "Aye. It'll take more than a wee fall to drub me."

"If that was 'a wee fall'"—Leslie pushed himself off the ground—"then I do not wish to know the kind of fall you would consider large."

Elle smiled and, satisfied they weren't injured, started walking left. The walls of the castle were great. It was grandiose to the point of egotism. Hatred lit her chest: a stray spark from the fire that burned through her dream-self.

Her dream-mother?

The calm of the castle pervaded the air. In her dream, the castle walls, with their excessive thickness and intimidating height, had already been conquered. Her mother had blown a hole in the wall somewhere to the left of the door, and if this really was the same place . . .

She looked for scorch marks or a patch of lighter, newer stones. What she found was the same breach from her dream. Weeds sprouted in the debris and vines snaked up the wall into the castle, but the hole itself hadn't changed. Disquiet blossomed in the pit of her gut, questioning why they hadn't fixed it.

A castle like this was made for a strong defense. It wasn't just pretty. It was fortified. She crept up the pile of rubble to peek into the dilapidated hall. Cold wind whistled past, and the answer clicked. The wall hadn't been mended because it wasn't what protected the king.

That was the beast.

Elle swung around, a warning on her tongue. She smacked into another person. Her nose flattened against hard pecs, the impact painful but quick, and she stumbled back. Strong hands caught her by the arm and waist. She opened her eyes.

"Cypress."

Dread laced her blood. Fear tensed her muscles. He leaned closer, and it was only in standing a hair's breadth away that she understood the truth of his eyes.

It wasn't the cold of death she had been seeing, but the cold of isolation. It was a promise of treasures untold coupled with the knowledge that once her soul was his, there would be no escape. She would be trapped, forever denied entry into the next cycle of life, and drained of her humanity. He would keep her there, in the horrible depths of his eyes, and siphon her energy *(her memories, her emotions, her experiences)* until she was nothing but a shell. Even then, she would be aware, and he would push on. He would take her shell, a perfect representation of what she once had been, and grind it into dust.

An ingredient in a potion. A salve on a superficial wound.

He would take and take and *take* until Elle ceased to be, and if she had ever existed at all, who would know?

Elle took a shuddering breath and accepted that the unnatural glow of his eyes came not from magic, but from lightning. From souls. The dark, unnatural blackness of his soul reached out, tasting, and she felt the impossible thrum of a connection. A promise. *A deal.*

They'd already made a deal.

She jerked back, horrified. He smiled, boyishly sweet. Cypress opened his mouth *(maybe to whisper an intimate secret, maybe to rip the flesh from her throat)*, and Honeycutt's sword thrust between them.

"Back, demon!"

Frigid blue eyes flicked down to the blade, unconcerned. He caught Elle's eyes again and, like the fate of her soul was some clever game meant just for them, winked. He released her. She rushed down the rubble to join Honeycutt and Leslie while Cypress raised his hands in a mocking show of surrender. Honeycutt pointed her blade directly at Cypress's face.

"Woah there, hoss." Cypress spoke to Honeycutt, but his eyes never left Elle. "You wouldn't hurt an unarmed man, would you?"

"Ye are no' a man."

"Fair." He used one finger to push the blade down and away from his face. "I'm also not here to fight. At least, not if you don't want to."

"Lies."

"Nope. I think fighting here would be counterproductive to our overall goals, so I'd like to offer you a deal instead."

Honeycutt jerked her sword back into position. Cypress leaned away to avoid getting hit. She said, "We are nae selling our souls."

"If only it were that simple." Cypress offered an apologetic smile, and Elle hated that it was charming. "You see, I had kind of counted on there being four of you and, no offense, but Adair was your ticket in. He would have been strong enough to hold me off while the halfling killed the hellhounds, and I'd have no choice but to retreat."

Elle's blood ran cold. "Hellhounds?"

Cypress blinked a few times, feigning innocence, then pointed over Elle's shoulder. Vicious growls erupted from the silence, making Elle jump and spin. Behind them stood four large black dogs. The beasts came up to her abdomen, and their jaws looked like they could snap bone. Thick drool dribbled from their lips, emphasizing their rabidity. Clawed paws scraped the ground, ready to leap.

Unnatural fear made the hairs on her arms stand on end, and she knew that these dogs, much like the lesser demons she'd encountered in the House, were predisposed to breed terror. Leslie huddled closer to Elle's side, both fists wrapped tightly around the strap of his satchel. She held one arm out toward the dogs, prepared to blast them with whatever magic necessary, and turned her attention back to Cypress.

Honeycutt pointed her sword at the hellhounds and said, "Dinnae worry, lassie. I can dispatch these pups."

"You could." Cypress canted his head. "But if you attack them, I'll attack these two, and my pups are almost guaranteed to outlast your clan."

Honeycutt swung her sword back around. "Then I'll kill ye first."

"That's a better plan. It is. Except then the positions are reversed, and the hellhounds go after the girl and the heart. Do you think they'll survive long enough for you to kill me? If you even can kill me?"

Honeycutt looked first at Elle, who did her best to seem brave, then at Leslie, whose arms were already trembling. She held the sword closer to her chest, her only show of indecision.

Elle squared her shoulders, confidence false, and said, "We can take them."

Honeycutt shook her head. "Hellhounds are a type of demon. Ye would need the sword to kill them." Honeycutt clenched her jaw and, begrudging to the point of fury, asked, "What do ye suggest then, demon?"

Cypress hummed. "So glad you asked. As I said before, this would be different if there were four of you—"

"Then we'll leave." Elle stepped forward, toes bumping the rubble. "We'll get Adair and come back."

"No can do, cupcake. You're here now, and unfortunately for you, that means I've got a job to do." He shrugged like there was nothing he could do about it, and maybe there wasn't. "Your choices are to fight me and my hellhounds here or to play nice for a little longer and let me lead you to Perun."

Elle blinked, stunned. Leslie asked, "Why would you do that?"

Elle slid her foot closer to Leslie's, so the side of her heel touched the tip of his boot. She said, "He wouldn't." She looked at Cypress, dread sinking deep. "You said deal, not favor. What do you want in return?"

"Smart girl." Cypress grinned, proud in a way that made Elle's stomach turn. "You're right in that it's not quite as simple as I've made it out to be. In actuality, I'm willing to take two of you to Perun. The last one stays here." He pointed to the ground. "With them." His finger moved to the hellhounds.

Elle shouted, "We're not sacrificing someone to your stupid dogs!"

Honeycutt said, "I'll stay behind."

Leslie released his satchel to lay a hand on each of their shoulders and, tears already glistening, said, "You cannot."

Elle twisted her neck to look at him. "What do you mean? There's no way we're doing this."

Leslie shook his head, eyes on Cypress. "He is changing the setting, not the situation. Someone still has to fight him, and someone still has to fight the hellhounds. The best use of Honeycutt's skill is fighting the higher demon."

Frustration bubbled. "But that's not fair."

"It is, though. It is exactly fair." Leslie dropped his hands to his sides. He didn't rub his palm against his thigh or tap on his satchel. An odd sense of calm pervaded, and Elle found she hated his stillness more than his nervous ticks. He said, "If we fight here, the two of us against the hellhounds, it is likely both of us will die. If we take his deal, one of us gets a free pass while the other is guaranteed to die. A life for a life."

"We can't—"

"You must go."

"What?"

Leslie kept his focus on Cypress as he said, "I am your escort, and yet you have been the one protecting me. Allow me to return the favor."

"Leslie, no."

Leslie looked at Elle, eyes dry. He smiled, as gentle as she'd ever seen, and her frustration turned to grief. If the cost of retrieving her memories was Leslie's life, she didn't want them. She shook her head hard, ready to argue, but he was a step ahead. Leslie brushed her hair from her eyes and said, "My Clarrissa is already dead, Elle. It will do me no good to reach Perun. Honeycutt can still retrieve the counter-curse. You can still discover your past. I am the obvious choice."

"Leslie." Elle clenched her eyes shut, and tears spilled over. She turned to look at a blurry version of Cypress. "Give us a different deal. We aren't leaving him."

"A different deal?" Cypress grinned, vicious and mad. "What a gorgeous sense of entitlement you've got. Tell me, Elle, do you think I run around helping little girls fulfill their dreams for free?" He took a step forward. Elle took a step back. The hounds snarled. "Right now, I am working incredibly hard not to break your neck. This is not because I want to break your neck, necessarily, but because another deal is compelling me to do so. Do you understand?" Another strong step forward. Honeycutt's blade at his throat. The fingers on his left hand curling into a fist. "The deal I've offered is beyond generous. You should take it, and you should take it now. Before I decide to cut my losses."

Desperation beat a drum in Elle's chest. She tried to calm down and think—to find the loophole she knew they were missing—but everything moved too fast.

Honeycutt sighed, low and defeated. "I hate to say it, but Leslie's right. I have to be the one who fights the demon, and ye need to face the god. We should take the deal."

Elle balked. She took a step away from Honeycutt, unwilling to believe the choice to sacrifice their friend could be so cut and dry. Her back bumped Leslie's front. He laid his hands on her shoulders and squeezed. "It is alright, Elle." Soft lips kissed her scalp. Tears wet her hair. Sorrow raked its claws down her spine, ruining her. She swiveled to plead with him, to say they could dive off the edge of the floating platform if need be, but his decision was already made. He stepped around Elle to face Cypress. "I have a request, demon."

Cypress's gaze flicked over to Leslie, interested but not invested. "And what's that?"

"A head start."

Elle tried to get between them, but Honeycutt grabbed her arm and tugged her back. Elle said, "No."

Cypress shrugged. "Sure."

Leslie turned to look at Elle. Contrary to the courage in his voice and the confidence in his posture, his eyes glistened. She saw fear there—powerful and all-consuming—and he smiled. "Good luck, Elle."

Leslie sprinted past Cypress, through the hole in the wall and out of sight. Barely a second later, Cypress gave a short, sharp whistle. The hellhounds followed.

Elle thrashed in Honeycutt's grasp, hot tears streaming down her cheeks as she screamed for Honeycutt to let her go. "Can't you see he's scared?"

"Of course he's scared!" Honeycutt yanked Elle's arm hard enough to hurt. "He's also smart. Out here, they'd have had him in minutes. In there, he can find a narrow passage. Force them to take turns. Buy himself some time."

Elle almost asked, "Time for what?" but the answer was obvious. Adair.

"Well, that was fun." Cypress stuffed his hands in his pockets, caustically casual. "Do you girls need another minute, or shall we go?"

Elle gritted her teeth, equally unwilling to disrespect Leslie's sacrifice by starting a fight and unable to swallow her rage. Heat gathered in her palm, eager to *raze this place to the ground*, but she didn't light the flame.

Honeycutt squeezed her arm. "Come on. There's only one way we can help him now, and it's no' out here." She gestured toward the castle with a tilt of her head. Elle sniffled and wiped her face on her sleeve.

They followed Cypress inside.

42

The Perun of reality and the Perun of Elle's dreams were indistinguishable. He wore the same white pants. His torso bore the same tattoos. Elle meant to say something poignant and threatening, but what came out was, "You don't look like a god."

Perun turned from the sphere of lightning with exaggerated slowness. His shoulders were lax, and his expression bored. His magic bled anger. Despite the time that must have passed since fighting her mother, he hadn't aged a day.

He folded his hands behind his back and said, "You said that last time, too."

"Last time?"

"Don't tell me you still don't remember." Perun's gaze flicked to Honeycutt and back again. "Though I suppose that does explain her."

"What about her?"

Perun ignored Elle. He turned to Cypress and said, "You should've killed them at the gates. Not all lambs should be brought to the altar."

Elle stepped forward, demanding his attention. Perun's magic slithered across the room and opened up around her—a flower in bloom. It snapped shut with her inside. His magic adhered to her skin, threatening suffocation. She responded by coiling her magic around her core and doing exactly what Adair had warned her not to do when passing through a barrier.

She clenched her fist and leaned into her rage. Her magic exploded outward, so violent and protective that even the air shifted to give her room. Perun's magic shirked away, its surprise a palpable thing, and retreated.

The short burst of wind ruffled Honeycutt's hair. She adjusted her grip on her sword, never taking her eyes off Cypress. The demon, in turn, crossed his arms and leaned against the wall, exactly as uninvolved as he'd been in Elle's dream.

Elle said, "What did you do to me? To my mom? What happened last time?"

Perun narrowed his eyes. "Your mother . . . ?" He glanced at Cypress, who shrugged, then said, "You really are confused, aren't you? Poor, blasphemous thing. You never were meant for this world." He lifted a hand, magic flexing with malice. "Next time, I'll make sure you don't escape, so you're never forced to suffer this earthen plane again. Next time, I'll take your legs."

His magic lashed out, an arrow loosed from its bow. Elle slid her foot forward in a call to the earth, and the stone of the castle responded. A wall rose between them, blocking his path. His magic swerved. It wrapped around her throat, following not a single command but a stream of consciousness, and she realized too late that he didn't only fight with his magic.

He fought with his soul.

Elle raised her hand to her throat, grasping at nothing. His magic tightened, cutting off her breath, and she reached out to the earth. Panic requested help, but anger was stronger. She asked for *vengeance*. Cypress must have felt her intent because he pushed off the wall, eyes on Elle. Honeycutt intercepted the demon with a slash of her sword. A spike of stone burst from the ground, aimed to impale Perun through the jaw.

He jumped away, and his magic fled. Elle sucked in air. To the right, Cypress and Honeycutt danced. The runes on her sword glowed, blade determining the distance between them, and Elle had no choice but to trust Honeycutt could hold her own.

Elle dropped to one knee and splayed both hands against the stone. Perun's magic reared back, preparing for another strike, but if Adair's lecture had taught her anything, it was that soul magic required concentration. She closed her eyes and imagined spikes beneath his feet. Always beneath his feet, wherever he moved. Rising. Piercing.

The castle responded with vigor. Perun's magic sped toward her. The ground beneath his feet cracked and jutted, attempting to spear through him. He darted to the side, and his magic went with him. Spikes formed under Perun as he went, every step a peril, and it was only in watching him dance that she realized he didn't know the steps. Just as Elle wasn't experienced in using soul magic, he didn't seem to be able to sense the earth's intent until it was already moving.

She raised a hand, imagined the heat of dragon fire, and flexed her wrist. Fire materialized at her fingertips, and she thought of Leslie's sacrifice. Of her mother's death and her time in the House. It fed off her anger, red turning blue, and spread.

If Perun were like Elle or Adair, he'd grab the flame and send it back. He dodged.

She barked out a laugh, arrogance tangling with disdain to form righteous justice. "You can't control any elements."

Perun opened his mouth. Elle inhaled, commanded the air in her lungs to *storm*, and blew. A gust of wind filled the room, sending Perun tumbling.

A loud curse from her right reminded her that Honeycutt, too, was blind to magic. Cypress appeared in front of Elle, blue eyes bright. He kicked her in the stomach. Pain splashed up her abdomen and cricked in her spine, knocking the air from her lungs. She flew clear across the room.

Her back hit the wall, but she didn't feel it. She coughed up blood. Cypress joined her in a blink, fingers glowing with a thick black smoke, and she knew this was the part where he tore out her soul. Fear tried to take her, to force her to grovel, but she would rather die. She spat blood onto his shoe.

Cypress crouched, then vanished. Honeycutt's sword nicked the stone where he'd stood. Honeycutt didn't berate Elle for her carelessness, and Elle didn't thank her for the save. There was no time. No need. They turned back to their opponents.

Perun stood by his sphere, chest heaving. Elle pushed herself off the ground. Her arms shook and her spine ached. She licked the blood off her teeth, canted her head toward Cypress, and said, "Maybe he should be the god. He's a lot better at it."

Perun's magic whipped toward her, out of control. Invisible tentacles smashed into the ground, cratering the floor. She rolled out of the way. The stone cracked as blows rained down, and she apologized for the damage. The earth responded with a stiff thrum, relaying no expectation of repair. Castles crumbled, as all man-made things crumbled, and the earth carried on.

Elle thanked the earth for its patience, then requested its strength. She dipped her fingers into the stone floor and, easy as lifting a carpet, tugged a layer of the floor from under Perun's feet. He stumbled and cursed, concentration flagging.

His magic fell back. Elle surged forward. She lashed out with fire, wanting nothing more than to see Perun burn. His magic flexed, alarmed, then curved. It formed a protective barrier not around him, but the sphere beside him.

Perun's weakness flared like a beacon in the night, and she changed targets. Whatever the purpose of the sphere was, it was important enough for him to protect it over his own body. She grinned.

Sure would be a shame if something happened to it.

Elle called upon the air, this time overly aware of where Honeycutt and Cypress were trading blows, and commanded it to *rush*. "It's you or the sphere, Perun!"

Perun froze mid-step. The air caught him—suffocating him the same as it had suffocated her—then threw him into the wall. His head hit the stone with a satisfying crack, and the lightning in the sphere brightened.

Elle met Cypress's eyes from across the room. He twisted out of the way of Honeycutt's blade. Elle strode toward Perun. The man-god was taller than her, though not as tall as Leslie or Adair, and lithe rather than muscular. She stopped in front of him, and he made no attempt to struggle. Despite the inherent power imbalance in their positions, it was him who reeked of arrogance. Him who said, "You are a fool."

"Better to be a fool than to be defeated by one."

"You believe me defeated?" His grin held more demeaning implications than teeth. "I am a god, and you are a worm. Writhing in the dirt, drowning in the rain, living in the darkness which I created."

She compressed the air around his throat just to hear him choke. "Tell me what you did."

Red tinted his cheeks as he gasped and wheezed, but his eyes never left Elle's. She loosened her grip on his neck. He said, "I have a proposition."

"No."

"Instead of what I did to you, how about I share what you did to me?" He lifted a hand without magical intent, and against her better judgment, she let him. He pressed his fingers to his stomach, where a long, thick scar on his abdomen cut through the tattoos *Indra* and *Chaac.* "You gave me this scar."

Elle stared at him, uncomprehending. She'd seen the scar before, given it before, but only in a dream.

"No. My mom—"

"Whoever your bitch of a mother is, I've never met her. The woman who gave me this scar is you. Right here. With that sword." He pointed across the room, toward Honeycutt, and Elle turned. She saw her friend fighting off the man who'd tortured Elle for a decade, and she saw the sword from her dreams. Her heart thumped in her chest. A migraine blossomed behind her eyes. Her control over the air flickered. He asked, "Do you know what happened next?"

Elle threaded her fingers in her hair, head pounding. She took a step back. The air holding Perun to the wall wavered and, without Elle's will there to guide the way, lost interest. It dissipated. Her instincts screamed at her to take action—to attack, defend, or prepare—but the void in her chest was louder. It yawned open with care for only one thing.

Knowledge.

She shook her head, a willing participant in Perun's sick game, and he smiled. He said, "I resurrected myself. I took your sword from you, and I used it to rip you to shreds." He closed the space between them, for the first time resembling the god he claimed to be. Tattooed fingers caressed the scar on her jaw, gentle as a lover. It was with a near-reverence that he whispered, "I wish you could remember how you screamed. The pitch of it. The pain. It almost made your insolence worthwhile."

Elle jerked back, horror dawning. Perun caught her by the nape and pulled her closer. She said, "You're lying."

"I am a god. I have no need for lies."

"But that would mean—" She cut herself off.

"That would mean?"

"That would mean Honeycutt and I are . . ."

Perun shook his head, eyes every bit as cold and cruel as those of the demon he employed. He dug his nails into her skin, magic flaring with the euphoric desire to *ruin*, and said, "Not just her."

43

Adair stared at the burned remains of what must have been a home some centuries prior.

It had been magically preserved by Perun because, according to the locals, the house had once been his. That, of course, was before he became a god. When Adair asked how Perun had "become a god," his worshippers zealously referenced destiny. Perun's parents had known *(must have known)* when they named him. The other gods had confirmed it by striking his home with lightning, effectively burning everything and everyone within.

Everyone except Perun, that is.

According to legend, Perun had been a child at the time of the fire and, despite having shown no predisposition to magic, emerged from the blaze unharmed. His parents and sister were mortals and, as such, had died. But even that was supposedly beneficial, as their sacrifice was the kindling required to birth a god.

It sounded a lot like accidental magic to Adair—stressful situations highlighted magical abilities a lot better than peaceful ones—but he supposed it was reasonable for backwater, magic-fearing societies to mistake surviving a fire for divine right. The only genuinely puzzling part of their folklore was the focus on lightning.

These people believed lightning striking across was an honor reserved for those approaching divinity. They scoffed at the thought of it being a natural phenomenon, instead insisting Perun personally selected those souls to join his court after death. And while Perun having a court of souls was as ridiculous as his godhood, it also made sense.

Everything Adair had learned thus far pointed to Perun being steeped in soul magic. If he'd somehow found a way to use other souls to preserve his youth, it would give the illusion of godliness. Strong, magical souls would last him longer, but if he'd really been alive as long as the stories said, he'd have had to restock.

Perun would need to find new victims, force their souls to strike across instead of up, and trap them for future use. Adair couldn't imagine what kind of twisted sorcery could do that, but he was willing to bet someone as magically ignorant as Elle might mistake the containment apparatus for a sphere of lightning.

Which begged the question of whether Adair's hypothesis had any merit. If it did, then Clarrissa's lightning had struck across, and he had wasted ten years not saving her. At the same time, it seemed like Perun needed to visit his victims personally in order to curse their souls, and Adair would have noticed if a soulmonger had entered his home.

Then again, noticing meant nothing without the ability to remember.

From what Adair could tell, the gaps in his memory extended for years before Clarrissa's death. He remembered her getting sick and them buying the cabin. He remembered seeking every doctor in every neighboring town to no avail. Then the details blurred.

He wanted to say he'd considered traveling to find a cure and that Clarrissa's begging had convinced him to stay, but the conversation was more of a concept than a definitive memory. The next few years had been spent keeping her comfortable while seeking a miracle, but he couldn't recall a single example of how he'd done those things.

And when Clarrissa had finally succumbed to death's pull, where had she been? In bed? In the garden? At the table? Adair remembered crying by her bedside, but was it next to her corpse or after her funeral? If he'd seen her lightning flash across, as he technically knew he had, they must have been both together and outside when she'd died.

But were they?

He didn't have the answers, and the next thing he could remember with any clarity was standing in front of the portrait, ready to step through. The months he'd supposedly spent creating the enchantment were hazy. The moment he'd decided to create it was lost.

And if that weren't complicated enough, he still had no idea how Elle fit into the puzzle.

She had a connection with Cypress and, by extension, Perun. Perun was connected to both Adair's and Honeycutt's Clarrissas. Everyone involved had a Clarrissa, which was improbable verging on impossible. Cypress knew more about Adair's Clarrissa than should have been possible without seeing her soul. That lent to the theory that Adair's Clarrissa had been taken by Perun, as he and Cypress appeared to have a deal. Of course, Cypress could have gotten the same information while cursing Adair's heart, but that begged the question of how it had gotten into and out of the painting.

There were too many coincidences to be natural, but Adair couldn't for the life of him figure out how they were connected. The secondary tear in his soul explained his blurred and missing memories, but it also left the burning questions of when, why, and how.

Adair wasn't weak. It would take a hell of a sorcerer to tear his soul, and that was without taking into account the power necessary to corner him in the first place. And if someone actually had bested him *(as they apparently had)*, why take a piece of his soul and leave? Why not kill him?

He frowned and rubbed his temple, warding off the beginnings of a headache. His thoughts were blurring again, no doubt the result of a compulsion. The more information he gathered, the harder it became to put it all together. Nothing made sense, and nothing he'd found out about Perun had made it any clearer.

"Mister! Hey, I've been looking for you." Adair turned to see the bartender from Perëndi's Pub jogging toward him. "Where are your friends?"

Adair shrugged, overtly aware that the townspeople wouldn't take kindly to a group of strangers setting out to kill their god, and said, "I don't know."

"Well, are you meeting up with them again?"

"Probably."

"Could you give this to the girl?" He held out an old, folded-up piece of paper. "Not, uh, not the dwarf. The other one."

Adair accepted the paper. "What is it?"

The bartender scratched the back of his neck, a soft blush dusting his cheeks. "It's that wanted poster I was telling you about. I got to thinking, and nobody should grow up without seeing their mum. I know it's just a picture but, well, it's something, you know?"

Adair looked from the crinkled square of paper to the apparently family-oriented bartender. He nodded. "Thanks. I'll get it to her."

The bartender stuffed his thumbs into his pockets and waited, friendly smile plastered to his face. Seconds passed in what Adair assumed was awkward silence before he remembered the large sum of gold Elle had traded for a few measly sentences of information. The assumption that they were both foolhardy and rich slid into view, and the bartender's newfound role as a good Samaritan made sense. He didn't want to comfort a grieving girl. He wanted a reward.

Adair said, "I don't have any gold."

The bartender flicked his wrist. "Oh, that's alright. Couple of silvers will do."

"I'm not giving you any coin."

The bartender's smile dropped. "Now look here—"

Adair summoned electricity next to the bartender's face. It shot to the ground and burned the grass. The bartender skittered to the side, cursing, and Adair raised both brows. "Anything else?"

Brown eyes flitted to the patch of scorched earth, then back up again. The bartender waved. "Give your friends my best." He left without waiting for a response, which was fair, as Adair hadn't planned on responding. Adair turned his attention to the thin, age-yellowed paper in his hand. He unfolded it.

Elle stared out from the wanted poster, gaze dismissive. She was older by a decade and missing the white scar on her cheek, which might've lent credence to the bartender's mother theory, except she also carried a sword.

Honeycutt's sword.

The white leather hilt peeked out from behind her back, distinct and unmistakable. His headache returned. Something akin to fear stained the void in his chest, warning him that the compulsion on his soul shouldn't be reacting to information about Elle. He gripped the page too tight, crinkling her picture, and read the description.

The name was just a letter. A simple, nondescript *L*. The compulsion charm on his soul tried to tell him that whoever had made the poster couldn't spell, but the truth was simpler. They'd only written a letter because she'd only given them a letter. Because she was a bounty hunter, and the only way to protect those she held dear was to leave her name at home.

Dread weighed down Adair's stomach for half a second. Pieces of Honeycutt's past and the information on the poster aligned. Impossible as it was, Honeycutt was a missing piece of Elle's soul. And regardless of how young she appeared, Elle was the one who had rampaged through Ferron a decade prior. It made a certain amount of sense, considering Elle's connection to demons and Honeycutt's knowledge of them, but it also meant that *Elle* was the one who had a Clarrissa.

A Clarrissa who'd been taken by Perun right around the time Adair's Clarrissa had died.

His headache turned into a migraine, powerful enough to nauseate. He skimmed over the list of transgressions to read the notes on her magic. Earthmonger. Airmonger. Firemonger. Lightningmonger. *Lightningmonger.*

If he'd had a heart, it would've dropped into his stomach.

There were two types of lightning: soul and electric. Souls only looked like lightning as they left the body, and few were powerful enough to be seen with the naked eye. That left electricity, which was also impossible because Adair was the first and only sorcerer to have harnessed electricity as an element. If someone else had done so, he would have heard. He would've—

"Your soul is torn on two sides. He's one of them." Honeycutt pointed at Leslie, *"Where's the other?"*

Adair balked. He wanted to come to another conclusion—any other conclusion—but his blurring thoughts and pounding headache were as good as confirmation. Her talent for magic. The way her magical signature mirrored Adair's. Her curiosity and brashness and determination. They were all his.

Or, more realistically, they were all hers.

The fact that Adair had retained a large chunk of their memories meant that he was a piece torn away, not the core. If they were to merge, his personality, abilities, and memories would meld with the whole. He would cease to exist.

A flash of panic lit Adair's chest, brief but vivid, and he wondered almost blandly if that was how his heart felt about merging with him. It would make sense, he supposed, since they were the same. They were *all* the same.

His thoughts muddled again, but the compulsion charm could only ward him away from information, not make him forget what he'd already learned. He turned his eyes to the sky and blinked through the pain. Now that he knew the truth—the real truth—he had to tell the others.

He scanned the seemingly empty air for earthen magic. When he found it—to the left and far, far above—he commanded the air to deliver him there. It swirled around him, ruffling his hair in its eagerness to bend to his will. He waited an extra moment for a spark of something *(happiness, fear, comfort, anxiety)* that would never come.

Then he flew.

44

Honeycutt's muscles protested the effort of keeping up with Blue Eyes.

The demon was fast. Faster than she could ever be. Without magic to sense where it would appear next, her maximum effort resulted in barely keeping up. It didn't help that her sword was too long or that Elle's magic was blinding to the point that Honeycutt could only activate her second-sight intermittently. To make matters worse, Blue Eyes seemed to have picked up on her Elle-centric issues. It repeatedly refused to be led from the room.

The only upside of the fight—and "upside" was being generous—was that she had already found Blue Eyes' magical core. It was known as the most powerful higher demon for a reason, and the number of souls attached to its core was staggering. Honeycutt would need to cut it out from basically every angle if she wanted any chance of actually killing the thing.

Thus far, she hadn't even grazed it.

"Demon! Restrain the spare."

Blue Eyes paused to look at Perun, and Honeycutt used the distraction to charge. The chant slipped easily from her lips, even more so considering Elle wasn't actively using magic. Her soul extended until she and the sword were one. She lunged. The demon disappeared.

It reappeared behind her, one hand snaking around to clutch her jaw. Strong fingers forced her mouth shut while its other hand grasped her wrist. It squeezed hard. Her nerves pinched. Her bones ground together. Pain raced up her arm, and her fingers spasmed. She dropped her sword.

The runes on her sword ceased to glow. Her second-sight faded. Humiliation tore a hole in her pride as the demon's grip lightened, constricting rather than painful. For all that she had been attacking with everything she had, the demon was just fooling around. It could have killed her twenty times over, no effort required. The hand on her jaw moved to her shoulder, gentle but threatening.

Blue Eyes turned Honeycutt so she faced Elle. Honeycutt didn't know what'd happened between Perun and Elle, but they'd stopped fighting. They stood close, and Perun used a hand on the back of Elle's neck to lift her head. He forced her to look at Honeycutt. "Look at that." He raised one long, tattooed arm and pointed at Honeycutt. "That is your guilt. It's angry and impatient. Useless. It's the fallout from the mistakes you made, which you no longer have to suffer for. Because of me."

"What?" Honeycutt bared her teeth. "Dinnae listen to him, Elle."

It was the demon who said, "Now's not the time to protest. She knows."

"Knows what? Whatever trickery ye have come up with—"

Blue Eyes patted her shoulder. "Look around, Honeycutt. Where's the counter-curse?"

Honeycutt gave the room a cursory once-over. "Ye moved it."

"Did we? Or was it never here to begin with?" It drummed its fingers on her shoulder, sounding bored. "Face it. There's no counter-curse because there's no curse to counter."

Honeycutt squeezed her eyes shut, desperate to remember the last time she'd been in this castle and where the counter-curse had been held. Her thoughts blurred. "Stop."

"Come on. You must have figured it out by now. Must have suspected from the moment you touched that sword."

"Stop it."

"The sword you made for yourself, to your specifications. And yet it doesn't feel like it was made for you, does it?"

Honeycutt jerked in the demon's unrelenting hold. Her head throbbed. Anxiety sprouted from nowhere, and she shouted, "Stop it!"

Blue Eyes met her furious, frightened gaze without sympathy. It voiced the fears that'd been plaguing her for nearly a week. "It feels like it was made for her."

It canted its head toward Elle, and Honeycutt's body moved out of sync with her mind. She looked at Elle, who stared apologetically back. Shame dropped into the humiliation pooling in her stomach, causing it to splash up her chest. *Elle knew.* Knew that Honeycutt was a part of her. Knew that Honeycutt had the memories, and that any part of Honeycutt not in-line with Elle was false.

Angry, sorrowful tears burned behind Honeycutt's eyes as she accepted not only that she was never going to see her clan again, but that her clan had never existed in the first place. She wasn't even an actual dwarf. It was a side effect of the curse. And her entire life—past, present, and future—was built on a lie.

She gritted her teeth and refused to blink. If she blinked, she would cry, and she'd be damned if these bastards saw her cry.

Perun said, "I tore that guilt from you, girl. Just as I tore your selfishness and your arrogance. I purified you. And now that you're here, you have a choice." He took a solid step away from Elle, releasing her. "Go to your guilt, if you wish. Return to your life of shame and anger. Or do what you came here to do all those years ago and join Clarrissa."

Elle swiveled from Honeycutt to look at Perun. "Clarrissa is here?"

Perun gestured to the sphere in the center of the room, and Honeycutt's heart shattered.

Clarrissa was real.

Clarrissa was dead.

"Only the pure are fit to give themselves to me. I judged her worthy, and she has been dutifully, faithfully serving me every day since." Perun spread his arms wide, as though he really were bestowing an honor. "When you came here last, you were unworthy. I struck you down, deservedly, but you're different now. Better. Pure. If you wish to join your true love, I will allow it."

Elle's eyes dilated, and despite her being the only one to never have had a Clarrissa, her entire body softened with want. "How?"

Perun's venom-dipped lips stretched in a predatorial smile. "You need only step into the sphere. I will do the rest."

Panic pulsed in Honeycutt's blood. She reached out. "Dinnae do it, Elle."

"Shh." Blue Eyes tugged her back into place, eyes on Elle. "This is the best part."

Elle turned toward the sphere, trancelike. She walked toward it, thin figure bathed in its light, and panic morphed into fear. If Elle went in there, she would die. Part of Honeycutt would die. And as much as Honeycutt was terrified of what would happen to her if they merged, it had to be better than her current hell: forever wandering with no clan, no purpose, and no way to know what was real.

"Dinnae do it, lassie. Ye are—*we* are better than that!"

Intense, invisible pressure on Honeycutt's jaw forced her mouth closed. She screamed through her teeth, but without magic of her own, there was no way to combat the spell. She stomped on Cypress's foot with the heel of her boot. It only held her tighter.

Elle stood in front of the sphere, too small and young to be making such a heavy decision. Honeycutt wriggled, trying to catch Elle's attention. She only needed one look, one shake of the head, one single *moment*. Elle pressed her hand against the sphere, and on the other side, a soul took shape. It flickered, gaining human form.

The soul was taller than Elle and undeniably feminine. It aligned its hand with hers, shimmering fingers flush with the barrier. Something deep inside Honeycutt broke. Even without real memories of the real Clarrissa—even without knowing who she, herself was—Honeycutt knew that soul. Perfect and loving. Brash and bright.

"Clarrissa?" Elle spoke, voice agonizingly quiet. "I'm sorry I don't remember you. And I'm sorry I let this happen to you."

Clarrissa's soul flickered brighter, though what that meant was lost on Honeycutt.

Elle nodded. "I thought you might say that. And I hope you're right. I also hope this really is true love because . . . because that's the only way you'll understand."

Elle angled closer, chin tipped up to gaze in the direction of Clarrissa's face. Clarrissa flashed, then dimmed. Sparks lit the air around Clarrissa's soul, a million tiny fireworks, and Honeycutt didn't know what to think. Part of her wanted to kick and scream, to never quit fighting, but another part wanted to beg. *(One more day with Clarrissa. One more hour. One more second.)* So long as it meant joining Clarrissa again, no matter how short or painful the experience, Honeycutt wanted it.

She would always want it.

Tears glittered in Elle's eyes, and she said, "That's just it. I like myself." She lifted her hand from the sphere, hesitated, then let it drop. "I like that I'm arrogant, and I like being selfish. And if I feel guilty, well that means I cared, doesn't it?" She licked her lips and, with more pride than Honeycutt could ever remember possessing, let her tears fall. "I really am sorry."

Clarrissa's soul glimmered. The entire room glowed, warm like sunset in summer. Elle took a step back.

Perun sneered. "How disappointing."

Elle stiffened, likely sensing something Honeycutt couldn't. She sent a gust of wind toward Perun and, without waiting to see it hit, started running. "Honeycutt!"

Honeycutt didn't have to ask what Elle wanted. She met glistening brown eyes, and she knew. Honeycutt threw her elbow back, hoping to take Blue Eyes by surprise. Its grip on her vanished, and she hit empty air. Surprise delayed her an extra second, but she sought no explanation for the demon's disappearance. There was no time, no point. She took off toward Elle.

They met in the middle, hands outstretched, and even without preparation, the process of merging was easy.

She extended herself to Elle the same way she would to her sword, and like a key slotting into place, Honeycutt was home. The fear of losing herself melted away because *this* was her. Brash, impatient, offhandedly kind, and lazy. Curious, fun-loving, angry, and smart. She was perfection.

And she was pain.

Elle fell to her knees as information stuffed itself into her head, ruthless in its efficiency. Memories of a clan she'd never had and beliefs she'd never held paled in comparison to the ones of her travels. Knowledge of different societies. People she had met and cultures she had experienced. The exotic magics she had studied and the ruins she had scavenged, all in search of Clarrissa's cure.

Clarrissa's cure.

She had found it. Really found it. Deep in the bowels of a forgotten tomb, locked away for its dark nature. A curse that would transfer the sickness of one living organism to another. Clarrissa would never have approved, but Elle hadn't cared. What Clarrissa didn't know wouldn't hurt her.

Except Elle had returned to their cabin, and Clarrissa was already gone. It'd been a year—a full *year*—since Clarrissa's death, and Elle hadn't known. Hadn't thought to question it, even when the letters had stopped.

Sorrow and guilt tore holes in Elle's heart. She remembered spiraling, too angry with herself to care about the damage she caused, and finding comfort in the bottom of a bottle. Drinking had numbed the pain, and drinking a lot occasionally allowed her to see Clarrissa. She remembered numerous nights spent lying on the couch, poisoned with alcohol but finally happy as Clarrissa ran her hand through Elle's hair.

Clarrissa would say, *You can't keep doing this,* and Elle would agree. She would promise never to drink again. She'd even mean it up until she awoke, devastatingly alone. It was Clarrissa's father who'd eventually brought Elle back to reality *(though he'd probably been hoping for sobriety)* by mentioning Clarrissa's lightning had struck across.

And that had been odd, hadn't it? Elle had learned enough in her travels to identify when magic was interfering with nature. She'd recognized the signs, and she'd turned her self-destructive spiral into a quest for revenge.

Any witch or wizard powerful enough to re-route a soul was dangerous, but Elle hadn't cared. She'd sought the fight with no preparation, eagerly adding to the odds stacked against her. She'd gone in drunk. And when she'd met Perun, when she'd realized he was strong but his magic was limited, her recklessness had only increased. She'd allowed him to corner her, to take her sword and do with it as he pleased.

For the pain of Elle's loss was unbearable. Clarrissa had died, scared and alone, because of Elle. And no matter Elle's official, superficial reasons for seeking Perun, the truth was she'd wanted to die. Craved it, even. She'd thrown the fight, expecting death, and was torn apart instead.

That was how she'd fallen out of the sky, into Cypress' dollhouse. She'd spent a decade there *(de-aged, magic held in constant check, unaware)*, and she'd spent a decade on the boat, too. And all the while, Clarrissa had been—

Self-hatred swirled in Elle's stomach, nauseating in its intensity. The rush of memories concluded with the last time she'd seen Clarrissa.

It'd been a fight, louder and angrier than any before. Clarrissa had begged Elle not to go, and Elle had slammed the door behind herself, never bothering to look back. She'd been unable to consider Clarrissa's side, unable to see a future where she didn't return triumphant, and arrogantly agreed to pay without looking at the price.

Tears swam in her eyes and marked paths down her cheeks, and *that was it*. She'd never seen Clarrissa again, and the years of research—the cure—had been for nothing.

Elle shook with heavy, hyperventilating sobs. The stone floor scraped her knees and palms as her body finished reshaping itself. She felt both odd and familiar: an older, healthier version of herself with arms muscled from years of swordplay and legs swift from constant travel.

The torrent of emotions slowed, and Elle lifted her head. Past and present blurred as Perun lifted a hand and declared her, "Pathetic."

Whether the two men standing above her were recollection or reality was unclear. Then Perun's magic crashed down around her, forceful enough to break the already weakened floor, and Elle fell to the room below.

She hit the ground hard. Pain resounded. *Not a memory.* Her tired body begged her for rest, and her sluggish thoughts agreed. Instinct pushed her to her feet. Perun's aim was to kill her, and without the rest of her soul, he would likely succeed.

She took advantage of the castle's labyrinth-like halls and, praying she could still save Leslie from the hellhounds, ran away.

45

Leslie couldn't feel his legs. His lungs ached, his sides screamed, his throat burned, but none of that mattered because *he couldn't feel his legs*.

He was going to fall. He was going to trip, and he was going to fall because that was what happened to people who couldn't feel their legs. Then, because he couldn't feel his legs while being chased by hellhounds, he was going to die.

Tears blurred his vision as he rounded another corner, shoes sliding against stone. He'd always been a good runner, but "good" and "good enough to outrun hellhounds" were two very different things. He sobbed and stumbled. The ground was uneven, his feet uncoordinated. He was going to die.

He was going to die.

He was going to die.

He was going to die.

A crater-like crevice dented the bottom of a nearby wall. He dove for it. The hole was barely wide enough for him to slide in sideways, and he hit the back far too soon. The hellhounds tried to follow, but their large, muscled torsos were too broad to squeeze in after him. Sharp teeth snapped at thin air, noses perilously close to touching his slacks.

He hugged his knees to his chest, relief leaving him weak. A wide maw lined with steel-tough teeth latched onto the wall, tearing stone like bread. Cold fear seeped into his bones. More of them joined in, as smart as they were vicious, and his tears returned. He was still going to die. Just slower.

He hid his face between his knees and cried. Quick, hyperventilating sobs pushed his back and neck against rough-hewn stone. One of their wet snouts brushed his ankle. Cold fear evolved to dizzying terror. He curled himself tighter against the back of the fissure, hard clumps of rock digging into his side.

The largest of the hellhounds growled. Leslie peeked up from his knees to see the others retreat, giving the singular beast more room. The remaining hellhound backed away, then rammed itself against the wall. He heard the stone crack, and dust showered down. Hot breath filled the small space with the smell of rotten meat. Saliva speckled Leslie's skin. The hellhound's shoulders were still too broad, but it was a near thing. A fixable thing.

He covered his eyes.

Leslie didn't want to die, and he didn't want to watch himself die. He heard the hellhound slam into the wall again and felt the dust sprinkle his face. He whimpered as teeth grazed his calf.

His thoughts spiraled around how badly this was going to hurt. Fear urged him to regret his sacrifice, but he didn't want to die a coward. He thought of Clarrissa, instead. She would be proud of him, if she knew. She would say, *That was so brave, Les!* and *You did the right thing. They're alive because of you.*

He pretended she was there with him, sitting beside him in the hole. Her hand gripped his own in silent reassurance that they would be together soon. He felt the warmth of her body at his side and the weight of her head on his shoulder. She didn't worry or cry. She didn't mind the wait. She was calm because she'd done this already.

Dying, Clarrissa said, *is the easy part. It's living that's hard.*

Leslie nodded and cried harder, desperate for that to be true. "I do not . . ." He sobbed. "I do not want to—"

But how could he complain about dying to someone who was already dead?

Leslie scrunched in on himself as he heard the stone crumble and the wall give way. He tried to squeeze Clarrissa's hand, but there was nothing there.

The hellhound breathed hot, damp rot directly onto his face. The blunt side of one of its large slick teeth indented his cheek. He thought he remembered reading something about lesser and intermediate demons feeding off fear, but then its maw opened wide, and maybe the book had said *flesh* not *fear*.

Its tooth sliced his cheek. He squeezed his eyes shut, not yet ready for the end. A thundering crash extended his life an extra second. The hellhound yowled, high and sharp. The scent of decay cleared from the air, but Leslie refused to look. If he looked, he would see them, and if he saw them, he'd gain a front row seat to what they could do.

He didn't want to watch himself die.

"Leslie?"

Leslie opened his eyes. Adair crouched in the mouth of the crevice, bright light streaming in around his dark figure. Fearful tears turned joyous. Leslie shimmied and squirmed, dragging himself from the breach. He stretched out his arms, knees touching stone, and tackled his other half.

"Adair! Oh, Adair." Leslie hugged Adair as tightly as he could, face buried in the crook of his counterpart's neck. He cried fat, heavy tears into the soft material of Adair's shirt, chest heaving. "I thought I was going to die. I thought, I thought—" He wept harder, trauma leaving him weak.

Adair hugged Leslie back. Strong arms wrapped around his middle, and a hand rubbed comforting lines down his spine. Leslie leaned into the embrace, desperate for some semblance of safety, and Adair provided. Leslie's fear leaked out of his eyes. He bathed in Adair's strength. They huddled on the floor, two halves of a singular whole, right up until Adair said, "Merge with me."

Leslie shoved him away.

The light behind Adair brightened, and Leslie squinted at the fresh stream of sunshine. Where once there had been stone, now there was air. A human-sized hole gaped in the wall directly across from Leslie's hiding space. A similar hole decorated the wall behind that, and the wall behind *that*, too. They opened the castle wide, cleaving a straight path to the outside world.

"Did you . . . ?"

"The dogs were in the way."

Leslie blinked, reality catching up in a rush. He grabbed Adair by the shoulders. "They are not dogs, they are hellhounds. Demons. We need the sword."

"Hellhounds can't fly, Leslie." Adair spoke slowly, like he was explaining a simple concept to a small, dimwitted child. "Regardless of immortality, they're not getting back up here."

Leslie opened his mouth to argue, but *oh*. That actually made sense. He pulled Adair into another hug, wildly thankful to have his rational mind back in action.

Adair once again ruined the moment by saying, "We need to merge."

Leslie's high spirits dipped. He ended the hug. "I will not merge with you until we help Elle and Honeycutt."

"If we want to help them, we need to merge now."

"No. You will leave them. I know you will."

"I won't—"

"You will! In a choice between helping someone else and helping yourself, you always choose yourself. Right?" Leslie scooted away until his butt touched the wall by the crevice. He shook his head. "I have said it before, and I will say it again. I am not you."

"Neither am I."

"No, you—What?" Leslie stared at Adair, dumbfounded.

Adair said, "You're not me, and I'm not me, either. We're Elle."

Leslie blinked, slow and stupid. "Say again?"

Instead of repeating himself, Adair pulled a crumpled piece of paper from his pocket and passed it to Leslie. The wanted poster depicted a woman who looked a lot like Elle, though she was older and, judging by her name, a bounty hunter. Leslie tilted the page so the sunlight hit it better, then stopped. Discomfort squirmed in his gut. "Is that Honeycutt's sword?"

"It is. She's one of us, too." Adair tapped the third section down. "Read this."

Leslie did, though he didn't understand why until he got to her apparent affinity for lightning. The discomfort dug deeper. His head started to hurt. "That is not possible."

"My soul is torn on two sides, remember? One is from separating with you. The other"—Adair tapped the paper again, over the picture this time—"is from separating with her."

"But she cannot be. . . . She has no memories. That would make her—"

"The original. Yeah." Adair laid his hand over Leslie's, neither forceful nor comforting. "I know this is hard to process, but you need to do it quickly. We have to merge and find Elle before it's too late."

Leslie's thoughts spun in circles. He didn't know what to focus on. He didn't know what to ask. He looked away from both the wanted poster and Adair, trying to clear his head. "Why must we merge?"

"Because Perun is powerful. I don't know how or why, but he did this to us. If we want any chance at beating him, it has to be together. Really together."

"But if you merge with her, you will disappear." Selfish worry disguised itself as altruism. He crumpled the poster in his fist. "We will both disappear. Does that not bother you?"

"It did. For a moment, I was terrified. And I understand now that's how you must feel all the time, but we can't let fear stop us. This isn't just a fight for our soul. It's a fight for Clarrissa's."

Tears welled in Leslie's eyes, unexpected. "What do you mean?"

"You were right. Clarrissa's lightning struck across, and it brought her here. She's waiting for us."

Slow, heavy tears fell from Leslie's eyes. He wanted to see the real Clarrissa again so, so much, but the longer their conversation drew, the less it seemed that would happen. Not for him, anyway. A headache throbbed behind his eyes, making it hard to think. He asked, "And Elle? Honeycutt? Do they know?"

"I don't think so. Which is why we have to hurry." Adair lifted his hand from Leslie's and held it out like an offering. "I don't know what will happen to you after we merge, but I know my magic was always at its strongest when fueled by emotion."

Terror and anxiety sloshed in Leslie's gut. As much as he knew it was the right thing to do, he didn't want to disappear. He didn't want to die.

"Please, Leslie."

Leslie's turmoil stuttered. He rewound the plea and played it again. He met Adair's eyes. "You called me Leslie."

Adair furrowed his brows, both impassive and impatient. "That's your name, isn't it?"

Gratitude blossomed, then spread: dandelion puffs in a fresh spring breeze. He smiled. "You have never called me Leslie before."

"I didn't think you were a person before." Adair stared into Leslie's eyes, technically apathetic but with an air of apology. "I was wrong."

Leslie's heart soared. His hands shook and his vision blurred. He was still afraid, yes, but he no longer had to face that fear alone. Leslie bypassed Adair's hand to pull him into a tight hug. He extended his reach to Adair's soul, and his other half hugged him back.

Lips pressed to his scalp. Bliss consumed. Adair whispered, "Thank you."

Merging with Adair felt like waking in a warm bed after a restful sleep. It was calm and perfect, and Leslie's fear of disappearing melted away. They were not two people fighting over one body, but a single soul learning to play a new tune. And Adair wasn't taking over. He was making room.

Adair tipped forward as the body in front of him faded to nothing, and for the first time in a decade, he cried.

He sobbed as the pain of Clarrissa's death sunk into his spirit, and he remembered why tearing his soul apart had seemed like a good idea in the first place. The woman he loved *(his best friend, his family)* was gone. Taken from him by a diagnosis. Taken from him too soon. Loss dug a hole in his chest fit to match the hole where his heart had been, but with that loss came love.

The years he'd spent with a living Clarrissa were suddenly brighter. Kindness and devotion colored his memories, returning joy to the sound of her laughter and remorse to the sight of her tears. And Elle. The mild interest he'd felt for her intelligence and talent swelled to bursting, splattering his insides with pride. She was so smart and kind and young. An Adair who hadn't been embittered by life. A version of himself who knew no loss or guilt. A clean slate.

His tears slowed as he realized he loved her—he loved himself—and that if she didn't want to take the pain of their memories or bear the weight of their mistakes, he wouldn't force her. For as much as he yearned to be whole—to know the truth of the gaps in his memories and to save Clarrissa once and for all—the other parts of his soul were more than slivers of self. They were people. And as his heart had pointed out over and over again, they had the right to decide whether they wanted to stay that way.

He pushed himself up on shaking limbs. His thoughts flitted to the sphere, the demon, and the god. There was no way of knowing how this journey would end, and for the first time in a long time, he worried. Adair wasn't used to anxiety. He no longer knew how to deal with fear. He pressed a hand to his chest, seeking guidance. His heart thumped encouragingly on the other side.

"Wait for us, Elle. We're coming."

46

Adair had forgotten how much he loved the feel of magic.

He called to the air, which responded with a breeze, and ordered it to guide him to Elle. The air mussed his hair as it contemplated his demand, but they both knew it had nothing better to do. It gave in and blew to the left. He followed the wind through the labyrinth-like halls of the castle, sprinting where he once would have walked. Halls and chapels and chambers. Stairs and suites and vaults. He told the air to take him the *most direct route*. It swirled around him, bored even by the suggestion, and took yet another turn.

A familiar magic signature approached from the left. Elation unfurled within him, so much better than the sorrow and the guilt. He ran even faster.

Elle rounded the corner at a similar pace, sentient earth leading her way. She looked taller and healthier. The scar on her jaw seemed even more pale. She stopped when she saw him. "Adair?"

Adair barreled into her, too excited to stop. He hugged her around the waist, lifted her from the ground, and swung her in a circle. She clutched his shoulders, stiff and confused. He buried his face in her wild, unbrushed hair and held her tighter. "I was so worried I wouldn't make it in time."

Adair squeezed her again, just because he could, then leaned back. He brushed her hair from her eyes and admired the rest of his soul. She furrowed her brows and parted her lips, more perturbed than pleased. "Leslie?"

Adair grinned and added a second hand to her hair, pushing all the frizzy flyaways from her face. "Leslie Adair, at your service."

Her lips quirked in an odd little smile, and she wasn't just taller. She was older, too. Her previously too-thin frame had filled out, though not enough for Adair's liking, and she seemed more grounded. If not for the white-white scar and the missing half decade, he could have mistaken this Elle for the one on the wanted poster.

He squinted. "Honeycutt?"

"Sort of. Honeycutt was my surname." Elle tilted her head, face still framed by his hands. She tapped the spot on her hip where Honeycutt's canteen had once hung. "And don't freak out, but I think Leslie was my given name."

Adair straightened, surprised that she knew. Then he smiled because she *knew*. He nodded. "Yeah. Yeah, you're right. We're the same." Pride swelled within him, and he wished he'd recognized himself sooner. If he'd known he was her, he would've had more faith in her ability to figure out the puzzle on her own. He released her face, allowing her hair to do what it would, and used his thumb to wipe a smudge of blood from her cheek.

She scrunched her nose. "This is so weird."

"Being the same person?"

"No. Well, yeah, but I more meant you being nice. You still, you know, look like the heartless Adair." She kicked at a stray piece of rubble, still shoeless. Without waiting for a response to her first comment, she asked, "What does this mean for us?"

"Us?"

"Yeah. I mean, are we going to merge, too, or . . . ? I know Leslie, um, *you* weren't too keen on it before . . ." She gestured to Adair as a whole, and he understood.

Nervous butterflies nestled in his stomach. He told the truth. "I want to merge with you. I want to find out what really happened to us, and I want to be whole again."

Dark, pernicious magic saturated the air, signaling Cypress had arrived. Both Adair and Elle tensed, apprehensive, but the demon didn't appear. It could've been down the hall, around the corner, or in a room above them. It could've been invisible, less than an arm's length away. Adair looked around, trying to pinpoint its location, but just as he hadn't been able to feel it enter his cabin, he couldn't feel it here.

Seconds trudged by, motionless. Adair said, "It's waiting for something."

"What?"

He shook his head. "I don't know. But whatever it is, it can't be good."

"Then let's hurry up and merge." She held out her hand, impatient. "Before whatever he's waiting for arrives."

Adair caught Elle's eyes, and his love for her grew. He ignored her hand and said, "We don't have to merge, you know. Our memories are wonderful, but they're painful, too. They're full of loss and regret, and if you aren't one hundred percent sure you want to carry those burdens, you can wait. Another hour, another day, the rest of your life. If you'd like to continue on as you are, a new Elle with a fresh start, I'll support you." He held a hand to his heart, and it beat its agreement into his palm. "We'll support you."

Elle stared at Adair for a long minute. The curve of her upper lip declared him stupid. The way she rested her hand on her waist, hip cocked, reinforced that opinion. Then, as if her body language hadn't screamed it loudly enough, she said, "That's dumb." She held her free hand out, palm up, and motioned to the castle around them. She spoke to Adair like he was *slow*. "I came here specifically to get my memories back. Why would I stop now?"

"I don't think you understand. The mistakes I've made—"

"They're my mistakes, too, Adair. And unless you're going to pull a Leslie and demand we go on some far-flung journey before merging, I'm ready." She re-extended her hand, fearless.

Adair said, "You have no idea how much this is going to hurt. Clarrissa was more than the love of my life. She was my best friend, my confidante, and my family. Losing her was . . ."

"I already lost her, Adair." Elle tapped the side of her head with her middle finger. Her eyes were older than they had any right to be. Her tone was bland. "I've got all the memories from after her death. I know how I felt when I failed to cure her, when she died, and when I failed to rescue her from Perun. What I don't know is how I felt when she lived."

Adair opened his mouth to dissuade her—to say that their wonderful memories with Clarrissa would only emphasize the pain—then he met her eyes, and the battle was lost. He recognized that stubborn look from the mirror. He knew that once he put it on, all arguments contrary to that of his goal turned to white noise. Regardless of what was said, Elle would insist on diving in head-first, just as Adair himself would do. She was him.

And he was her.

He nodded, accepting their eccentricities for what they were, and offered a lopsided farewell grin. He accepted her hand. Their souls fit perfectly into each other, euphoria upon bliss, and the void in Elle's chest finally filled. Pleasure twirled her, promising eternity, then passed her to pain.

Adair's half of her life pried her open and stuffed her full, injecting oceans of information into her overwrought brain. First came magic—so much magic—and Elle was surprised by her own wealth of knowledge. Every new class of magic had been seen as a challenge, and while she rarely liked something enough to master it, she almost always gave it a try.

Earth, fire, water, air, and electricity. The soul magic in her sword. The soul magic in the painting. Teleporting short distances. Illusions. Compulsion charms. Healing magic. Potions and herbs. They filled Elle's mind more quickly than she could process, and the list of concepts she recognized disappeared beneath a slew of more obscure magics. Color magic. Containment magic. Transferal magic. Impact magic. Time magic. Her education expanded until she felt she could vomit knowledge, and when the last piece of information finally dropped, the flood of memories began.

The false memories lit up, their inaccuracy as pronounced as the full moon on a clear night. Her life began to piece itself together. Elle remembered growing up. She remembered her family, accommodating but not comprehending, and the magic-restricted society. She remembered leaving them behind for the Impossible Markets, and she remembered Clarrissa.

Clarrissa.

Love and loss colored Elle's world. She'd stopped Clarrissa from making a deadly deal and had helped acquire the medicine for Clarrissa's father. Both Clarrissa and her father had taught Elle how to fight. They'd spent nearly every day together, gratitude melting into friendship, then blossoming into more.

Before Clarrissa, Elle's life had revolved around learning magic. After Clarrissa, she'd learned to love. While Elle hadn't often understood Clarrissa's need to be kind and helpful to everyone, she'd admired it. She'd basked in Clarrissa's attention and affection, always yearning for just that one minute more. Elle would do dishes by hand and let someone without magic punch her in the face. She would apologize when she wasn't in the wrong and leave the Impossible Market. For a single extra minute – a single extra smile – she would do anything. And when Clarrissa, who'd always been better with emotions than Elle, called that desire to be together 'love,' Elle had believed her.

The butterflies, the desire to make Clarrissa happy, and Elle's unconditional devotion were all love.

It was Clarrissa who'd taught Elle to embrace her emotions rather than smother them, and together they'd dreamed of traveling the world. Clarrissa had yearned to experience new cultures while Elle had ached for more impossible things. Their love had been strong. Their goals had aligned. Then Clarrissa fell sick. They'd postponed their departure but didn't cancel anything. *It's just a bad flu*, they'd thought. *It'll pass.*

It didn't.

Clarrissa had only grown weaker, and talk of travel made room for home-buying discussions. Elle shuddered as the memory ripped through her: Clarrissa hiding her tears as she adjusted her dreams to fit her reality. Elle scorning her for the effort. Elle heard her own voice echoing through her head, furious and unforgiving.

We're not buying a house! You want to see the world, don't you? Then you have to get better. Not settle in to die!

And that, in hindsight, was when Elle should have left. If she'd gone earlier, maybe she would have found the cure in time. Maybe her love would still be alive, and none of this would've happened. Except she'd never genuinely considered losing Clarrissa to be a possibility, and that baseless arrogance had cost more time than they could spare.

Clarrissa must have known, even then, that she was going to die. But she never said it. Instead, she let Elle rave on about healing and their idealized future. It took another year before Elle gave in and bought the cabin, and another year after that before she stormed out, determined to find the cure.

False memories of giving into Clarrissa's pleading and staying to take care of her shattered. The memories from Honeycutt connected to the ones from Adair, and Elle was forced to accept that she'd really left. Clarrissa had begged and cried, terrified to die alone, and Elle had walked away.

Her travels had led to Cypress. Before the House and before Clarrissa's death, but after her search for the cure had begun. Elle had been in a bar. Cypress had sensed her desperation. He'd offered to save Clarrissa in return for Elle's soul, and Elle?

Elle had laughed.

I don't need your help, she'd said. *I can save her on my own.*

Cypress had given her his card—a plain black rectangle with no writing—just in case she changed her mind. She'd left it with her tip for the bartender.

A pained whine slid from Elle's throat, agonized and mourning, as she understood that her arrogance had cost her not only time with Clarrissa but Clarrissa's very soul. Perun could only curse his victims in person. If Elle had stayed home, she'd never have been taken.

Tears burned Elle's eyes and strained her throat. She would trade anything to go back in time and cherish Clarrissa while she had the chance. Her broken heart bled anew, and it wasn't until her final memories slotted into place that she was able to accept the wound was old.

Clarrissa had died more than a decade prior. Elle had already gone through her breakdown. She'd spiraled. She'd drank herself to the bottom of countless bottles. She'd torn her soul apart. And now?

Elle sobbed into the stone floor, remembering the way Clarrissa's soul had flashed in the sphere. Warm and loving. Weak and desperate. She'd been waiting for Elle to come save her, and it was thanks to Elle's selfishness that she continued to wait.

The last time Elle came to the castle, her mission had been self-centered. If she ever wanted to move on—not to forget her past, but to remember it with the love and kindness Clarrissa deserved—then this time had to be different. Rather than seeking vengeance or reclaiming her lost love, Elle had to accept their journey together was over. She had to place Clarrissa's needs above her own and do the most harrowing thing of all.

She had to let go.

47

"I see you've managed to pull yourself together."

Elle frowned from her place on the floor, still unsteady from her merge. "You have my sword."

Cypress smiled and tapped the tip of the blade against the floor. "I do."

Elle felt the magic of her sword in Cypress's hand. The metal and leather were as familiar as her own body, and the thought of someone like Cypress commanding any part of her left a rotten taste on her tongue. She raised a hand to call it over. The steel recognized her request, remembered her care, and responded with vigor.

Cypress let it.

The hilt hit her hand with a satisfying clap. Elle adjusted her grip with an appreciation she couldn't have mustered as either Honeycutt or her younger self. This sword was made for her, and she for it.

She leaned against the wall and asked, "Why'd you wait?"

"You seemed busy."

"I can't imagine your master would approve."

"He only cares if you're threatening him. Talking to yourself is more off-putting than threatening."

Elle frowned, unamused, and activated the sword with a precision the magicless Honeycutt could never have achieved. She felt her soul wrap around the blade like a second coat of steel. The souls Cypress had taken brightened the glow of his magical core a hundred times over. The magic in the air and earth shimmered, blurring the distinction between animal and element. Elle flexed her will, narrowing her second-sight until she only saw souls. Her surroundings went back to normal. Cypress's litany of souls continued to glow.

She pushed herself to her feet and looked past Cypress, in the direction she knew Clarrissa to be. She readied her sword. "Move."

"You know I can't do that."

Elle shot forward, aiming for a single strand of a single soul. Cypress's intent to dodge glimmered in his soul. *A step to the left. A twist.* She countered by calling on the stone beneath his feet, requesting it entrap him. The floor dipped, sludge-like in consistency, and swallowed his shoe. Her sword cleaved air as he teleported away.

His magic flashed behind her a half-second later. She met his reappearance with her blade. The tip of her sword pierced flesh, muscle, and a single strand of soul. He leapt away, too late. The freed soul vanished.

Blood stained Cypress's shirt, though Elle doubted the wound remained. The demon bared his teeth, more beast than man. Caution bled into his will.

Elle returned to the center of the hall, where her reach was greatest. "Is it worth it, Cypress? Harvesting Perun's soul will only give you so much energy, and I promise fighting me will cost more than you'll gain."

"Expenditures are considered when agreeing to terms, not negotiated in the aftermath." He rolled his shoulders, tension genuine, and Elle understood. Free will was a human's game. Cypress's will was on loan. He could no more go back on a deal than she could choose to quit breathing.

Still, she asked, "What use is protecting Perun if it gets you killed?"

"All games have rules, Elle."

Disgust curdled in Elle's gut. *Of course this was a game to him.* She lunged. He disappeared, then reappeared behind her. His magic gave him away. Long, talon-like claws came down over her. She blocked. He curled his hand around her blade, uncaring of the way it cut into him, and Elle felt his soul bearing down on her own. Fear spiked, involuntary. She strengthened her resolve but didn't fight back, well aware that Cypress's soul, reinforced as it was, would rip her apart.

Elle held her sword steady and reached out to the air. She imagined static on her fingers and storms in the sky. The possibility of electricity sparked in the air, wild and wonderful. It threatened everything in the immediate vicinity like fire gone feral, and Elle encouraged it to *burn*. Cypress's eyes dilated. He doubled down on her soul. He yanked her sword down, blood dripping to the floor, and she felt her soul waver. Pain spasmed in her leg, a physical force. The hallway filled with lightning.

Portions of the wall exploded. The ceiling shook and cracked. Electricity skipped over the leather hilt to surge down her blade, and Cypress jerked away. She sped after him, lightning an extension of her blade. When she swung her sword next, it was with the knowledge that no, Cypress wasn't willing to die for this.

He dodged too much when, if he stuck around and sacrificed a few souls, he'd probably be able to pull one over on her. The demon, after all, could heal himself. Elle could not.

She called to the air beneath her feet, requesting speed. It coated her soles and launched her across the hall. The balls of her feet touched the wall first, to the right of and directly above Cypress's head. Killing his body was less effective than cutting away at the souls, but it would force him to waste excess energy. She shoved off the wall and aimed a clean swing at his neck.

Cypress shape-shifted, adult body abruptly trading out for that of a small boy, and Elle's blade sliced empty air. She twisted to land on her feet, then swiveled, sword pointed low.

"Elle?" The electricity in the air died. Bright, frigid blue eyes stared up at Elle through straight black bangs. Skinny fingers twisted in an overlarge shirt. The cloth that'd once been tied around empty eye sockets hung around his thin neck, and he said, "You're still gonna come find me, right?"

Hurt and betrayal stuck their hands into her stomach, long fingers scraping her back and spine. Her heart beat in her ears, deafeningly loud. "Quincy?"

He smiled, and she saw Cypress in the jut of his cheekbones, the curve of his nose. The odd shiver of familiarity she'd felt in the dragon's den clicked with the underdeveloped curve of Quincy's jaw, and she saw that they were not only the same demon but the same shell. Quincy was a younger version of Cypress.

A little voice in the back of her head called the whole thing a hoax, insisting that he could shift into any form he pleased, but if Cypress had wanted to hurt her with a shift, he would have chosen Clarrissa. Her heart iced and sank. Years of trust and care hollowed, her only friend a fraud. Elle tightened her grip on her sword, but she didn't attack. She let it fall to her side, spell fading. "Why are you showing me this?"

"Because I don't want to die, and you don't want to kill me."

"Oh yes I do."

"Not yet you don't." Quincy lifted his hand to pluck at an invisible string. It resonated in Elle's soul, an echo of the isolation in his eyes.

"What did you—"

"We made a deal, remember? I helped you escape the House, and in return, you're supposed to find me again. We're going to go on an adventure." Quincy grinned wide enough to turn his eyes into crescents, purposefully childish.

Elle said, "I didn't know you were a demon."

"And? The only requirement of making a deal is that we agree on an exchange." Quincy brushed his hair from his eyes, casual and callous. "You should consider yourself special, Elle. It isn't often I offer my services for anything less than a soul."

Elle's fist trembled, and her sword trembled with it. "If the deal wasn't for my soul, why should I care?"

"Because I'm a demon. Souls are our currency, and while I've agreed to accept a different form of payment, your soul acts as collateral. If you don't come through on your end of the bargain, your soul is forfeit."

"All the more reason to kill you."

"The only thing killing me will do is guarantee you can't fulfill your requirements. Our deal won't be dissolved. It'll just be handed off to someone else. And I assure you, Elle, other demons don't treat their pets nearly as well as I do."

Elle looked down at her blade. She didn't know enough about demons to say exactly how their deals worked, but she wouldn't doubt for a second that some convoluted, demon-killing loophole really did exist. She pressed her lips into a thin line, nodded, and activated the blade.

She was there to save Clarrissa's soul, not her own.

Elle drew a line from the floor to Quincy's heart. She met his obsessive gaze, unflinching. "So be it."

She thrust her blade forward. Quincy disappeared. He reappeared behind her, younger form discarded, and she imagined heat around her elbow. Images of sunshine turned to fire and flame. She threw her burning elbow backward, intending to nail him in the ribs.

Cypress caught her elbow, fire and all, and held her there. "That's the spirit, Elle. You've got this."

He let go, and by the time she finished turning, he was gone. His magic faded from the hall within seconds, signaling he'd genuinely left, and she didn't know whether to curse or laugh. Even with two deals and his own life on the line, the idiotic thing insisted on playing games.

She kept her soul wrapped around the sword, taking no chances, and used her magic to caress the earth. It thrummed, offering strength. She declined, requesting knowledge instead.

Where is the demon?

The earth's magic swelled, then rippled, searching the grounds. It returned with the notion of a sphere.

Elle sheathed her sword without deactivating the spell and strode toward the center of the castle. The magic around her *(in the flow of the air, in the solidity of the ground, in the possibility of everything else)* pressed butterfly kisses to her skin. They didn't ask what she wanted, but they waited to hear what she'd say. She flexed her will, appreciative.

When Elle entered the room with the sphere of souls, she felt calm. Perun's magic lashed out, a child throwing a temper tantrum, but Elle only had eyes for the sphere. She heard him say, "Demon. You were supposed to kill her," like they were in separate rooms. Separate universes.

Cypress said, "Sorry," but made no effort to rectify the situation.

Elle turned toward Perun. His aura was large but not impressive. The colors flowing throughout belonged to souls not his own. She pursed her lips, neither a martyr nor a hero, and said, "Let Clarrissa go, and we can part ways."

"We'll part ways, regardless." Perun twisted his magic into a whip, malicious intent sharpening the line. He lashed out, aiming to slice her down the middle. She sidestepped. It smashed into the floor where she'd stood, then curved to swipe at her from the side. She used her own magic as a shield. His magic smashed into hers, painful and heavy, but she didn't let it show.

Perun was a sadist and a bully. A narcissist with no plan B. So long as she could keep her reactions to a minimum, he'd do the rest of the work himself.

She tapped the ruined floor with the ball of her foot, returning strength rather than requesting it. "Pure magic and soul magic, huh? Interesting choices." The magic of the earth spread through the castle, granting Elle a picture of how it used to be. She realigned the stones and raised the rubble from the floor below. Then, specifically because she wanted him to feel inferior, she fixed his table, too. As the room restored itself, she said, "They're powerful in their own right but practically useless in a fight."

Perun widened his whip into a wall, then bludgeoned her with it. Pain exploded in her side—a bruised rib or a light bleed—and her silly, fearful heart tried to surface. Her shield had withstood the blow due to magic capacity alone. She wouldn't be able to take many more hits.

Elle licked her teeth, just in case there was blood, then grinned. She said, "You know, if you'd sent more than one of those golems, you might've actually killed me. Or part of me, at least." She took a careful step forward, on the hunt for a skittish animal and needing it to run just the right path. "Does it sting to know you could've gotten rid of me, if only you'd tried a little harder?"

His magic reared back, shaping itself into something long and sharp. Not a pointed whip or a blunt object, but a full-on blade. Elle watched it form, disquiet rising, and knew her shield would never hold. If that pierced her magic, it'd pierce her body, too.

Perun said, "I offered you eternity."

"You offered me death. How long's it take you to drain one of these souls? A decade? Two?" She took another step, bolder this time, and grasped the hilt of her sword. She goaded. "I bet it's less. You don't strike me as the rationing type."

"It is an honor to serve me."

"An honor my ass."

Elle drew her sword, and Perun's blade of magic shot toward her. She dove and rolled. It smashed a gaping hole in the floor where she'd been. She ran for Perun, adrenaline pumping, and waited for the perfect moment. His blade rose again, too slow. She readied her sword. They made eye contact, and Perun, despite his endless claims of godhood, did what any human would do.

He dodged.

Elle raced past him, blade swinging. Her sword sliced through the sphere like a knife through paper. Perun shrieked, magic flaring. Malice filled the room, but there was nothing he could do. For Perun's attacks were uselessly large, and his sphere was fragile. With Elle standing so close, his hands were tied.

She carved a line clear through the center of the spell, then twisted the blade to sever Perun's connection, too. The sphere shattered, magic dissipating like dust in the wind. The captured souls sparkled, then expanded. Blinding light filled the room.

The souls she'd freed caressed her, filling her with their joy, fervor, and gratitude. The air in front of her shifted, and though it wasn't any brighter than the rest of the room, she could imagine Clarrissa's outline. Elle tilted her head up to look where she thought Clarrissa's eyes would be. She meant to stand strong and reassure Clarrissa that they'd be okay, but all that came out were tears. Letting Clarrissa go meant releasing her from pain, heartache, and sickness, yes. But it also meant *letting her go.*

Elle dried her eyes on the heel of her palm. It didn't help. "Sorry I'm late."

Clarrissa's soul flashed with laughter. Her will flexed like an *I love you.*

Elle's throat constricted. Her chest ached. She wanted to hold onto the moment forever, but life was never that simple. It was never that fair. She opened her mouth and, knowing she'd never get to say it again, forced herself to whisper, "I love you, too."

Clarrissa shimmered, both grateful and forgiving. Elle wanted to beg for more time. To bask in Clarrissa's attention and affection for just one more minute. But then, that was the thing about "one more minute." One never really meant one, but more always meant more.

Clarrissa's lips pressed to Elle's, the ghost of a memory.

Then she was gone.

48

Perun choked on fear as the light—the souls—in the room vanished, leaving him alone with the woman and the demon. He skittered backward as the woman turned, and the scar on his abdomen ached. Her eyes were red-rimmed and puffy. Fresh tears glistened on her cheeks and darkened her shirt. She met his eyes, and despite all her displays of vulnerability and weakness, she stood strong.

He didn't understand it.

The woman raised her sword, and though it no longer glowed, it was more dangerous than ever. Perun raised a thick shield of magic between them, aware that he could not best her in a physical fight, and said, "Demon. Protect me."

The demon lounged in Perun's throne, legs crossed at the knees and hands folded in its lap. It canted its head and said, "I'd rather not."

Terror caught in his throat. His heart rabbited. The woman looked at the demon, dismissive, then strode toward Perun. He reminded himself that he was a god: chosen by lightning, protected by fire, guarded by the dead. His voice still cracked as he said, "You must protect me until I die. You are bound."

The demon smiled, faux apologetic. "Would that I could. Unfortunately, the terms of our agreement only compel me to protect you until the day you die. Unless I'm wildly mistaken, which I rarely am, that day is today."

Dread dropped into Perun's stomach. He touched the scar on his abdomen and felt the truth of it in their bond. Hatred burned in his blood, and the knowledge that this was all because he'd collected some sickly farm girl stuck like a knife in his brain.

She hadn't even been a good power source. Hell, she'd barely been worth the trip. The only reason Perun had wanted her in the first place was to spite the demon who'd failed to land a deal. If the demon hadn't told Perun about her—

If the demon hadn't told Perun about her.

Perun's thoughts slowed, and panic ravaged. He jerked his head to look at the demon, unable to believe anyone could play such a long game, especially when pitted against themselves. The demon caught his eyes, and despite there being no way for it to know what he was thinking, it winked.

Perun's head spun. His chest felt too full, and he couldn't breathe. The woman stopped in front of him, and her eyes were backlit with gold. The runes on her sword glowed. Fear of death placed pleas on his tongue, but pride swallowed them down. He said, "This is blasphemy. I am a god."

"A god?" The woman lowered her weapon. "That's too bad."

"If you understand your transgressions, then—"

"Not for me. For you." She slid her foot toward Perun. The ground lurched beneath him, flinging him into the air. She readied her sword, every bit as beastly as the demon, and said, "If you're a god, there's no one for you to pray to."

Perun fell toward the woman. Her blade met him halfway. She cut through his shield like child's play, then his chest and innards, too. Pain clapped him. Agony drowned him. He felt the assault both in slow motion *(the burn of metal parting skin, muscle, and bone to cleave his heart in half and come out on the other side)* and all at once. His vision blurred as his body stopped responding, and the realization that he'd died felt more like a sidenote than the exclamation it should've been.

He knew his body had hit the ground, and he saw the woman pulling her blood-slicked sword free, but the sensations that should've accompanied those actions were absent. Despite the oddness of his situation and the panic he'd been drenched in moments prior, Perun felt calm. Contentment settled around him, warm and light. His soul prepared to disconnect from his body, and *yes*. This was how it was meant to be.

The universe opened to welcome him, and with its call came the knowledge that he was not a god. He was a human—a small cog in an infinitely large, unfathomably complex machine—and his job was done. Rapture flowed in as the universe reached out, eager to shuttle him to his next life. He floated upward, a few measly layers of cells between him and the universe.

He bumped into his sternum.

Confusion touched him, and he shimmered, requesting guidance. The universe pointed to his deal with the demon, which had wound itself around every bone in his body, warding against his passage.

His body was a prison, his bones the bars. They locked him down, refusing him entry into the next life. Perun tried to scream, but he had no voice. He tried to plead his case, but it already knew. The universe, aware of everything and accepting of all consequences, began to close. Perun struggled harder, desperate to become one with the world.

The woman kneeled over him. Her face and wild hair blocked his last glimpses of the universe. Her hand shone bright with the glow of her soul. Perun recognized the magic in her fingers, instinctive, and knew at once that she intended to rip him out.

Panic returned, and though he had no idea what she would do to him, he knew it would be terrible. The demon appeared behind the woman in an instant. It used the bottom of its shoe to flatten her hand against Perun's lifeless chest. "Much as I'd love to see you harvest a soul, and believe me when I say I would love that, this one's mine."

The woman looked up at the demon, expression indecipherable. She pulled her hand from beneath its shoe and stood. The demon crouched to take her place. Perun flashed as far from the demon as he could while still being stuck inside his body, the light of his entire being molding to the sole of his foot. The demon seemed to see as much because it smiled.

"Are you ready?"

Perun thought the word *no* over and over again. His soul glinted and gleamed. The demon placed a hand over Perun's sternum, and like a moth to the flame, he went.

He touched the demon's palm, and their deal unwound itself from his corpse. When the demon moved away from Perun's body, it took Perun's soul with it.

Outside his body, his soul took the shape of a sphere barely larger than a grapefruit. The demon's fingers curled around him, keeping him in place. He flashed and flickered, terrified, but the demon only smiled. It stood, and Perun saw the woman standing off to the side, arms crossed. The demon lifted Perun above its head and craned its neck.

It grinned wider, then wider still, the cut of its lips reaching deep into its cheeks. Nauseating fear caused Perun to brighten. The demon opened its mouth to reveal infinite rows of sharp teeth. Perun thought for a second that he was going to be chewed up and torn apart, then the demon unhinged its jaw, and its maw opened wide enough to swallow him whole.

Perun didn't need to breathe, and yet he felt close to hyperventilating. His nonexistent lungs felt too full, and his actual soul trembled. He was so scared that it hurt. The beast dangled his soul over its mouth. Perun stared down the cavern of the demon's throat, impossibly aware that *this* was where the cold of the demon's eyes came from.

Then it let go.

Perun tried to flash to the other side of the room, but he was frozen. He fell past rows of sharp teeth, into an endless black void. It was empty in a way nothing should be *(in a way only true Nothing could be)*, and if Perun had lungs, he would've screamed. This place was the death he feared, and it knew so. He felt the darkness, the Nothing, close in around him like a physical thing. He wished he could cry.

Before the Nothing could touch him, he hit the ground. Perun blinked, then, surprised that he had eyes and eyelids to blink with, did it again. He was back in his body, or at least what felt like his body, and he was inside. He pushed himself off the floor, arms trembling. He felt weak.

An intense surge of pain took him back to the floor, every molecule in his body seizing. He scraped lines in the wooden floor and choked on air. His physical form flickered, reminding him that he was nothing but light. Agony traced his cheekbones and ran its hands through his hair, then let him go.

Instinct informed him that a little piece of his soul had been drained. A happy memory with his sister had disappeared, though he couldn't say which one. He waited to see if the pain would return, and when it didn't, he used the wall to help him stand.

He was on the upper floor of an empty gray house. There were four bedrooms and one small, seemingly broken bathroom. There were no people. The staircase creaked on the way down.

A wooden door with a brass handle greeted him at the bottom of the steps. Three planks were nailed over the door, and he could feel the warding on the planks from where he stood. Without a decently high level of magic, they would never come down. He bypassed the planks to search the downstairs. On the left sat another bedroom and a kitchen with no hearth. On the right was what looked to be a living room and a long hallway leading to another boarded, warded door.

There was no furniture. There were no amenities. He stood by the back door, and it was only in pressing his hand to a plank that he realized something else was missing, too. He had no magic. It'd been dampened, tampered with, sealed away. And without it, he was trapped.

Dread settled in his chest like a lead weight. Sorrow whispered in his ear. And he understood—finally, *fatefully*—that this was his grave.

Five dank, gray bedrooms. One cold, hearthless kitchen. One small, broken bathroom. One bleak, useless living room. Two glorious wooden doors: boarded shut.

Forever.

49

Elle watched Cypress's mouth return to normal, equal parts interested and disgusted. She still wanted to cut every soul from his core and carve out the hard black lump he called a heart, but exhaustion dulled the need. With her soul in his grasp, it would take some maneuvering before she could safely end him. Not killing him now didn't equate to not killing him later. She said, "I knew demons were called devourers of souls, but I didn't think the title was literal."

"It's not literal. It's theatrics. You only get to send a soul to the Nether Realm once." He paused, then swept his gaze over Elle. His smile was cruel. "Usually."

"I'm not selling my soul."

"We'll see."

She narrowed her eyes. Much as she wanted to go home, curl up on the guest bed, and cry, there would be no better time to clarify the bounds of their deal. She asked, "You can't prevent me from completing my end of the bargain, can you?"

"Unfortunately, no. I can make it harder, but any attempt to directly impede you would nullify our contract."

Elle hummed. "What was the exact phrasing of our deal?"

The lilt of Cypress's smile said that was the right question to ask. He said, "I help you escape, and in return, once you're strong enough, you find me again. Take me on a huge adventure."

"When you say I'm supposed to find you, does that mean it doesn't count if you come to me?"

"All terms are up for interpretation, but it's unlikely we'll be in a situation where we go on an adventure together and the contract remains unfulfilled."

She asked, "What counts as an adventure?" Cypress smiled but said nothing. Irritation itched in her lungs, and she went on. "Up for interpretation then. How about we go on an adventure right now?"

"Do you have something in mind? Adventures tend to be rather fantastical endeavors. Though I suppose wandering around together until an adventure occurs could be fun."

Elle grimaced. She'd rather have her soul ripped out than spend an unspecified amount of time just *hanging out* with Cypress. She asked, "How do I find you?"

Cypress held out his hand, and a plain black card appeared between his pointer and middle fingers. Elle didn't have to look at him to know he was getting some sick sort of satisfaction out of forcing her to accept the card she'd once declined. She took the card, careful not to touch his hand.

A spell similar to the one on her sword echoed out from the card, letting her know she was supposed to wrap her soul around it. She flipped the card over, looking for engravings. Both sides were blank.

"How'd you enchant this?"

"Do you really want to know?"

His smile promised a dangerous exchange. Elle rolled her eyes. "No." She stuffed the card carelessly into her coin pouch and, with a mocking echo of Cypress's two-fingered salute, made her way out of the castle.

Cypress followed. "What are you going to do next?"

"Go away."

"Will you go back to your cabin?"

"Go. Away."

"I'm curious is all. It's odd for someone as powerful as you to be so aimless."

"I'll aim my sword at your soul if you don't go away."

Cypress leaned closer, unafraid. "You were nicer without your memories."

Elle summoned electricity with a twitch of her fingers. The dark hallway filled with violent shocks of light. When it dimmed again, Cypress had gone.

She walked on, content in the silence. The sun brightened her path as she reached the breach in the castle's wall. Elle fixed the damage behind her as she stepped out. While the earth held no particular care for the rise and fall of human constructs, she felt better for it.

"What'll I do next, huh?"

Wind tousled her hair as she strode to the edge of the castle grounds, and she admitted, if only to herself, that she didn't know.

Even with victory fresh on her tongue, she felt empty. Elle was whole, she was powerful, she was free, and she was alone. While that had been fine when she was a child, still wide-eyed and ignorant of the ways of the world, living with Clarrissa had changed her. Life alone *(stuck in the House, stuck on the boat, stuck in the painting, stuck in the cabin)* had proved unfulfilling. Even her time exploring the world in search of Clarrissa's cure paled in comparison to the months she'd spent traveling with the other parts of herself.

And maybe that spoke more for how much she liked herself than it did her propensity to appreciate the company of others, but it was worth considering. She could find another group to travel with, or maybe seek out an apprentice. She could move on.

Elle stared out at the skyscape, at the sun rising on the endless horizon, and for the final time in her life, fell out of the sky.

FINAL NOTES

If you enjoyed this book, please consider sharing it with your friends
and leaving a review on Amazon.

Thanks again for all your support, and keep a look-out for the next
installment in the Impossible series, *Two for Flinching*.

About the Author

Jackary Salem is a fantasy author from Kingsport, Tennessee. She majored in neuroscience at Berea College with equal emphasis in biology and psychology. Her passions are writing, editing, and her cat, Chihiro. She currently works as an author and developmental editor. To connect with Jack, you can follow her on Twitter, Facebook, or Instagram, email her at jackarysalem@gmail.com, or sign up for her newsletter at www.jackarysalem.com.

www.ingramcontent.com/pod-product-compliance
Lightning Source LLC
Chambersburg PA
CBHW031324210726

48287CB00005B/1677